I0772324

FOR NOTHING IS HIDDEN

A Novel by John A. Valenti 3rd

Inspired by One of the Oldest Unsolved Missing Child Cases in U.S. History

For my brothers, Jim and Rob

*And for my father John Jr. and late mother Dorothy,
who, despite the times we wanted to kill each other, were
always there when I needed them*

With many thanks to my love, Elizabeth Eser Jose. And to my family and confidantes, first and foremost my son, Jarek, who makes me proud, and to Tony Mills, who, for going on five decades has been a far better friend than I've been. With untold thanks to Jenn Stauder, Rachel Coyne, Toni Munna, Jerelyn Zontini, fellow *Newsday* colleagues, past and present, Lynn Petry, Joan Gralla, Cecilia Dowd, Mark Harrington, David Reich-Hale, Elaine Vuong, Dandan Zou and David Cassidy, and to Frank Nappi, novelist and former teacher extraordinaire at my alma mater, Oceanside (N.Y.) High School — all of whom read the raw manuscript and made invaluable suggestions. Eternal thanks to Monika Atsuko Taga for years of friendship and professional mentoring and for helping get the 2016 reissue of *Swee'pea,* as well as this book, to the finish line.

Also by John A. Valenti 3rd

13 POETS FROM LONG ISLAND

*Swee'pea, The Story of Lloyd Daniels and Other Playground Basketball Legends**

Library of Congress Cataloguing-in-Publication data pending application.

Hardcover ISBN: 979-8-9889193-5-3
Trade Paperback ISBN: 979-8-9889193-6-0
E-Book, Kindle ISBN: 979-8-9889193-4-6

Artwork

Cover: Based on the search for Steven Damman, November 1, 1955, Ike Eichorn, *Newsday*.
Title Page: Based on Steven Damman's tricycle, October 31, 1955, Tom Maguire, *Newsday*.
Dedication Page: Dorothy and John, Jr., Putnam Avenue, Bushwick, Brooklyn, 1956.
Post-Epilogue Page: John A. Valenti, Sr. (back to artwork) with officials.
First two sketches based on photos used with rights obtained from *Newsday*.

Swee'pea was originally released by Michael Kesend Publishing, Ltd., in November 1990.
Reissued by Atria Books, a Simon & Schuster Company, July 5, 2016.

FOR NOTHING IS HIDDEN

For All Those Missing Children and Their Families

This Story is a Work of Fiction

For nothing is hidden, except to be revealed;
nor has anything been secret, but that it would come to light.

— Mark 4:22

Prologue

The old woman was on her deathbed.

She had been battling cancer and, under sedation, drifted in and out of consciousness, trying hard to speak, at times incoherent.

She seemed so much older than she was, now. He had never seen her like this, though he had imagined it more than once.

"Come close," she said.

And with that the sturdy but otherwise ordinary looking man leaned in so he could hear, ever wary the distance.

He had never cared for her much.

Truth be told, he had never cared much for anyone in his family: not his father, not his sister; not any of the lot of them.

He had always felt like an outsider, he would later say, and had never felt loved. It wasn't love now that made him strain to listen.

"What?" he said, matter-of-fact.

"Your life," the old woman said, haltingly. "About your . . . "

She reached out best she could, near blind, motion restricted by the intravenous tube and monitor connection that covered her index finger.

He sat unwavering, unyielding. A tear welled in her eye.

"There's so much . . . " she said, gasping for breath. "There's so much you don't know."

He stared at her, old before her time. Her pain apparent, he felt anything but sympathetic. He'd had to endure so much for so long.

He thought about the car ride, the one so long ago now.

Him, tucked hard into the back seat, wondering what was happening as the days and nights passed along with the countryside.

One minute he lived in a beautiful suburban home. One with a yard, a swing made out of an old tire hung from the biggest tree branch he'd ever seen. He had a mom and dad who loved him. Or so he thought.

He had a baby sister. Or so he recalled.

Then just like that it was all different. His world, changed.

Those people — whoever they were, whoever they'd been — were long-gone. That life, gone. And then he had new parents, a new family. A new life. One he had never quite been comfortable with.

One he'd grown most-uncomfortable with.

Fifty-one years old, Robert Charles Landsness had lived a vagabond life. His father had been an Air Force man; his family, forever on the move. Once it was over, once the time had come for his father to leave the service, to move on, all of them had moved one more, one last, time. His father called it going home, home being Kenosha, Wisconsin.

Robert Landsness knew it had never felt like home to him.

He drifted, aimless. Uncertain about his past, undecided about his future. He left home after high school, took work on a farm in the Upper Peninsula, hated it, came back to Kenosha, sought employment any place that might earn him a hard-won paycheck.

He found a job with American Motors, on the assembly line, building cars in town. It was good work, steady work. The kind of place a man could make a life. And then American went under, bought by Renault; not long after, sold off to Chrysler. Then Lee Iacocca shut it all down, called his decision "irrevocable." And just like that he was gone. Just gone.

He was in his thirties then, no future in sight.

He took unemployment, lost his house, lost his wife. Lost it all. Took odd jobs, bounced around, drank too much. Eventually, he became a janitor. Mostly, because he didn't know what else to do.

He rented a trailer, a single, then once he'd saved enough, bought it. It wasn't much. Wasn't much of anything, really; home.

Then again it wasn't quite that, either.

Throughout it all he'd never been able to come to grips with any of it. What had happened, what was happening. Where it all went, where it was all going. He glared at her. She didn't have much time.

"Tell me," he said. "And this time tell me the God-damn truth."

Gertrude Landsness was sixty-seven.

She had never been an easy woman. Her mother died young. Her father, once a respected shopkeeper, had fallen into alcohol.

Had become a drunk — and a mean one at that.

Even back in junior high school, right after the tragedies began, she'd envied the girls who seemed to have it all. They had parents who were there for them. She had no one. They had looks. She was never going to be beautiful. They were carefree, able to go with the good times. She learned early on to keep it all in check, if just to hold the middle ground.

A half-century down the line she was drawn, gaunt, what was left of her sandy-blonde hair matted and gray; her eyes, long-faded.

"Robert . . . " she said.

She thought to that evening back in Panama City, Florida.

November, 1955.

A light breeze blew in from the Gulf, across Spanish Ante, across St. Andrews Bay, fighter planes landing off in the distance at Tyndall Air Force Base. Somewhere back in town a freight train from the *Atlanta & St. Andrews Bay* rumbled down the Bay Line, hauling north to Dothan in the fading, faltering, light. She had an infant daughter, but for the longest time, it seemed, had felt this sense of indescribable loss.

It was all she'd ever wanted, this lost little boy.

It was the night Robert had come to her. Come, oddly enough, in the crammed back seat of that 1951 cream-yellow-and-white Nash-Rambler Custom Country Club hardtop — a Rambler built back in Car Town.

Her home, Kenosha. A car she knew well.

That car pulled up outside the small cottage house, the one she and her husband, George, had landed off-base.

Within moments she was exchanging hugs with her brother Thom and his wife Marie and then she was peering into the back seat to see the little boy. He was tired, confused. She tried to coax him out, taking him by the hand. Reluctantly, he stepped forward.

Toward her, toward his new life.

She and the boy eyed each other for what seemed a lifetime. George was on duty, the baby carriage down the driveway.

"Hello Robert," she said.

He didn't say a word.

"We had quite a trip," Marie said. "Quite a trip."

Thom leaned in. "He needs time, Gertie. Give him time."

Just then the baby cried. And Robert looked around, puzzled.

He spotted the carriage, back down a ways. Ignoring Gertrude, ignoring them all, he ran toward it and, once there, stood staring; just staring, transfixed almost. When Gertrude reached him Robert was standing on the curb, peering over the carriage side.

He gave her a look she'd see many times in years to come.

"Your baby sister," she said.

He shook his head. "Don' *thing* so."

He was three; her, barely nineteen. It all seemed like yesterday.

Gertrude fought to turn and face Robert, seated at her bedside in the Kenosha Hospital Medical Center. Spent, she couldn't.

Such a beautiful boy," she said, a bare whisper.

"What?" Robert said. "What the hell did you say?" He grabbed her arm, shook it. "Mom!" The very word stung him.

The old woman forced what she could of a smile.

"You were, my Bobby," she said. "You were a good son . . . "

An alarm sounded.

As Robert sat in stunned silence a doctor and two nurses rushed in; looked at the old woman, looked at the monitors, looked for a pulse.

"She's gone," one of the nurses said, finally. The doctor — Robert never bothered to ask his name — leaned in and, with a hand placed firmly on his shoulder, said: "I'm so very sorry for your loss."

The next thing Robert Charles Landsness knew he was out in the hall, alone. Still not knowing. Still not understanding one damned thing.

With no one around he punched a wall.

"Damn it," he screamed. Then: "Motherfucker."

For the longest time he stood seething, not knowing what else to do. He wasn't about to turn to his sister. Not a chance.

And his dad? That was a good one.

No, if he was going to resolve this, the questions, after all this time, he would have to do so himself. Angered, he turned to leave.

As he walked down the hall he made himself a promise then: to get some answers; to finally figure the damned thing out.

1

Monday, October 31, 1955

The carriage was gone.

The carriage, her kids. That's what she said. Just gone.

Moments before she'd stepped out of the IGA into the midst of a crisp autumn afternoon, had seen the foot patrolman headed toward her swinging his billy club, whistling, on the stroll — a catalogue cop, if ever someone had ordered one. Then, before anyone knew a thing, anything at all, she'd bolted to where the carriages sat, lungs ablaze.

"Officer! Have you seen a boy and a blue baby carriage?"

The patrolman stared, dumbstruck.

Blank, like the night he was acting the maggot, stumbled in on that poet, blind drunk and already half-dead, down at the White Horse.

"In a carriage?" Officer O'Reilly said, finally.

"No!" the woman shouted. "A boy *and* a blue baby carriage."

This was when she'd turned, pointing to the strollers near the door.

"I left my little boy *here,* watching his baby sister in her carriage. I just went in to get a few things and came out to find he's gone."

Emphatic, she said then: *"They're* gone."

"How old's the child?" O'Reilly asked, still unalarmed.

As she spoke, spoke a mile a minute, she ran toward the lot. The shopping center was huge. Ten stores, more than a dozen cars. Clad in the uniform of the local Hempstead Plains Police, not the larger county department, O'Reilly stood looking about. To him, all seemed normal.

Still, she was yelling, "Bobby!" as he went to the carriages.

"And none of these are yours, are they, then?" he said.

"No!" she said.

"Look, Misses," he said, as she raced back toward him, brown paper shopping bag bouncing about in her arms. "Misses . . . "

"Goodson." She fought to catch her breath. "Colleen Goodson."

"And how long is it then you were off collecting the messages?" he said, to be met with the blankest of blank stares — soon reconsidering the question he'd offered to ask how long it was she'd been in shopping.

"Just a few minutes," she said, then. "Maybe ten."

"I'm sure it's a lot of nothing, then," O'Reilly said, "and the child's just wandered off."

"He's a good boy," she said. "He doesn't wander."

O'Reilly scanned the sidewalk. "How's the child look?"

"He's about this tall," she said, holding a hand to her waist. "Blonde hair, blue eyes. He has a little lisp."

"And this carriage?"

"Blue." And, after a pregnant pause: "A regular blue carriage."

"We'll find it, then," O'Reilly said. "We'll find them."

They couldn't have gone far.

The metal counter was clean, spotless, and it glistened in the brightest of incandescent light that shone down from overhead.

Arm's length from her shopping cart Colleen Goodson thought the brushed stainless surface reminded her of the instrument table in her doctor's examination room, cold and somehow achingly antiseptic.

Trying hard not to think about all she was thinking about she glanced at her wristwatch. Close to 2 p.m. She looked toward the double doors that led to the back room but could not see anyone working. She reached out, pressed down on the ringer atop the call bell on the countertop.

No one came. On the butcher block, all slabbed up, lay a side of beef. Dark red, it was layered in bands of thick, unctuous, subcutaneous fat — assortment of knives, laid, at the ready. She turned, not wanting to look.

Moments earlier she had been in produce, lost in thought.

"I said, 'Hello, Mrs. Goodson,'" he said.

Startled, Colleen had turned to see the smooth-skinned teen.

Down on one knee, he was hunched over a crate.

"I'm sorry, Jimmy," she said. "I don't know what . . . I mean, Hello."

She hadn't understood when he said: "They're ripe as can be." Then she noticed the smirk as he offered the apple, bright and red.

Under normal circumstances she might have lingered, made small talk; maybe even picked through the crate with him. This afternoon she found herself oddly aware of time. She glanced at her watch.

"Next time, Jim," she said. She forced a smile.

Jimmy Dodge thought it all odd. She always called him Jimmy, never Jim. But he shrugged, went back to unpacking Red Delicious.

Down the aisle Colleen grabbed potatoes, an onion, garlic; tossed them all into the cart. Most afternoons she spent time sorting, careful to make sure there were no cuts, no bruises. Not this afternoon.

She reached out, hit the bell clapper again.

It felt like forever before the door swung open and old man Katsch stepped out wiping blood from gnarled hands.

"But don't you look lovely today my sweet little *maideleh*," he said, as Colleen tried to look embarrassed. "What can I get for you this afternoon, Mrs. Goodson?" the butcher said, pointing to the slab of beef.

"It would be my pleasure to cut for you a nice steak."

"It's Monday, Mr. Katsch."

"Special meat loaf night," the old man said, as Colleen forced a smile.

As the old man ambled from the counter, headed for the meat grinder in the back room, Colleen scanned the counter, again caught a glimpse of that bloody, slabbed side of beef. Again, she turned away.

When old Katsch returned Colleen was sure not to watch as he placed the butcher paper with the fresh-ground meat on the scale in front of her.

"Everything is good with you, Mrs. Goodson?" he asked, as he handed her the package. Getting no reaction, he said: *"Nisht gut?"* Not good?

"I'm fine, Mr. Katsch. Really, I am."

"For bending your ear." He winked. "No extra charge."

"You really are so good to me, Mr. Katsch," she said.

For a briefest moment Colleen felt almost at peace with herself.

"Tomorrow, my dear?"

"Maybe," she said. "Probably."

Over at the register Colleen made small talk with the cashier, Myrtle, making it a point to change a dollar for two fifty-cent rolls of pennies.

"I'll need them for the kids," she said.

"Halloween. They'll be ringing your doorbell all night."

"A bunch of little terrors," Colleen said, then thought better.

She thanked the girl who bagged her groceries, made sure to leave a twenty-cent tip. Then Colleen Goodson stepped out into the clear but chill afternoon. She took one more look at her watch. Already 2 p.m.

It was then that she saw him.

The patrolman turned, headed for the far end of the shopping center. Colleen turned and ran back inside the IGA.

"Did you see Bobby?" she yelled.

Startled, Myrtle turned from the register. "Why no."

The girl who bagged her groceries was already down the far end, working with Edith, a cashier old enough to be her grandmother.

"Have you seen Bobby?"

Hearing the commotion, Edith turned.

"No," she said. "Not since the other day."

Colleen shot the girl a look. But the bag girl said no, too.

Colleen ran out; ran into the shoe store next door. No baby carriage, no Bobby. She ran next to the florist shop and then to the 5-and-10; ran past the luncheonette counter that stretched straight along the far wall there, past a handful of late lunch customers seated on swivel soda shop stools, ran aisle-to-aisle until she was back at the front door.

No one quite understood what was going on. Colleen knew.

There was no sign of her son.

Back on the sidewalk Colleen Goodson stopped to catch her breath. She was still standing there, drained, when O'Reilly came waltzing up.

The officer said he had been to the barber shop, the bakery, the men's shop, the appliance store. North of forty with an Irish face and a tuft of reddish-blonde hair peeking out from under his patrolman's cap, O'Reilly said no one had seen the carriage. That no one had seen her boy.

"And how far are you, then?" O'Reilly asked.

"Just three . . . " she said, caught herself. "Four blocks."

"Go home, then, Misses. See if the children . . . What's your little girl's name?"

"Jo," she said. "Johanna."

"Go home then," O'Reilly said. "See if the children are there at your dwelling. 'Til then, I'll see what I can see of it here.

"If you don't happen to find them . . . "

"If I don't find them?"

"Look, I'm certain your little Bobby and Jo are just fine, there, Misses. Happens all the time, it does, a child wandering off like this."

"I told you, Bobby doesn't . . . "

The officer drew a hand, mid-sentence.

"Trust me, Misses," he said. *"Boyos* wander."

He thought he saw her shudder, though maybe it was the autumn air.

"What was it, now, that the child was wearing?" he asked. "What kind of costume, being how it's Halloween and such."

"I was going to get him dressed later. After dinner."

Then, after a moment lost in thought, she said: "He was going to be an Air Force pilot. His father's stationed over at Meadowbrook Field."

Two blocks from home Colleen stopped at a corner, looked to see if anyone was around; she saw no one, kicked off her pumps.

They hurt; she was tired of them.

She ran the last two blocks, tearing holes in her nylons.

Her block was quiet, though down the far end she thought she saw trick-or-treaters. She jumped the two steps to the house, stood briefly on the gray cement stoop searching her pocketbook for keys and, juggling the grocery bag, opened the door. Inside, she stood in near-total silence.

She'd seen no sign of the carriage. She knew she wouldn't. She had seen no sign of Bobby. She'd known that, too.

She saw his tricycle off in the corner, Halloween bag hanging from the handlebars. It was tough to look at.

The house was dead quiet save her own hard breathing and the noise the groceries made as she dropped the bag to the floor.

Colleen tossed her pumps down next to it.

She ran to the bedroom closet, searched for a pair of flats. She tried on one pair, then another before making a decision. She grabbed a light sweater from the closet as well. It was cool out. She'd need it.

She tried hard not to look at the pictures on the dresser.

She'd gone through the photographs that morning once her husband left for work, had placed pictures of Bobby and Johanna on the dresser, along with a nice family shot. Now, she couldn't bear the thought.

She turned, pretending not to notice any of it.

Back in the living room she thought about what needed to be done.

It was close to 2:30 p.m. Her husband wouldn't be home for almost three hours. She ran across the street to Margie's.

Marjorie Woods was her best friend on Long Island. Years older, in her early thirties, Margie was the older sister Colleen never had, maybe even the mother she never had. She could tell Margie anything, everything almost, and they often talked for hours. They talked a lot of girl talk, the two of them did. Cooking, clothes, husbands. Men.

Margie was from California, a small town north of Bakersfield. But her parents were from Long Island — from farm country; out on the East End, North Fork — having left decades before. Margie always said it was odd then how she'd ended up in New York. Out here, on the Island.

She'd met Taggart one summer at Pismo Beach, just after the big one. He was on leave, having decided to re-enlist, and was hanging around with a handful of buddies. She was working in a beach-side cafe.

She brought him breakfast one morning. He told her it was something he could get used to. They'd been together ever since.

Tag was older than Margie, was an airplane mechanic over at Meadowbrook Field. Now, he'd had it with military life.

His papers had come through. By the end of the week he and Margie would be free and clear. They'd talked of going back to California, though said they might try Las Vegas. It was just the two of them, no kids.

Colleen often wondered what it would be like having nothing, having no one, to ever slow you down.

Margie often spent time watching Bobby and Johanna.

Colleen was ever-thankful she never seemed put out but always seemed keen to do so. She wondered what her friend would say now.

Colleen crossed the street, knocked on the door. Nothing.

She was about to leave but Tag's car was in the driveway.

"Hey there," Margie said, suddenly opening the door, fixing her white blouse and dark brown skirt as she did. She started to say something.

"I was at the IGA," Colleen said, stopping her cold. "I came out — and my kids were gone."

"Gone?"

"I couldn't find them anywhere, Marge."

Marjorie stepped onto the stoop, closing the door behind her. Once out on the front lawn, she caught Colleen staring at the car.

"Tag was just going to run out for some boxes, for the move," Margie said. She told Colleen she'd head to the far end of the block, search the four blocks to the shopping center. She told Colleen to go back the way she'd come. "We'll meet back over at the IGA," she said.

As the two headed off in opposite directions Margie yelled over her shoulder. "They've got to be somewhere, Coll . . . I just know they are."

2

Colleen Goodson ran toward one end of MacArthur Terrace headed for Mitchell Avenue, Marjorie Woods ran toward the other headed for Glenn Curtiss. Near the corner Colleen called out for Bobby, got no response, looked around, saw nothing. Not a soul.

She ran up the block to Lindbergh Place.

The avenue was lined with stately oaks, thick with widespread branches that overhung the road, their leaves shielding all beneath them in smothering shade. It had been a hot humid summer with lots of rain and those leaves had hung on for the longest time. Autumn now in full persuasion, temperatures dipping chill into the cooling nights, all that foliage had turned from lucid green to flaming red, golden yellow, burnt umber and fading brown — some of it fallen, most still threatening to — and somewhere in the back reaches of the neighborhood drums filled with dead stuff burned smokey, sweet. Burned, unmistakable.

The surrounding blocks were mostly military housing and the streets all had some military connection, or ties to aviation, named for notable civil aviators, armed forces fliers, war heroes, U.S. generals, ambassadors and presidents. Mostly, it seemed, for dead men.

The houses were simple and neat, with tidy lawns and gardens.

Almost all had a U.S. flag hung near the door, accompanied by a squadron guidon or some other military standard. Halloween decorations filled most of the windows this time of year; carved pumpkins, with knifed, cut-out faces, anchoring otherwise bare concrete stairs.

The cool autumn air made Colleen glad she'd thrown on the light sweater. She considered the consequences of having taken the time, then dismissed the thought almost as soon as she'd thought it.

Lindbergh was a short block, not a through-street, and it ended in a cul-de-sac. Colleen ran toward the dead end calling for her son.

She noticed a woman watching over a handful of young children trick-or-treating outside one of the homes and ran to her.

"Have you seen a little blonde-haired boy, this high?" Colleen asked, hand held to her waist. "He was with a baby carriage."

"Pushing a carriage?"

"You've seen them?" Colleen said.

The woman surveyed the cul-de-sac, then turned back.

"Sorry, no," she said, after a moment. "We've been up and down a few blocks. Roosevelt, Rickenbacker. A couple of others. But we haven't seen a thing other than a few lions and tigers and the cutest little bear."

"If you do," Colleen said, "I'm on MacArthur."

And before the woman could muster an answer she ran off.

A short time later Colleen found herself back in front of the IGA, watching as shoppers walked to and from their cars as traffic, what of it there was this time of day, moved easily out on Eisenhower Boulevard, the main drag through Hempstead Plains. Another otherwise ordinary afternoon, you could hear the airplanes not far off, over at the base.

Colleen checked her watch, again. Almost 3 p.m.

He'd be home in a matter of time.

Then she saw them down at the far end of the shopping center, Officer O'Reilly — and Marjorie. Her friend was pushing the carriage.

Colleen wondered what it was they'd found. She took a few steps, decided it better to run. She reached them in front of the bakery.

"The kiddo's just grand," Officer O'Reilly said.

The young mother peered hard into the carriage. There was Johanna, covered by her blanket, fast asleep. She bent in, unfastened the girl.

She cradled Jo in her arms. "Where did you find her?"

"Around the corner," Marjorie said. "On Hughes."

"What about Bobby?"

Officer O'Reilly looked concerned. Marjorie forced a weak smile.

"We couldn't find anyone who'd seen him," she said. "Just Johanna."

The three of them stood there, no one knowing what to do next.

The silence almost untenable, Marjorie moved to Colleen, gave her friend a comforting hug. "I'm sorry. I just know it's not your fault."

A tear rolled down Colleen's cheek, then another.

She sniffled, her nose ran. Pressed hard by Margie, Jo locked in her arms between them, Colleen couldn't even reach for a handkerchief, wasn't sure if she even had one in the pockets of her cardigan.

Sensing the moment, Marjorie reluctantly released her grip and Colleen reached into the carriage, set Johanna down, took a drool cloth — and blew her nose. As the two stood there — Colleen, wiping tears from her reddened blue eyes — O'Reilly decided he could wait no longer.

"I'll call over to the station, then," he said.

And he disappeared into the store.

"Was the sergeant I spoke to," O'Reilly said, upon his return.

"And?" Colleen said.

"And he's going to send a unit to take the lot of you home. Said he's going to ring up the county cops. Standard procedure, Misses."

"What then?" Colleen said.

"County will send a couple uniforms, no doubt. They'll want to ask questions, will want to know everything is you remember, put out an alert. That being, they'll alert all their precincts, their captains, the whole fine lot of them, they will. They'll tell them to be looking out.

"One more thing," he said. "Would you happen a photograph?"

"Of Bobby?" Colleen said. "I'm sure I can find one."

"Good then, that's good."

The patrolman remembered what it was his sergeant had told him and reached into his back pocket, took out a small notebook.

"And the child, what was it he's wearing?" he said.

"A . . . a plaid shirt," Colleen said. "A blue plaid shirt, dark slacks. Navy blue. Dark socks. Shoes . . . Brown shoes, I think."

"Good, that's good. And he's named Bobby Goodson, is he?"

"Robert," Colleen said. "Yes."

The officer was still writing notes on Bobby's height, weight, hair color and the rest when the car arrived. It was a white two-door Pontiac police coupe with a light and siren on the roof and black lettering on the side that read: Hempstead Plains Police. A uniformed officer got out.

Shorter than O'Reilly, he was younger, heavier. Colleen thought he didn't wear the uniform well: shirt, stretched tight over his belly, buttons taut; the band of his slacks rolled where he bulged at the waist.

She watched as the officer walked over to O'Reilly, began in a hushed voice, words indecipherable. The officer said some things. O'Reilly said some things. O'Reilly went through his notebook, pointing out things he'd written down. The two of them turned, gave Colleen and Marjorie the once-over; looked at Johanna asleep in her carriage.

They turned back, talked some more.

Colleen could only imagine what was being said.

When they were done the younger officer moved to the passenger door, moved the seat forward, motioned for the women to get in. Colleen lifted Jo, got into the back next to Margie. The officers took the carriage, placed it in the trunk. Slammed the lid. Marjorie flinched.

The younger, shorter officer walked around to the driver's side, got in behind the wheel. Moving to the passenger-side door Officer O'Reilly put his hand atop the door frame — and leaned in to face the women.

"Officer Ricks here will take you home, wait 'til county comes to call." Then, to Colleen, he said: "I'm sure all of it will work out fine, Misses."

"Officer O'Reilly? Could you do one thing for me?"

"Sure now."

"Call the base operator and ask for my husband, Driscoll Goodson," Colleen said. "He works in the main building at Meadowbrook.

"The Requisition Control Office."

"He's not a pilot is he, then?"

"Oh, no," she said. "Driscoll's a clerk. He's afraid of flying."

"Imagine that?" Ricks said, shooting O'Reilly a look.

It seemed like O'Reilly was going to close the door. Instead, the patrolman realized he'd forgotten to ask one important question.

"One more thing, Misses. What's the birth date?"

"My husband?"

"No," the officer said. "I'm meaning the child."

"October Nineteenth, Nineteen Fifty-Two."

She stared at him as the color drained from her face. "He's three." Then, in the barest of whispers, she said: "He's only three."

The bulb in the old lamp on the corner table tinged the living room in a languid yellow light as what was left of the fading sun crept through the open blinds and drawn-back curtains of the front picture window.

Marjorie sat uncomfortably on the sofa next to Colleen; Johanna, in a back room, was asleep in her bassinet.

Officer Ricks paced about agitated, looking at everything and nothing at all: the television console, the carpet, at scratches in the legs of the coffee table. Marjorie thought the patrolman about to have kittens.

Stoic, Colleen seemed not to notice. She simply stared at the wall clock, waiting on the county police to arrive, waiting on Driscoll.

Waiting on a train.

The doorbell rang, startling everyone. Marjorie rose to answer and Officer Ricks watched her cross the room, smoothing her dark brown skirt as she went. "Trick or treat!" children yelled as she opened the door.

On the doorstep a handful of school kids stood jockeying for position. Almost swallowed up by the howling mass, a little blonde-haired boy, half the size and age of everyone else, stood, no costume at all.

Behind him was a uniformed policeman.

The shock of blonde hair startled Marjorie and she let out a gasp, sending Colleen and Officer Ricks running toward the door.

"What?" Ricks said, before realizing it was nothing at all.

The kids yelled as Marjorie stood, transfixed; transfixed, as if she'd seen a ghost. The kids were holding out their bags, now. And pocketbook in hand, Colleen slid past her stalled friend as she fumbled for the rolls of pennies buried in it. She'd known without looking the blonde-haired boy wasn't her son, the "policeman" an older trick-or-treater chaperoning the young kids, and as she looked over the muddle of schoolchildren, Colleen began dropping a few coins into each of their bags.

Fast as they'd arrived they were gone. Colleen quietly closed the door. Officer Ricks watched Marjorie turn, give her friend a hug. He studied the two as they moved back to the sofa and tried to settle in.

It was a few minutes before they heard the car door slam.

Officer Ricks answered the door this time, extending his hand for a professional handshake. The two county officers gave him the once-over; one snickered as they instead blew past. The officers were tall, ordered.

Colleen was struck by their presence.

The Hempstead Plains Police Department had but fifty officers.

The Nassau County Police Department, meanwhile, had a force of more than a thousand, manning seven precincts from the Long Island Sound on the North Shore to the Atlantic Ocean on the South, from the citified Queens border in the west to rural Suffolk in the East.

They didn't have the history or mystique of their city brethren, the NYPD. But they were far from a bunch of Keystone Cops. Their newest precinct had opened months earlier to meet the demands of what had become the fastest-growing suburban county in the United States.

Once almost all farmland, summer homes, surf-side beach bungalows and country estates, Nassau County was fast filling with tract homes and emerging neighborhoods and a constant, seemingly endless, influx of new residents in search of greener pastures. The grandiose harness horse track, Roosevelt Raceway, was built at the eastern edge of old Roosevelt Field, a stone's throw from the modern drive-in movie theatre.

One of the new developments, a so-called "planned community," had been christened a few years earlier. Built by Levitt & Sons, Inc., they'd called it Levittown. And though Roosevelt Field, the once world-famous airfield that had seen Lindbergh off to Paris, had closed in 1951, a huge modern shopping mall of the same name was now under construction in its stead — the future home of F.W. Woolworth, Gimbels and Macy's.

"Ladies," the shorter of the officers said, removing his cap.

The taller one also removed his hat, placed it under his arm, nodding toward his fellow patrolman.

"This is Officer Spence," he said. "I'm Johns."

Holding a notebook and a pen he clicked, almost in cadence, Johns asked matter-of-fact: "Which of you is Mrs. Goodson?"

Officer Ricks started to say something. Spence shot him a look and the Hempstead Plains policeman instead bit his tongue.

Johns never wavered. He just continued his focus on the two women, clicking his pen as he waited, unperturbed, for his answer.

"I'm Mrs. Goodson," Colleen said.

Johns nodded.

"We're going to find your little boy," he said, scanning the living room before turning his attention back to Colleen. "I just need to get some information, Ma'am. Details for our incident report, a picture of your son, so we can get started . . . Is there someplace we can talk?"

She motioned for the officer to follow, then headed through the dining area back to the small kitchen. She stopped in the far-most corner, turned to face Johns. The officer opened his notebook. He seemed a bit more at ease now, though not quite relaxed.

"Anything you can remember will be very helpful, Ma'am."

Colleen forced a weak smile. "Thank you."

Johns began to ask questions: Where did the incident happen? What time was it? How long was she in the supermarket? Did she see anything out of the ordinary, anything suspicious? What was her son's name? How old was he? How tall? What was he wearing? When was the last time she saw him? Did he ever talk to strangers? Did she think he might have just wandered off? Had he ever wandered off before? Could he have pushed the carriage? Was he protective of his baby sister? Would he have left her? Who found her daughter? Where was she found? Did she appear harmed in any way? What did Colleen think had happened to her kids?

Was it possible her son could be with a family friend?

Colleen answered each as best she could. Johns seemed to give each question — and each answer — thought before writing it all down in his notebook. He studied her reactions. Noted them, noted the time.

It was obvious he had done this before.

Colleen thought the very notion of that unsettling. She couldn't help but wonder what was going on out in the living room, especially each time the doorbell rang. She thought Driscoll might suddenly walk in, assail her with that disapproving look of his, demand she explain something she couldn't rightly justify to him or anyone else right then.

Just as the interview was about to conclude Officer Spence walked in, startling Colleen. The patrolman motioned to Johns.

Johns said to Colleen: "Do you have a photograph of your son?"

"In the bedroom," she said. "I'll get it."

"You see the tricycle, Mike?" Spence said, after Colleen had gone. He looked at his watch. "Just after four and the bike's in the corner, an empty Halloween bag hanging from the handlebar."

"Empty?"

"Yeah. I checked."

"Got to wonder when she was going to take him," Johns said. "If."

The two officers still wore curious expressions when Colleen returned, photograph in hand.

"It's the best one I have," she said, handing it to Johns.

It was a big black-and-white photograph, a studio shot, hand-painted after the fact. In it the little boy was seated, posed, wearing a dress shirt, a sleeveless sweater over the top, slacks and fresh-shined shoes. His blonde hair was fresh-cut, combed neat. His eyes were very blue, teeth straight and white. Studying it, Johns thought he looked on his Sunday best.

"This will be good," he said.

He seemed about to ask another question, then thought not.

"I know this isn't easy," he said, finally. "But the detectives are going to want to go over this again with you."

The young mother was just about to say, "Okay," when she heard the front door open. Then she heard Marjorie say, "She's inside."

Colleen felt her heart skip a beat. Before she knew it, Driscoll turned the corner and was standing in the kitchen.

"I had to wait for them to let me off base," he said, to no one in particular. Then, damn-near vacant, he said: "Someone please tell me what's going on?"

3

To the kids at Chase County High School back in Cottonwood Falls, Kansas, it was a romance as inevitable as it was improbable. Though not the most-striking girl in class and far from the most-popular, Colleen Tetherwood no doubt had distinctive beauty and, just as certainly, seemed the most-ambitious. Not ambitious in the sense she had ambition.

She didn't.

She had no aspiration of ever becoming the best student, had no intention of going on to college or of ever finding herself a career.

Her lone desire was to find a husband. And, to that end, Colleen was near-shameless, almost to the point of calculation. She was a catch. Or so she often made it known, with a knack for doing so. She had the ability to seem like she wasn't trying even when she was.

And, she almost always was.

Those who knew her thought her shallow, transparent; those who knew her best just thought her manipulative.

Boys mostly seemed destined to look past it all.

Driscoll Goodson had been the last — or maybe, the latest — in that line. He was a farm boy, though maybe this was a misnomer, since it implied he was somehow dirt poor, maybe even a hick, and had not a lick of upbringing or refinement. Truth was his father was one of the richest men in town. And though Norman Goodson had no real need to get his hands dirty he still believed it a right-honorable thing to do.

His farm was south of town, closer to Bazaar than to Cottonwood Falls. It stretched over four-hundred-fifty acres.

His family first farmed wheat on a smaller tract of land, though, after the crash and the following drought that hammered the Plains with *Oklahoma Rain,* black blizzards and the woebegone Dust Bowl days of *The Dirty Thirties,* he had switched to livestock and soy bean.

Many farmers and farms faltered then. Not him, not his.

The Goodsons had connections. Namely Howell Goodson, Norman's older brother, president of the Cottonwood Savings & Loan. When the *Roaring Twenties* hit the skids that Thursday in October 1929 word had it Howell had maneuvered Goodson money out of the vault before the town folk made a run and it all went belly-up. No one knew for certain if this was true or if Driscoll's grandfather, Howell and Norman's father, simply had been hedging against dry-as-dust days for quite some time.

What most knew was Chester Goodson did not believe much in banks, certainly had no faith in Wall Street or the market.

Indisputable was that cash in hand — or, in a safe somewhere in the root cellar of the Goodson family home — the brothers bought up land while those around them lost theirs, often in heartbreaking fashion.

A shrewd move, made by the Goodson boys at pennies on the dollar, it enabled what had been a modest hundred-acre East Kansas spread to swell with each new failure and foreclosure.

It was 1854 when a wandering trader first settled his ranch along the Cottonwood River, a stone's throw from Diamond Spring Creek, and Cottonwood Falls began life, literally, as a one-horse town.

Then came the railroad, the *Atchinson, Topeka and Santa Fe* building a junction in 1871, followed by Chase County Courthouse — a stately building built at the end of a wide brick street called Broadway.

As America raced into the 20th Century Cottonwood Falls blossomed into a town of hundreds, complete with a dam on the Cottonwood River, a truss bridge to span the South Fork down near Bazaar and an arch bridge at the Falls. Soon folks were calling it "Where the West Begins."

Though, even after a hundred years, Cottonwood Falls was in reality no more than an indistinguishable, indistinct dot on a map between a bunch of other indistinguishable, indistinct dots on a map.

It had, however, earned an inglorious footnote in American history.

That would the events of March 31, 1931.

Which, luck had it, was the very day Driscoll Goodson was born.

Harriet Goodson had spent much of the night in labor and her husband sent for the midwife. Together they had all made it through to dawn. But the sun had come up and the child still had not come and soon Norman Goodson was wondering whether it was more painstaking being a father or ushering a new calf into the world. He made a pot of coffee, drank it, made another, drank that, had eaten breakfast and still, mid-morning in full bloom, not one blessed thing had gone on.

Except, that is, for Harriet's moaning and bemoaning, his spare comforting words falling on her tired, deaf ears.

Then came the thunderous crash, a ground-shaking swell that rocked the house. His wife hard in the throes of childbirth Norman nevertheless ran outside. Off in the distance black smoke was rising from the land.

Pending parenthood or certain disaster, Norman fast explained to Harriet and the midwife something fierce had happened. He had to go.

He hopped into the pickup, drove like the dickens, and when he reached the site could hardly believe his eyes.

There, dead in the middle of the winter wheat field the next farm over, was the smoldering wreckage of an airplane.

A plane that had fallen square out of the sky, left that field filled with scattered bodies and incongruous debris.

The crop, a hundred feet around, was flattened and scorched.

The air hung thick with the smell of oil, gasoline. And death.

Though he hated to admit it Norman's first response was to heave. He was a tough son-of-a-bitch, everyone who knew him knew that. But, witnessing the scene at hand, he simply could not help himself.

After the purge he dug in, trying to find anyone still alive.

It was futile chore, one that last a lifetime, Norman soon joined by friends, neighbors, acquaintances, then by police and the volunteers.

They'd found eight bodies; some intact, some not.

No one knew until much later. But, the crash that had befallen Bazaar and Cottonwood Falls at 10:45 a.m., a scant ten minutes before Driscoll Goodson entered the world, marked the death of a national hero.

An American icon.

The plane was a Fokker F.10A Tri-Motor owned by Transcontinental and Western Air. Operated as Flight 599, it had been en route from Kansas City, Missouri, to Los Angeles, California, with six passengers, two crew, when it literally came apart in midair, went down.

One of the dead was the 43-year-old football coach at the University of Notre Dame, Knute Rockne.

It was all such ignominious history, one that made national headlines, humbled an indomitable collegiate might.

One that caused Norman to miss the birth of his only child.

But it made for a good story in years to come. One Norm Goodson would tell over and over again, often sealed with his take on the infamous Ronald Reagan line: "Couldn't you win just *one* for the Gipper?"

It also was the one, Driscoll would later confess, that first made him afraid of flying. As if his birth were somehow inextricably linked to tragedy. Strange thing was Driscoll grew to have an uneventful childhood. He worked the farm, went to school, did his chores.

Was an obedient son.

His father was strong but often silent. He could be demanding and, surely, he had his moments, often when no one was around.

But despite his presence, despite his rules, he also was the kind of man who believed he had to give his son room to breathe.

Had to give him just enough rope.

Driscoll's mother didn't always agree with this, but she also wasn't the kind to make a scene. A fine woman, a dedicated housewife and mother, she appreciated that Norman was a good husband, a good provider.

So she doted on her only child, learned to be tight with her emotions, take the good with the bad. She held her tongue when she had to.

With no brothers or sisters and no one around for miles Driscoll often spent much of his time alone. Not that he minded.

He was introspective, awkward almost, and far from sociable. He was well-mannered, polite, but he wasn't a talker. It wasn't that he didn't like people. He did, for the most part. He just wasn't very good with them.

He was an average student, didn't play sports. He was neither good-looking nor bad, but rather average, nondescript.

He was remarkable in the fact he was so unremarkable.

If the Goodsons had stature in Cottonwood Falls the Tetherwoods had none. Colleen was from the wrong side of town, raised in the southwest corner of the Falls, known with some disdain as "Benderville."

Locals said it was where the "hoodles" lived. The troublemakers, the *hoodlums.* Her daddy was a railroad man, working the yard for the *Atchinson, Topeka and Santa Fe.* He was a hard drinker, a roughneck, a man with a mean streak who often let his fists do the talking. Most who knew him, or knew of him, didn't think much of him at all. To them he was a bad egg in a bad box who was bad medicine. Most thought his wife not much better and, in some ways, worse — a pot-boiler, who lacked cow sense. Gossip around town had it she was a bit odd, even a bit off. As tight-wound as her husband was she seemed every bit as loose. It was little wonder their daughter had grown up ramshackle and dreams.

Colleen was a year younger than Driscoll, one grade his junior. Together they'd gone to the same school their whole lives, though it wasn't until high school she'd barely even noticed him. By the time she set her sights on him Driscoll was a senior and Colleen had been through a slew of boys, not that there had been much of a selection.

Despite the fact it drew from the surrounding towns and townships there weren't a hundred kids at Chase County High. Barely half were boys and half of those didn't interest Colleen in the least.

Most lasted exactly one date.

That seemed long enough for Colleen to get the lay of the land, get out while the getting was still good. Rumor had it she'd done more than that. But though boys talked Colleen wasn't the kind to kiss and tell or at least kiss and tell the whole truth —just the most-convenient parts.

Boys said one thing, she said another.

Actualities were buried somewhere in-between, deep in the brush, and it was here Colleen's own initials betrayed her.

All the jealous girls in school, which was mostly all of them, soon took to calling her C.T. The *cock teaser*. No one said this to her face. But almost everyone, it seemed, said it behind her back.

For her part, Colleen didn't seem to care.

No girl wanted a reputation. Except, it seemed, her.

If she'd learned anything from the failures of her mother and father it was her way around the block. As she figured it, a reputation created opportunities and opportunities were what she was looking for.

A boy would do just about anything if he thought he had a chance. She promised one and it got her to the rodeo, the County Fair, the State Fair a hundred miles over at the fairgrounds in Hutchinson, and even a few nights out to the brand-new Community Drive-In over in Topeka.

In a year's time she'd seen *Sorrowful Jones* with Bob Hope and Lucille Ball, *The Third Man* with Orson Welles, Trevor Howard and Joseph Cotten, *Every Girl Should Be Married* with Cary Grant and *The Search* with Montgomery Clift. But none of it was going anywhere, at least not anywhere with a destination that interested Colleen.

Which was out of Cottonwood Falls.

Fast running out of boys, she took note of Driscoll. He was neither short nor tall, muscular nor fat. His face was round but not too round. He had light brown hair, blue eyes and he didn't smile much.

Still, she thought he seemed pleasant enough. Even if he was painfully quiet, with just one or two close friends.

He was different. And, his family had money. That was a start.

And, unlike most of the boys at Chase County High, he didn't seem to care if she lived or breathed. He didn't seem to care about her at all.

It was mid-spring of her junior year when Colleen decided on Driscoll. The circus would soon come again to Chase County. She wanted to go and Driscoll had a car, even if it was an old pickup truck.

He didn't have a girlfriend.

She started with a few small smiles when she passed him in the halls. Soon, she was smiling and saying, "Hi, Driscoll."

At first Driscoll had no response at all. He just walked on by, almost as if he didn't hear her. Or was pretending not to.

The truth was he didn't much know much what to say.

As the days turned into a week, then into two, he began to nod hello, though she thought he seemed self-conscious doing so.

Then one morning, when the time was right, she made her move. It was just before lunch. Driscoll was at his locker.

"You know," she said, "the circus is this weekend."

Driscoll turned around, face bright red, more nervous than any boy Colleen had ever known. "Uh," he said. That's what he said: "Uh."

Then, after a moment, he added: "It is."

Her brown hair, shoulder-length with a slight wave, was pinned back on one side. She cocked her head, to the opposite, looked at him with the softest blue eyes she could possibly muster, pursing her lips.

"Well," she said, "are you taking me?"

Uncomfortable, Driscoll looked around, looked up and down the hall, looked at the other kids busily going through their morning routines, looked anywhere he could but at Colleen.

He reached into his locker, set his books down, closed it. She was still staring at him, patiently waiting, when he turned back.

She raised an eyebrow as if to question if she were going to get an answer to her question in this or any other lifetime.

Then, after the longest silence, he said: "I guess."

She smiled at him. "Good. You can meet me here Saturday, out front of the school." She smiled at him again. "One o'clock."

That Saturday Driscoll arrived at Chase County High in his rusting old pickup, the same one his father had driven some eighteen years earlier to the site of the Knute Rockne plane crash the day he was born.

He arrived at the school a few minutes before 1 p.m. More than fifteen minutes later he was still sitting there, waiting for Colleen.

She came walking up about twenty past.

She was young but knew enough to know it was never bad to have a boy wonder but good not to have him wonder too much.

She smiled at Driscoll as she opened the door and got in.

"Hi," she said, again with a smile. "I was hoping you'd be here."

Standing in the crowded kitchen Driscoll wore a look of angst.

No sooner had he asked the question than Colleen ran to him, a tear in her eye, hugged him tight. She kept pressed up against him, holding onto him, her face buried in his chest, as Johns, the Nassau County Police officer, explained to him all that had happened.

When he was done Johns thumbed through his notebook, checking to see if there was any detail he'd missed. The room was filled with deadly silence. Colleen could hear her husband's heart beating so loud, so forceful, she wondered if anyone else heard it, too. Driscoll was trembling. She could feel it, knowing he was trying to hang on as it all sank in.

She squeezed him tight, then tighter still.

She looked up at him. "Please, tell me it will be alright."

Her husband just stood there and soon she relinquished her hold.

Driscoll turned from her, from all of them, and stared out the back window into the yard. It seemed so tranquil as dusk settled in. So empty. He saw the old tire swing hanging from the tree branch.

"Didn't I warn you not to leave them alone?"

Colleen started to cry.

Officer Spence handed her a linen from the counter.

"Now isn't the time, Mr. Goodson," Johns said.

His back to the three of them Driscoll took his hand, wiped his face. After a few moments he turned back to the room. His eyes were red.

"So, what do we do?"

Officer Spence was working on an answer when the doorbell rang.

It had rung a few times during the conversation in the kitchen, Halloween trick-or-treaters making the rounds before dinner. Each time Marjorie had gone to the door, greeted the kids, dispensed with a few pennies, sent those kids packing. Expecting to see more children, instead Majorie answered to find two men wearing dark suits.

One was older than the other by years. An easy guess was mid-to-late fifties, the other middle-aged. The older one had gray hair, slicked neatly, the younger dark black, cut tight. Both wore white shirts, ties. The older man, shorter than the younger, wore a navy blue jacket and slacks. The younger wore all black with black shoes, long in need of a shine.

Before Marjorie could ask both flashed a badge.

"We're looking for the Goodsons," the older man said.

Marjorie ushered the two men in and, as they walked into the living room, Johns and Spence walked in from the kitchen followed by Driscoll and Colleen. The two detectives nodded to everyone, matter-of-fact.

Then the older detective looked at Ricks, the Hempstead Plains officer, who was still hanging around.

"Thank you, patrolman. You can go now."

Officer Ricks started to say something; the older detective cut him off at the knees. "Thanks, patrolman," he said. "We've got it from here.'"

The detectives paid little attention as Ricks headed out, more intent on sizing up the scene. Johns stood motionless; Spence again snickered.

The older, shorter detective was Newbury Farmer. A veteran of the department, he was seasoned, grizzled. His partner had many years under his belt, too, not to mention his fair share of steak and potatoes.

His name was Jones.

The detectives asked Driscoll, Colleen and Marjorie to wait on the sofa. They took Spence and Johns back to the kitchen.

The patrolmen explained the situation. Johns made sure to point out the tricycle. When they'd finished Farmer thanked them and told them to get back to the station house so their captain could get things going.

He wanted an alert sent to all precincts, all radio patrol cars, all of Nassau County. He wanted to find the boy.

It was a little after 5 p.m. when the two officers left. Farmer and Jones were in the living room, Farmer seated in an armchair, Jones standing. Jones studied the nervous faces as his partner got comfortable.

There was still much work to be done.

A little boy was lost out there, somewhere.

Farmer got ready to plow.

4

"There's no one who'd want to hurt your boy?"

It was a question, though Newbury Farmer didn't ask it as one, and once asked he sat back and did what all good detectives did having asked a question meant to be asked not as a question but rather as live bait set out there just because. He pushed slightly back into the armchair, sure. But that was it. When you had as many years on the job as he had you didn't get anxious, didn't press. You sat casual, played the old lion.

It was tried-and-true detective work with years of hard knocks behind it. Ask the question, wait for the answer. Be confident, even smug.

Watch what happened next; make them sweat.

Lost for an answer Driscoll sat silent.

Colleen turned to Marjorie. "I can't think of anyone. Can you?"

Marjorie never looked at her friend, never even looked up. "Who would want to hurt such a good little boy?" she said, finally.

"I'm not saying anyone would," Farmer said, pondering the answer. Then, raising an eyebrow, he said: "Though, you'd be surprised."

Turning to Colleen, Driscoll seemed about to say something, saw she seemed shaken, instead didn't say a word. Farmer thought the husband might move to comfort his wife, maybe throw an arm around her shoulder, pull her in close. Instead, he never moved an inch.

The detective shot his partner a quick glance. Jones reacted ever so slight. Farmer noted it, turned his attention back to the sofa. Eyes reddening, Colleen sat hands folded in her lap. Her husband stared, blankly, straight ahead. Marjorie, meanwhile, still appeared agitated, at least uncomfortable. Maybe she knew something, maybe nothing.

Farmer couldn't really tell. It was all too soon.

The detective settled still deeper into the cushioned chair.

"What's the boy like?" he asked.

A slight smile crossed Driscoll's face. "He's a good son."

Colleen fought back a sniffle.

"He's . . . he's the kind of boy who pays attention to everything, who pays mind to what you say. The kind who listens to his mother."

"He's quiet," Marjorie said. "He can't put it all into words yet. But you know he's thinking about what he's heard, what's been said, and you never know if he'll say something when you least expect him to."

"You seem to know the boy well," Jones said. "You close?"

"I sit for him, sometimes. For both Bobby and Johanna, when Coll has errands to run. Or an engagement. I love him like he was my own."

"You have children?" Farmer asked, curious.

Marjorie's smile vanished. "I . . . I can't have children."

The detective watched as she dabbed her eyes with a tissue.

"I'm sorry. I can't imagine that can be easy," he said. "You sound like you're good with kids."

While all was being said Jones sat, watching Colleen. He'd been bothered by something for more than a few minutes now, it seemed.

"You cooking something?" he said, finally.

"No. Why?"

"I smell it, too," Farmer said, turning to Jones.

The detective was walking the room now — Driscoll, Colleen and Marjorie watching him with curiosity, even interest. Like a bloodhound trying to find the trail, Jones had a scent he couldn't quite place. He went to the kitchen but soon returned, then headed for the back of the house. He walked into the main bedroom, then into the room where Bobby and little Jo slept. Back out into the living room he motioned to Colleen.

"Your daughter needs changing."

Marjorie jumped. "I'll get it."

But it wasn't the odor of some dirty diaper that bothered Jones and he continued toward the front door. Toward the upstairs staircase.

"What's up here?"

"The attic," Driscoll said.

Jones seemed just about to climb the stairs when he looked down, saw the brown paper bag leaned hard against the warm radiator. He took one look, thought he saw a dark maroon blotch on one side, thought it looked like seepage, blood. He took a deep breath.

As the pungent air filled his nostrils, his look was one of revelation.

"Ground meat," he said, as he opened the bag.

"Oh," Colleen said to the detective, taking the parcel from his hand.

"I don't know where my mind was," she said, as she turned for the kitchen trash. "Mondays are meat loaf night. That was dinner."

Inside, Johanna was now crying. Marjorie called for a bottle.

"I'll be right back," Colleen said as she headed in with formula, leaving Driscoll alone on the sofa in front of the two detectives.

Farmer thought the husband strangely calm.

"The officers said you were upset your wife left the children outside the market unattended, Mr. Goodson," he said.

"It was one of her bad habits."

"Do you blame her?" Jones asked. "You know, for what happened?"

Quietly, he said: "She just doesn't think."

As he sat there looking lost Colleen and Marjorie walked back into the room. Colleen held Johanna, nursing a bottle.

The detectives thought Driscoll almost overwhelmed at the sight of his daughter, watching as he reached for her, taking the little girl in his arms, cradling her with the first real tenderness he'd shown.

"Coll told me what happened," Marjorie said. "You all must be famished. I still have leftovers. From the weekend party. I'll go get them."

"Thanks Margie," Colleen said. "Thanks."

It was a few minutes before Marjorie returned with a platter of white bread sandwiches. Her husband came, too, two bottles of cola in hand.

"I'm sorry," he said, nodding to Driscoll and Colleen as he walked in.

"I had to run out, get boxes and a crate. If I had known."

The detective watched as he set the soda on the coffee table. He reached out to shake hands, but Farmer just laid a stare on him.

"Boxes?"

Before the man could answer Jones chimed in. "A crate?"

He stood frozen, eyeing the two men.

"I'm sorry. And you are?"

Stone-faced, the elder detective returned the hard once-over.

"I'm Detective Farmer, this is Detective Jones. We're Nassau County Police . . . And *you* are?"

"I'm Marjorie's husband, Taggart . . . Taggart Woods."

Farmer shot Jones a quick glance, turned back to the new man.

"What's this about boxes and a crate?"

Taggart stared smug at the gumshoe dick. "Air Force. I just retired . . . We're moving end of the week. Back to California."

"Or maybe Las Vegas," Marjorie said, back in from the kitchen.

"Or maybe Las Vegas," her husband said, corrected.

"I see," Farmer said.

As Marjorie handed out plates and poured soda for everyone, Taggart leaned in and grabbed half a sandwich. So did Colleen, Marjorie, then Farmer. Jones grabbed two: one tuna fish, one ham and cheese.

Driscoll, Johanna still nestled in his arms, passed.

"If there's anything we can do," Taggart said to Driscoll and Colleen, chewing on a bite as he said it. "You know you can count on us."

"Thank you," Driscoll said, his voice a bare whisper.

Farmer turned to Marjorie.

"You found the carriage, Mrs. Woods?"

"You found the carriage, Margie?" Taggart said, surprised.

"Yes." She gave her husband a nervous glance. "Over on Hughes."

"There was no sign of the boy?" Jones asked, jumping in.

The woman shook her head. "No. Just Johanna."

Farmer thought for a moment.

"Did you see anything else? Before that? After?"

Again, Marjorie glanced at her husband.

"What is it, Mrs. Woods? Did you see something?"

"Well . . . But I'm sure it's nothing."

"How's that?"

"Tag and I went to the shopping center. Earlier in the day."

Colleen gasped. "You did?"

Jones took another quick look at his partner. "What time?"

Marjorie turned to her husband seeming not to want to guess. He shrugged. Cool as a cucumber, he said: "One-fifteen, one-thirty."

"And?" Farmer said.

"There were carriages outside the IGA," Marjorie said. "There were more, down near the . . . I think it was down near the Five and Ten."

"And?"

"And there were these Negroes."

"Two niggers," Taggart said, interrupting.

Jones went fishing. "Two Negroes?"

"Two *niggers*," Taggart said, again, this time for emphasis. "Man and a woman. *Darkies*. Standing around, just hanging around. Loitering."

This time Farmer raised an eyebrow.

"What made you notice them?"

"Do I need a reason? They were there. That's why."

Turning to Farmer, Colleen said: "You don't think . . ."

The detective raised a hand, cutting her short. "Did you see them by the carriages, Mr. Woods, these *Negroes?*"

"Not exactly."

"Why not exactly?"

"Because . . . " Taggart started. "Because we had things to do. I had errands to run . . . I mean, if I'd have known."

"Right."

"What time was that?" Jones asked.

Taggart turned to his wife, shrugged again.

"Maybe one-forty-five?"

Detective Farmer stared at Colleen. Driscoll sat, taking it in. "About the time you got to the shopping center, Mrs. Goodson?"

"About."

Farmer took the temperature. Marjorie, Taggart. He pointed to Colleen. "And *you* didn't see *her?*"

"You usually go up Mitchell, don't you, Coll?" Marjorie said.

"Yes," Colleen said. "That's how I went."

"That's why," Taggart said. "We drove out on Eisenhower, went down Glenn Curtiss and came home. We must've just missed each other."

"Must have," Jones said, shooting Farmer a look.

"So," Jones said. "What was it these two *'darkies'* were wearing?"

Taggart thought.

"Nothing special. The man had dungarees, a loose shirt. Dark blue, a work shirt. The woman, I can't remember. A dress? Beige, maybe?"

"Anything else?" Farmer said.

"There was a car."

"A car?"

"An old Plymouth. In the lot. Remember, Marge?"

"Oh, yes. I recall you pointed one out."

"It was gray. Medium color," Taggart said. "That battleship gray color. I remember thinking, 'That looks like a car they'd be driving.'"

"Why's that?" Jones said. "What made you think . . . "

"I don't know," Taggart said. "I don't know for sure. I just did."

"Do you remember the license Mr. Woods?"

Again, Taggart thought for a moment. "No. Can't say I do."

"The year?" Farmer said. "What year?"

Taggart shrugged. "I couldn't place it if I tried."

Farmer stared holes through the man. "Try."

"Somewhere in the Forties. Maybe late . . . Probably late."

"What about you, Mrs. Goodson? Did you see these Negroes?"

The young mother seemed a bit unraveled as she tried to recollect the scene. "I'm sorry," she said. "But, I didn't. I had a lot on my mind. I had no idea anything bad could happen." She started to cry.

In the barest breath she added: "I just had no idea."

The doorbell rang, again. Marjorie answered to find more kids.

As Colleen moved to hand out more pennies, Farmer asked for the phone. Without a word, Driscoll pointed to the kitchen.

Then, he went inside to put the baby down.

Farmer was still on the phone long after the trick-or-treaters had gone and a good ten minutes passed before he returned to the living room. He'd called headquarters to tell his squad commander about the Negroes and the Plymouth, just in case. He'd also called Meadowbrook Field.

He wanted to talk to the base commander.

Walking back in Farmer turned to his partner, shook his head.

"I'm sorry," the detective said to Driscoll. "There's no news."

"Nothing at all?"

Farmer seemed momentarily lost, then said: "I'm afraid not."

He looked around the living room. All eyes were on him, now.

"This is how it goes, sometimes. You can't read into it. Someone could have found him and they're trying to figure out who to call.

"You just don't know," he said. "Until you do . . . "

"Until we do, what?" Colleen said.

"Until we do we do what we can to find him."

"And, what's that?" Driscoll said.

"We have patrols out all over the county, officers on the look out."

Then, turning to Driscoll, Farmer added: "I just got off the phone with your base commander."

"You called General Johnson?"

"Yes. And he understands the situation and is calling in all available personnel. We're going to search every neighborhood, every block, every house, every yard. We'll go door-to-door deep into the night if that's what it takes to locate your son." He gave his best look of reassurance.

"We're going to find him."

As Farmer spoke, Taggart moved next to Driscoll and, standing over him, reached down and placed a hand on the man's shoulder.

"We can go, too?" Taggart asked.

"I'd expect nothing less," Farmer said. He motioned to the two men. "Better grab some coats. It's cold out and we may be a while."

As Tag ran across the street to grab a jacket, Driscoll went inside to get something warm from the closet.

Colleen remained seated, Marjorie arm's length.

"One more thing Mrs. Goodson," Farmer said. "Before we go."

"Yes," Colleen said, looking up at the detective. "What is it?"

"The tricycle. I couldn't help but notice it in the corner. You've got an empty Halloween bag on the handlebars. How come?"

"I . . . I was going to take him after dinner," she said, finally.

As she answered Driscoll walked back in wearing his service jacket. He stared at the bike, off in the corner.

"I thought you were going to take him in the afternoon?"

Colleen bit her lip. "I was. Then I thought maybe you'd want to go trick-or-treating after dinner. That we might all go as a family."

For a moment Driscoll seemed at odds what to do. Then he stepped over to his wife, placed a hand on her shoulder, squeezed.

Just as fast, he pulled away. "We'd better go," he said.

As the three men headed toward the door Colleen got up from the sofa, ran to Driscoll and gave him a big hug. It seemed to surprise him.

"I love you," she whispered, barely loud enough for everyone to hear.

Almost reluctantly, he said: "I love you, too."

No sooner had the men all left, headed for Meadowbrook in the black unmarked police car, than little Johanna began to cry. Knowing Colleen was a ball of nerves, Marjorie went to grab Jo.

Returning to the room, baby rocking in her arms, Margie said to her friend: "I think she needs another bottle."

Colleen got up and went to the kitchen, got a bottle, handed it to Marjorie. Then, she stood — just staring at the front door.

"You should try to get some sleep," Marjorie said.

"How can I?" Colleen said, still blankly staring.

"Look," Marjorie said. "You need time. I'll take Jo for the night."

"Would you?" Colleen said.

"You know I'd take them any time." She turned to Colleen, looking as if she might cry. "I'm sorry. I didn't mean it like that. You know . . . "

"I know," Colleen said, as she forced a weak smile. "I know."

Colleen went inside to pack a bag for her friend: a sleeper, diapers, ointment, safety pins, a pacifier. A few bottles of formula.

As she packed, Majorie said: "Look, I have to ask."

"What?"

"You had nothing to do with this, right?"

"Margie," Colleen said. "How could you? Of all people . . . "

Marjorie squeezed her friend tight as she could.

"I'm sorry," Marjorie said. "I really am, but I had to ask."

"You should know better," Colleen said. She sounded angry now. "You know better than anyone, Marge . . . You know the answer."

Forcing a weak smile, Marjorie shook her head yes. She gave her friend one last hug, grabbed the bag, took the baby — and left.

5

General Leon W. Johnson was a man of reputation and regard. A hero of the first order, he looked it: fit, lean, handsome. Dashing. He had a full head of dark hair, though it had begun to salt in a handful of places.

He wore a thick, bristling brush mustache, one that hid what, after all these years, remained an undeniable boyish smirk.

A graduate of the U.S. Military Academy at West Point, recipient of a master of science degree in meteorology from the California Institute of Technology, Johnson had commanded the heralded U.S. Army Air Forces 44th Bomb Group, the *Eight Balls,* in World War II.

He not only survived the daring low-level raid on the German-occupied Rumanian oil fields at Ploesti, one of the bloodiest air battles of the war, he had also been a leader of it — piloting his high-altitude four-engined B-24D Liberator bomber barely a hundred feet off the deck in the face of fierce German anti-aircraft fire and Luftwaffe fighter opposition that doomed a third of the almost two-thousand men around him.

He had been awarded the Silver Star, the Legion of Merit, not one, but two Air Force Distinguished Service Medals, two Distinguished Flying Crosses, four Air Medals. He was recipient of the French Legion of Honor, the Croix de Guerre from Belgium *and* from France, a Distinguished Flying Cross from the United Kingdom. He had the U.S. Congressional Medal of Honor. That, for his unbridled heroism at Ploesti.

Rising through the ranks from Second Lieutenant to Colonel, then General, Johnson organized the Third Air Force after the war, then commanded the Fifteenth Air Force in Colorado Springs, Colorado, to provide the backbone necessary for the Berlin Airlift that brought food and supplies to a war-ravaged post-Hitler nation.

Near the start of the Korean War he was named Base Commander at Meadowbrook Field, heading the Continental Air Command.

There, he oversaw the Air National Guard and the Air Force Reserve. His Cold War warrant was the steadfast protection of America.

Though Driscoll had served three years now at Meadowbrook, his rank was still that of Airman Second Class. He was a clerk.

He piloted paperwork, flew a desk; had never been in battle, not even over the phone, and was certain he never would.

He had nervously saluted the Commander on the random occasions when their paths unexpectedly crossed in the hallways of the stately brick Headquarters Building built three decades earlier to house the U.S. Army Quartermaster Corps at Meadowbrook. But in all that time he'd never had a real conversation with Johnson. Not one; not two words. He hadn't imagined any circumstance in which he actually ever might.

Now he found himself in Johnson's office, no more than an arm's length from him. Johnson stopped him dead as he began his salute.

"No need, son," the General said. "We've got better things to do."

Driscoll looked relieved. Johnson shook his hand, gave the man a reassuring smile; gave Taggart and the detectives the once-over.

"We'll have a thousand men here within the hour," he said. "We'll get them anywhere they need to be to help find the boy. They're yours."

"It's much appreciated, General," Farmer said.

"Not a problem . . . I've got two girls of my own."

The office was filled with old black-and-white photographs from the war. Pictures of Johnson with his old crew, pictures of his war-wearied bomber, *Suzy Q.* Pictures of him with influential statesmen.

Pictures with Presidents: Roosevelt, Truman *and* Eisenhower.

The General walked past all of it, taking no notice, to a big aluminum canteen-style coffee urn off in the corner.

"I made us some Joe. Grab yourselves a cup."

He poured black coffee, handed it to Driscoll.

"You and your wife are from Kansas?"

Nervous, Driscoll said: "Yes, Sir."

"Whereabouts?"

"Cottonwood Falls, Sir. Over near Emporia."

"East Kansas. Good folk," Johnson said. He smiled.

"Ad Astra per Aspera."

Driscoll stood dumbstruck. The General looked over the other three, thought all seemed more than a bit confused.

He decided to let them muse for a moment. Then, he said: "Latin."

He turned back to Driscoll. "Go on, son."

The young father dropped his head, overwhelmed. When he looked up all eyes were on him. His voice quavered.

"It . . . it means, 'To the Stars through Difficulties.'"

"Exactly," Johnson said. He placed a firm hand on Driscoll's shoulder. "You've got to plow on through hardship toward your goal."

He gave the other three men a look. "Kansas state motto," he said with a wink, as he turned to face the burdened man.

"I'm from Moline, son. A hundred miles south of you . . . God as my witness, I'm going to do all I can to help find that boy of yours."

The largest search in the young history of Nassau County, of modern Long Island, began with almost two thousand men.

A thousand, maybe more, were Air Force men: pilots, mechanics, crew, doctors, nurses, cooks, clerks, drivers from the motor pool.

Anyone who was not needed to man the base that night.

Most came in voluntarily, foregoing off-duty hours, foregoing sleep, to help find Bobby Goodson. Some brought wives or girlfriends, others brought friends and neighbors. There were police officers and firemen. Foot patrolmen, desk sergeants, detectives, chiefs, captains, marshals. Anyone and everyone who thought they might lend a hand.

Anyone who'd just heard of the ordeal.

General Johnson had pulled out all stops. He'd called in the National Guard. He'd activated reservists. He had even contacted the New York

State Police, located a K-9 Unit in upstate Westchester, north of New York City. Asked them to come.

The Suffolk County Sheriff's Office, which teamed with the State Police to enforce the law on eastern Long Island, sent deputies.

Local departments sent officers, too.

The Garden City Police pledged to search their upscale enclave, north of Hempstead Plains. The Freeport Police and Long Beach Police, which patrolled those South Shore waterfront communities, said they'd search parks, boats, beaches. Hempstead Plains, Glen Cove, Southampton Town, East Hampton Town, Sag Harbor, Southold, Greenport. Amityville.

The list went on and on. And on.

Roadblocks were set on all major roads throughout the county. Officers arranged a checkpoint at the toll booths out on the Southern State Parkway, near the Queens border. The NYPD did as much on the highways into and out of New York City. Harbor patrol units were on alert for suspicious activity. No stone would be left unturned.

Driscoll had never seen anything like it. He found himself greatly moved by the Herculean effort being undertaken to find his son.

Blocks, yards, parks, woods, churches, schools, houses, garages, sheds. Nothing was out of bounds. Searchers would knock on every door, stop every car, question every resident. Some would search streams that crisscrossed the county. Some were instructed to shine flashlights into roadside sewers, to crawl down into them if need be.

Others would search the corridors of the Long Island Rail Road.

One team was even sent to the construction site for the highway being built not far from the off-base housing area for airmen at Meadowbrook Field. Those searchers were to comb through the heavy equipment being used to build Meadowbrook Parkway, the new, modern road that would eventually run from the South Shore up into central Nassau, dividing Hempstead Plains. They were to sort through piles of construction debris, through piles of bulldozed trees and bushes and undergrowth.

The K-9 Unit, their officers armed with search dogs trained for such an event, were headed to the supermarket, hoping beyond hope to track a scent. The detectives, Farmer and Jones, were going with them.

So were Tag and Driscoll.

It was about 8 p.m. when the teams set off. Some headed out on foot, others loaded into buses commandeered from local school districts. Still more headed out in canvas-sided troop carriers used to transport airmen at Meadowbrook Field. Farmer, Jones, Taggart and Driscoll set off in the unmarked car. They arrived at the shopping center minutes later.

Stepping from the car into the darkened lot, a lot illuminated only by the glow of a three-quarter moon, a handful of dim streetlights and a million faint stars, Driscoll walked uneasily to the IGA and stood there like some punch-drunk prizefighter battling to keep his feet. He breathed the chill autumn air in deep but couldn't catch his breath.

His heart pounded as he took in everything at once — and nothing at all. This was the very spot where his son had last been seen. He imagined his boy, curious or frightened, innocent or overwhelmed by circumstance, at the carriage, standing watch over his baby sister, waiting for one door to open, somehow passing through another instead. Driscoll envisioned a world of possibilities. And yet, he could envision none. He felt weak in the knees, a little Leon Errol, as if hit by one last invisible punch.

And just like that he collapsed to the pavement, falling before Taggart, Farmer or Jones could even think about moving in to catch him.

"My God," he said, sobbing so hard he might never stop.

As the three men knelt there to comfort him, Driscoll, still in uniform, stared at that supermarket door, simply overwhelmed by it all.

"Where is he?" he cried. "Where did he go?"

Alone in the darkened living room Colleen sat on the sofa, lost in thought. She'd wandered aimless after Marjorie had taken Jo, had walked out to the backyard trying to escape the silence, sat down in a lawn chair

— eyes drawn to the swing until finally she went back inside. Try as she might she kept seeing the damn tricycle. And the Halloween bag.

And Bobby's face.

So she went to the kitchen, trying hard not to notice the telephone on the wall near the door. She got some ice, poured herself a glass of scotch. Turned out the lights, fell pressed into the sofa. She thought about how her life had become such a mess, everything gone so wrong.

When she reached the bottom of the glass Colleen pulled herself off the couch and walked back inside for more.

She stood in the dark dialed in on the telephone, barely visible in the shadowy light that crept in through the back window. She thought about making that call, dismissed it, not knowing what even to say, then having pondered some more, moved to the phone — and dialed the number.

It rang and rang. It rang long enough that she damn-near hung up. Before she could change her mind the call went through.

He answered.

"Hello," she said. "It's me."

She listened hard, more disquieted with every word. "I know what you said. But I had to. Please. We have to talk."

As she listened Colleen wandered to the dining room, stretching the cord. On the far side of the table, line taut and at its limit, she almost knocked over the vase as she hit the end. She was most *uncalm* now.

She swirled her scotch, exhaled hard, took a sip.

"I know. But I need to see you. Please."

She hated arguments, had seen enough of them to last her a lifetime, and she wasn't looking for one now. She wanted to cry.

She took another sip of scotch, instead.

"Fine," she said. "I understand." She caught her breath. "I just wanted to tell you Bobby's gone. He's disappeared."

This time as she turned, Colleen caught the vase with the phone cord, knocking it over with a crash. "What do I mean, 'He's gone?'

"I mean gone, disappeared. When? This afternoon."

She pulled out a dining room chair, the one at the end of the table, nearest the back wall, collapsed hard into it still listening. He sounded annoyed, as if he didn't honestly believe her. As if she were lying.

As if it were all a game, a ploy. A damn dodge.

"Please," Colleen said. "Don't do this . . . Not now."

She started to cry. She was sure he could hear her as she did, using her free hand as she tried to wipe away the tears.

"I know it doesn't change anything, but . . . Just see me."

Before she could say another word the line went dead. Left with only the dial tone buzzing in her ear Colleen dropped the phone.

Just like that she was alone again, forever a girl in the dark. Dazed, inconsolable, she wandered back to the living room, fell onto the sofa.

"My God," she uttered. "What a complete mess."

She took a long drink, let the scotch settle in, swallowed hard.

Oh, Colleen, she thought. What have you done?

66

6

The Royal American Circus rolled into town with eighteen brick red rail cars trailing an old black steam locomotive belching smoke, cinder and ash. There were box cars and flatbed cars and coach cars and even a little red caboose, all of it a sight to see. Each coach had a silver roof and cream-yellow sash band mid-section, window-high. Below, in Carolina blue outlined in black: Royal American Shows.

Above, the boast that made the circus a favorite of families and fans throughout the Midwest: World's Largest Midway.

Within hours the hands had unloaded it all: lions, tigers, elephants, bears, horses, ponies; an assemblage of trained dogs.

Tent poles were pulled from flat cars, loaded onto trucks, carried off to the fairgrounds. Canvas tents followed, as did mechanical rides, crates filled with games and attractions, grills for cooking, boxes of programs and tickets for hawking everything from admission to sideshow acts. The twenty-four-hour man had advanced it, making arrangements, marking the route, scouting the grounds, setting the layout of what tent went where and where went what ride, game or vendor. What wonder.

And overnight a patch of land had been transformed into an ethereal marvel of light, sight and sound that had drawn forth most of Cottonwood Falls. Had drawn the curious from places as far as distant Emporia.

The circus wasn't like the State Fair or the County Fair. Or even the 4-H Club Fair, with its agriculture exhibits, cattle shows, craft sellers and homemade pie stands. It was strange, seductive. Indescribable.

Driscoll and Colleen arrived not long after the first crowds, after a short but mostly silent drive in the old pickup from the parking lot at Chase County High. On that ride she'd said, with enthusiasm, how great it was to have the circus back in town and he'd said, "I know," and that was it. She didn't think it was because he was angry or even upset she'd been late. She simply thought it was him being him, quiet and reserved, and maybe more than a little nervous and so she looked out the window as he drove along, for the first time in her life unsure what to do. Or say.

After they parked and walked to the entrance, neither too close or too far from one another, Driscoll paid their admission and then they were in. But not before the man at the gate sized him up, made a joke at his expense, saying: "You look like you just walked in from Kansas, son."

To which the second gate man said: "Wait, y'all did."

Her new boyfriend didn't even laugh. She wanted to, if but to lighten the mood, then fought it off not wanting to embarrass him.

As they walked through Colleen took Driscoll by the arm.

"Well," she said. "We're *not* in Kansas anymore."

Looking around the midway it almost seemed true. Colleen noticed Driscoll smirked, briefly pulled her arm in tight, before catching himself — and, so she thought then for the first time it all might work. That there was a shot. She felt good about that and it made her relax. She had at least a day to find an answer and, if all went well, maybe more.

She decided for once to let it play out.

The midway stretched almost to the horizon, a low wide tent at the entrance, a row of smaller tents in a line on either side. Between them there was a long tent, with open sides, then another. And another.

Near the back end of the lot, past the last of those open tents, a giant ferris wheel with red, white and blue seats, towered over it all. Not far was a merry-go-round with a calliope that seemed it could be heard for miles. There were children's rides, miniature cars that went around on a small circular track, and hand-crank cars that rode on train rail. There was a stand selling custard called "Frozen Delight" and another selling roasted peanuts for five cents a bag. There was an odd, sensational-looking ride like a ferris wheel except it had enclosed cage-like chairs that tumbled and twirled, end-over-end. And, of course, there was the Big Top — a huge red-striped tent whose peak soared high above the grounds.

Colleen asked Driscoll if he wanted to go on the ferris wheel. He looked at her with an uneasiness and said: "Don't think so."

Instead, they bought admission to the sideshow tents.

Driscoll forked over two quarters, one for each, and soon they were wandering, tent-to-tent, taking it all in.

There was a sword-swallower and a fire-eater; a ventriloquist with a wooden boy on his lap who said the most-inappropriate things. One tent had a bearded woman, another a midget barely the size of a kindergarten child who called himself "The World's Oldest Smallest Man."

There was a man, covered from head-to-toe with hair, who claimed to be a werewolf, and another who was so thin that when he sucked in his chest Driscoll and Colleen thought they could see his spine outlined against his stomach. It all seemed just so inhuman.

The strangest of the strange acts was the two-headed baby.

It was tiny, not very big, and it was obviously dead, if it had ever been alive at all. It sat, floating in this big mason jar filled with some sort of liquid that was clouded and murky and not quite clear. It had a body that appeared normal in every way, except that it had not one but two heads. It was hard to tell from looking if they were one in the same, if it really was one little boy with two heads or if it was something else altogether.

They watched the blonde hair float in the liquid.

One woman fainted, straight away, onto the hay-strewn floor.

"Do you think it's real?" Colleen asked, finally.

"Can't be," Driscoll said. "More like a doll."

"It's a . . . What do you call, that? A hoax?"

"That'd be my guess."

"But, it looks like a real baby boy," she said. "I wonder how he got like that. You wonder how someone could let that happen."

"Yeah," Driscoll said. "You would."

Having stared at the boy for the longest time Driscoll and Colleen decided to move on. They walked out into the afternoon sunlight, to folks milling about, to clean, fresh springtime air. They each took a deep breath, relieved the boy was now somehow behind them.

Colleen wanted to see what was inside the tent with a banner that read: "Fabulous Mary Jane and Brother Bob, The Double-Sexed Wonder Twins. Exposed in the Nude!" But before they could enter Driscoll asked if she wanted cotton candy and they walked to the concession, got some, ended up with sticky fingers, then decided on the Big Top, instead.

They found seats near the front of the dirt-floored ring. There were jugglers and hoopers and clowns. There was an elephant act the ringmaster billed as "Pachyderm Pulchritude." There was a man on a unicycle, trained horses that moved in cadence; even a woman who rode bareback, jumping on and off a white stallion at will, doing somersaults and then standing astride it in defiance as that horse ran around — all, as her virginal white dress flowed carefree in the breeze.

The high-wire routine saw a man navigate a tightrope above the crowd. Blindfolded, he did so without a net. Once, when the walker took a stumble, Colleen latched onto Driscoll tighter than she'd ever held onto anyone. She was surprised he didn't pull away, but seemed to enjoy it.

He gave her a smile. Or what passed for one.

Moments later a couple was launched from a giant cannon across the ring and into a net, ending the show. Driscoll seemed to be having fun.

Truth be told so was she.

Walking out of the big tent Driscoll and Colleen found the midway a myriad of lights. Night had fallen, the stars were out.

The circus had a whole new feel. They walked the grounds, got a cola, pitched pennies but failed to win a prize. They walked past that strange new amusement, the one with cage-like seats called the "Rock-o-Plane."

Colleen asked Driscoll if he wanted to ride. He looked at her, again suddenly tense, and shook his head no.

They went on the merry-go-round, instead. On one pass he managed to grab a brass ring, handed it to her. She smiled, thinking it sweet.

Not long after they walked to the pickup truck, a full day behind them. Before he could ask Colleen told Driscoll to drop her in the lot at Chase County High. He said he'd rather not, that he thought he should take her home, but she said, "Please?" and, reluctantly, he agreed.

When they stopped at the school neither of them said much.

He looked at her, said: "It's okay. I understand."

She waited a moment thinking he might make a move like all those other boys had tried. But he didn't. She smiled at him sweetly.

"I hope we can go out again," she said.

He nodded. "Sure."

She leaned over, gave him a small kiss on the cheek.

"Great," she said. And then she was gone.

Down in Barnum Creek something in the dark caught the attention of Officer Johns. He was walking the shallow creek bed about a mile or so west of where it was Bobby had somehow gone missing, had vanished.

It was after 9 p.m. when he turned his flashlight on the object.

"There!"

The small creek ran next to the new Meadowbrook Parkway. It started up north, in a small reservoir on the western side of the road, then ran south past the edge of Meadowbrook Field before it crossed under where the road was being built and continued along the east side. It crept through a small flat stream bed, no more than ten feet at its deepest and no more than fifteen feet at its widest. It was surrounded by dense scrub oak and pine and grassy, weeded undergrowth that made going tough. The water in the stream this time of year was barely knee-high. As Johns waved the flashlight to attract the attention of his fellow searchers he moved toward the object along the water's edge, heart pounding. Soon they were all shining their lights on a shirt, caught up on a small rock.

"What do you think?" Johns said, as one man reached it.

The other searcher, a volunteer fireman, lifted the shirt.

He shook his head in disappointment. It was too big to be that of a little boy and it was obvious it'd been in the water too long to have belonged to anyone who might have taken Bobby that afternoon.

"Damn," Johns said, under his breath. Then: "Okay. Let's get back to work." Somehow, this already was beginning to feel futile.

Over at the IGA luck seemed to be running better for Farmer and Jones. Before leaving the Goodson house Jones grabbed a sock and an undershirt belonging to little Bobby to bring for the canine team.

He had given it to the handler and almost immediately the hound found a scent. Agitated, the dog pulled on his leash. Farmer, Jones, Taggart and Driscoll in tow, the handling officer and his dog moved down the sidewalk of the shopping center toward Glenn Curtiss. There they turned, walking down the wide street until they reached Hughes. The dog sniffed around, confused. He sat down, not knowing where else to go.

"What's wrong?" Jones asked.

"He's lost the scent," the handler said. "This might be it."

Jones looked at the handler, turned and stared at Farmer.

"The carriage was found down the block," Farmer said. "But not the little boy . . . You think it's possible he didn't push it there?"

"They could have been split up," the handler said.

"What's that mean?" Driscoll asked. "You think . . . "

"Don't jump to conclusions," Farmer said. "None of this means anything yet. We still have a lot to do before we find answers."

Driscoll shook his head okay as Jones reached into a bag for a sleeper belonging to Johanna. He gave it to the handler, who held it for the dog to gauge. Just like that the hound was off again, pulling them all down Hughes. About a third of the way down the block, not far from a big oak, the dog again stopped cold. Everyone looked around. All they could see were houses, porch lights, light seeping out into the street from inside living rooms. Not much else. The handler shrugged.

"This must be where the carriage was."

"We should knock on some doors," Jones said.

Farmer agreed. "Let's see if anyone saw anything."

As the handler stood, dog at his feet, the detectives went to knock on doors, leaving everyone there. The first few houses turned up nothing.

One older woman said she'd been running errands all afternoon; a man said he'd been at work. Another resident said he was retired, said he and his wife had been for a walk in the nearby park. No one answered the door at still another house and a stack of mail and newspapers on the front stoop made it apparent whoever lived there had not been home for days, at best. Finally, a few houses down, the detectives caught a break.

The older man who answered said he lived with his son, who was stationed over at Meadowbrook; said he'd been in the garden most of the afternoon. The detectives asked if he had seen a blue baby carriage.

"I saw a woman with a baby carriage," he said.

"Around what time?" Farmer asked.

"I don't know. Just before two?"

"Before two o'clock? Are you sure?"

"I think," he said. "I was working in the garden, pulling weeds, so I wasn't wearing my watch. But I remember the siren, the one from the firehouse . . . It sounds off every hour on the hour, you know."

The detective studied the old man. Easily in his seventies he seemed the active type, in good physical shape for a man his age.

That is, he seemed alert enough.

"The woman. What did she look like?"

"Average height, average weight. A nice enough figure."

"White? Or Negro?" Jones asked.

"Negro?" The man stared at the detectives, the strangest expression all of a sudden crossing his face. "What do you mean, Negro? Not in this neighborhood, Detective. Of course, she was white."

"Of course she was," Farmer said.

"What did she look like?" Jones asked. "What was she wearing?"

The old man thought for a moment.

"She was pretty far away and I only saw her for a moment, since I was busy working in my garden, you know. But she had brown hair, maybe about shoulder length. She was wearing a blouse. And a skirt."

"What color?"

"What color? Let's see . . . The blouse was white. I'm sure it was white. The skirt? The skirt . . . I could swear it was dark brown."

Farmer glanced at Jones, looked back at the old man.

"Dark brown? Are you sure?"

"Yes, yes. Brown. Dark brown. I remember it now."

Jones turned to Farmer. "Sounds like the neighbor."

"Yeah, I know."

"What is it detectives?"

"Are you sure it was before two, not three?" Farmer asked.

"I think. But, like I said, I wasn't wearing my watch . . . It's a beautiful watch. I got it in Cuba. During the Spanish-American War."

A remembering smile creased his lips.

"I was young back then. We went in at Siboney, with General Shafter, east of Santiago de Cuba. It was late June and not quite July, if I recall, and it was God-damned hot, like being in a brick oven, you know."

The detectives were growing impatient. They didn't really care about the war or about him landing in Cuba or about any of it.

"I'm sorry," the old man said. "I'm rambling, aren't I?"

"It's okay," Farmer said. "We just need to know if you're certain it was two — or if it could have really been three."

"I mean, it could have been three. It might have been. I heard the siren, from the firehouse. They sound it every hour, you know."

"Yes," Jones said. "We know."

"But did it sound twice," Farmer asked, "or three times?"

"Now, I could have sworn it was two times," he said.

Then, after a minute lost in thought, he said: "To be honest, I wasn't listening all that close. I was working in my garden. And I wasn't wearing my watch . . . Beautiful watch. I got it in Cuba. During the war."

Farmer nodded. "Okay. That's okay."

"What's all this about, anyway?"

"A little boy went missing this afternoon, up on Eisenhower. His baby sister was in that carriage — found by a woman in a dark brown skirt."

Jones added: "She found it just before three."

"Oh. I see," the old man said.

"And you didn't see a boy with them, right?" Jones said.

"No. I didn't see a boy. Just the woman and that carriage, right out there . . . Like I said, I could have sworn it was before two. But, come to think of it, it might have been closer to three. Maybe three . . . "

"Thanks," Farmer said, as he turned to walk back.

The old man waved goodbye. "Glad I could help you boys."

Jones mumbled. "God-damned terrific."

The detectives were still shaking their heads when they reached Taggart, Driscoll and the canine officer out near the old oak.

"He see anything?" Taggart asked.

"Yeah," Jones said. "He saw your wife."

"No?"

"She was wearing a dark brown skirt, right?"

"I'm not sure. Why?"

"He thought he saw her just before two o'clock," Farmer said.

"Before two?" Driscoll asked.

"That's not possible," Taggart said. "Couldn't be."

"He wasn't sure," Jones said. "First he said before two, then he said it might have been before three. He couldn't really . . . "

"Three sounds more like it," Taggart said. "That's when she found the carriage, right? I'm sure it would have been there closer to three."

Farmer gave him a look. "Yes, Mr. Woods. Closer to three."

"Did he see my son?" Driscoll said.

"I'm afraid not."

"So, we've got nothing," the handler said. "Nothing at all."

"Appears that way."

Driscoll seemed crestfallen. "What now?"

The detective ran his hand through his hair. "We keep knocking on doors," he said, finally. "We keep looking for your boy."

Out at the toll booths on the westbound Southern State Parkway in Valley Stream half a dozen officers had their guns trained on a gray 1947 Plymouth. "Where's the boy?" one of the officers yelled.

Inside the car Osias Storm and his wife Alile sat frozen, terrified, hands above their heads, shaking, no idea just what was going on.

"Don't y'all move," Osias whispered. "Just *set* all still-like."

He didn't dare take a breath, turn his head, move a finger. Didn't dare do anything at all. Moments earlier he'd been driving the Plymouth toward the booths, Roosevelt dime in hand for the toll, headed back to the old Weeksville section of Bedford-Stuyvesant, Brooklyn.

Alile was a domestic for a white family in exclusive Garden City; Osias had just taken employment as a sanitation man in Nassau County. Her mother had a small home in a colored neighborhood in Roosevelt.

The two had decided to leave their tenement in Brooklyn, where they lived with his mother, brothers and sisters, an aunt, and move in with hers. To start anew. Money was tight, but this was their chance. It would take hard sacrifices. But they were young, knew how to maneuver.

No matter what, they would make it work.

Night fallen, Osias had driven the old Plymouth onto the Southern State headed to Brooklyn. He would drive the Southern to Laurelton Parkway, take Shore Parkway past Idlewild, head up Pennsylvania Avenue and cut over on Atlantic to Bedford-Stuyvesant. There he and Alile would load what they could into the old car for the trip back. Osias had just pulled into the toll plaza when he saw the police. Before he or Alile even knew what was going on, a half-dozen officers were pointing .38-caliber revolvers at them, one screaming: "Get your damn hands up, *now!*"

Amid the commotion Osias dropped his dime onto the floorboards of the aging Plymouth. And Alile, she began crying something fierce.

"Where's the boy?" the officer yelled, again, revolver aimed squarely at Osias. "And don't you move a God-damn lick! Hear me?"

"The boy?" Osias said, voice a tremble.

"The boy. Where's the boy?"

"He . . . he be in the back."

"Where?"

The other officers still had guns drawn, pointing at the young Negro couple. Still crying, Alile had begun to sing *Jacob's Ladder,* low, quiet, barely above her breath, trying to calm them all. She sure hadn't been this scared since way back in Alabama, back when she was just a child, and the men had come, cloaked in white, setting nighttime skies ablaze.

Her mother and her sisters, her aunts and their families, had all hidden in an old root cellar then, praying for daybreak.

And she'd found herself singing, over and over, that simple spiritual tune: *Sinners do you love your Jesus? If you love him, why not serve him?* Found herself singing it loud enough so only she could hear.

She recalled as she sang it again now how daylight had come and how she and her kin had walked out of that cellar, thankful to be alive.

How then word came that two men — two Negro men; one of them, the local jack-leg preacher — had been found hanging from a length of hand-tied rope off the branch of the biggest, oldest tree in town.

They had been stripped, those men had; left naked to the world, the nooses fitted tight around their necks, another length tied tight around their testicles. It was all a wretched sight. She recalled as she sat singing again now how they had not been much older than she was here and look what happened for no reason at all — except the color of their skin.

"Tell her to shut up!" the officer pointing the gun yelled. "Now!"

Without turning, Osias, still trembling, whispered to his young wife.

"Please 'Leale. Hush now so the man don't think to shoot us."

Alile did, though the lyrics still echoed inside her brain.

"Good," the officer yelled.

"Now, tell the boy to step on out of the car. *Now!* And don't you move, *nigger!* Or, God as my witness, I swear, I'll shoot you dead."

7

It was a little after 10 p.m. when the doorbell rang. Alone in the darkened living room it startled Colleen. She was almost done with her third scotch, was contemplating a fourth, and jarred from her ponderous state her mind raced. It was too late for trick-or-treaters. For the briefest instant she considered it might be Driscoll, with news of Bobby. Then she remembered the door was unlocked. As she walked across the room, out of sorts, Colleen stumbled in the dark, banging into the coffee table.

She opened the door somehow expecting to find Jake.

"Colleen Goodson?"

Confused, Colleen stood staring at the girl, trying hard to figure just who she was. Barely in her twenties, she was simple but attractive, with dark brown hair cut in a bob just above her shoulders. It was full, with a natural wave that took the edge off, softened it. Still there was something tomboy about her. Something confident, something no-nonsense.

"I'm looking for Colleen Goodson?" the woman said, again.

"Yes," Colleen said, still in a haze. "I'm Colleen."

"Lenore Terranova," the woman said. "Sorry to bother you so late, but I'm a reporter for *Newsday*. I'm working on a story about your son."

"The newspaper?" Colleen said.

Almost before Colleen stepped back Lenore stepped in. She wasn't about to give her a chance to change her mind, shut the door.

"From what I've heard you've had a rough day," Lenore said.

"You have no idea," Colleen said, finding the table lamp.

As Colleen turned on the light, Lenore shut the door.

"Why don't you tell me?"

It'd been a day that began with a shooting that might be a murder and was ending with the case of a missing kid that might be a kidnapping.

The very kind of day, Lenore Terranova thought, that first made her want to become a reporter to begin with.

It was about 2 a.m. Sunday, the 30th, when Ann Woodward called police to tell them she'd shot her husband. It was all a mistake she said, still in tears. She thought he was an intruder. That he was naked and silhouetted in the doorway of his bedroom when she fired the shotgun blasts, striking him once, was not the relevant part, she said. Neither was the fact she'd suspected him of having affairs, maybe since before they were first married. She loved him. He was the love of her life.

It was all *so* accidental, she swore.

William Woodward Jr. was a socialite; a sportsman, the emphasis, it seemed, on sport. Thirty-five years old, heir to the Hanover National Bank, owner of the wildly-successful thoroughbred farm Belair Stud, his estate, even by conservative estimates, was worth a cool $20 million. A Harvard grad, he'd been a Navy hero in the Second World War.

He was young, tall, good looking. He also was dead.

Though his body was barely cold, the newspapers, news services and their reporters were already having a field day with it all. *The New York Times, Associated Press, United Press International, The Daily News, New York Post, Long Island Press, The New York Herald-Tribune, New York Journal-American* and *New York World-Telegram* had all sent reporters. And photographers. So, of course, had *Newsday*.

All descended upon the twelve-room mansion in Oyster Bay Cove on the North Shore of Long Island, the Gold Coast, in pursuit of the story.

One day later what a tale it was turning out to be.

Like Colleen, Angeline Lucille Crowell had come from Kansas. And, as she'd told friends there, all she ever wanted to become was famous.

Oh, and rich. Which made perfect sense.

Growing up poor-as-dirt she was deserted by her father and raised by her mother, who was twice-divorced. They lived in a tumbledown shack in a town called Pittsburg, tucked hard into the far southeast corner of the state. When she was old enough Ann Eden, as she'd taken to calling herself, had fled Kansas across lots, come to New York, taken work as a model. She was dancing as a showgirl at Fefe's Monte Carlo in New York City when she married Billy Woodward Jr. in March 1943.

She'd once been called "The Most-Beautiful Girl in Radio." Rumor had it she'd also once been the mistress of Billy's father, William Sr.

Billy and Ann had married to the objection of pretty much everyone, mostly to the objection of both his parents and high society, and with her he had two children, both boys. But Billy had a playboy heart, police told reporters, deep on the QT, with "sources" saying that Ann had suspected "numerous" affairs for years, had even hired a private investigator to tail her husband in what proved a profitless attempt to gain information.

Not that Billy Woodward seemed to care one way or the other.

He had an endless slew of admirers, women *and* men, who barely seemed to notice he was married at all. He had the right friends, entree to the right parties, was living a right life. Or so he himself truly believed.

And who, exactly, could argue that?

Under the direction of his father, who'd once rubbed elbows with King Edward VII of England, Belair Stud won the Kentucky Derby with Gallant Fox in 1930, Omaha in 1935 and Johnstown in 1939.

When he was shot to death Billy Woodward owned the best racehorse in the land, Nashua, the two-year-old horse of the year in 1954.

Now Nashua was on his way to being named champion three-year-old, having won the final two legs of the 1955 thoroughbred racing Triple Crown, after a heartbreaking loss to Swaps in the 81st Kentucky Derby.

Young and eager, Lenore wanted in on the story.

The socialite shooting had all the elements, as they said in the trade. It was the biggest story of the year, almost certainly of the decade. Some said maybe it was even the shooting of the century on Long Island.

Started in 1940, *Newsday* was the new kid in town.

Still, it was coming off its first Pulitzer Prize, had a newsroom filled with veteran reporters. And so the best reporters on the staff were sent to chase it. That is, the supposed best reporters. Meaning men.

All of which left Lenore back in the cluttered office over on Stewart Avenue in Garden City, wearing a rut in the chessboard linoleum floor between her desk and the morgue — the place in the office library where old newspaper clips were kept on file. Her task was research. To pore through every story written about Ann Woodward, about Billy Woodward, about his horses, his father, his history, his life, about his obscene wealth; about everything and anything at all, no matter how inconsequential.

About whatever it was that might add even just a line to the finished stories about a rich man somehow shot to death by his poor wife.

All day Sunday Lenore made phone calls, talking to operators who might connect her to someone who could tell her something and to police who might be willing to share information no one else had.

She'd worked late into the night, caught a few winks of fitful sleep, had come back Monday, Halloween, to work it some more.

Twenty-four hours in her legwork began to pay big dividends.

Sometime in the afternoon Lenore heard police were searching for a vagrant suspected of breaking into Gold Coast mansions. They suspected he had a shotgun, stolen from a priest in nearby Kings Park. They also suspected he'd broken into the boathouse and the garage on the estate owned by the Woodwards. She learned police told the Woodwards there was a prowler in the neighborhood the evening before the shooting, not long after they'd returned home late Saturday from a dinner in nearby Locust Valley hosted by Wallis Simpson, Duchess of Windsor.

She learned Ann had told police both she and her husband had gone to bed that night, each in their separate bedrooms, with loaded shotguns at their sides. She learned Billy and Ann were avid hunters, though one official, asking to remain anonymous, said the circumstances of the shooting were most-incredible because, as that source confided in Lenore:

"Mrs. Woodward was known to be a terrible shot."

It was all good stuff. The kind of stuff Lenore dreamed of as a girl reading all those grand Nancy Drew mysteries: *The Hidden Staircase, The Clue in the Diary, The Mystery of the Tolling Bell, The Clue in the Old Album* and *The Ringmaster's Secret*. But it was still office work. And she wanted to be out there in the field. Out there with the boys.

On her side was that, unlike most of the dailies, *Newsday* was an afternoon paper. Which meant it had obscenely late deadlines, most early in the morning, long after the other daily papers had been put to bed.

It also had a somewhat small staff, which meant if you were in the newsroom late and something good broke, you had a chance to work a story. Especially the day after a rich socialite who stood to inherit millions had shot her husband in their million-dollar mansion.

In his bedroom. In the nude.

Further on her side was that *Newsday* was owned by a woman.

Alicia Patterson was herself a socialite, from a long line of newspapermen. Or, maybe more correct, newspaper owners.

Her great-grandfather, Joseph Medill, had turned *The Chicago Tribune* into a force in journalism. Her father, Joseph Medill Patterson, had founded *The Daily News* in New York City. Her aunt ran *The Washington Times-Herald*. Still, though from money and married to money, her third husband being Harry Guggenheim of the millionaire Guggenheims, Alicia Patterson had a no-nonsense air to her.

That is, she didn't mind the notion of women in the newsroom. After all, she had a fierce streak of tomboy, herself.

So when a captain in one of the Nassau County Police precincts told Lenore, well on the QT, a massive search was underway for a boy who'd gone missing in the afternoon from outside a market in Hempstead Plains, she found herself in the right place at the right time: at her desk, in front of her old Remington Paragon typewriter.

Before anyone could get an inkling of what was going on — and, after everything that'd occurred, no one seemed eager to think about anything but the shooting death of Billy Woodward — Lenore walked over to the editor, Bill McAllister, said she was going to work the story of the search for a missing child. Before McAllister could say a word she was out the door, headed to MacArthur Terrace to find out how a three-year-old boy had disappeared in broad daylight. Had vanished into thin air.

"Y'all go on, son," Osias Storm said, the policeman still pointing a .38-caliber revolver at his head. "Step it on out now, all slow-like."

With that the little boy in the back of the Plymouth reached up from where he was crouched low on the floor, grabbed the door handle, pulled it open. Got out. He was scared. He had no idea what was going on. As he stepped onto the pavement and stood frozen in the parkway lights, he saw all the policemen. Saw all the guns. Terrified, he wet himself.

"What's this, a joke?" the officer pointing the gun yelled, seeing the little boy. "You think this is all some sort of God-damned joke?"

He cocked the trigger, to show he was serious.

"I said, 'Where's the boy?'"

"He . . . he be right there," Osias said, hands still raised.

"The white boy, *nigger*," the policeman demanded. "Where's the white boy at?"

Daring not move too fast, Osias turned his head just enough so he could see Alile. His wife had tears streaming down her cheeks.

Barely audible, he said: "What's he talkin' 'bout? What white boy?"

"Got no idea, Ozzie. Got no idea at all."

"Well?" the cop yelled. "Where is he?"

"Don't got no idea what y'all mean," Osias said. "This here is my boy. He be the only boy me and mine got in this here automobile."

As little Josiah Storm, all of five, stood shaking alongside the gray 1947 Plymouth sedan out at the toll booths near Exit 13 on the blacktop of the Southern State Parkway, a half-dozen officers stormed the car.

Osias went to say something, but an officer told him to shut his *fucking* mouth. The cops looked through the windows, saw nothing.

"God damn it!" one said.

Before Osias or Alile knew what was happening the policemen had dragged them from the Plymouth, thrown them to the ground, slapped on the handcuffs, pressed knees down upon their necks — and, started going through the car. They went through the front seat, back seat, trunk.

"Are you trying to tell me," the officer said as he stood above Osias, laid out on there on the road, whatever cars out that late rolling past, "you didn't take no white boy this afternoon in Hempstead Plains?"

"What white boy?" Osias said.

"Here," Colleen said, as she walked back into the living room, handing a black-and-white photograph, colored after the fact, to Lenore.

"This was just two weeks ago. We didn't have any real nice pictures, so I got him dressed up and took him to a studio."

A tear beginning to well, she said: "It was his birthday."

"He's adorable, Mrs. Goodson."

"He is cute, isn't he? He was so sweet that day, the sweetest little boy, even though I could tell he wasn't in the mood to pose for pictures."

"How do you mean?"

"Do you have children?"

"Me?" Lenore said. "I don't even have a boyfriend."

"A cute thing like you?"

Lenore forced a smile. "I'm married to my work."

"Oh," Colleen said. "Then maybe it's hard to understand. But one's tough enough. With two there's a lot of days you've got your hands full, really full, especially with a baby. My son, he's into everything. Restless, relentless. Bobby's a good little boy. A real momma's boy. But at that age, well . . . boys just don't like to sit still. Not for long, anyway."

"I see," Lenore said.

She studied the photograph. Bobby hardly seemed restless. He was seated, posed, clothes immaculate, hair neat, perfectly combed.

He wore the sweetest smile.

"You said, 'With two there's days you've got your hands full.'"

"With two children, yes."

"Is that what you meant?"

"Why? What did you think I meant?"

Lenore stared at the young mother. "Nothing . . . I just wondered what you meant by that, 'With two you've got your hands full.'"

"I just meant with a three-year-old and a baby there's never any time. There's always something. It's hard to explain if you haven't done it."

"Do you feel like you're overwhelmed? Like it's all too much?"

Colleen shook her head, no. Began to cry.

"What is it, Mrs. Goodson?"

Tears rolling down her face, Colleen looked at the young woman.

"Please. Call me Colleen."

"Okay. What is it, Colleen? What is it you're not telling me?"

"What do you mean?"

"I mean," Lenore said, "what is it you haven't told me? We've been talking more than a half-hour now and you've told me how you went to the store, how you were only inside a few minutes. How you came out and your children were missing . . . You've told me a story. But what is it you haven't told me? That's what I want to know."

Without a word Colleen rose from the sofa, walked through the living room to the kitchen, leaving Lenore sitting in silence, alone.

It was a minute, maybe more, before she returned. She had a handkerchief in one hand, another glass of scotch in the other.

She took a sip from the glass, set it down on the coffee table. She took the handkerchief and dabbed her tears until they were mostly gone.

Her eyes were red. She took another sip of scotch.

"How old are you?"

Caught off guard, Lenore said: "Twenty-three."

"Same age as me . . . You know, I've been trying to figure out who you remind me of and I've finally got it. Audrey Hepburn. Only, tougher."

Lenore gave her a look.

"I'm sorry. I didn't mean that how it came out."

"It's okay," Lenore said. "I didn't take it badly, I think."

Colleen took another drink, folded her hands in her lap, tucked into the pleats in her skirt. "Can I ask you something?" she said.

"Sure," Lenore said.

"Have you ever been in love?"

"Maybe," she said. "Probably."

"I'm sorry. I take it it didn't work out."

"It's a long story."

"I understand."

Colleen leaned forward, pondering a question.

"If I tell you something can you promise you won't print it? Can you do that, keep it between us girls?"

Reporters didn't like to go off the record unless it was absolutely necessary. But there were times when it could help to understand the story. Lenore asked herself what Nancy Drew would do.

She thought the girl detective would want to understand all she could about the mystery she was chasing no matter how it came about.

She closed her notebook, put it on the coffee table. "I guess."

"Love isn't easy," Colleen said. "Marriage is harder. Driscoll and I are trying. It's just there's days when I'm not sure we're in love, anymore. At least, not in love how we were when we first met back when. Everything was different, then. Just different." She stared at Lenore. "Have you ever made a mistake, wondered what it was going to cost you?"

"Sure," Lenore said. "I guess."

"Well, I've made a lifetime of them. I've been thinking about that, wondering, all afternoon. All night."

She reached out, put her hand on Lenore's, squeezed it.

It was a move that startled the young reporter. She moved her hand away and reached for the notebook, taking it, opening it again.

"I want to ask you something. On the record."

"Yes?"

"Do you love your children? Do you love your son?"

Without hesitation, Colleen said: "What do you think?"

Lenore studied her for the longest time. "Honestly?"

"Honest as you can be."

"Honestly, I want to believe you do."

The young mother gave her a hard, cold stare. "But?"

"But, right now, I don't know what to think."

With that, Colleen began to cry.

8

Inspector Cuthbert Caldwell was in a mood, one worse by the minute. Chief of Detectives for the Nassau County Police Department, he'd spent all day Sunday overseeing the investigation on scene at the Woodward mansion, then, after what little sleep he'd been able to muster, had spent much of the day Monday doing pretty much the same.

He was tired, exhausted, frustrated — had been living on coffee, cigarettes, donuts and stale sandwiches — and couldn't remember the last time he'd eaten an honest-to-goodness sit-down meal.

He hadn't seen his wife and kids in two days.

Then came word of the Goodson disappearance and word of the traffic stop out on the Southern State.

It made him wonder if he was just getting too old for this shit.

He had a sensationalist case making international headlines: a dead millionaire and a wife who'd admitted to shooting him. On accident, of course. During a late-afternoon news conference one reporter asked him: "Are you at all suspicious of this death at this time?"

Now, what could you say to that, exactly?

"No," he'd said. "However, my opinion is subject to change."

Asked if that meant detectives had discovered evidence that might change that opinion the Inspector began to feel claustrophobic.

"We have come across nothing," he said, "to indicate it is anything but what it is. A terrible, tragic mistake."

Caldwell knew he didn't believe it. Not for a second. And he knew that, not two days into the investigation, it was beginning to eat at him.

Now, on top of it, he also had a missing three-year-old boy — a kid who'd simply disappeared in broad daylight.

What kind of crops were they raising in Kansas, he wondered.

The Inspector was at his office window, pondering the very question, when the phone rang. He lifted the receiver, hoping for good news.

"I see," Caldwell said, as he paced a circle around his desk. "And you searched the entire house? Uh-huh . . . What about the neighbors?"

More exasperated with each and every answer, Caldwell scuffed his feet. "So the boy isn't there and never was . . . And you're sure?"

He stopped for a moment in front of the window, stood staring out at the darkened boulevard illuminated only by the street lights.

"Yeah, terrific. So what we've got is nothing. That's what you're telling me, right? That I've got two *spades* down the hall in interrogation who had nothing to do with anything and that I've got to let them go."

He took his right hand, slammed it on his desk.

"Yeah, I'm frosted," he screamed. "You bet your ass, I'm frosted. I've got no little boy, no leads. I've got no answers, only headaches."

He took the receiver, slammed it, too. "God damn it."

He kicked the garbage can next to his desk. It crashed into the wall with a thunderous thud, sending trash all over. He grabbed a pack of *Lucky Strikes* from his desk, lit one, took a long drag; sucked the smoke in deep, trying hard to relax. He turned back to the window, muttering.

"I'm getting God-damned creamed."

Lenore barely hit the newsroom when McAllister stopped her.

"What've we got?"

"Here," she said, handing him the studio shot of Bobby Goodson.

McAllister gave it the once-over.

"How old?"

"Three."

"What's the deal?"

"Vanished from outside the IGA on Eisenhower in Hempstead Plains," she said, moving toward her desk. "Around two o'clock."

"And?" McAllister asked over the clattering of typewriters as he followed her. Lenore stopped, turned to the editor, raised an eyebrow.

"And his mother said she left him outside watching his baby sister while she ran inside a moment. Said she came out and they were gone."

"The cops believe her?"

"Hard to tell."

"You believe her?"

"Haven't decided . . . I think I might."

"You *might?*"

"Like I said," Lenore said, continuing toward her desk.

"What about the sister?"

"A neighbor found her carriage next block over."

"She hurt?"

"She's fine," Lenore said, tossing her bag alongside her desk.

She tossed her notebook onto the desktop, pulled out the chair. She looked up at McAllister, pointed to the photograph of Bobby Goodson.

"But there's two thousand volunteers searching for him, right now."

"Two thousand?"

"At least." She reached for two sheets of paper, sandwiched a carbon between them, loaded them into her old Remington. "Cops, firemen, Air Force. Guardsmen, reservists . . . You name it, they're out there."

"If you don't mind me asking, what the *hell* are you doing here?"

Glancing up Lenore shot McAllister a long, hard look.

"I knew you'd be a Nervous Nellie, Bill, if I didn't file some notes."

She took a quick glance at the clock. Not quite midnight. She looked back at McAllister, flashed a weak smile.

"Now, let me do that, okay? Then I promise, I'll grab a photographer and we'll get back out there to see what's going on."

"Good," he said. "Then I'll get out of your way."

"That'd be nice."

As Lenore began to type, McAllister turned to walk away. She made sure to let him get a few steps.

"Oh, and Bill," she said. "We're the only ones who have this."

She was already typing away furiously when McAllister turned back. She pretended not to notice he was grinning, ear-to-ear.

"How's he doing?" Inspector Caldwell said, as he nodded toward the black boy on the bench down the hall from the interrogation room.

The Negro woman seated next to the child glared at him.

"Jus' fine. Thank you for askin'."

Caldwell wondered what he'd done to incur such a look.

She'd been cleaning bathrooms at headquarters when the boy and his parents were brought in, the child obviously scared. Caldwell asked if she'd sit with him while his parents were being questioned by detectives.

She'd graciously agreed.

The Inspector had seen her around the building forever, it seemed, since she worked with the late-night cleaning crew. But even after all that time he didn't know her name. Thinking back on it, he wasn't sure he'd ever even said hello to her. He was sure, in fact, he hadn't.

"Look," he said to the cleaning lady. "I'm sure he's been through a lot. I appreciate you taking the time to sit with him like you did."

She put an arm around the boy, gave Caldwell a cold stare.

"No need to talk me up for doin' the right thing here. This boy, name's Josiah in case you was wonderin', he told me all about his night."

"He did?"

"Yes, Sir. He *mos' suredly* did."

Hundreds of cases under his belt, hundreds of bad actors behind bars and the Inspector had never seen someone so trenchant.

"I trust you'll be doin' the right thing by his folks?" she said.

Caldwell held his tongue, turned away.

Down the hall in interrogation, Caldwell found Osias Storm on one side of the old wooden table, Alile on the other, both still visibly shaken.

He went to say something.

"Where's my boy at Inspector?" Alile said, before he could.

"He's down the hall," Caldwell said. "He's fine."

"Fine? You think he's . . . "

"Look," the Inspector said, interrupting. "It's been a rough night for everyone here. This was all a misunderstanding and, on behalf of the department, I want to tell you both we're all very sorry for any inconvenience." He gave Alile a look. "By all accounts . . . "

"By *y'all* accounts," Alile said.

Fighting the urge to be anything but diplomatic, Caldwell stared hard at the floor. When he looked back he could see the woman's blood still rising, too. "I've got a missing three-year-old boy on my hands."

"A missin' white boy," she said.

"Yes. A missing white boy. But, by all accounts, the officers had reason to stop you. A witness told us he saw a gray Nineteen-Forty-Seven Plymouth in the lot where the boy disappeared. A car just like yours. We have an obligation to investigate any possible involvement with this missing boy. We'd do the same if it was your son."

"Would you?" Alile said.

"Yes, Ma'am," he said. "I'm afraid we would."

As Caldwell stood staring at her the door opened and Josiah came running into the room. He ran to his mother, grabbing onto her with all his might. She hugged him, fiercely, eyes suddenly welling with tears.

The Inspector watched as the two continued to hug, until the boy and his mother loosened their grips and the little black boy turned to face him — his mother still with her arms thrown around his shoulders, cradling her child tight as she could against her comforting body. She was staring straight at Caldwell. The child was staring straight through him.

"Look," Caldwell said. "You're free to go."

Osias stood and immediately moved to his wife and son.

"C'mon now, Leale," he said. "Y'all said 'nough, now. Let's get."

But, Alile wasn't about to go like that. Not after all of it.

"So, you say we're free t'go?" she said.

"Yes," Caldwell said.

"Like that?"

"Look, Ma'am," Caldwell said. "No one wants trouble here. You don't. I don't. I trust you understand what I'm saying here, right?"

"Leale. Let's get," Osias said, again.

But Alile motioned to her husband to let her be.

"You know, I thought I left all this behind me back down in Alabama," she said, still cradling Josiah in her arms. "Now, I'm thinkin' I was wrong. But we're goin' to walk out a here and we're goin' to 'understand,' as you put it, what it is happen to us. By way a sayin', Inspector, what it is *your* men done. We didn't come lookin' for no trouble. As you said, we still ain't lookin' for none. But, I want to call on a favor, 'fore we leave."

"What's that?" Caldwell said, continuing to seethe.

"When you go home t'night to you an' yours," she said, her glare at the Inspector still one of utter condemnation, "I want you to *aks* yo'self how you all'd feel if *you* been *us* . . . If *we'd* been *y'all.*"

"I wish I could tell you something," Caldwell said, as he rifled his desk drawers for a cigarette. "But honestly I've got nothing. And that's off the record, Lenore. I've had a bad enough day already with all this."

"Understood," Lenore said.

She was seated across the desk, notebook in hand, watching as the Inspector went drawer by drawer, more annoyed with each dead end.

"Finally," he said, pulling a half-empty pack from the bottom drawer. He took a *Lucky,* lit it. Took a drag, smiled. "Let it be said I actually solved one mystery today." Caldwell shot Lenore a look. "That's off the record, too. You'll have me looking like a fool, writing I said that."

She smiled, ever so slight. "Would I do that, Inspector?"

Caldwell exhaled a long stream of grayish-white smoke overhead.

"Don't look a gift horse in the mouth, Lenore. Name your price."

Lenore smiled.

"You've told me what you haven't got. Now, tell me what you have."

Caldwell stood, turned, stared out the window. A light rain had begun to fall. The boulevard glistened, eerily, in the midnight glow of the incandescent street lamps. Tears for the damned, he thought.

"Okay," he said, still turned. "Here's what I've got."

He told her what he knew about Colleen and Driscoll Goodson, what he knew about their little boy. He told her about the IGA, about the other carriages, about the story Colleen told his detectives about running into the store for just a few minutes. He told her how the neighbor found the carriage, how the search dogs tracked a scent then lost it. Told her about the old man who'd seen a woman, likely the neighbor, and the carriage; how he thought it was before two then thought maybe it was really before three. How a witness said he saw the Plymouth, saw these 'Negroes' hanging around the shopping center; how officers stopped a car fitting the description, interrogated the man and woman inside. How they searched that Negro couple's home; searched their street, their neighborhood. He told her how all of it, how everything, kept coming up craps.

"What about these two 'Negroes'?" Lenore said.

"Nice folks," Caldwell said, pulling out another *Lucky*.

"I see. They're 'nice folks'?"

"Lenore," the Inspector said. "Yes, they're nice folks."

"Well then, why did you stop them. I mean, if they're nice folks?"

Caldwell searched for an answer.

"They were just in the wrong place at the wrong time. They matched the description given us by a witness. Turns out, they're not involved."

"So there's no other reason?"

"No," Caldwell said. "I have to believe it was just that."

"Do I?"

"Do you *what?*"

"Do *I* have to believe that? Should *I* believe that? I mean, your men would never have stopped them just because they were black, right?

"They'd never do *that?*" she said.

"Lenore!" Caldwell said, shooting a look. "No. They'd never do that."

"What about the old man?" Lenore said, finally.

"My guess," Caldwell said, as he flicked ashes into the dirty ashtray on his desk, relieved to change the subject, "is he got the time wrong. That he saw the neighbor woman find the carriage, instead of how it got there."

"So you think the neighbor woman is telling the truth?"

"You got reason for me not to?"

Lenore pondered her next question.

"And you believe Ann Woodward accidentally shot her husband, too? Is *that* right? That she didn't just murder him for his millions?"

"Don't do that," he said.

"Do what?"

"You know what," he said, as he took one last drag on the *Lucky,* pressed it out in the ashtray. "Look . . . I'm trying to be honest here."

"Then be fucking honest," Lenore said.

The Inspector seemed taken aback by the very forthrightness. He hated all this second guessing, having to be a diplomat. Being forced, all in the public eye, having to choose his words. He leaned across the desk, staring down the young female reporter, his eyes drilling holes.

"Put down the notebook."

"Put it down?"

"Yes, damn it. Put it down. And if you ever repeat any of this, I swear I'll make your life so miserable you'll wish you'd never been born."

Lenore was staring back at him, now, giving him a hard look, too.

She wanted to say something, but bit her tongue. She wanted the story. The real story. Against all instinct, she closed the notebook.

"Be honest," she said.

Caldwell leaned back, eyes still locked on Lenore.

"You think I'm some sort of hayseed, Lenore? You think I really haven't been around the block enough times to know Ann Woodward didn't shoot her husband on accident, thinking he was a burglar? I wasn't born yesterday. Give me some credit. But you know I can't say that, not without proof. And, right now, Lenore, I've got no proof.

"I've got nothing I can take to the bank."

He reached for another cigarette, lit it.

"You want honest? I'll give you honest. I've had two miserable days. Two of the most God-damned miserable days, pardon my French, I've ever had. I've got the Commissioner breathing down my neck, wanting me to pin a murder on a millionairess who I'm sure shot her husband in cold blood. I've got the press breathing down my neck, acting like my detectives are a bunch of Keystone Cops who can't put two and two together and come up with four. On top of it I've got a missing kid; a kid who vanished into thin air. I don't know whether he's missing, kidnapped. Dead. I don't know whether he just wandered off or if his mother knows something she's not telling us. I've got neighbors who said they saw Negroes who might be involved — what they told my detectives — and I don't know if that's real, imagined, or something else all together. I don't know what to think. I just know I've got two nightmare investigations, a million God-damned questions. And that I've got exactly no answers."

The Inspector took a drag of the cigarette, flicked more ashes into the overflowing ashtray. Some missed, landing on his desk. He swatted at them, sending them flying. "How's that for fucking honest, Lenore?"

Lenore stared at the chain-smoking Inspector.

"What does your gut say?"

"My gut? My gut says it's tired of muddy black coffee that tastes like it was brewed on a cattle drive, that it's tired of stale donuts and soggy roast beef sandwiches. My gut says I'm getting sick of all this bullshit. That maybe I have a murder and a kidnapping on my hands or maybe even two murders . . . But you know I can't tell you that. And you know if you ever say I told you that I'll call you a God-damned liar and say you made it all up." He snuffed out another cigarette. "That's what my gut says."

"You're not threatening me?" Lenore said, opening her notebook. "Because, I've got to be honest, that sounded a lot like a threat."

She moved the notebook, making certain Caldwell saw it.

"That's not what you meant, right?"

Caldwell leaned back from the desk, face ashen.

"I'm . . . I'm just blowing off steam. It's just I'm really frustrated, like I need to go on a buster or something. You know what I mean?"

"I think."

"Newbury Farmer's one of my best men. A good detective, a real old-school detective who doesn't miss much, if anything. But I still feel like there's something — and, I just can't put my finger on it. That none of us can. This kid didn't just get abducted by a UFO from Roswell."

"I understand," she said.

"Do you?"

"Yes. I do."

The Inspector took a deep breath. "Look. Here's what I can give you . . . Police, aided by volunteers, are conducting one of the most thorough and intensive organized searches in the history of Nassau County, looking for a three-year-old boy who went missing from outside a supermarket in Hempstead Plains on Halloween. We have every belief he simply wandered off. We're leaving no stone unturned in our efforts to find him and to return him safe to his parents, who are concerned for his well-being." He reached for another cigarette. "You can say we've interviewed witnesses, that we're following every lead, that we questioned a Negro couple in connection with the disappearance, are satisfied hey had no involvement whatsoever. That we don't believe, at this time, that this is a kidnapping, since we have no notes, no ransom demands, no indication. That we remain hopeful Bobby Goodson will be found safe and sound."

As Lenore finished scribbling in her notebook she glanced up at Caldwell as the Inspector took another drag of his cigarette.

She almost felt sorry for him.

"Okay," she said. "I can make this work."

She closed the notebook, stood to shake hands with the Inspector. "Thanks. I know you had a rough day, so I appreciate it."

"Look, no hard feelings, okay? I know I was tough on you."

"You were a bit of an ass," she said. "Pardon my French."

"I'm sorry. It's . . . it's nothing personal. I'd give all of Billy Woodward's money to find out what happened to this kid."

"I'm sure you would, Inspector."

"Good. Because I really wish I could tell you where he is."

As Lenore turned to leave, headed out to meet with her photographer and check on possible new developments, she pointed to a New York Yankees pennant hanging on the wall under some photographs.

"You're a Yankees fan. You must have loved the Series."

Caldwell scowled at her.

"You know," Lenore said. "My parents are from Brooklyn. I grew up rooting for the Dodgers." She smiled, feeling cocksure.

"Wait 'til next year, huh?"

She'd almost reached the door when Caldwell called out.

"Berra got Robinson stealing home. You know that, right?"

She turned and gave Caldwell the biggest smile.

"Sure he did, Inspector. Sure he did."

9

Driscoll Goodson stood alone in the darkened backyard, misting rain glistening on his Air Force jacket like a thousand teardrops.

Can of *Schlitz* in hand, amid the murk, he took a mouthful of working-class beer thinking back on what had been the single-worst day of his life. He wasn't one to drink, at least not often, but tonight it was hard not to argue a reason. Several times it seemed the search team had been onto something. Each time that promise had gone unkept. With every failure, every dead end, he felt like he'd died one more small death.

All of it so inscrutable, so insurmountable. Soon he was overcome with the realization he'd never felt so profoundly, unfathomably, lost.

Coming home he'd walked to the back bedroom at 3 a.m., flicked on the light hoping against hope for a miracle; that he might find Bobby tucked deep into his bed, asleep. Instead, he found the room empty. Not only wasn't Bobby there, Johanna was gone, too. When he saw the note at the bottom of the bassinet, he stood frozen, not knowing what to do. He remained like that until, finally, he forced himself to turn back toward his own bedroom. Throwing open the door he found Colleen in bed, out cold, dead to the world. Slowly, carefully, he closed the door and turned again toward the other room. This time he willed himself to the crib.

He picked up the note:

> *Marjorie took Johanna. I'm sorry. Not sure what*
> *else to say. But I can't say that enough. I love you*
> *and hope you can forgive me.*

He closed his eyes. When he opened them again it was all still there; the vacant bed, the empty bassinet, the undeniable void. Mindless, he wandered to the kitchen. He flicked on the light, went to the refrigerator, took out the beer, turned back to the living room. Before he could shut the light he saw the tricycle, still alone in the very corner of the room.

He walked to it, set his beer on the table, bent down fixated.

He ran his hands over the frame, hand to cold metal, recalled the night he'd brought it home, little more than a year before, Bobby's second birthday. He remembered how Colleen looked at him, delighted.

How then she'd said to Bobby: "It's your bicycle."

How good it made him feel, how he and Colleen sat and laughed, as Bobby tried to repeat the word, stumbling out with: "Icicle . . ."

It seemed so long ago, now, yet gone in the smallest instant — like the flash of a lightning bug in the field on a late-summer's eve.

He fought back tears, unsuccessful, fell back onto the floor and, leaned hard against the wall, sat there sobbing uncontrollably he was so overcome. He cried like that for ten minutes, maybe twenty, until he could cry no more. Finally he stood, grabbed the beer, shut the light, walked out into the darkened backyard to be alone with his thoughts.

He found himself standing in the rain.

Under normal circumstances he liked rain, maybe even loved it. He was a farm boy, after all; rain was a farmer's best friend. He remembered the look a good, solid soaker brought to the face of his grandfather, to his mother and father, and he could remember joyous days when he would go out in it and simply walk the field, watching for hours as it watered the crops, nourished the soil, cleansing, renewing, all it touched.

This night, he thought, it felt like sadness. Tears from a crying sky.

He considered himself a God-fearing man. Not a church-goer, not a true believer, whatever that was, but still a good Methodist. At this moment, though, he almost hated a God who could do this to him. He thought at this moment that he also hated his wife, hated she could have been so careless, so reckless, with their children. Could have left them unguarded, unattended. Alone. He hated himself for being so impotent, for not being able to do more. For not being able to do anything to find his son. Hated the fact he had no answers, had only numbing questions.

It all felt so ruinous.

So incomprehensibly, indecipherably, tragic and sad.

Marjorie Woods was still awake when her husband returned from the long night of searching. She had been packing boxes, getting on with the move, wondering the entire time what clues were being uncovered.

She demanded an answer no sooner had Taggart come in.

He'd walked home with Driscoll from several blocks over after the detectives came to the conclusion there wasn't much else could be done. They'd knocked on the doors of every house in the area, had talked to mothers, fathers, grandmothers, grandfathers, school kids. They'd heard a lot of stories, a lot of theories. In the end all of it was a lot of nothing.

Walking home, Taggart urged Driscoll to keep his chin up.

"I know Bobby's out there," he said. "Don't ask how, but I just know. You have to believe no one would have hurt him. Trust me."

The worried father forced a weak smile, didn't answer. Taggart put his arm around Driscoll's shoulder, trying to be a good friend, trying to show support. He couldn't tell if Driscoll believed him, believed any of it.

"Talk about a night. We had a lot of close calls."

"But nothing?" Margie said. "No one knows anything?"

"I don't think so. At least from what I could tell listening it seems that way. But there were a few moments when . . ."

"When what?"

"When it seemed they might start pointing a finger at us."

"Really?"

"Really. Some old geezer over on Hughes told the cops he saw you outside with the carriage around two . . ."

"Around two?"

"Yeah, around two," Taggart said. "Then he said how it might have actually been around three. He wasn't sure . . . Something about firehouse sirens and some watch he'd gotten somewhere in Cuba."

"Oh, my God. And what did the detectives say?"

He walked past her into the kitchen to grab a beer.

"Taggart," Marjorie said. "What did they say?"

He popped the top with a can-opener, took a gulp.

"I think they thought he was senile, just some old kook."

"That's it?" She felt weak in the knees.

"That's it," he said, leaning back as he took another swig. "But it was pretty nerve-wracking for a while there."

He set the can down, pulled her close. She hugged him tight and, as she did, he felt her body shaking. He tried to hide his was, too.

"Look," he said, finally. "It's all going to be alright."

"Do you really think?"

"You have to trust that, Margie. You just have to."

He forced a smile.

"I told Driscoll we'd be there for him and Colleen . . . I even told him we'd be willing to hold off on the move if they needed us to."

Marjorie pulled back, surprised. "You did?"

"Why not?"

"What do you mean, 'Why not?'"

"Relax. He said he was thankful to have friends like us, but knew we needed to leave at the end of the week."

"He did?"

"Did you really think he'd say anything else?"

Marjorie leaned in and hugged her husband again.

"You know," she said. "I took Johanna for the night."

"I figured you would."

"I had to. Coll was drinking. I thought she might do something stupid. She told me she felt really guilty over everything."

"You knew she would."

Still holding onto her husband, Marjorie looked up. She looked sad. "I know. It's just . . . it's just it made me feel so guilty, too."

"You can't look at it like that, Marge."

Tag took another sip of beer. "Besides, we can still figure something out . . . And a week from now we'll be out west getting on with our lives, just like we planned. It won't be our problem anymore. None of it."

He pulled her in tight. She was no longer trembling.

"Do you really think it's all going to work out?"

Taggart smiled. "Just like we said, hun. Just like we said."

Back in the office over on Stewart Avenue in Garden City Lenore was at her desk pounding out the story on her old black Remington Paragon. She'd never learned to touch type and so typed with just a few fingers — her right index finger and two fingers and thumb on her left, to be exact. Still, when the words were coming at a steady rate and everything made sense, the keys produced a rhythm that wasn't just clatter. Or chaos.

It was the sound, she thought, of music.

Not quite Mozart. Or Beethoven. But a rhythm she could feel, hear. When she heard that she always sensed she was onto something good.

"It isn't Shakespeare," she'd joke. "It's not even Capote."

But she knew it wasn't pulp, either.

She was hearing it now, despite a newsroom abuzz.

Across the room the teletype machines incessantly chattered away, transcribing stories from wire service reporters working the far corners of the globe onto continuous streams of off-white roll paper. Every so often the copyboys would tear off a section of it, take it to the appropriate desk where editors would skim it all for pertinent news. Not far, over on the rim, where stories were edited, desk editors endlessly checked for errors: mistakes in grammar, in fact, spelling errors, syntax errors, typographical errors; anything that might reflect badly on the job at hand.

Some cut sentences, others entire paragraphs, thinking they fit better elsewhere or maybe not at all.

They would cut out the section in question with scissors, cut through the draft where they wanted it moved, then tape the section in place like some mad scientist slapping together a newspaper Frankenstein. It was all workingman's ballet Lenore thought as she paused for a moment to take a sip of lukewarm coffee and catch her breath, taking in the scene. She was twenty hours into her day now. Honestly, she didn't care.

She was done reporting, done writing. All she needed to do was read back on it, checking details against her notebook to make sure she hadn't missed anything. She felt good about it, good as anyone could feel about such a story. McAllister hinted she might even get the front page.

A night editor was yelling for a copyboy she watched as the boy, a young man in his twenties, ran to the desk, grabbed the edited story, full of pencil marks and heavily cut and taped, and raced down the hall to the composing room. There the back-room crew would read it all and, letter-by-letter, pull the appropriate piece of lead — the lead typeset block — from a huge wooden box filled with alphabetized blocks, spacers and grammatical symbols and, according to the determined layout, stick them in a jig frame to form the proof pages needed for printing.

It was far from mindless work.

A good back-room man needed to read back-to-front, because every letter, every sentence, every story, had to be set in reverse when typeset. It was the only way to do it, positive-to-negative-to-positive again.

Lay it down in order and it was ass-backwards in the paper. Doing it ass-backwards was the only way to get it right.

Just another quirk of the business Lenore thought as she finished the last of her coffee, settled in to read. Out of the corner of her eye she could see McAllister skulking, wondering how long before he got to read it, too. She gave him a quick smile, but he turned his head, pretending he wasn't growing anxious and impatient, pretending he hadn't been watching her at all. She still had time and knew it was a big story and she wanted to make sure it was right. Once in print you couldn't take it back.

She had to be certain she'd chosen the right details, the right order, the right quotes. That she'd set the right tone. All the things that would make her readers understand the magnitude of what'd happened. That would make them understand that somewhere out there, on their Long Island, a three-year-old boy had gone missing. That his parents, that police, that thousands of volunteers, were out there trying to find him.

Finally satisfied, Lenore got up from her desk. She thought about calling a copyboy to take the story to Bill McAllister.

Instead, she took it herself.

"Here," she said, standing over him as he finished pencilling his way through another piece. "I know you've been waiting for this."

"It's done?" he said, without a glance.

"You decide," she said.

He took the story from her, began to read. He gave her a look as if to say, "What are you still doing here?" But, she didn't move. Every now and then he drew his pencil, went to make a note, reconsidered, pulled it back. Reaching the end without making a single mark, he went back and read it over again, just to make sure. Only then did he turn to Lenore.

"It isn't Shakespeare," he said, shooting her a look.

Lenore was about to say "Thanks" when McAllister took his pencil and scribbled something across the top of the story. He looked up at her again, this time a smug look on his tired, wearied face.

He didn't say a word, at least not at first.

"What?" she said, suddenly nervous. "What is it?"

"As I recall," he said, "Terranova has two R's."

He held out the story so she could see the correction.

"You spelled it with one."

10

"So, what'd you think?"

"Other than I'm shot?" Farmer said, fighting to stifle a yawn.

"You had to go do that, didn't you?" Jones said.

Unable to stop the impulse Jones began to yawn now, too.

Both men were dog-tired, both wore a look of disgust. Spread out on the wooden desk between them were stacks of papers, incident reports, all of them freshly typed, all related to the Goodson disappearance.

Farmer glanced at the clock. It was pushing 5 a.m.

"I think," he said, "Caldwell's going to be breathing down our necks if we don't figure what all this means, what's going on here."

"You bet your asses he will!"

Startled, the detectives turned to find the Inspector walking through the door of the Detective's Bureau, cigarette in hand.

"You'd better have answers," he said.

He dropped the butt onto the worn linoleum floor, pressed it out with his foot. Walked to the coffee urn on the desk against the wall, poured himself a cup, black, turned back to face the two weary, frustrated men.

"What do we have, exactly?"

"Honestly?" Farmer said.

"No," Caldwell said. "Feed me a line of shit . . . Of course, honestly."

Farmer gave the stack of reports the once-over.

"Honestly, we've got a lot of nothing."

He expected an angry response. Caldwell was up against it, had been for days now, what with the Woodward shooting coming up blanks and now the case of little Bobby Goodson proving much the same.

Instead, Caldwell took a sip of coffee then reached into his coat pocket for his trusted *Luckys* — lighting another, taking a long solid draw.

Farmer was thankful the Inspector bit his tongue.

Caldwell tossed the *Luckys* onto the desk, set his coffee down next to the dwindling pack. He grabbed an ashtray, took a seat at the end of the table. Sitting there, he sucked the smoke deep into his lungs, exhaled. He watched as it rose toward the ceiling of the stark, drab room.

"I've talked to the General, what's his name . . . "

"Johnson," Farmer said.

"I've talked to General Johnson over at Meadowbrook Field, notified all the precinct commanders that come daylight we'll restart the search, double-checking, triple-checking, every place we've been in one last effort to find this kid. Officers will hand out fliers at all the major shopping areas across the county. We're going to canvas stores, schools . . . "

As the Inspector reached for his cigarette, he saw Farmer shake his head. "What is it, Newb?" he said, taking a draw.

"You know, this Goodson kid didn't just wander off, Cuth."

This time, the Inspector didn't hold his tongue.

"I'm not going to take the chance some fucking housewife finds him asleep under a tree blocks from the house and have us looking like horses asses. We'll run the search until mid-afternoon, long enough to show the proper concern — and we'll exhaust every reasonable chance he didn't just walk away from that market. Even if we all know the answer to that."

He took a sip of coffee, watching the cigarette smolder. "But once that's done we've got to know what we're looking at here. So, that's the sixty-four-thousand dollar question. What the hell are we looking at?"

He turned to Farmer. "There anyone we can rule out?"

"The father?" Farmer said, as he grabbed another coffee.

"You don't sound . . . "

"Convinced? I'm not, other than his alibi."

"Agreed," the Inspector said. "Anyone we like?"

"I like the mother," Jones said.

"I don't know," Farmer said. "I'm still not sold on the story from the neighbor woman, finding the carriage like she did and all."

"Do we even know if the kid was ever at the market?" Caldwell asked. "Have we talked to anyone who even saw him there?"

The detectives both said no.

"Then let's go there first thing," Caldwell said, "talk to everyone who works there, who works in the other stores. To customers, anyone in the parking lot, anyone waiting for a bus. Let's talk to that patrolman, the one who first talked to this Mrs. Goodson . . . What's his name, Reilly?"

"O'Reilly," Farmer said.

"Let's talk to this Officer O'Reilly and that other guy, the one who drove her home. See what's there, what's not. Then, let's figure out where we go from there. By afternoon I'm going to have everyone breathing down my neck: the Commissioner, the press. Probably, the God-damned FBI. I've already got enough headaches with this Woodward shit."

He stood, pulled off his tie, stuffed it into the pocket of his rumpled coat. Gave each of them, his men, a furtive glance.

"Don't fuck this up," he said.

Farmer and Jones each let out a tired sigh.

Caldwell knew he had no choice. Turning back, he said: "And start pulling files on every known pervert, every convicted child molester, every possible suspect — anyone who seems even the least bit suspicious — just so we all know we've covered every damn angle here."

Before either could say a word Caldwell reached over and with the biggest shit-eating grin pushed everything off the desks. As it all went crashing to the floor, he said: "You're going to need a place to sleep."

The first light of November found Driscoll still in the back yard, in a lawn chair, staring through the early-morning haze at the swing he'd built for his son — the rain ceased, clouds clearing, sun on the rise.

He had awakened to find himself draped in a big red lawn blanket. He didn't have the foggiest notion where it had come from, how it had gotten there, but it was warm and he was thankful to have it, the chill autumn air nipping as it was. He couldn't help but wonder how his son had gotten through the night; had fallen asleep envisioning a million possibilities.

Mostly, he'd thought about the night Bobby was born.

Morning had broken rain-soaked, gusts howling across Seneca Lake, whipping its surface into frenzied white-capped waves that went crashing drunkenly onto the shore. The wind was blowing so hard you could hear it; had knocked a fall mix of dead leaves straight from the trees. It made the grounds of the old Seneca Army Depot, hard on the eastern edge of the lake, seem far less inviting than they'd ever seemed before.

Driscoll thought it a terrible day for an arrival.

Colleen was due on the morning train from Buffalo, a day he'd been waiting for since he'd first set off for Geneva, for Sampson Air Force Base. That had been weeks earlier, before tiresome days of never-ending drills and mind-numbing exercises; days of being screamed at and abused.

Driscoll had long-since traded his farm clothes for a uniform; his head shaved, like a boy in summer at the hands of a maniacal mother. He'd been questioned, tested, berated. Had been knocked down; had gotten up, only to be knocked down again. All of it, the drill sergeant reminded him in no uncertain terms, in the name of training. All, Driscoll thought, in the name of trying to make him something he'd never intended to be in the first place: a member of the United States Air Force.

Driscoll had never once envisioned himself a military man.

High school behind him, he'd enrolled in classes at Arkansas City Junior College. This for the fall, 1949.

He wasn't keen on school but it offered courses in agriculture and he was a farm boy from Kansas and his parents thought the education might prove useful, do him some good. Besides, he had family down in Arkansas City, a hundred miles or so southwest of Cottonwood Falls.

His parents figured the distance might be good, too.

Founded in 1922, the college held classes on the bottom floor of Arkansas City High School. Locals called it "Basement University." But it was affordable and the distance meant he could still see Colleen. As deals went, Driscoll thought it a good one, all things considered .

Between his first and second year war broke out in Korea. This was June 1950. Not long after the feds reinstated the war-time draft.

Across America men faced conscription having come of age. But college students were exempt, their status deferred.

Driscoll's best friend, Robert Hinkson, hadn't gone to college. He'd stayed home to help run the family farm. When the draft came Robert was nineteen and he was taken, summoned into the Army. Driscoll had known Robert since grammar school. They'd grown up together, played games together, gone camping together, fished the Cottonwood River together. Robert Hinkson was his one, true, close friend. Then one morning Robert was off to war. A cruel blow, Driscoll thought; one that shook him.

He saw his friend off on the train, said he'd see him when he got back. Meanwhile, he continued to go to school, work the farm, see Colleen; tried hard not to think about the draft, about the war. About any of it.

Colleen thought about it all the time. Her brother Franklin had also been among the first taken. Aimless, unmarried, twenty-two years old, Franklin found himself dead square in the sights of the draft and in late 1950 his ship came in — just not how he'd pictured it.

Called into the Army, which made him a soldier of sorts, in March 1951 he found himself on a troop-carrier out of the U.S. Army Depot in Oakland, California, on the first leg of a trek down through San Francisco Bay and out across the Pacific bound for South Korea.

It was months before the investigators arrived in Cottonwood Falls to tell Colleen and her parents that, on arrival at the Subic Naval Station in the Central Luzon Province north of Manila, days from a voyage to the Korean Peninsula, Private Franklin Tetherwood had disappeared.

Gone AWOL: Absent Without Leave.

The Army said he'd jumped ship, wandered off into the Zambales Mountains, had vanished in the shadow of volcanic Mount Pinatubo.

Now, they wanted to know where he was.

The question caused Chardon Tetherwood, whiskey in hand, to tell the two investigators: "Get the fuck out of my house!"

Colleen's mother, adrift amid the wreckage of her own miserable life, barely reacted at all. Except, to light another cigarette.

And pour herself another drink.

But Colleen knew better. She knew the truth.

A week earlier she'd gotten a letter, the one and only letter her brother had ever written. Would ever write. Postmarked out of the Philippines, in it her brother wrote of his voyage aboard the U.S.S. General H.B. Freeman, a Military Sea Transportation Service ship, T-AP-143. More than thirty-five-hundred would-be soldiers, young men soon no longer boys, had been crammed onto the 522-foot-long single-stack, single-screw steamer. It was gray, it wasn't much to look at. And, it was awful.

He wrote how the men slept in hammocks, three and four deep. How the belly of it smelled like sweat; how most got seasick, the rotten stench of stale puke worse than that of the worst, most-wretched Sunday-morning bar. He'd written how he'd hated it all from long-before the entire mess had even sailed; hated it with all he had still left in him before the Freeman made port in Subic Bay. He said he'd made his mind up from the get to leave it all behind first chance he got. He was homesick.

But, he wrote, no matter what road he took, war or desertion, he was certain he'd never see Kansas again, so the choice had become clear.

For the longest time, for the times she'd still think of him, Colleen imagined her brother as some down-and-out Bogart character in a wayward Korean War cross between *Passage to Marseille* and *Tokyo Joe*. That is, she could almost picture him, drunk in a bar somewhere in the back alleys of downtown Manila, a Filipina, maybe even two, on his arm, just daring the Military Police to find him, fight him, haul him in.

Whatever the case, Colleen knew he was gone, a casualty of war in the unlikeliest sense. She wouldn't let Driscoll chance such familiar fate.

Driscoll had no designs on continued education.

But Colleen convinced him, with the help of his mother, who proved a willing ally, to enroll for the 1951 fall semester at the Kansas State College of Agriculture and Applied Sciences over in Manhattan, a little more than fifty miles from Cottonwood Falls. Soon Driscoll was making the round trip, most times five days a week, in his father's rusting old pickup.

All of it was far from ideal, Colleen thought.

After all, there were other women at Kansas State. So it wasn't the worst that could happen, Colleen figured, when she sat Driscoll down after Thanksgiving and broke the news: she was pregnant.

For months Driscoll had wondered what he wanted. He loved Colleen, but knew his parents had their doubts. It was why they'd pushed college in the first place, trying to drive that wedge. Now Colleen was pregnant. There was only one choice. He made it. Within a week he and Colleen married, moved into the same bedroom where he'd lived his entire life.

Driscoll decided to finish the school year, then start work full-time for his dad in the summer of '52. Just after Christmas, Colleen sat him down again. This time she delivered bad news: she'd had a miscarriage.

The baby was gone.

Driscoll was devastated. He'd been looking forward to fatherhood and vowed that as soon as Colleen felt well enough about everything they'd try again. He was thankful she was fast to recuperate and soon seemed eager for another go. Late in the winter, just before spring, she announced she was pregnant again. Driscoll thought it great news. So did Colleen.

She also thought it time for them to move out of the house. She was still worried about the war and reminded Driscoll of this. She told him she was fearful he might soon be called up, be shipped out.

Though married men received paternity deferment, rules change in time of war. And, in 1952, they did. Colleen reasoned a U.S. Army soldier might find himself boots on the ground, in the war zone; that a U.S. Navy seaman might find himself on a transport or combat ship off Korea.

But the Air Force? He might remain far from the front, maybe even stateside, she said. For obvious reasons Driscoll feared planes, had vowed never to set foot on one. Still, Colleen argued, the Air Force was their best chance for a normal life. So, why shouldn't Driscoll consider that?

If the Knute Rockne crash and the stories his old man re-told *ad nauseam* scared him, irrational or not, the Glanville crash of '44 had left Driscoll dead-certain of his fate. That July morning was like any other — Driscoll doing chores, lending his father a hand fixing the tractor — until that big old Boeing B-29 bomber fell straight out of the sky.

It was just before noon and over at the Glanville place, southeast of Cottonwood Falls and not far north of the Goodson farm, Jack Glanville and his sons were working the field. The Misses had just stepped outside to check laundry drying on the line when, lo and behold, that four-engined heavy bomber *augered* right in.

Glanville was second-generation in the Falls, his family having settled the land just over from England. The bomber, the kind that a year later would drop atomic bombs on both Hiroshima and Nagasaki, was being flown cross country out of Memphis, Tennessee, piloted by a commander named Lyman W. Draw of the 59th Ferry Squadron.

Driscoll and his father heard the explosion.

By the time they made the Glanville place the house was gone, the barn and shed in flames; what was left of the B-29 was laid up against a grain silo. Five of the six men on board were dead, Lyman Draw among them. Somehow no one in the Glanville clan suffered even a scratch.

But as he stood looking on — Fat Andy, Digger Dave, Doc Mills and his old man all doing what they could to lend a hand — little did Driscoll know the events still to come. Not long after, a single-engine monoplane was dispatched from nearby Herington Air Base and it landed without incident in the adjacent field, the men aboard working the crash scene.

But hours later it failed to clear a fence on takeoff and it, too, crashed and burned; all, a few hundred feet from the wreckage of that B-29.

His mother later tried to convince him all planes didn't crash, go down in flames. It was the only time he didn't believe her.

Now all these years later here Driscoll was, his own wife trying to make him believe his best interests lay in the U.S. Air Force.

And he wasn't buying it now, either.

But Colleen wasn't his mother and she could reach him in ways his mother never could. She wore him down; he succumbed to her wishes.

Trepidation aside, he finally enlisted, left his pregnant wife back in Kansas. Set off for the unlikeliest of war-time destinations — on a passenger train bound for Geneva. Geneva, New York.

Recruits usually went to Lackland outside San Antonio, Texas. But there were only so many Lackland Air Force Base could take. When the onslaught of enlisted men swelled the ranks, most thinking along with Driscoll, the Air Force resurrected the aged Seneca Army Depot — and sent them off to the sleepy Finger Lakes region in upstate New York.

Basic training in the mirror, Driscoll sent for Colleen and arranged for a room at the grand old Hotel Seneca down on Seneca Street.

It was a wondrous hotel, six stories high, with turreted window bays and magnificent awnings that shaded the scores of glass panes that adorned its beautiful beige street-front facade. It was brick-sided, it was charming. Even Driscoll could tell it was a swell romantic backdrop for a long-overdue reunion with Colleen. Even if she was eight months pregnant and they were so achingly far from Kansas. From home.

Driscoll arrived at the Lehigh Valley Railroad Station just past 10 a.m., a good half-hour before Colleen was due.

It was an elegant station, as small-town railroad stations went. Built of red brick, it had a tower at one end, near the street and trolley line, and a spacious outdoor waiting area covered by a long, high, pitched roof supported by banks of columns so passengers could stand out alongside the track. Driscoll brought a cup of coffee and the *Finger Lakes Times*. He drank the coffee but found he couldn't concentrate on the paper what with the news about the war and all. After what seemed the longest time he saw black smoke from the steam locomotive rising in the distance. And then it was there, with its dining car, sleeper cars and coaches, coming to a halt right in front of him. Driscoll scanned the platform, searching.

The wind howled, teeming rain pelting off the station roof.

Colleen was far down the platform, stepping down off a coach, one porter helping, another carrying her bags. Driscoll thought her face as beautiful as ever, maybe more beautiful than even that. But, he was surprised how her coat stretched tight over an expectant belly.

In a moment he was before her. She looked at him, there in uniform, and said: "Don't you look handsome, Mr. Goodson."

He thought she reminded him of a prized heifer at the 4-H Fair back in the Falls, but didn't dare say it. He reached out, gave her a big hug.

"I missed you," he said.

"I missed you, too," she said.

She squeezed him as tight as she dared, then let go, moved back a step and unfastened the coat to reveal herself.

"Just don't get any ideas."

Soon the two of them were in the car, the second-hand '39 Ford he'd bought the week before down in Hayt Corners. He drove out to Sampson, just to show her around, then stopped at this quiet old restaurant nestled amongst a stand of tall trees over in Seneca Lake Park.

She told him all the news from home.

Greetings from his parents, the latest gossip about some of the boys and girls they'd both gone to high school with. They were already back in the Ford, headed to the hotel along Route 20, just east of downtown Geneva, when Driscoll asked the question she'd long dreaded.

"Has anyone heard from Robert?"

Colleen didn't answer. Driscoll glanced at her. She seemed about to cry. "What is it?" he asked, face ashen, as he pulled off the road.

"I'm sorry," she said.

Hands trembling, she reached into her pocketbook, took out the article from the local paper, handed it to her husband. **'BOBBY BOY' HINKSON KILLED IN KOREA,** the headline read. It was weeks old. Colleen said she was sorry, but no one had known how to deliver the news. Not over the phone, not while he was so far from home.

For the longest time the two of them sat there, in unbearable silence. Then, without a word, Driscoll began to drive. He drove back to the hotel, carried his wife's bags to the room, set them down. Took her coat, hung it. Still, he didn't say a word. She wanted to hug him, hold him. She knew he was hurting. He didn't let her get that close. She didn't try.

Soon he'd excused himself, said he was going for a walk.

The wind was still screaming and the rain still at full squall as Driscoll walked down Seneca Street past Schine's Geneva Theatre, past the home appliance store, past The Norge. He walked past the U.S. Post Office over on Castle Street, past City Hall, walked past the Methodist Church over on Main. He walked like that for hours, lost in thought. He walked like that until night had fallen, until he could walk no more, returning to the Seneca a tired mess. He was drenched, soaked clear to the bone, and he was shivering, though he barely seemed to notice. As he walked, vacant, across the lobby, headed for the stairs, the *maitre d'hotel* approached.

"Mr. Goodson?" he said. Driscoll stared right through him, blank. "Mr. Goodson?" the *maitre d'* said, again.

"Yes?" Driscoll said, finally.

The *maitre d'* told Driscoll his wife had gone into labor; had been taken to General Hospital. He offered a car to deliver him.

All still a blur, Driscoll found himself in the Maternity Ward, a doctor in full hospital gown explaining to him.

The doctor said something about premature labor, the delivery being a tough one, about how the umbilical cord had wrapped around the baby's neck. It had been quite traumatic; the boy, born blue and weathered from distress. Everything was fine now, the doctor said, seeing as how the new father appeared quite overwhelmed. The color had come back, the vital signs seemed normal. But, the doctor said, it had been quite a scare.

He ushered Driscoll into a room. There he found Colleen, in bed, their newborn son resting upon her chest. He was pink, he was beautiful. He was fast asleep. Colleen looked at her husband. He offered a weak smile. She knew he had suffered through a most-terrible day.

She wished it all had been so much different.

"Do you want to hold him?"

"Do you think . . . "

Before he could finish, Colleen said: "I think you should."

Driscoll reached down to pick up his new son; lifted him, cradled him, looked at her and seemed so moved, fighting hard not to cry.

"You weren't here and the nurses asked me for a name."

He gave her a look.

"Please don't be mad. I know we had one already picked."

A tear was rolling down her cheek, now. Driscoll just stood there, staring. She looked so overwhelmed, too, he thought. He wasn't sure what to say. He looked at his newborn son. It was all so incredible, he thought, and he felt a connection he hadn't once felt in his entire life.

He also felt such loss. He was so confused.

"I'm sorry," he said, finally.

"It's okay. I understand."

"What did you tell them? About his name?"

"I wanted it to be special," she said. "I hope you understand."

She looked at him standing there, holding their son.

"I told them," she said, "his name is Robert."

Still staring out at the swing, lost in thought, Driscoll never heard the door. Before he realized it Colleen was there in front of him.

She offered him a cup of coffee.

"I thought you might want some," she said.

She was wrapped in a bathrobe; tired, from the long night.

He didn't say a word. Not thank you, not sure. Just took it, trying hard not to look at her.

"I didn't want to wake you," she said.

Driscoll stared straight ahead.

"I brought out the blanket. You looked cold."

He took a sip of coffee, steam rising off the top in the chill air.

"Do you want to talk?" she said.

He shook his head, no, again without looking.

"I didn't think so. But, well . . . I just thought I'd ask."

She stood amidst the long, uncomfortable silence, not knowing what to do. She moved beside him, put a hand on his shoulder.

He flinched.

He was still staring out at the swing, the old black car tire, covered in morning dew; hanging, unmoving, from the thick strand of rope. She wondered what he was thinking, what he had been thinking. She thought he probably hated her. Maybe it was her guilty conscience. She thought she truly had a lot to feel guilty about. She hated herself for all that'd happened. She hated herself for all she'd done wrong. She had no idea how to fix it, any of it. She had no idea even where to start.

Colleen took her hand from her husband's shoulder, stepped around in front of him. He didn't look up, didn't move.

He just stared right through her.

"Driscoll?"

He closed his eyes.

"Look," Colleen said. "I made some eggs, in case you were hungry. I made toast . . . I thought you might want some breakfast."

He breathed deep, took another sip of coffee. "I can't."

He looked up at the sun, now just clear of the horizon. He looked back at his wife, glaring at her now.

"Have you even wondered where he is? How he is?"

Her hair was a mess. Tears welled in her eyes.

"How can you even ask me that?"

He shrugged his shoulders. "You tell me."

"I'm worried sick," she said. "You should know that."

"Then you should know I don't have time for breakfast," he said. "I have to go back out and search . . . I have to search for our son."

"I know," she said, suddenly self-conscious. She leaned down, kissed her husband gently on the forehead. He didn't move.

"I know," she said, again.

Then she went inside.

11

Seated at the back of Joe's Luncheonette, Inspector Caldwell and his detectives were talking over the events of another fruitless day.

For Caldwell things couldn't have gone worse — or been a bigger annoyance. The news conference had been a free-for-all. A lot of loaded questions, a lot more second-guessing. All, aimed squarely at him.

Held out in front of the IGA, the news conference attracted hordes of reporters — print, radio and even from the fledgling TV stations.

But the first question everyone wanted answered was not about the lost little boy. It was about Ann Woodward and the swirling rumors that a vagrant arrested after midnight had admitted to prowling the grounds of the Woodward estate the night Ann shot her husband dead.

Hans Wurtz was twenty-one, a six-foot-three blonde-haired German immigrant who spoke broken English and smiled a lot, as if the entire fiasco he'd become embroiled in was no more than a game or joke, maybe both. He'd been drinking black coffee around 2 a.m. at a diner on Main Street in Huntington, just over the county line into Suffolk, when three Huntington Town Police officers, all rookies, strolled in, saw him there, blessed their good fortune — and, slapped on the handcuffs. Police were calling Wurtz "a no-good burglar," as if there were some other kind.

But though the cops found a shotgun in the trunk of a car parked outside — the shotgun stolen from that Catholic priest, of all the masses — they couldn't figure what, if anything, any of it had to do with Ann Woodward killing her husband. Sure, it confirmed reports a prowler had been stalking the Woodward estate before Misses shot Mister.

But, it didn't change the circumstances. Ann still pulled the trigger. Her husband still had been standing, buck naked, a few feet from her, his own shotgun still at the side of his bed, when she'd fired.

And, of course, Billy Woodward, Jr., was still dead.

The Inspector tried to explain the rumors were just that; that all of it was some misunderstanding, a misstatement of fact.

That the truth was far different from how it had been portrayed in the wildfires of dog-eat-dog big-city journalism.

Police thought Wurtz was on the estate grounds the night of the shooting. Caldwell said that wasn't the case. The German's clear lack of English had confused things. When detectives finally got to the bottom of it, the Inspector said, it turned out Wurtz had admitted to breaking into buildings on the Woodward estate long *before* the shooting. On Friday night, not Saturday; certainly, not early Sunday. The truth, Caldwell said, was Wurtz was breaking into the clubhouse at a local golf club miles from the estate at the time Ann shot and killed Billy Woodward.

Which meant it was all a dead end. Literally.

But the reporters weren't buying it, that there was no connection. They wanted something more from Caldwell. When the Inspector wouldn't give it to them they thought he was hiding something, that maybe he was incompetent or careless. Maybe even both. They wanted to know why he wasn't putting more of an effort into making a connection between the no-good German and the shocking Woodward case.

"Why," one reporter asked, "are you neglecting the killing of William Woodward to concentrate on this missing boy?"

"Neglecting?" the Inspector said. "Did you say *'neglecting?'*"

"Yes," the reporter said. "Neglecting."

The Inspector could feel his blood beginning to boil. It was a dumbass question. One thing he hated was dumbass questions.

"You understand what dead means, right?" Caldwell said.

The reporter was dumbfounded. "I think so."

"I'm not sure you do," Caldwell said, all belligerent. "So let me try and help you, here. Billy Woodward's *dead.* We have every reason to believe the boy's still alive. Who, exactly, would *you* have me help?"

Thinking back on it as he sat in the booth drinking coffee with Farmer and Jones, Caldwell shook his head in frustration, all of it still under his skin. He knew it was all hang-the-expense. Six of one, half-dozen of the other. Even hours later it still irked him. Just fucking irked him.

"What is it, Cuth?"

"Nothing," the Inspector said, taking a sip of his coffee.

"You sure?"

"Just thinking about the news conference, Newb." He reached down, grabbed a *Lucky*. "That reporter was a real prick . . . *Negligence.*"

He stared across the table, flicked ashes into the ashtray. "Do I look like I'm being fucking negligent here? Do I?"

Farmer shot a glance at Jones.

"What?" Caldwell said.

"Nothing."

"C'mon, Newb. What is it?"

"I was just thinking what a lucky woman that wife of yours is."

"You got no idea," Caldwell said.

The detective flashed a wry smile. "Oh, I think I do."

The day began with thousands of volunteers fanned out across Long Island searching for Bobby Goodson.

It began with investigators from the Detective's Bureau chasing down all known perverts and child molesters, interrogating anyone who might be even the least bit suspicious; with officers posting fliers with a photo of little Bobby and other information that might help someone identify him — and call the cops. It began with Farmer and Jones running down leads at the shopping center, asking questions, conducting interviews.

It was soon certain the kid wasn't lost.

Though Farmer and Jones hadn't fared well they did uncover curious details. The stock boy, Jimmy Dodge, told them Colleen Goodson seemed preoccupied, constantly checking her watch. The cashiers thought Colleen tense, maybe nervous. The girl bagging groceries recalled Colleen left a twenty-cent tip; recalled her saying kids were "a bunch of little terrors."

"Little terrors?" Jones asked.

"Almost like she didn't like children," the girl said.

"You thought she didn't like children?" Farmer asked.

"Well, yeah. Maybe. I mean, maybe she was just having a bad day? But she certainly sounded like kids were a nuisance."

None of the women seemed to like Colleen. No one said that, exactly. But Farmer and Jones thought all of them hinted it, that some downright implied it. One called her "a flirt." Another said she wasn't "motherly." A few suggested she always seemed to have an ulterior motive.

Others thought her manipulative.

But the detectives thought the oddest thing was that no one could recall seeing Colleen with the carriage. Or with her children.

They remembered her being panicked, saying the kids were gone. They remembered her making a scene. But no one ever saw Johanna or Bobby. Even Officer O'Reilly thought Colleen had been "dodgy."

Though none of it seemed like much these were all useful tidbits, if not proof. They raised questions, doubt, as to whether Colleen — or even Marjorie and Tag, for that matter — had been telling the truth.

Or telling some sort of tale.

But what to believe? Who to believe?

If Farmer and Jones thought the old man at the butcher counter would make it all clearer, they were sadly mistaken.

When they told him Bobby was still missing after a long night of searching the old butcher appeared visibly shaken.

"Good God," old man Katsch said, then mumbled something under his breath. The old man stared at the two detectives at the counter before him. They appeared confused, having not understood a word of what he'd said. "Sorry" he said. "Yiddish. From the old country . . . It is just I feel I should want to cry. It makes me very sad, this news."

"Why is that?" Farmer asked.

"*Ei,* a real *goyishe kop,*" the old man mumbled.

"What kind of cop?" Farmer said.

The old butcher seemed sheepish, realizing he'd been heard.

"Not cop," he said.

"Not cop?" Jones said.

"Please, forget what it is I said," he said. "What I am asking is what do you mean when you say 'why is that?' This is just a small boy, Detective. A little boy, how should I say? A boy taken from his family . . . Do you understand what this must be like for a boy like that?"

"And how is it you understand how the boy must feel, Mister . . . "

"Katsch. I am Hevel Katsch."

Farmer asked him to spell his name, wrote it down — K-A-T-S-C-H, H-E-V-E-L — inside a little pocket notebook he carried.

"Okay. So how is it you know this, Mr. Katsch?"

"The war, the wars. Trust me, *tsores* I know."

"Sorest?" Jones said. "What's sorest?"

"Not sorest, Detective. *Tsores,* with a *'T'* . . . As in troubles." He took the rag, wiped his face. "With troubles, I am long-acquainted."

"And what kind of troubles would those be?" Farmer said.

"You've heard of Adolf Hitler, the Wehrmacht . . . the *Nazis?*"

The detectives studied the old man. His age was indeterminate. Farmer later said he thought him pushing eighty, Jones thought him even older than that. He wore a blood-stained white apron. He was stoop-shouldered, weathered. Hands gnarled. He looked like a man who carried the burdens of a lifetime. And now it all seemed to make sense.

With a nod, Farmer said: "I'm sorry. I didn't . . . "

"It's forgotten, Detective."

Everyone took a deep breath.

"The cashiers said you know Mrs. Goodson as well as anyone here," Jones said, finally. "That true?"

"I should think."

"Any idea what happened to the boy?"

"I haven't the faintest. Though, I wish I did."

"What can you tell us about Mrs. Goodson?" Farmer said, as old Katsch considered the insinuation. "Can you tell us about her?"

"I am an old man," he said. "An *alter kocker,* an old fart. Understand I don't want to speak out of turn, here. It's . . . it's not my place."

"But?" Jones said.

"But since you ask, I should say Mrs. Goodson may well be a lot of things. That is, as you or I may be a lot of things. Some of the folks . . . well, some folks here might not think kindly of her, I think."

"How so?" Farmer asked, as the old man raised an eyebrow.

"The women," he said. "They *kibitz,* they *kvetch.* Worse than old washer women they are, sometimes. To them Mrs. Goodson could well be *a maidel mit a klaidel.* How should I say this? No more than a cutie-pie, showing off a new dress. Some think her beyond help."

"And you, Mr. Katsch? Do you think Mrs. Goodson is . . . That she is what it is you said she is, beyond help?"

"Detectives," he said, and how he said it made it clear he believed the question answered itself. "I rather think her a . . . " He said something in Yiddish, caught himself. "A good soul," he said, this time.

"A good soul?" Farmer said, staring. "So, you don't think she could have done anything to the boy, then?"

"Can I say this for certain? Only God knows the truth. What I say is this: You can't pee on my back and tell me it's raining outside."

"What the hell does that mean?" Jones said.

"There are some people," Katsch said. "They see what they want to see, what they wish to see. Me, I think that if Mrs. Goodson were a bad person she would be a bad person, no matter. She wouldn't be a good person, she couldn't be a good person. And I have already said I think this Mrs. Goodson is a good soul . . . That she is a good-soul person.

"That is, I think she could not have hurt this boy, her son."

"But the truth is you don't know Mrs. Goodson well, do you?" Farmer said. "All you know is she comes to buy meat."

"This is correct, Detective."

"I mean, you don't know her socially, right?"

"This, too, is correct . . . Detective."

"So," Jones said. "What makes you so sure, then?"

Katsch shrugged. "I can't. I should call it a feeling."

"A feeling?"

"A feeling. From what I know of her, of people."

"I see. So if . . . "

"If?" the old man said. "Oh, '*if.*' This '*if,*' this changes everything."

"Doesn't it?" Farmer said.

The old man smiled, ever so slight.

"Perhaps, I should say this, Detectives. There is this expression, in Yiddish. Please, beg me my pardon for being so crude. But, if my grandmother had testicles, she would be my grandfather."

Jones leaned in. "Like if the Queen had balls she'd be the King?"

"Exactly," the old man said, in mock revelation.

Farmer stared at Katsch. He believed the old man believed what he believed. Still, he knew what all detectives know and that is that truth is in the eye of the beholder. That the perception of truth, even as a man might know the truth to be, doesn't make it true. Not even in the very least.

"You think Mrs. Goodson is what then, Mr. Katsch?"

"Do you know the story of the boy who cried wolf, Detective?"

"I do," Farmer said.

"This Mrs. Goodson. Perhaps you must consider — and, this is no matter what you've heard, what you will hear — but perhaps she has been calling like the boy who cried wolf. Not understanding the cost when the *shtayer-moner* — the tax man — comes and the bill is due. Like it is when the wolf comes and scatters the sheep and the boy calls out, only to be left to wonder why it is no one has come to answer his cries for help."

The old butcher thought the detectives confounded.

"What I am trying to say is Mrs. Goodson is a woman who, for whatever reason, could be begging for attention. She could be lost, could be lonely. She could be, how should I say? She could be *farblondzshet*. Misguided, confused. But I think, in my heart, no more than any of us. No more maybe than you, no more than I. From what I know, from what my eyes have seen, I trust Mrs. Goodson loves her children. No matter how much anyone thinks she might not. That she is a good mother, no matter how much those might say she is not. But truth is I am just a man, an old man. And you detectives, you are only men, too.

"So I will say just this: Is it a fault the bride is too beautiful? Truth is the bride is not too beautiful; others are merely jealous. Do you see?"

Neither detective said a word.

Katsch said: "Then I should say a thief's hat burns."

Jones and Farmer stared at the old man. Katsch smiled.

"The thief acts as if everyone knows it is he who has committed the crime. But the truth is no one knows; they merely suspect. In Yiddish, we say: *'Got vaist.'* God knows . . . If you think the boy is not truly lost, detectives — if you think this is foul play — I should suggest you look for your thief. Because if you look hard enough he will reveal himself.

"God knows this. You will know this, too."

For the longest time the detectives stood there pondering what the old man said. Finally, Farmer said: "That's fair enough, Mr. Katsch."

He shot a quick glance at his partner. Jones shrugged.

"Thank you," Farmer said.

He pointed to his head. "Even if I am an old *goyishe kop*."

Old Katsch appeared embarrassed, suddenly aware that his mumbled criticism had been understood, after all. "Please," he said.

Farmer cut him short. "One of the phrases I learned with the NYPD back in Brooklyn," he said. "It's okay. I've been called far worse."

Katsch forced a weak smile.

"Thank you," the old man said. "I should hope you will find this boy. I should trust you will find this boy and whoever it is took him."

The detectives were still sharing a laugh at the Inspector's expense when Joe arrived carrying a pot of murky black coffee.

"*Youse* guys need a refill?"

Looking up, all three pushed out their cups.

Joe Monti was the Joe in Joe's. In his forties, he was of average height but still lean, if not quite athletic, and good looking, if not handsome. He wore a white T-shirt, with rolled-up sleeves, a white apron and had dark Sicilian skin, a prominent Roman nose. Down-to-earth, without pretense, he knew how to schmooze, was what you would call a regular guy.

He was instantly likable. His customers loved him for it.

He'd fought in the war with Patton's Seventh Army, found himself, strangely enough, tramping through his hometown, Menfi, during the Invasion of Sicily. He'd come home, left the Canarsie section of Brooklyn, opened his luncheonette in Hempstead Plains.

Like him, the place was without airs: counter service lined with spin stools, a handful of tables, red vinyl-clad booths. He served breakfast and lunch, the basics. And, he did good business since he sold an honest sandwich at a fair price, but also because his place was a stone's throw from Meadowbrook Field and straight across Eisenhower from the shopping center and IGA. The cops all knew him, a lot of them were regulars. Joe liked having them. They stopped in when they could.

As he topped off the coffee, Joe stared at the copy of *Newsday*.

The front front screamed: **LITTLE BOY LOST.**

Beneath it the sub-headline read: *Intensive Search into the Night for Three-Year-Old, Who Disappeared as Mother Shopped.*

"*Minchia!*" Monti said. "What a cryin' shame."

"That's what it is," Caldwell said. "A fucking crying shame."

The story by Lenore Terranova had a photograph of Colleen Goodson seated alone in her living room looking pensive, tricycle in the background, the trick-or-treat bag still dangling from the handlebars.

Inset was the studio photo of little Bobby.

"Heard *youse* caught a couple of *schvartzes* out on the parkway last night," Joe said, as he emptied the last bit into the mugs.

The detectives all laughed. Toward the back room an old white-haired woman hovered over the big, black gas stove, making sauce.

Caldwell took his cigarette, what was left, snuffed it out.

"All a lot of nothing," the Inspector said.

Joe nodded towards the paper. "You know, I seen her."

"Who?" Farmer said.

"I seen her. She's been in. A few times."

"You're shittin' me," Caldwell said.

Joe set the empty coffee pot down on the tabletop.

"I kid you not. She was right here, in this booth."

Turning toward the back room, towards the aging woman standing guard over the marinara, he motioned with his hand.

"*Matri! Ma!*" he yelled to her, then turned back to the cops. "I'm tellin' *youse*. That broad, she was right here."

As Joe talked the old woman came ambling up.

She was short, heavy-set and wore an apron spattered red with sauce. She had a mass of white hair pulled not quite neat into a bun. Squinty-eyed, she came off tough, with crooked teeth and a weathered face that warned no-nonsense. It was obvious she'd had a hard life. And yet when she reached the booth she grabbed Joe, gave him a big hug.

"*Youse* know my mom, right?"

He said something in Sicilian and his mother turned to the detectives, gave them all a gap-toothed smile.

Joe pointed to the picture of Colleen on the front page.

"*Ricordi? Quello lei chiamato una puttana?*"

Squinting, the old woman leaned in, stared hard at the photo.

"*Stronza!*" she screamed, spit on the floor. "*Squaldrina! Sorca!*"

The suddenness of the outburst caught the detectives off guard. Joe seemed embarrassed. He knew what she'd said.

"Ma? Mamma? *Per favore, sia bello.*" Please, be nice.

"What?" Caldwell asked, as the woman continued her rant in Sicilian.

Joe put his hands together as if seeking divine intervention. "Ah, *marrone,*" he said. Oh, shit. He pointed to the photo of Colleen.

"My mother, she called her a bitch, a whore, a . . . uh. Um." Joe leaned in low amongst the detectives, whispered: "Called her a . . . "

He thought the detectives still stunned over the God-awful slur that had been lost in translation.

"I told her be nice. She said she knew this broad was no good."

"How'd she know that?" Farmer asked.

Joe turned to the old woman, who pointed to her ring finger.

"She got a wedding ring," he said.

The detectives all looked at each other, shrugged.

"Yeah?" the Inspector said. "She's married. So what?"

Before Joe could say a word the old woman waved her hand at the trio. "*Idioti!*" she screamed — and went off again, in Sicilian.

Embarrassed, Joe Monti said: "Ma?" He turned back to the detectives his mother had called idiots and smiled, weakly. "She said 'cause she was with a man. And this guy, he ain't her husband."

"A man?" Caldwell said.

"And he ain't her husband."

The three detectives exchanged quick glances, intrigued.

"You see this guy?" Farmer asked.

"Big guy. Good lookin'. Like Elvis. Looked like he was *sittin'* her."

"Sitting her?" Jones asked.

"*Sittin'* her." Joe made a fist, punched an open palm. "*Chiavata, cosina veloce. Farsi un ragazza. Youse* know. . . *Bangin'* her."

He stood smirking, as the cops broke into laughter, again.

"You know this guy?" Caldwell said, finally.

"Nah. But he's a flier."

"A pilot?"

"Yeah. Had them wings. Had the uniform and everythin'."

"Either of you catch his name?" Farmer asked.

Joe shook his head no. He asked his mother something in Sicilian, but she shook her head no, too. The detectives asked why she thought there something was going on. Joe asked; the old woman launched into a long diatribe, Joe laughing at times, as he translated it all, what she'd said.

"She thought the guy was trouble. That he was *int'rested* in one thing and it wasn't the meal . . . It was the dessert."

The three men smirked.

"How about the missing boy?" Farmer said.

Joe asked. Again, the old woman seemed furious. Slut, bitch, Joe said, translating. She knew the woman was no good. She bet she had something to do with it. The Inspector was about to ask another question when the old woman turned, spit on the floor again, headed back to the kitchen.

"*Porca! Donnicciola! Faccia di merda! Figlio di puttana! Sopata facile!*" she screamed to no one in particular as she walked.

"I won't even ask."

"Don't."

"She thinks the mother did it, huh?" Farmer said.

"She *knows* the mother done it."

"How's she so sure?"

Joe gave them a look like how should I know? He yelled back to the kitchen again. His mother didn't look up from her sauce.

"*I cani abbaiano, i buoi pascolano!*" she yelled back.

Joe broke out laughing.

"What?"

"She says, 'Dogs bark, oxen graze.'"

"What the hell does that mean?" the Inspector asked.

"Means a tiger don't change his spots," Joe Monti said.

"Spots?"

"What?"

"Tigers have stripes," Jones said. "Leopards have spots."

"Whatever," Joe said, as he grabbed the empty coffee pot, wiped where it had been with a dishrag. *"Youse* know what I mean."

"How many times the two of them been in here?" Farmer asked.

Joe Monti thought for a moment. "Three, maybe four."

"Hmmm. And the last time?

"Thursday, maybe Friday. I think it was Friday."

"And?"

"And it looked like they wasn't havin' such a good time."

"How's that?"

"Looked like things wasn't goin' so good, like a fight or somethin' . . . The broad, she seemed real upset. The guy, he looked pissed."

"Really?" Caldwell said.

"You couldn't really hear 'em. But, it didn't look too good."

"And this was Friday?" Farmer asked.

"Thursday, Friday. One of them days."

Detective Farmer glanced at his partner then at Caldwell. Both looked intrigued. Farmer knew he was. It was all very interesting.

"Look, I got to get back to cleanin'. *Youse* want somethin' else?"

"No," Caldwell said. "We're good."

And just like that Joe was gone, back to closing down. The Inspector chuckled. "Tiger spots. That's fucking great, huh?"

The three of them laughed.

"We certainly heard a lot of theories today," Farmer said. "The employees at the IGA, that old butcher."

He glanced at Jones, who rolled his eyes. "Now this."

Caldwell flicked ashes into the ashtray. "And?"

"They're coming from all sides. Some think the mom, some think the kid was kidnapped. Some think maybe he really wandered off, that we're still going to find him. The butcher? He thinks the mom's a good woman, that we should be looking at other suspects. Joe's mom. She's a pisser, huh? Well, we know all what she thinks . . . Me? I've got no idea."

"I know what I think," Caldwell said.

"What's that?"

"I think the husband's in the Air Force, but doesn't know *Snuffy Smith* from fucking *Bodacious Idjit and H.T.* That he's a clerk who came here from Kansas on a God-damn train. And our dutiful, adorable mother of two? Suddenly, she's in an Air Force town with scores of cock-hard airmen. Pilots, real men." He pushed back in the booth.

"She's never been out of Cottonwood River, Cottonwood Falls. Wherever, whatever, the fuck that is. She's got men and God knows what else, all in her backyard. She's friendly, probably throws a good spread, and I'm not talking special meat loaf of hers. Maybe she's willing to share the gravy with anyone who'll show her a good time, like this pilot guy."

He took a last draw from his smoke, tamped out the *Lucky*.

"The kid's what? Three?"

Jones and Farmer nodded yes.

"So, he's really learning to talk, now. Maybe he heard mom talking on the phone. Maybe she got worried, turned on the boy."

"Maybe this guy had something to do with it?" Jones said.

"Or maybe this guy had something to do with it."

"We need to find this pilot," Farmer said.

"Exactly. And let's see what that neighbor lady knows, if she knows anything. First thing tomorrow, you guys go talk to her, see what she's got. Check out her house, too. Just to make sure. Then go talk to the mother again. Get a name. Let's find this guy, talk to him . . .

"Let's see what the hell he knows."

The Inspector reached for one last cigarette.

Out back, Joe Monti had finished and his mom had taken her sauce, stored it in the refrigerator. Was busily wiping down the stove.

Watching, Caldwell shook his head.

"What is it Cuth?" Farmer said.

The Inspector half-laughed.

"Just thinking, fellas. I mean, we got this God-damned Woodward shooting. We got this missing kid. What else could go wrong?"

"They say bad things happen in threes."

"Yeah. Just fucking terrific, Newb."

Newbury Farmer smiled. "Well, it has been a month since we had a plane crash over at the base," he said.

If looks could kill, he'd have been dead on the spot.

"Fuck you, Newbury," the Inspector said. "Fuck you."

He wasn't smiling when he said it.

12

"Amazing, huh?"

"How's that?"

Seated passenger-side Jones motioned to the morning paper, to the latest on the Woodward shooting. There was a photo of Ann Woodward lying in a hospital bed, surrounded by doctors, nurses, aides, attendants.

It was almost glamorous. All, a publicist's dream.

"This Woodward bitch," Jones said. That's really what he said: This Woodward bitch. "She shoots her husband, kills him. Dead. She's got twenty mil, easy, coming to her in insurance and inheritance. And what's she do? Goes off to the hospital complaining how she's got 'anxiety.'

"It's ridiculous. Just God-damned ridiculous, you ask me."

"Yeah," Farmer said. "Sure as hell is."

He pointed to a story about Colleen. "And now this Goodson woman. Makes you wonder who's the victims — and who's trying to be."

Jones stared out the window. "Tell me about it."

On the day her husband was to be buried Ann Woodward remained under care of the professionals at Doctors Hospital in Manhattan, where she'd been since the morning of the shooting, a victim of "anxiety."

And now Colleen Goodson had been placed under "observation" at Meadowbrook Hospital, suffering from both anxiousness and stress.

The hospitals were worlds apart; the effect, much the same.

The police wanted answers. Under observation and care neither Ann nor Colleen would be readily available for questioning. The doctors said the cops would have to understand. The cops thought it all infuriating stuff, a game of cat and mouse. They didn't appreciate being mice.

"Anxiety?" Jones said. "I got nothin' but damned anxiety."

Behind the wheel of the unmarked cop car, Farmer snickered.

"You got to love it. You really do."

Not that anyone in the Detective's Bureau was surprised that Ann Woodward and Colleen Goodson had gone into seclusion.

Suspects always had a dodge. Cops knew that. It was just that no one expected hospitalization, if you could call it that, to be involved.

Not for some condition as nebulous as "anxiety."

Inspector Caldwell and Nassau District Attorney Frank Gugliotta had been at the Woodward estate that Sunday morning when the ambulance arrived. This was scant hours after the shooting, barely moments after investigators finished processing the crime scene. It was always a crime scene when someone was dead and there were still answers to be had.

As Caldwell and Gugliotta looked on men from the Medical Examiner's Office carried William Woodward, Jr., wrapped in a body bag, from the house and placed him in the transport.

Ann Woodward was obviously shaken. Which was understandable, since she was now a widow. Since she'd killed him.

Then, out of nowhere, came the luxurious private ambulance, white and unmarked, no affiliations noted. It drove in, as if on cue.

As the cops, the Inspector and the District Attorney watched, medics in crisp white coats stepped out, brushed past them, entered the house. Not long after they ushered poor Ann out the front door and placed her gently, gingerly, into the back of the waiting vehicle — and drove off toward their exclusive, posh Manhattan hospital.

The Inspector and District Attorney had the law on their side. They knew at that moment it all meant nothing, not a damned thing.

"And they say the rich are just like the rest of us, huh?" Gugliotta said, as medics hauled Ann away hot on the heels of her stone-cold Billy.

"I tell you, Frank. You've got to wonder."

"Don't wonder, Cuth," Gugliotta said.

Truth was, Caldwell and Gugliotta knew where it was all headed.

That is, Doctors Hospital wasn't a hospital in the sense most hospitals were a hospital. It was, in fact, more like some swank hotel.

When it opened twenty-five years earlier Doctors did so with a board of directors that included a Hayden, a Whitney, a Rockefeller.

It was a hospital that had no wards, but rather private rooms. Those private rooms had private baths, private refrigerators, private blackout curtains — all for privacy from paparazzi, of course. Ordinary hospitals had doctors and nurses on call. The "on-call" staff at Doctors included a florist, a barber, a tailor. There was a stenographer, a telegraph office and an elegant restaurant, instead of some common make-do cafeteria. The gymnasium came complete with barbells, rowing machine and hot-steam sauna; the library, with a collection of rare leather-bound works.

There was a solarium for much-needed relaxation and a floor of suites reserved solely for the employees of those who'd been admitted.

Most of all, there were no patients at Doctors.

All admitted were considered "guests."

The cops and the District Attorney decided that when it came to Ann Woodward the overkill served to add insult to fatal injury.

Testament to that was the manner which questions could be asked of the pitiable millionairess in the wake of the entire bloody mess.

The District Attorney and the Inspector were to travel to Manhattan if they wished to question poor Ann. To her private private room.

Two days after the shooting, they sat at the grieving widow's bedside, a dozen high-priced attorneys and aides at Ann's side, interrupted by the medics when it was believed things got too "strenuous" for her.

Which, of course, was often.

The night of the shooting Ann told the cops she'd fired her shotgun at a "shadowy figure" in the darkened hall of the 12-room mansion. She'd wakened to a dog barking, grabbed the loaded shotgun, opened her bedroom door, seen the outline. There was word of a prowler.

She was sleepy, she was scared. So she'd fired. *Twice.*

Two full days after the fact, however — after two days of treatment, two days of conversation with her closest advisors — that shadowy figure, the sinister, menacing outline of some unknown burglar, was really not that at all, Ann said. She now claimed she'd blasted buckshot at a strange "sound." A sound, she now claimed as she lay in her billowy linen bed at Doctors suffering greatly, that tragically proved to be her beloved Bill.

The new version of events relayed to the proper authorities, those high-reputation doctors told the humble public servants the interview was over, finished. Done. Mrs. Woodward, after all, was in ill health.

She'd suffered enough, had suffered too much.

The District Attorney later told reporters he had no opinion of the new account, would let a grand jury decide.

"I'm not buying any of this, Frank," Caldwell said on the way back to Nassau. "This whole thing sounds like a crock of shit, you ask me."

The Inspector later said the frustrated D.A. told him: "Remember Cuth, the lie of a millionaire is more-believed than the truth of a beggar."

At the telling, Caldwell added: "Ain't *that* the fucking truth."

Now, as he drove toward Mitchell Avenue, Farmer thought back on the conversation recounted that morning by the Inspector as only he could recount it. Jones was back to staring out the side window.

It was just after 1 p.m. Wednesday — three days after Ann Woodward fired wild into that darkened mansion hallway, had shot and killed her husband; two days after Bobby Goodson had just up and disappeared in the broad daylight of suburbia. The detectives had hoped to get an early start on the day. Then they learned Colleen had been taken the night before to Meadowbrook, had been held overnight.

Word was she was to be released sometime that afternoon.

Their whole timetable thrown into a maddening mess, Farmer and Jones spent the morning sifting through calls to the hotline — calls generated by the thousands of fliers handed out across Long Island — in the vain hope someone knew what really happened to Bobby Goodson.

There were hundreds of them, those call sheets, with hundreds of theories regarding the disappearance. These, too, were a veritable shit-show; calls about Negroes, about the afflicted, about the insane.

About pretty much anyone and everyone.

One man suggested the government was behind it, considering the father was in the military. Another wondered if the boy had been abducted by aliens. Someone urged the police to look harder at Hans Wurtz, the German, who'd admitted to prowling the Woodward estate — as if the cops hadn't at him looked hard enough already.

Report after report, the detectives read. Report after report, the more disgusted they became. Reports of sightings that seemed too unbelievable to be believed. Accounts of shadowy figures and elaborate kidnapping plots. Suggestions that Communists might really be to blame; suggestions it was all a hoax. One caller wondered if the case might be tied to the Lindbergh baby. Even if that kidnapping had happened in Jersey.

Had happened back in '32.

Just when the detectives were about to give up hope they came across two promising leads. One was from a woman in Brooklyn, the other from a woman working at a roadside farm stand on a rural road out in Suffolk County. The woman from Brooklyn said she'd seen a blonde-haired boy fitting the description of little Bobby on Tuesday, walking with a woman under the Myrtle Avenue El, the elevated train, near the border of Ridgewood, Queens. She'd followed them down Wyckoff to Putnam Avenue in nearby Bushwick. There she saw the woman and child enter a house. She gave the cops an address. Investigators were dispatched to the scene. Turned out the boy looked nothing like Bobby Goodson.

Far from upset, his mother found the entire episode comedic. She provided them with a birth certificate, family photographs. Just in case.

Investigators were sent to the farm stand, too. Not far from the grass-strip aerodrome in Bayport, police interviewed the woman.

She'd been working Monday afternoon when she saw a car, driven by a woman, stop just down the road. She found it curious when another car pulled up and a man and a boy got out and walked to the car in front.

The man placed the boy into the back seat, talked to the woman, returned to his own car. Then the cars drove off in opposite directions, she said. The car driven by the man headed west, the other east.

The investigators were intrigued. They asked questions, hoping for details. No, the woman said, she didn't get a license plate. No, she didn't know what kind of cars they were other than one was gray and one was green. No, she didn't get a good look at the man, the woman or the boy, though she did tell the cops she thought the man looked like he was — or had been — in the military. Why was that, she was asked.

"I can't really say," she said. "Just the way he carried himself."

Sensing it might be something the detectives went to a pay phone back down the road. One called the Detective's Bureau, got Farmer.

"This could be our pilot," Farmer told Jones, off the phone.

"You think?"

"Only one way to find out. Let's go."

So the two headed out to talk to Marjorie and Tag, then catch Colleen when she got home. They needed to find out about the pilot. Who he was, where he was. What color car he drove. They needed answers, straight or otherwise. As he waited at the light to turn onto Mitchell Farmer exhaled a deep, frustrated sigh. Hearing him, Jones turned to his partner.

"What?"

"Just thinking," Farmer said, as he tapped his fingers.

"About?"

"What Caldwell said, that scene out at the Woodward estate. He said the rich were different from the rest of us."

"And?"

"And other than money, I'm not so sure that's true."

"How's that?"

"Ann Woodward's been holed up in that hospital in Manhattan since she shot her husband, right? Like you said, she's got 'anxiety.'"

"All bullshit. But, yeah."

"Now this Goodson woman . . . She goes to the hospital, too, the stress of her kid being missing too much for her."

"More bullshit."

Farmer turned. "You tell me, what's the difference?"

"Other than a couple ten million bucks?"

"Yeah. Other than a couple of ten million bucks."

Jones thought for a moment, shrugged his shoulders. He turned back to the window, still glum. "Nothing," he said. "Nothing at all."

The light changed. Farmer turned onto Mitchell bound for MacArthur Terrace. "People really are terrible, aren't they?" Jones said.

He was still looking out the side window when he said it.

The elder detective thought for a moment.

"At least a lot of them sure as hell are . . . Then again, you and me, we'd both be out of work if they weren't."

Jones never turned his head, but he sounded beaten.

"Yeah, Newb. I guess we would."

"You look like shit."

Bags under his bloodshot eyes Jake Johnson took a tired hand and ran it through his uncombed jet-black hair.

"Much obliged," he said, his tired voice stung with sarcasm.

"Don't blame me. You really look like all hell, Jake."

"Feel like it, too. 'Bout feel like trouble lookin' for a place to happen."

Holt Hamilton took a deep breath. "What now?" he said.

Johnson stood there, not saying a word. Then he tossed the afternoon paper onto the Ready Room table. For the second-straight day *Newsday* had a front-page story about the disappearance of Bobby Goodson.

Hamilton studied it, not quite understanding.

Johnson pointed to the front-page photos of Bobby and Colleen.

"I'm . . ." He said it, *ah'm.* "I'm *envolved.*"

"Involved?"

"Envolved."

"With this kid gone missing?"

"Hell no, Jethro. Why y'all gone say that for?" Jake said.

"What then?"

"Her." Jake reached down, tapped his index finger on the photograph of Colleen. "The mom. I'm *envolved* with the mom. Least, I were."

Seated at the table Hamilton stared at Johnson. "How involved?"

"Let's just say I *knowed* her."

"You know her? Like?"

"Like I *knowed* her."

Hamilton shook his head.

"What did I tell you about the married ones? Huh?"

"I know."

"You know?"

"Don't get your dander up, Holt. Y'all gettin' ugly, nose out of joint, not knowin' to the *sarcumstance.* I mean, I didn't go to do it.

"Least, not directly."

"You've never seen a girl you didn't think you couldn't get into bed, Jake . . . Lieutenant Jake Johnson, Kentucky Colonel Casanova."

Jake grinned, sheepishly. Hamilton never cracked a smile.

"Why y'all faultin'? I already feel like I up'n died." He motioned again to the paper. "When I see'd that there . . . I mean, I were like I'll be dog."

"This kid's gone, Jake. It's sounding like a real shit-storm."

"Sure come up a bad cloud, Holt."

Hamilton got up, walked to a row of metal lockers in the Ready Room, stood facing them, his back to Jake. He thought to haul off and slam his fist into one, but didn't. He turned back.

"The cops are all over this. They've searched high and low for this kid, looked under every rock. They're talking to everyone ever talked to this woman. There's even talk of the FBI. How long before they get to you?"

Johnson shrugged. "Beats the heck out of me."

"That's it?"

"Don't go makin' a mountain out a molehill, Holt. They ain't got nary none. I didn't done it. Had nothin' to do with it. When I *see'd* that paper, when I *see'd* what'd happened to that there boy, Holt . . .

"I mean, I'm feelin' *awfullest.*"

"You sure you had nothing to do with this?"

"Bite your tongue."

"I'm just asking."

"Y'all barkin' up the wrong tree, Holt. I know they're gone be *frog-giggin'* on my butt. But that dog won't hunt. Ain't got no call."

"So they've got no reason to think you had a hand in this?"

"Nah. I'm *gooder'n* grits. Ain't got no dog in this fight."

"Okay. Good then. That's good."

Holt moved his chair, sat down, motioned for Jake to do the same. He glanced again at the paper, shook his head.

"Of all things."

"Believe me, I'm fit to be tied. I just never *thunk* it'd all get this out of whack, me knocked off 'n my high'n mighty like . . . "

"Look," Hamilton said. "Tell me what happened."

After thinking for a time, Johnson said: "First off . . . "

It had been a couple three months before, Jake said. He was at the shopping center, the one where little Bobby supposedly disappeared, buying flowers for a girl. He'd come out of the florist shop, run smack into Colleen. In uniform, he looked handsome. Embarrassed he'd almost knocked her over, he began to extend his apologies.

She beat him to the punch.

"You're in quite a big hurry," she said. "Lucky girl."

"Might a been," he said. "If I hadn't met y'all."

He smiled at her. "I tell her, 'She ain't half near as *purty* as y'all are, Miss. Even on her Sunday best.'"

He said she reached out, admiring his pilot's wings.

"Is that what they say to tell a girl in the pilot's manual?"

"Nah. Come up with that one myself."

She laughed. Soon the two were cutting up like kids.

"Hit it off, right quick, Holt. Peas in a pod, possums in a pie. Y'all know me. I got radar. *A'fore* long I were feelin' happier than a dead pig in sunshine." He grinned. Said she said it must be nice to have a man bring you flowers. He told her she could find out sometime. She said maybe, then said sure. Before he knew it he'd handed her his number.

"I tell her give me a call."

He stared at Holt.

"I had no idea she were married, Holt. No idea 'bout she had them kids. Never said nothin'. Not a God-danged word."

"You really expect me to . . . "

"I *swear'n,*" Jake said. "God as my witness."

"C'mon Jake. You're talking to me, now."

"Wasn't 'til later, Holt. Didn't *knowed* nothin' 'til later. 'Til late."

As Hamilton listened he thought all he knew about his friend. Son of a miner and moonshiner, Jake Johnson had been hard-born, second of four, into a small hollow town in the mountains of eastern Kentucky.

"A mile in off the hard road," Jake told him.

Off the pavement, Route 40, just outside Oil Springs.

Growing up dirt-poor, pay-no-never-mind, his world was backwoods Appalachia; Flatgap and Paintsville, Minefork, Mashfork and Manila, named by men home from the Philippines and the Spanish-American War. Barnett's Creek, Oil Springs. Down the road a piece, Van Lear.

Lexington, Louisville and Bowling Green might have been on the Moon. All of it, Hamilton knew, a million miles from his own insulated childhood out on the West Coast, in sun-soaked San Diego, California.

Holt learned to swim at two, surf at six, fly at sixteen.

By that age Jake had been helping his daddy run white lightning a good five years, sometimes driving the back roads at night — sometimes by himself, *hisself;* sometimes with his brother — lights out, *lift-a-rag,* when his Pa was off doing whatever it was he'd done: working for a paycheck, doing time or simply laying out. That is, down in the coal mines or in jail; the calaboose. Maybe, just catting around. *Spreein'.*

All along, Jake said, he'd pondered something better; better than a tin-roof shack — tumbledown, tucked into a hillside holler, no running water, no indoor plumbing. No future. Then come the second war, World War II. Jake was too young. But as it got along he grew older and just into '45 he turned eighteen and thought it his time. He started talking at 'em at the table one night; that is, *conversatin'* with his Ma and Pa, saying he wanted to join up. Enlist in the Air Force. He said he'd figured — "I *figgured,"* is what he'd said — flying might could be fun.

"Why not for?" Jake said. "Already *knowed* I could drive a lick."

Still, he and his daddy near come to blows over it, he said. Least, that's how he'd told it. Jake said his father had gotten *"mad as far"* — fire, that is — saying how he'd come off "biggity, above his raisin'."

Said Jake thought he was better than.

When cooler heads prevailed, which was all easier said than done, Jake convinced his Pa it was all just 'cause. Men were needed, opportunity was awaiting. And he wasn't scared — "I weren't *askeered"* — to go ruckus. To go fight. Certainly, he wasn't too scared to learn to fly.

Or die trying.

It turned out Jake was a day late and a dollar short; the war, over before he could get in on it. He took work with Consol, the Consolidation Coal Company, over in Van Lear, as his daddy before him done.

Instead of flying Jake went to digging underground, pulling block coal from the bottom of the Paintsville Field.

It was dark, dirty, nasty. And Jake, he hated it with all he was, with all he wanted to be. Good thing it, too, was over almost before it begun.

Within a year Consol sold off to Farwest and Jake again went to odd-jobbing, to whatever he could get. Back to running shine.

Years passed. One, two. Three. Jake growing *sickerer, tireder* of it by the day. Then, he come home one night, said he'd had enough. He was twenty-one. He was signing himself into the Air Force.

They couldn't stop him if they tried. They didn't try.

So, he said goodbye to his brother, his sisters, to his Ma; his father drove him off on Forty out of town, headed for a recruiting office north in Cincinnati. They'd stopped up the road a stretch in Twentysix, not far from Ezel, which back at the turn of the century had been Ezell. *"Spelt with two Ls."* Then, Jake said, he and his Pa, they drove on north through the Daniel Boone, the national forest, and cut west across Paris.

"Paris?" Hamilton had asked at the telling.

"On Stoner Fork, Licking River," Jake said. "Not France."

His Pa had kin all the way over in Rabbit Hash, at the upper edge of Kentucky, south of Cincinnati, somewhere between Big Bone and McVille, hard by the Ohio River straight across from Rising Sun, Indiana. They went there, *clear to* Jake said, to see more relations and take a last few days fishing the Ohio. They'd caught some catfish.

"Caught us a mess." Drank some beer. "Drunk us a heap." Then they'd driven on to Cincinnati, where Jake, he up and joined.

"Come'n go," Jake said to his father as he prepared to head off on the train to Chicago bound for another to Lackland Air Force Base outside San Antonio, a thirty-two-hour trip, all-told. That is, he'd said his goodbye. He told Holt his Pa slapped him on the shoulder, shook his head — his *haid* — took a deep breath, turned and walked back to the car.

Nary otherwise a word.

Two years down the road, when he got a shot at Korea, Jake found himself assigned to a cargo plane with Holt — the two flying missions, side-by-side. Now, after a lifetime in the cockpit with Jake Johnson, Holt Hamilton knew what he knew to be all more than true.

Jake was a good pilot. A darned good one.

One he trusted with his life.

Sitting there in the Ready Room at Meadowbrook Field, a stone's throw from the flight line and the A-26 Invader they needed to check-ride, Holt pondered all Jake had told him so far about what happened with Colleen. Jake could sell bacon to a butchering hog farmer, could charm the dress off any girl he set his mind to charm the dress off of. Holt also knew Jake had never, in all the time they'd flown together, lied to him.

Exaggerated, yes. And, often. Lied, no.

"So what then?" he said, turning back to Johnson.

Jake said he met Colleen at a bar. They'd had some drinks, some laughs. Made small talk. He'd told her about Oil Springs, about his Pa running shine. He'd told her about flying, about how he was last of a dying breed of death-defying men flying dangerous piston-engined airplanes in a world fast into the jet age. About how being up there, in the blue, was the only thing had ever been able to keep his attention.

How she'd told him: "'Well, we'll see 'bout that.'"

Colleen didn't talk a lot about herself, mostly just listened.

"She tell me I could charm the fur off a cat. I tell her I reckon I'd sure like to try."

When the two got to his car he asked if she'd like to go for a ride. She said sure thing. They went driving, then parking. He went to kiss her.

"She says she *cain't*. I ask her why not for?"

She told him she didn't want to talk about it. Not right then, anyhow. She said she would walk home, that she needed time to think. But, she'd said, maybe they could still go out again sometime. She said she'd call.

She promised to tell him everything then.

Jake looked at Holt. Looked at him with hound dog eyes.

"I felt like a big ol' river cat, hook in mouth, hard on the trotline," he said. "Couldn't shake it, couldn't find a mud hole to lay up in.

"So finally I says to her, 'Okay. We might can.'"

"Dumbass."

"I reckon, Holt. Believe me, if I'd had a lick of sense then . . . "

"Instead you kept seeing her, didn't you?"

Jake looked almost embarrassed. "I did."

Colleen called. The two of them got together. She told him about Cottonwood Falls, about her life there. About her husband, her kids.

She said she felt trapped. That life just wasn't what she thought it would be back then. Her husband was a clerk. It was just so routine.

She told him she wanted excitement. At least, she said she thought she did. She said how it'd be nice to have someone to laugh with, someone she could talk to. Really talk to. About anything; about anything at all.

It had been a long time, she said. Forever, maybe even.

"I ask her what she *thunk* of him. Her husband."

"And?"

"She tell me, 'He's a good man.'

"So I says, 'That's a cheatin' line ever there were. A woman loves her man, she say, 'I love him. We snug as a bug.' ' Soon as I say it she done got her feathers all ruffled an' she give down the country on me."

"She started yelling?"

"Were hotter'n two Julys in the middle a August, she get so addled, riled. It were all *upscuddle*. She were like, 'How could y'all say that?'" He looked at Holt. "Then she gone to bawlin' somethin' fierce. I get so out of kilter, feelin' like country come to town. I mean, I'd like to have died were so embarrassed. I tell her *I's* sorry for makin' her cry, that I weren't tryin' to get all *briggity* britches on her. When finally she calm herself down she says she *knowed* I were right as rain. That's what get her such. That I were right 'bout all of it. She says she ain't got no idea what do."

"And?" Hamilton said.

"She were a sweet-talkin' thing, Holt. Had some ideas, sure did. Had me *hornier'n* a two-peckered billy goat on a hill full a ninnies."

"You slept with her?"

"Didn't say I did." He winked. "Didn't say I didn't, neither."

Jake said he and Colleen continued to meet for drinks, for drives. For lunch. He was working her, but she kept bobbing and weaving. He'd never had a girl he couldn't pin down, least not one he wanted to.

She was the first, he said; she was it.

"*A'fore* I *knowed* it, Monday a week done passed, then 'nother Monday a week, *purty* much all of it the same. An' I get to thinkin', her runnin' 'round on her man like she were, *strollopin'*. Me, in a no-win. It *throwed* me, Holt, it did. Y'all know, by the doin's. I were more'n a mite taken. But, I thunk 'bout that *ignert* man of hers and I tell myself I wouldn't want to be'n that doggone fool's shoes for his socks."

"I bet."

"I know, right? And none of it were gone change. It start off forty goin' north. *A'fore* long it were still better'n a poke in the eye with a stick, but not by much. I get to thinkin' how maybe it were just too much pie for a nickel. Like if y'all *cain't* race it or take it to bed, y'all don't need it." He gave Holt a look. "I tell myself *t'aint* no reason to re-lick the dog."

"So?" Hamilton said.

"So, I tell her it come time to fish or cut bait and *I's* tired of the tail waggin' the dog. That it weren't workin' and I gone doggone skedaddle."

"You ended it?" Holt said. "That doesn't seem so bad."

Jake shrugged. "I reckon it wouldn't a been. But it weren't. 'Cause then she says to me, 'Tell me, Jake. What *if 'n* I didn't have no kids?'"

"No kidding?"

"Sure as day, Holt. I were like, well I'll be tarred an' feathered."

"You might just be . . . I mean, if you're involved." He gave Jake a hard stare. "You said you're not involved, right?"

"What'd I tell y'all?"

"I know what you said. But, I'm still asking."

Jake glared at him, eyes ablaze.

"Y'all ask me again we gone have us a go, we is, *fray'r fraction.* I ain't storyin', Holt. I ain't. So don't think twice, 'cause it ain't so. Come by it honest, I did. And, truth'll stand when the world's on *far,* all I could think were every tub got its bottom. So I tell her, 'Y'all made your bed, now lie in it.' An' I walk out on her then'n right there."

Holt Hamilton took a deep breath. "How long ago was that?"

"'Bout a week . . . Couple of day, give or take."

"So. You think she did something? You know, to the kid?"

"I don't know. That's what *throwed* me. I just *knowed* what she says to me. Then, come Monday, well . . . her kid, he just up'n disappear.

"Like a *haint.*"

"A haint?"

"A ghost, Holt. That boy become a ghost."

13

Seated at the dining room table, Colleen had just finished telling Lenore Terranova: "If I'm lying, may God strike me dead." As she waited for a response it seemed he had willingly taken her at her word.

One second Lenore was mid-reach for a glass of water, pondering the next question. An instant later the front picture window imploded, shattered glass, lethal shrapnel, careening throughout the room, both of the women knocked from their chairs, pounded straight to the floor, their eardrums ringing, their bodies stinging in searing pain as they were assaulted with debris. There had been a thunderous roar like a runaway train and a shrill whine that was a thousand whirlwinds untamed. Before any of it could register the Earth jumped, almost literally leapt. Lights flickered, then went out, the room cast sudden into semi-darkness. The front door blew open; pictures, knocked straight from the walls. Plaster crumbled, its dust filling the air with unbreathable grit. The rear window blew out into the back yard, taking the blinds with it.

None of it made sense — not in the immediate, not in the thereafter — as a series of explosions deafened the room. The first sounds that followed, those first recognizable above that strange, unfamiliar, crackling sound, were the groans: unearthly, surreal, morbid.

Drifting slowly back into the present Lenore first believed she'd imagined it all. It was some time before she understood it was, in fact, very real. She fought to move. It hurt like hell. She tried to focus on the room, to no avail. She became aware her face was warm, almost wet. She moved best she could to touch it, all painstaking effort. She found herself covered in rivulets of blood. She searched for words, but couldn't form a clear thought. Seconds passed, minutes maybe.

She thought she heard a baby crying.

Then she heard it, that sound. Faint at first, then louder still.

It took what felt an interminable amount of time before she realized just what it was. The sound of sirens.

It was sometime after 1 o'clock when Farmer and Jones arrived on MacArthur Terrace to talk to Marjorie and Tag. What they saw surprised them. In the driveway was a gray late 1940s Dodge.

"Interesting," Jones said. That's what he said, interesting.

"I'd say," Farmer said, eyebrow raised.

Knocking on the front door, welcomed in by Marjorie Woods, the detectives found the living room a maze of boxes and crates.

Marjorie asked them to excuse the mess, said the movers were due in the morning. That there was so much left to be done.

"You don't realize how much you accumulate," Tag said.

"There's always something you overlook, too," Farmer said.

He smiled at Marjorie and Tag. So did Jones.

The detectives noticed a bassinet off in the corner, just inside the dining room. Marjorie said she'd taken Johanna for the night, what with Colleen in the hospital and all. She said Driscoll had called to say they'd be home soon. Farmer and Jones asked if they could take a look around.

Tag told them sure.

They searched the bedrooms, the closets, the basement, the attic, even the garage. They'd hoped to find some evidence Bobby had been there since his disappearance Monday. Instead, they found nothing at all.

Back inside they told Marjorie and Tag they needed to talk.

"We know Mrs. Goodson was having an affair," Farmer said, bluntly.

Tag gave his wife a look. "Go on," he said. "Tell them the truth."

Marjorie said Colleen mentioned a man she'd met, months before, up at the shopping center. A pilot. His name was Jake. She'd called him a friend. Said she'd needed someone to talk to, that Jake made her laugh.

Colleen said she'd forgotten how much she missed that. She'd said he was down-to-Earth, easy to be around. That he looked good in uniform.

"I asked her if she had, you know . . . "

"No," Farmer said. "I don't know."

Margie glanced at Tag. "I asked her, if she'd been with him."

"And?" Jones said.

"And she said, 'How could you ask me that?'"

"What do you think?" Farmer asked.

"By how she talked about him? Yeah, I think she did."

Marjorie said Colleen told her she and Driscoll were having "problems." No big deal, just the usual. Driscoll wasn't much of a talker. He could be, what was the word? Aloof. Colleen was frustrated about things. She wanted to have fun — or go home to Cottonwood Falls.

Majorie said she also knew Colleen drank. Often, too much.

It was then the doorbell rang and Tag answered to find Driscoll. He'd just brought Colleen home from the hospital, had come to get Johanna.

He seemed surprised to see Farmer and Jones.

Was there any news, he asked?

They explained they were still working leads; that, though it was difficult, he needed to be patient. He reminded them it had been two full days, now. That the two of them weren't going to find his son standing in his neighbor's living room. Farmer tried to say something. Daughter now in his arms, Driscoll said talk was just that. He didn't say it kindly.

He said he had to get home because his parents were coming in at LaGuardia Airport. He and his father had plans to search again.

"I expect you'll be doing the same," Driscoll told Farmer.

"Trust me," Farmer said. "We haven't given up on finding your son."

"It doesn't feel much that way to me," Driscoll said, glaring.

As he turned to leave, Marjorie ran to Driscoll, gave him a hug.

"How's Colleen?" she asked.

"Fine," Driscoll said. That was it, fine.

"Do you think he knows?" Marjorie asked once he'd gone.

"You'd think," Jones said.

Finally, Farmer asked Marjorie if she knew anything else about this Jake character. No, she said, Colleen had never mentioned a last name or even what kind of car he drove. She'd never told her much of anything, except how he talked "kind of funny." She'd found it amusing.

"What did she mean?" Farmer asked.

She said he had a terrible accent, like it almost wasn't English. At least, she said, not like any kind of English she'd ever heard.

Jones turned to Tag.

"You work on planes over at the base, right?"

"I did," Taggart said. "Not anymore."

"And you don't know this guy?" Farmer said.

Taggart gave him a look.

"There's hundreds of pilots at Meadowbrook," he said. "And hundreds more who rotate through on a damn-near daily basis."

"Who talk not quite English?"

"You can't know everybody. It's a big airfield."

"So you don't deal with pilots?"

"Not often. Least, I didn't."

"So you don't know this guy Jake?"

"What'd I say?" Tag said.

Farmer stared hard at Tag. Nothing. He turned to Marjorie.

"Mrs. Goodson say anything else?"

"She mentioned homemade alcohol. White lightning, I think she called it. And some place called Oil Can, I think."

"Oil Can?" Jones said.

"I think," Marjorie said, again. Then, thinking further, she said: "No, wait. That wasn't it. That wasn't that at all. It was . . . Oil Lake, Oil Pond, Oil Slick. Oil Springs . . . That was it. Oil Springs, Kentucky."

It began with a simple question, Lenore asking, "How are you?" An hour later it was a conversation that had uncovered hard-fought ground.

Driscoll had left for the airport just before Lenore arrived, unannounced, Colleen inviting her in.

Truth was Colleen, still overwhelmed by the events of the last couple days, was looking for an ear. Someone she could trust. Or thought she could. Lenore was willing to be that someone. The young mother told her about the day Bobby was born; about Geneva, about Seneca Lake. About Bobby Hinkson. She told stories about her son, growing up: first steps, favorite baby foods. His first smile, first word. "Ma," she'd said, proudly.

She said her son was a good-natured child, who liked attention; who hung onto his mother, but had his moments. His trials, her trials.

"Like any boy has," she said. "Like any new mother faces, I'd guess."

She recalled how Bobby had almost once blown up the house — one morning turning on the stove, the pilot unlit. She recalled how Driscoll had awakened to the smell of gas and somehow managed to open all the windows and doors, airing the place out, before it'd all gone South.

She said Bobby had a lisp but the doctor said it might just be the age and would likely go away. She said people found it cute but that it worried her. That she was working to teach him all the proper pronunciations because of it. She said Bobby was into everything, could be a handful.

She said it all became harder once Johanna was born. How sometimes, she said, she just felt overwhelmed.

"There's times when you felt trapped?" Lenore had asked.

"I didn't say 'trapped.'" Colleen said. "I said 'overwhelmed.'"

"I see."

"Do you?"

Colleen called Bobby "accident-prone," said Driscoll was always reminding her — "Telling you?" Lenore had asked; "Reminding me," Colleen had told her — to pay more attention, to keep a better eye on their son. She said Driscoll always wondered how tough a job it all really was since his own mother had made it all look so simple.

"She only had one," Colleen said.

"You told me love isn't easy, marriage is even harder," Lenore said.

"Did I say that?"

"Yes, you did."

It was pushing 4 p.m. Outside, the light was beginning to fade.

Colleen got up, offering a drink. "Just a glass of water," Lenore said.

In the kitchen Colleen poured water for Lenore, a glass of scotch for herself. Lenore thought it an attempt to delay the inevitable.

"What did you mean?" she said.

"By?"

"By what you said about love and marriage."

"He's a good man," Colleen said. "I always knew that, though maybe I didn't always understand what that meant, what it should mean."

Colleen said how growing up had been a struggle, how she'd always dreamed of something better back in Cottonwood Falls. She said how Driscoll seemed to have it all. Loving parents, money. How, even if he was quiet, she'd figured she could live with that. That he was good for her.

That his family was good for her.

"What I never understood until too late," she said, then, "was that there's always something."

"How so?"

"I was young. I'm still young, though these days I don't feel much like it, after all that's happened. Do you know what I'm trying to say?"

Wiping her eyes, she the held the glass close, breathing it in.

She gave Lenore a look. "No matter how perfect your life seems," she said, "you think there's always something that could make it more perfect. How if it could only be how you've imagined it, instead of how it is."

Colleen said she'd wondered what it'd be like to be Marjorie and Tag — without kids, without a care — or have a husband who brought home flowers once in a blue moon. If she might be better off with someone else.

If she was missing something important being who she was.

"Have you ever had an affair?" Lenore asked, point-blank.

"No," Colleen said. *"No."*

"Have you ever hurt your son?"

"How could you even ask?" Colleen said. "Of course not."

Lenore stared across the table at the young mother.

"Did you have anything to do with Bobby's disappearance?"

Colleen glared at her. This time, Lenore noted, there were no tears, no emotional outbursts. No theatrics. She just stared, anger building.

"No," she said.

She took one last sip of the scotch, set the glass down hard. It was 4:15 p.m. "If I'm lying," she said, "may God strike me dead as I speak."

Across the street Farmer and Jones had finished up their interview. They'd talk to Colleen and then, armed with more information, would return to talk some more with Mr. and Mrs. Woods. They knew they didn't have much time, that come morning Marjorie and Taggart were headed West. They had a bad feeling about that. And still there were all these allegations Majorie had made about Colleen — and even about how she may have hurt Bobby. That she'd done so more than once.

As Marjorie told it she'd found bruises on the boy one night while watching the kids. Marjorie said she'd been changing Bobby into his pajamas when she'd found them; that she'd asked Colleen about it, only to have her laugh it off, calling her son "accident-prone."

Weeks later Marjorie found more marks. On his legs, his chest, his backside — the last maybe from being beaten with a belt, she said.

Bobby was too young to tell her what happened, Marjorie told Farmer and Jones. Colleen gave her explanations, but she still wasn't sure.

The bruises, the drinking. Marjorie said she had her doubts and started to take the kids more often. Then came the moment, Majorie said. She'd taken the kids one afternoon when Colleen had an errand to run. Bobby wet his pants and Majorie said when she went to change his underwear she discovered a burn mark, right there on his backside.

"A burn mark?" Farmer asked.

"A burn mark. Under a bandage. His skin was bright red."

"What did you do?"

"I got salve, then bandaged it again," Marjorie said.

Majorie told the detectives that Colleen claimed her son had knocked over an iron. That she'd been ironing, had stepped away to answer the phone; that Bobby had come running into the room, hit the ironing board, had knocked the iron flying. That it'd burned him. Burned him bad.

"I take it you didn't believe her?" Farmer said.

"I didn't know what to believe," Margie said. "Bobby had all these bruises, all these marks. And then there was this burn. I wanted to believe her, I really did. But, I didn't know what to believe after a while."

She looked at the detectives, shaking her head.

"What was I supposed to do? She's my friend."

"Did you ask if she had taken him to a doctor?"

"She said, 'What, you think I've been beating him?' When she saw I wasn't laughing, she told me she'd gone to the pediatrician."

"There'll be a record. Do you know the doctor's name?"

"I've got it written down. It's in my pocketbook."

She searched her bag. "Here you are, Detective."

"Thanks," Farmer said, stuffing it into his pocket.

Saying they needed to get across the street to speak with Colleen, the detectives thanked Marjorie and Tag for their time. But, turning to leave, Farmer shot Taggart a look — saying there was just one more thing.

"What's that?" Taggart asked.

"That's your car in the driveway, right?"

"Yeah," Tag said. "So?"

"What is that? A Forty-Eight, Forty-Nine Dodge?"

"Forty-Nine. Why?"

"I don't know," Farmer said. "Just seemed to me it looked like the kind of car those *Negroes* might've been driving."

"What the hell's *that* supposed to mean?"

Farmer smiled.

"You said you saw a gray Nineteen-Forties Plymouth — a battleship-gray late-Forties Plymouth, you said — up at the IGA Monday."

"Yeah?"

"Then you said you couldn't help but think it was the kind of car the Negroes outside the store — *niggers*, you called them — might drive."

"What's your point?"

The detective glared at him.

"My point is we come here and you've got a Forty-Nine Dodge parked in the driveway. And it's gray. Battleship gray."

"Exactly," Taggart said. "A gray Dodge, not a Plymouth."

"Same car."

"Not exactly. Not if you said so a hundred times."

"Really?"

"Yeah. Really."

Farmer glanced at Jones. Jones said: "You ever been to Bayport?"

The detectives thought Tag even more surprised by the question than he'd been by the one about the car. So, they thought, was Marjorie.

"Where?" Tag said.

"Bayport."

"Where's Bayport?"

"Out East," Farmer said. "South Shore. Suffolk."

Tag shrugged. "Can't say I have."

"Can't? Or *won't?*"

"Can't. Why? What are you getting at?"

"See, a witness told us she saw a gray car with a man and a blonde-haired boy stop near her farm stand in Bayport Monday. Told us another car with a woman was there, that the man put the boy in that car . . . "

The detectives watched as Marjorie reached for Taggart's hand.

"What's any of this got to do with my husband?" she said.

"You tell me," Farmer said.

He didn't expect an answer. He didn't really get one, either.

"I don't know where you're going with this," Tag said, finally. "Where you think you are. But you're barking up the wrong tree, Detective."

"Why's that?" Jones said.

"Why's that? Because you are. Maybe you should be asking this pilot guy where *he* was Monday. Maybe you should ask Colleen."

"We plan to," Farmer said. "Where were you again Monday afternoon, Mr. Woods? You said you had to run an errand, if I recall."

"I said I was out getting boxes."

"And a crate," Jones said.

"Yeah. And a crate."

"Good," Farmer said. "You'll be able to tell us where, then."

"From a friend . . . A friend who works at a warehouse in Westbury."

Throughout the interview Farmer had been jotting down notes in his notebook. He turned to a clean page, handed it to Taggart.

"Go on," he said. "Give me a name, address and number."

He watched Tag scribble down some information.

"Look," Tag said, as he handed the notebook back to Farmer, "I don't want to get this guy in trouble. He could lose his job."

"The least of your worries," Farmer said.

He nodded to Taggart and Marjorie. Then the two detectives turned to leave. Headed for the door Farmer lifted the notebook over his head and, without turning back to face Tag, waved it in the air.

"You'd better hope this checks out," he'd said.

Then they were gone.

Standing on the front stoop, door closed behind them, Jones gave Farmer a knowing smile. "Think you made them nervous?" he said.

The elder detective breathed in deep, filling his lungs with the crisp autumn air. Daylight was fading, sunset not far off.

"Just a little," he said, with a laugh.

He turned to his partner. "Got them right where we want them."

"I was thinking the same thing."

"Now," Farmer said, pointing across the street to the Goodson house, "let's go see what *she* has to say about all this. Where *her* story goes."

Farmer stuffed the notebook into his jacket pocket, took a quick glance at his watch. Four-fifteen. It'd a been a long day. But, for the first time since the investigation began, he finally felt like he and Jones were getting somewhere. Somewhere good.

The two had just stepped off the porch, headed across the street, when they heard the thunderous roar.

Instinctively, both turned and looked skyward.

"Oh, shit!" Jones said. That's what he said: *Oh, shit.*

14

Propping herself up against the dining room wall Lenore Terranova gasped, trying hard to catch her breath. Breathing hurt, her body hurt. Gingerly, she touched a hand to her rib cage, winced as waves of searing pain shot from head to toe. She imagined she'd been stuck with a knife, blade twisted in, scraped against bone. It hit her she had broken ribs.

Still, she found herself awash in an odd wave of euphoria, the stark realization she was somehow very much alive.

In the dim light she could see the air thick with fine dust: the window blown out, front door knocked open, what looked like the blade of a sword embedded in it dead-center. Shards of glass littered the carpet and Lenore found herself staring at her arms, at the sleeves of her blouse, all covered in detritus and debris; hair, bestrewn with fragments. Blood trickled down the side of her face. She took a hand, tried to wipe it away.

On the other side of the table, stretched out on the floor, Colleen lay, unmoving. Lenore could hear her moan.

Somewhere in the back bedroom Johanna was crying.

Slowly, Lenore willed herself down the hall to find the little girl in her bassinet, somehow unharmed. Thinking it best to leave her as she was Lenore fought back to the dining room, in time to watch Colleen struggle upright, a gash on her forehead. Her dress was spattered with blood.

"Don't move!" Lenore shouted.

"The kids," Colleen mumbled. "How are the kids?"

"Johanna's fine," Lenore said. "Not a scratch."

Colleen stared past her, fixated on the tricycle.

"Bobby?" she said. "Where's Bobby?"

Lenore put her hand on Colleen's shoulder.

"Bobby's missing. He's been missing for days."

"We have to find him," Colleen said.

Outside there was shouting, the sound of engines, and for the first time Lenore noticed there was an eerie light bleeding into the room, dull white with a flicker of red that came and went as it danced in time.

Try as she might, she couldn't envision what it was.

Lenore saw Colleen's eyes had glazed over. Caked in white dust, she was rambling: "We have to find him. We have to find Bobby . . . "

"Look at me!" Lenore yelled, shaking Colleen to get her attention. "I have to get help. Sit there! Don't move until I get back!"

Slowly she made her way across the darkened room and at the front door stood staring at the blade embedded in the wood.

Three feet long, it was half as wide as her body, dull black, the shaft thinned at the edges like the hone of a knife. The front had driven straight through the door, splintering the wood. The other end hung broken, fire-scorched and jagged, as if snapped in half by a giant.

Lenore couldn't fathom what it was.

Stumbling out onto the stoop she stood aghast at the scene before her. The street was filled with police cars, fire trucks, ambulances. Firemen were in the midst of a frenetic, mad-hot scramble, racing here and there, dragging hoses, connecting hoses, shouting instructions, shouting replies. Torrents of water streamed from the lines onto a roaring blaze, as flames leapt a hundred feet into the twilight sky as fire beneath it danced. Again, Lenore heard the crackling and only now did she understand.

It was the sound of fire burning down the house, what was left of the house, across the street.

Snapping, popping, resin exploded in the timbers, a sound that strangely reminded her of popcorn over the burner of a stove. The house was all but gone, walls bowed outward, threatening to crash down on the neighbors. At its center nothing remained; nothing, except a twisted mass of burning wreckage the size of a flattened bus, jutting into the street. On it was a navy blue ball, a white five-pointed star dead-center.

Lenore thought it familiar, couldn't place it.

Everything seemed a blur. Some terrible, bad dream.

Lenore felt weak in the knees, thought she might faint, then crashed onto the steps, watching the scene unfold. As she did, it hit her.

She turned to the door, then back to the raging inferno.

"Oh God," she said.

The slab of smoldering metal stretching into the street like a bent and broken finger was the wing of an airplane. The burning, twisted mass ablaze on the lawn across the street, what remained of its fuselage. The blackened steel behind her, buried in the front door, the shattered shaft of a propeller blade. She was staring at the horror of a plane crash.

"Over here!"

Collapsed on the front steps Lenore saw the uniformed officer running toward her, full stride, out of the mayhem and confusion.

"Over here! I've got one, over here!" he yelled, frantically, as he waved to get the attention of the others.

Bending to speak, Officer Johns asked Lenore if she was okay as she strained to answer. As the medics came running, Johns yelled to them.

"She thinks she broke her ribs."

The medics set down to work on Lenore as Johns stepped back trying to assess the damage. Unlike the scene across the street the house had escaped the full brunt of the crash. There was no fire, save for a few small pieces of smoldering wreckage on the front lawn. Though a mangled engine nacelle the size of a refrigerator lay wrecked in the driveway, against all odds it had somehow stopped short, missed the house.

The house. Something about it seemed familiar. Johns looked back across to where firemen were battling the blaze, then looked at the number beside the door. He turned to Lenore.

"Inside," Lenore said. "Mrs. Goodson is inside." Before Johns could move, she added: "The baby's there, too. Back bedroom."

Inspector Caldwell had arrived on scene just as medics were loading

Colleen into the ambulance. Laid out on a stretcher, a blanket covered her to the neck. Near the back of the vehicle, Officer Johns stood silent. Inside, Spence sat, Johanna cradled in his arms. As the gurney was moved into position and locked down Spence gave him a weak smile.

"Good luck," he said, as Johns closed the door.

Banging on the side to leave, Johns turned to find the Inspector.

"What the hell happened?" Caldwell said.

"Plane crash," Johns answered, still stunned.

"I can see it's a . . . " Caldwell said, catching himself before he said fucking. Instead, he said: "Got it . . . Tell me what've we got."

Banks of floodlights, powered by portable generators that filled the air with a deafening clatter, illuminated the darkness with surreal white light that shone bright at the center then faded soft into shadows at the far, outermost edges. The ground was layered in an indelicate weave of tight-woven linen hoses stretched in each and every direction like earthworms brought to the surface by teeming rain. A hundred volunteers, maybe even more, raced about in their black rubberized firefighter slickers emblazoned with a myriad of alphabet letters: HPFD, WFD, LFD, MFD, BFD, SFD. That is, the Hempstead Plains Fire Department, Westbury, Levittown, Merrick, Bellmore, Salisbury. On and on, and on.

Red pumper trucks, ladder trucks, engines. All formed a haphazard maze choking down the street going back down the block, their flashing lights casting a sinister red hue on all within reach. Ghostly silhouettes danced, illusory, over the lawn and onto the facades of nearby houses, as shadows of firemen slid off the walls into the surrounding brush before fading into darkness, into the ethereal. Into pure nothingness.

Amid it all danced the fiery flame, burning yellow and burnt orange; white smoke, acrid black smoke, cinders, all roaring skyward until somewhere in the pall they met the invisible, then floated softly, minute particles of ash, back down to Earth. Like dirty snowflakes.

"Mike?"

Johns mumbled, almost inaudible. "It's just . . . "

"I understand," the Inspector said.

Fighting all emotion, Johns breathed in deep.

"Three survivors in the house across the street," he said, finally, pointing to the Goodson house. "One, a little baby girl."

He turned back, pointed to the house burning before them.

"No one's been able to get near enough to this one, Inspector, the one that got hit, to even know what we've got in there. It's all been going pretty good since I arrived, since we all . . . "

"So we don't know if anyone was inside?" Caldwell said.

"If there was, they're dead. I don't think anyone could have made it out alive, all the damage considered . . . It took the direct hit."

"Good God," Caldwell said.

"There's more."

"What's that?" Caldwell asked, turning to Johns.

"The woman they were taking when you walked up? That was the Goodson woman, the one whose son disappeared."

"No."

"She and her little girl."

"Damn," Caldwell said.

He stared hard at Johns. "You said you had three survivors so far. Who else? The husband? Was he the third?"

"A woman," Johns said. "There was two women and the little girl."

"The neighbor woman? The one who found the carriage?"

"Lenore something or other."

"Lenore Terranova?"

"I didn't ask," Johns said.

"Dark hair, cut in a bob?"

"Yeah. That's about right . . . You know her?"

"She's a reporter," Caldwell said. "From *Newsday.*"

"Her?"

"Yeah," Caldwell said, terse now. "How is she?"

"Looked worse than it was," Johns said. "Possible broken ribs, cuts from all the flying glass. The medics said they needed to check for internal bleeding, punctured lung. But, her vitals were good."

The Inspector pulled out his *Luckys*. Took one, lit it.

"Okay," he said. "At least we've got some good news." He pointed to the burning house. "We know who lives here?"

Johns said no. Amid the confusion he hadn't bothered to ask.

Making his way over to a small group of onlookers, he talked to them a few moments, then returned shaken.

"What?" Caldwell said.

"The Woods," Johns said.

"What do you mean the woods? What woods?"

"The Woods," Johns said. "The friend who found the carriage Monday. Her and her husband. That's what the neighbors said."

The cigarette fell from the Inspector's hand as he started toward the burning house. To the left was the smoldering hulk of a car, parked against the curb. He hadn't paid it any attention before. Now, he circled it, slow as could be. At the front of it he bent down, wiped soot from the license plate, so he could read. He sat there, frozen. Just frozen.

"Inspector?" Johns said.

"It's one of ours," Caldwell said, blankly.

"Ours?"

"One of ours," the Inspector said. "Farmer and Jones."

As Caldwell stumbled to the curb Johns turned and sprinted for his marked patrol unit a hundred feet down the block.

Reaching it he flung open the door, grabbed the mike.

"Fifty-One to Radio Dispatch. Ten-Ninety-One, MacArthur Terrace between Mitchell and Glenn Curtiss. Possible Ten-Seventy-Eight . . . "

"Repeat," the dispatcher said. "Did you say Ten-Seventy-Eight?"

"Ten-four," Johns said, breathing hard. "Ten-Seven-Eight at the plane crash on MacArthur. Notify Headquarters . . . Possible officers down."

"Did you say *officers?*" the dispatcher asked, confused.

"Ten-Four," Johns said, again.

For the longest time Johns stood silent, staring towards the crash. It felt like a lifetime, though maybe it was thirty seconds, not even. Soon the radio had sprung to life again, the dispatcher calling.

"Car Fifty-One," she said. "Car Fifty-One."

This time Johns could hear the emotion in her voice. In a small department, people knew each other. Especially, the dispatchers.

"Who is it, Mike?" she asked.

Fighting all emotion, he answered: "Farmer and Jones."

On the other end he could hear as she began to cry. Before he headed back toward the scene Johns took a hand, crossed himself.

"Please, God," he said. "Just let them be alive."

15

Inspector Caldwell looked in the mirror, adjusted his tie.

He had done so a half-dozen times now and still, he thought, it wasn't right. It was beginning to get on his nerves. Truth be told, everything was beginning to get on his nerves. He was running late. Yet, he couldn't bring himself to leave his office. Not even after a half-pack of *Lucky Strikes*, two cups of black coffee and a lifetime of stalling.

He hated funerals. He always had, even as a kid. Being a cop only made him hate them more. The suits, the ties; the tears. It was all too much emotion and it got him to thinking. Being a cop you didn't want to think too much. Certainly, not about death. About dying.

About what happened to everyone left behind.

It was all too much stuff. That's what it was, stuff.

He never knew what to say at funerals. He always felt like he said the wrong thing. That anything, everything, said at a funeral was the wrong thing. That bothered him. It got on his nerves when things bothered him.

It had been two days since the crash over in Hempstead Plains; two of the longest days of his life. He looked in the mirror one last time, adjusted his tie one last time. Opening the door he stepped into the hall.

He found himself face-to-face with Farmer and Jones and, frozen, didn't know what to do. He looked up and down the hall, strangely self-conscious. He was relieved to find it otherwise empty, not a soul in sight.

"Damn," he said. That was it: *Damn.*

He turned from the detectives not wanting to cry in front of them. As if any of that really mattered now.

"You shouldn't have to see me like this," he mumbled.

Turning back he tracked down the line of black-and-white photographs that ran the length of the hall, each handsomely framed.

Each a story; each, with a face staring out into nothingness.

Across the years, across a lifetime. Across eternity.

Patrolman John A. Hahn, Shield 28.

Thursday, September 24, 1925. Five months and one week on the job; five months and one week serving a department then not a day older than the time he'd been on the job. Motorcycle crash.

Lieutenant John P. Dowd, second in the line, almost four years on the force. Tuesday, April 30, 1929. Car accident. Patrolmen Fred S. Hirsch, shot by the driver of a stolen car. A car he didn't know was stolen until too late. May 6, 1931. A Wednesday. That was it, dead on an otherwise fine Wednesday. Caldwell thought it all a rude surprise.

Patrolman Alvin J. Borgwardt, Shield 646, wore his high-collared uniform smartly; with a knowing smirk that told you it was out of love, as well as a hint of boyish vanity. It made his partner, Patrolman Milton Verity, seem all serious by comparison, though Verity was twenty-six and Borgwardt had him by two years. None of which mattered, since both of them had been dead almost as long as they had been of the living. Killed together in an automobile accident, in their marked patrol car.

Hempstead Turnpike, Elmont. February 25, 1932.

John D. Kennedy took four years and thirteen operations to die after being shot by two suspects on patrol. One got death, fried in the electric chair at Sing Sing; the other got life. Kennedy's family got his badge and a half-assed pension check. Bad deal all around, Caldwell thought.

They were all bad deals: Naar, hit by a limousine. Yulch, killed in a freak fall against a curb on parade duty, of all things. Duncan, dead of a fractured skull when his police motorcycle was struck from behind by a drunk driver back in '35. David Murphy shot himself cleaning his service revolver in the back room at the Fourth Precinct in the Summer of '42.

John West, a tough son of a bitch if ever there was, was killed with his own weapon while transporting a suspect to the station in '46. Patrolman Arthur J. Klepper looked to be just a kid; Alexander N. Benedict, shot to death investigating a burglary, almost fatherly. That is, he looked like a priest. Patrolman Charles H. Shaw looked like a cop if ever a cop had looked like a cop. And yet, there they were; each of them, all of them.

Dead, dead and deader still.

Sixteen in all. At least that's what there had been; sixteen. From the darkest year in the thirty-year history of the department — 1932, when three of them died — to 1954, when Sellers and Sternberg got it in accidents less than three months between them.

Which had knocked them all for a loop, those who wore the uniform, those who walked these halls. And now the two fresh black-and-white photographs stared out at Caldwell from a spot empty and unclaimed when he'd arrived that very morning. The Inspector couldn't take his eyes off them, the two newest fallen. Off Farmer, off Jones. Off the faces of his two best detectives, two best men. His two best friends.

Killed. Wednesday, November 2, 1955.

Dead in a plane crash.

Police funerals are like no other funerals, save maybe firefighter funerals. The funerals of statesmen, of dignitaries; royal funerals, funerals of Presidents and Popes; funerals of movie stars and the Mafia.

When it came to pomp, all had cops beat.

But few things can match a police funeral for circumstance.

Caldwell was thinking about that as he stood outside St. Agnes, the Roman Catholic Church in the Village of Rockville Centre, waiting for the limousines and hearses to arrive. Thinking somehow police funerals were altogether different. It wasn't just the sea of blue that spilled out into the street, from the sidewalks and the lawns, for blocks around the church. It wasn't the crispness of the uniforms, the fine white gloves that covered every uniformed hand, the high-collared necks clasped with a single gleaming brass button, the stick-pin medallions — one, on either side of the collar seam. It wasn't the hats, wasn't the shields. It wasn't all the departmental ribbons or all the medals. It wasn't even that police funerals drew a cast of thousands, from public officials and fellow officers from across the metropolitan area, to the curious and the concerned. That they drew anyone who thought it simply their civic duty to honor fallen men.

It was, the Inspector thought, the overriding sense of violation.

Everyone knew cops died. Cops knew it, their families certainly did. They knew it came with the territory, was a risk they all faced. And still it wasn't hard to think it all somehow unfair. That no matter the job at hand cops should somehow be immune, should somehow be protected from the dangers of the world that surrounded them. From the fates, from harm.

That God did not afford them all some sort of extra protection, did not impose his will in the form of some shielding divine intervention, filled Caldwell with anger. Quite frankly, it pissed him off.

Four dead officers in little over a year; two good friends killed on an otherwise tranquil afternoon by an out-of-control airplane, of all things. Eighteen gone in the thirty years the Nassau County Police Department had been in existence. It all seemed like a lot, seemed like too much.

The Inspector looked out over the crowd, over the bluest sea, taking note of them all standing there, sullen and stoic. A light breeze was in the air, air gentler and warmer than it had been for days. The sun shone bright, an otherwise beautiful day. Try as it might it couldn't lift the sadness. Caldwell thought nothing could on a day like this.

He studied the faces. He knew more of them than he could've even imagined. He thought most of them so young and he remembered being that young once, standing there as they were now. He wondered which of them would be next. He knew someone among them had to be and he wondered if any of them were pondering the question and wondering the same exact thing. He knew each of them, maybe all of them, were trying hard not to think about it. He knew he was trying hard not to.

Then the first notes filled the air with that mournful tune and Caldwell turned to look at the spot where McGowan and the boys from the Emerald Society stood, in their kilts, cradling bagpipes, playing sweet and sorrowful as anyone ever played. He thought it terrible he knew what it was, the song, almost from before a single note had even sounded, and as he listened he turned from them to look down the block so he could follow the procession as it made its way to the church. As the hearses pulled to a stop the Inspector recounted the words to the bagpiper's tune. It was *The Minstrel Boy,* that 19th-Century standard by Thomas Moore:

> *The minstrel boy to the war is gone,*
> *In the ranks of death ye will find him;*
> *His father's sword he hath girded on,*
> *And his wild harp slung behind him;*
> *"Land of Song!" cried the warrior bard,*
> *"Tho' all the world betrays thee,*
> *One sword, at least, thy rights shall guard,*
> *One faithful harp shall praise thee!"*

The officers were all at attention, all in professional, determined salutes, as they had been since the pipes first sounded, since the procession first appeared. The Inspector knew each of them, all of them, were no doubt fighting their own inner turmoils as the drivers opened those limousine doors, as the families stepped out into the sullen street. Stepped into the vast, seemingly endless, saluting sea of blue. There was Farmer's widow, dressed in a formal black gown, veil covering her face, her tears, and then his daughter and son-in-law and their two children. Farmer's grandchildren. Caldwell thought how they'd all grown since he'd last seen them. How fast his friends had turned into a generation past.

At the door of the second car was Jones' wife and their three kids, all teens, the boys strapping and gangly, not at all like their dad. Caldwell thought hard to remember the bulky detective had once been so thin. The girl, his daughter, stood beautiful. Plain, simple, but with an elegance otherwise hard to describe. It crossed Caldwell's mind that someday someone was going to have to walk that girl down the aisle, now that her father was gone, and for a moment he wondered if the task might even fall to him. He watched as one of the boys pulled a handkerchief from his pocket, handed it to his mom. His two were just a few years older and he wondered if either would be so considerate, given the circumstances.

He fought hard to dismiss the thought.

The families were coming up the stairs now, the sea of mourners parting to let them through. They stood silent, eyes sneaking to follow the bereaved; desperate to see them, desperate to remain unseen.

The Inspector waited nervously on the crowded landing nearest the wooden doors leading to the inner sanctuary. He watched Nellie, Farmer's wife, childhood sweetheart, fight each step, knowing she must. When she got to him the Inspector moved to embrace her in a comforting hug.

As she held onto him, he could hear her crying. Could feel her body tremble. He wanted to tell her so many things, just then.

That he'd loved her husband, that he already missed him.

"Nell . . ." was far as he got.

Voice choked with emotion he began to cry. As he stood holding onto her, hanging onto her, he felt so embarrassed. So foolish.

He felt her squeeze him tighter, the widow now comforting the friend, and he didn't know what to do. When she stepped back to look at him his face was contorted as he fought his tears, a losing battle. He tried to speak, but couldn't. Instead he just looked into her eyes hoping she knew at that awful moment what he meant. What it was he wanted to say.

"You know he thought the world of you, Cuth," she said.

He stood, tears streaming down his face.

The rest of it was all a blur. A hug for the daughter; handshakes with the son-in-law, the grandkids, the hug with Jones' widow, their kids.

Every second of it muddling haze.

Long after most of them had gone Caldwell stood graveside smoking a cigarette in the warm afternoon sun, remembering what he could.

Everyone who mattered was headed over to McGee's to drink away whatever it was they could drink away — the hurt, the anger, the pain; the loss — and he knew it fell to him to get them all started down that road with a farewell toast. The service had been beautiful, if you could ever call anything about a funeral beautiful. The priest had spoken of the importance of their work; the work of the two fallen detectives, the sacrifices made in pursuit of it all. Not just the ultimate sacrifice, the one that led to the flag-draped coffins, but the sacrifice of family, of loved ones, of friends; of personal well-being, in the name of justice.

Sitting there listening to that Mass best he could had forced Caldwell to consider all he'd gone through his years on the force. All anyone who wore the uniform went through to do their work.

That is, it got the Inspector to thinking. About his shortcomings as a husband, a father, a friend; as a cop, as a man.

He wasn't the easiest guy to get along with, never had been. He knew he'd demanded a lot from Farmer, from Jones, knew sometimes he'd demanded too much. Knew that despite it all he would demand as much from the men who replaced them, maybe more. He knew he'd do so because he had expectations. Because, he expected a lot. He thought about why it was he wasn't very understanding when he didn't get what he wanted, thought he wasn't very understanding because what he wanted was hard to understand. He knew he wanted justice. He knew he didn't always get it. At least not as often as he thought he should.

Maybe if he'd done something different for a living it wouldn't have been so cut-and-dried. Maybe not. He tried to think of some other line of work he could have chosen where he might've been different.

Try as he might he couldn't imagine a situation when he wouldn't have cared as much about doing his job. About getting it right. Being a cop only made it worse. Being a cop meant there was no margin for error. Meant he had to get it right or the people he was sworn to protect weren't protected. If some out there in the world didn't understand how he could have such an unforgiving sense of right and wrong, what did he care.

He didn't believe cops should bend the rules, break the law, unless it was needed. He believed everyone involved in a case, other than his officers, than the victims, should be considered a suspect and be treated as such until somehow proven otherwise. Sure, he was coarse. He cursed a blue streak. Cursed far too much, far too often. Far too willingly.

He called people names, vile names, sometimes to their face.

He knew what it felt like to be called names but believed you had to earn respect. That it wasn't handed to you. His people had to prove it straight off the boat. Others should have to prove it, too. He believed once they did the name-calling stopped. It was why he hated politics, hated politicians, hated being political. Why he hated diplomacy, hated diplomats, hated having to be diplomatic. It all just rubbed him wrong.

If few understood, well so what. He knew he did.

There was a difference between suspects and criminals and honest God-fearing folks. You couldn't catch a criminal treating him like he was something better-than. A criminal could sense weaknesses a good man never could. If you weren't willing to get down there in the gutter, to see life through those eyes, with that mind, you were destined to fail before you'd even begun to fight. This was the outright problem with civilization, the problem with being civilized, he thought. Civilization demanded civility. He didn't see it that way. Not now, probably not ever.

Not all men deserved comity. Some were good, some weren't. Most fell somewhere in between. A bad man didn't deserve the same respect as a good one, no more than a good cop could be a saint and catch a sinner. It didn't work that way, not in the real world. In the real world you had to know what sin felt like. How to recognize it, how to thumb-down on it.

If you didn't, a sinner would get the best of you. Every time.

"Every fucking time," Caldwell said, as he dropped his cigarette butt on the ground, staring out at the fresh-shoveled dirt.

"You two knew that better than anyone."

He'd watched them lower the caskets as those bagpipers played *Amazing Grace;* had watched the honor guard hand the widows folded American flags and the badges of their dead husbands.

Gugliotta, the District Attorney, was there. So was the Governor, the County Executive, members of the county legislature. General Johnson, commanding officer at Meadowbrook, came in full dress uniform, along with his staff. He had two more funerals come Sunday, the funerals of his two dead pilots, and watching him Caldwell considered that between this, the second war and the hell he'd no doubt seen there, Johnson had suffered through a hundred lifetimes worth of funerals. More, certainly, than he could even begin to imagine. The dead men, lifelong friends, had been buried side-by-side in adjoining family plots at the insistence of their wives, of all people. The Inspector lit another cigarette.

"Odd who wasn't here," he said, out loud.

No, the Goodsons hadn't come. Not to the wake, not to the church, not to the grave. Not to any of it. Caldwell hadn't expected the mother. She'd been hurt in the crash, was still recovering from a torturous week. But the absence of the father certainly made him wonder. After all Farmer and Jones had done; after all they'd given trying to do so.

It had to make you ask yourself the question.

He took a long draw, scanned the rows of headstones that stretched to the horizons, far as the eye could see. He felt a chill run down his spine; shuddered. He knew Farmer and Jones were really gone, now. That he needed someone to pick up where they'd left off. Someone who could hit the ground running. He hadn't wanted to think about it. But he was a cop and there was cop's work to be done. He knew what that meant.

Bobby Goodson still hadn't been found.

Someone needed to find him — and do so soon.

He leaned down between the graves, as if he needed to get a stamp of approval from two dead men, knowing it had been their case.

Knowing now it always and forever would be.

He'd named Johns and Spence to replace Farmer and Jones, giving the two what amounted to a field promotion. There were detectives with more real experience. Caldwell still needed them on the Woodward case. Besides, Johns and Spence had dealt with the Goodsons from Day One. Cursory as their knowledge as investigators was they knew the lay of the land. He'd have to hold their hands, guide them. But they at least had a notion. An idea of what they needed to do. Caldwell reached into his jacket, pulled out a flask of Irish whiskey. He'd been due down at McGee's a while ago now. He couldn't make that toast before he made this one here. He poured one last taste for Newbury Farmer, one for Jones.

"I know you would have solved this," he said. "You would've because you took it personal, took them all personal."

He took a taste for himself, felt the burn as it slid home, punched his stomach. "These fucking guys, they'd better do half the job you two did. They'd better remember to always be looking over their shoulders at everything. To watch what they see." He felt about to cry.

Before he did, he turned and walked away.

16

The Inspector was in the middle of pouring himself another cup of black coffee when there was a knock at the door and Johns and Spence came walking in. They had news; he was eager for some.

It'd been a bad morning. Caldwell offered them some Joe — and, both said sure. Dumfounded, they watched as the Inspector instead strolled to his desk, sat down, fumbled around for his *Luckys*. Took one, lit it.

"I'm not your fucking wife," he said, finally glancing up.

The first order of business for Caldwell had been to call on over to Meadowbrook, to get General Johnson on the horn. Something about the crash was under his skin. He had questions, needed answers.

It was the pilots. That, far-fetched as it seemed, one might be the one Joe Monti and his mother saw with Colleen Goodson. He needed to know who was flying the bomber when it went down. Needed to know if the Air Force investigators, if the General, truly believed the accident had been an accident. That it might be something otherwise was almost too much to consider. But, try as he might, Caldwell couldn't shake the thought.

The General wasn't surprised by allegations of an affair. Shit happened. But Caldwell thought him unsettled by the possible scenario he'd described. To that end Johnson said both were good pilots, serious pilots with spotless service records. He'd checked.

He knew Holt Hamilton. Not well, but knew he was married, knew word around base was he was a straight-arrow. But the General admitted he'd heard stories about Jake Johnson, who was no relation. That he was single, played the field. That he was a handful, maybe even a headache.

And still. Still, Johnson found it difficult to fathom the crash a result of anything sinister. Though, the General said, there was one thing.

One strangely odd thing.

Indications were Hamilton was flying when it went down.

But evidence suggested Johnson had been on the flight deck, as well. That was unusual. That was what Johnson said, unusual.

It wasn't protocol for Johnson to be there, not in an attack-bomber flown by a single pilot. More than that Johnson couldn't say. But he swore he'd let Caldwell know as soon as he heard anything at all.

The Inspector felt his heart sink. Off the phone, the conversation echoed in his brain. The cause of the crash had been unusual. Hamilton was a straight-arrow, but Jake Johnson was a headache.

What the hell did all that mean?

Thinking about it Caldwell decided he'd never felt so damned lost. He sifted through the latest reports on the Woodward shooting, if just to take his mind off things. It was futile stuff. He couldn't come to grips with the thoughts he'd conjured up. And he was still trying to recover from a hard night of drinking down at McGee's, an all-too-painful reminder he was no longer as young as he once was. His stomach was in knots. He had the heebie-jeebies. He leaned over the trash can, tossed right there in the middle of his office. It was all a God-damned mess.

He'd gone down the hall to wash up, taken a look in the mirror, decided he looked like shit. That the job was killing him, just fucking killing him. That he needed to get a grip, focus on what was real, not invention. He'd also made himself a promise to not spend the entire morning looking over the shoulders of his two new detectives their very first day on the job. That he needed to trust them, trust their instincts. He wasn't sure he didn't, but was pretty sure he didn't know he ever would.

For now Caldwell still planned to be looking over their shoulders as much as he could stand to. Which was why he'd called Johnson in the first place. Down at McGee's Johns said he and Spence had already made arrangements to bring the Goodsons in first thing Saturday.

Why not start shaking the trees, Johns said.

"We'll make it clear we're working hard to find their son. That doesn't mean they're above reproach, that we're sold on their innocence."

"And why is that?" Caldwell asked.

Johns grabbed his beer, pondered the question.

"No boy, no body. No ransom note." Setting his glass down, he called for another. "We haven't found the kid, haven't found anyone who has."

Considering the explanation the Inspector turned to Spence.

"And what do you think?"

"We've heard the story once. We'd like to hear it again."

Snuffing out a cigarette the Inspector sized it all up. "I see."

As much as he wanted to find fault he hated to admit he thought it a good idea. To backtrack, see what in their stories held up. What didn't.

"Okay," he'd said, matter-of-fact. "Do it."

Now after a morning spent agonizing over what was going on Johns and Spence were in his office. He needed good news.

"How'd it go?"

"Curious," Johns said.

"Curious?"

"Very curious."

The Inspector swatted ashes from his desk, in no mood for games.

"How's that, Mike?"

The two glanced at each other uncertain who should answer. Caldwell pointed at Spence. "Not you." He pointed to Johns. *"Mike."*

The new detective cleared his throat. "We gave them lie detector tests, Inspector. The husband and wife."

"And?"

"Inconclusive."

"Inconclusive?"

"Inconclusive," Johns said, again. "The administrator said he couldn't tell if they were answering truthfully. Or lying. Said it was hard to tell."

"Both of them?"

"Both. He couldn't tell if they were involved, if they weren't. If they knew more than each had told us. If they'd told us all they knew."

"Damn."

"Yeah. That's what we thought."

Johns took a sip of his coffee. "You've got kids, right Inspector?"

"Yeah."

Johns flashed the back of his left hand. "Not even married."

"So?"

"So, I called my mom this morning," he said. Allowing that to sink in, he said: "Let me ask you this, Inspector. You're a parent, your kid's sick. Your wife feeds him dinner, puts him to bed early. What d'you do?"

Eyes locked on his new detective Caldwell said: "You go in and . . . "

"Right. You go in and check on him before you go to bed, make sure he's okay. I mean, that's what any good parent would do, right?"

"Sure," Caldwell said.

"And then before you go to work the next morning you probably poke your head in his room again to see if he's sleeping or if his color's good and maybe you say, 'Hey kiddo, how're you doing?' Maybe you feel his forehead to see if he's running a temperature, like my mom used to . . . "

"Right."

"Yeah, that's what my mom thought, too."

He walked over to the coffee burner, dropped another of sugar cube into his cup, spooned it around.

Turning back, he said: "Not Driscoll Goodson, Inspector."

Caldwell eyed Johns, curiously.

"And that's not all," Johns said.

Spence handed the Inspector a file. Caldwell dropped it on his desk.

"Curious, huh?"

"Very curious," Johns said.

"What about this pilot I told you guys about?" Caldwell said.

There was an uncomfortable silence as Spence turned to Johns. Johns stood there, squeezed his notebook tight.

"Tell me it wasn't one of the dead guys," Caldwell said.

"Sorry," Johns said.

Caldwell took a deep breath. "Which one?"

"Jake Johnson," Johns said.

"Shit."

The Inspector reached for another cigarette, lit it, just as fast smashed it into the ashtray. His chest was tight. So tight, just then, the Inspector even pondered the thought he might be having a heart attack.

"She denied an affair," Spence said, finally. "Said the two of them were just friends. That's how she described it. That they were 'friends.'"

"Bullshit!" Caldwell said.

Johns nodded, nervously. "That's what we thought, too. The husband said he knew nothing about it. Said he'd heard rumors. Said he didn't believe them. That guys had always talked about his wife, going back to high school. Said he didn't think she could do it. He just didn't."

"But?"

"But he told us he'd begun to wonder since the boy disappeared. Nothing concrete. Just that he'd begun to wonder, thinking back."

"Here's what I want you to do, Mike," Caldwell said.

The detectives looked at one another as if to say, Me? Caldwell wondered whose bright idea it'd been to team two guys with the same name together as partners. Wondered why he'd done it, too.

"Yeah, you . . . *Mike!*" he said, pointing to Johns.

He ordered the two back over to Meadowbrook, told them to poke around. To dig up whatever they could on Jake Johnson, on the relationship, on the crash. To figure out what role any of it had.

To figure out, he said, what it fucking meant.

"One more thing," Caldwell said. "We need to settle this whole Mike thing, right now. I'm not dealing with two God-damned Mikes. Got it?"

"You could call me Michael," Spence said. "My mother does."

"I could call you a lot of things, shit-for-brains," Caldwell said. "Fucking Michael's not going to be one of them."

He pointed to Johns. "You're *Mike.*"

He pointed at Spence. "You're *Ike.*"

"Like the President?" Spence said. He turned to Johns.

Johns shrugged. "I guess you're Ike, Mike," Johns said. "Like President Eisenhower."

"Not Ike like Eisenhower, asshole," the Inspector said.

"What then?" Spence said.

"Like those God-damned jellybean candies you get at the fucking movies. You two, you're *Mike and Ike.* Now get the hell out of my office!"

Johns went to say something, thought better of it — opened the door to find a young woman standing outside in the hall, about to knock.

Lenore Terranova eyed Johns. "You clean up well," she said.

Johns smiled. "You too, Ma'am."

A bandage covered the side of her head and she had dozens of marks that dotted her skin, wounds from the flying glass.

"Lenore," she said, wincing ever so slight.

"The broken rib?" Johns asked.

"I never knew something could hurt so much. My mother's been telling me it can't be worse than childbirth. I can't even imagine . . . "

Before she could finish Caldwell was at the door. He started to say something but she beat him to the punch.

"Can I get a few minutes, Inspector?"

"Barely back and already a pain in my ass," Caldwell said.

Sensing she'd walked into something she shot a glance at Johns and Spence, said: "I'll go grab lunch at the delicatessen, be back in an hour?"

Caldwell turned to his new detectives.

"Don't even think about it," he said. Then, he turned back to Lenore and said: "Like I said, a real pain in the . . . "

"Can't blame a girl for trying, can you?" she said, cutting him off.

"I don't want to say anything I'm going to regret," Caldwell said. He waved a finger at her, then said: "All of you. Out of my office . . . Now!"

As the three of them turned to leave the Inspector said: "And don't think I didn't see you out there yesterday, Lenore. It's appreciated you thought enough of everything to be there but not to get in the way."

He forced a half-hearted smile.

"I'll swear I never said that. So will *Mike and Ike,* here. Now, see you in a bit . . . And close the damn door on your way out."

The first statement was from Driscoll Goodson and at first it seemed the usual stuff. Twenty-four years old. Born March 31, 1931, in Bazaar, Kansas. [Caldwell noted the officer who took the statement typed "Bizarre," crossed it out, wrote the proper name in by hand.] It stated Driscoll was a member of the United States Air Force, held the rank of Airman Second Class, did clerical work at Meadowbrook Field.

Routine, routine. *Routine.*

If it was, and it was, what came next was far from it. Because Driscoll stated he had been off Sunday, October 30, his usual day off. That Taggart Woods, the neighbor, now dead, had come over to help him work on his car, mostly because Woods was a mechanic and because the car wouldn't start, Driscoll said. The car was a '39 Ford coupe. A *green* '39 Ford coupe. And Driscoll stated that once the car was running he took it out for a ride. He came home, found his wife feeding their son supper — the boy, Goodson called him; odd, he called him *the boy* — and said he turned on a new TV show called *Wide Wide World.* He watched, the boy ate.

His wife put the boy to bed, noting he'd been sick for days.

Driscoll never said he'd asked her how their son Bobby was doing. He never said he'd bothered to kiss him goodnight. He never said anything about any of it, just said he'd sat there and watched television; that he ate dinner with his wife, then wrote a letter home to his parents.

"I remember I mentioned in this letter something with regards to an argument my wife Colleen and I had, that we had been having some problems," Driscoll stated. "That some of it had to do with issues over the care of the children, especially the boy. I wish to state we have had many arguments of late over the punishment of this child.

"If he was being dealt with as he should."

All of which, Caldwell thought, sounded, well . . . curious.

Curious too was that after dinner Driscoll said he went back to watching TV while his wife went to check on the children, then went to bed. He said he sat up until about 10 p.m., went to bed, got up at 7 a.m., showered, shaved, ate breakfast then left for base at 7:30 a.m. Prompt.

"Thinking back on it," he stated, with strange explanation, "maybe I woke a bit before seven. The baby had aroused me. But I wish to state for the record that after four-thirty on Sunday afternoon, when my wife was feeding him dinner, I never saw the boy again."

The statement was signed Driscoll Chester Goodson, November 5, 1955. The Inspector read it over and over again.

The baby girl had "aroused" her father. Not awakened him, not roused him from bed. But "aroused" him. And what about the green Ford coupe; that Taggart Woods, of all people, helped him fix it? What to make of the fact that this Air Force man never inquired about the health of his son? Never checked on him, never kissed him as the kid went off to bed? That he never asked how he was? But he sat down, wrote a letter to his folks, mentioned arguments with his wife. Questioned how the children were being disciplined. Or, maybe, complained he'd been questioned over how he'd disciplined them. How he'd disciplined the boy.

That Driscoll made certain to state for the record he had not even seen his son in the almost twenty-four hours before he disappeared.

"What the . . . " the Inspector said, reaching for a cigarette.

For the longest time Caldwell sat at his desk reading and re-reading the statement, wondering how the pieces fit together.

Maybe Driscoll Goodson had a role in what happened to his son. Maybe there was more to the story than anyone first envisioned.

Maybe there was a darkness here none of them had considered, that sinister forces were at work inside the home, not outside of it.

Was Driscoll a cruel father, a violent abusive husband? Did he have reason to loathe his son, have some unnatural prurient interest in his infant daughter? And what of the admission of his own cool disinterest, the arguments over punishments, the letter home. The truth?

Or some amateurish stab at an alibi?

A witness had seen a gray car and a green car out near that farm stand in Bayport. Farmer and Jones said as much before they'd headed out for the last time. That raised intriguing questions. Turned out Taggart Woods had a gray car, Driscoll Goodson a green one. It might mean something — or nothing at all. Problem was it was all problematic.

The witness saw a man, a woman and a boy. Colleen Goodson didn't drive. Marjorie Woods drove, but couldn't have been there. She found the carriage. Driscoll Goodson was on base when everything happened, never left before being called home. Records and witnesses confirmed it. The whereabouts of Taggart Woods were unknown. But he and his wife were dead and, for the moment, that meant it was all a dead end — especially, since no one knew if the boy in Bayport was even Bobby Goodson.

He needed Johns and Spence to talk to the woman at the farm stand, to show her pictures. To see if anyone, if anything, looked familiar. Was what she saw. Was who she saw. Caldwell went to hit the men's room. Stepping into the hall he was again faced with those photos of Farmer and Jones there on the wall. It was like a shot to the heart.

"I wish you could tell me what we're missing," he said.

After the bathroom the Inspector found himself at the desk of the officer responsible for administering the lie detector tests.

But not before he'd taken a moment to go for a walk, then another to sit in one of the first-floor interrogation rooms. Just to think.

Interrogation rooms are never how you picture them. They're not dark; they're not lit by some single shadowy bulb.

Friends would always ask Caldwell to describe them, interrogation rooms, and he'd always tell them they were not at all like they are in the movies. He thought they always seemed so disappointed that after a while he'd started telling them they were exactly how they'd pictured them.

Truth was that while they were spartan, utilitarian for the most part, if they were anything they were well-lit. Usually there was a center table with chairs on either side, so the detectives faced the suspects. And there was another desk, with a typewriter and a tape recorder, where an officer recorded the interview, statements a suspect might give.

Detectives kept notes, jotting down important information — a key phrase, a curiosity — all for some future reference. But the true, most-ominous part of any interrogation room, any cop would tell you, was that anyone entering one knew they were about to be interrogated.

Which made it interesting how the officer who'd administered the tests described the Goodsons, Driscoll and Colleen.

The husband, he told Caldwell, was cool, calm. Almost detached. The wife? Nervous. And talkative. Real talkative.

She'd rambled on about the crash, about her friends being killed. About the pilots, the detectives. Her son. All as he set up the polygraph machine. "Then she said, 'And now my in-laws have come to town, they're waiting outside, and my husband . . . ' "

Here, the officer said, Mrs. Goodson stopped cold.

"What about your husband?" he said he'd asked. "'He thinks I'm to blame for everything that happened,'" he said she'd told him, finally, adding: "'I can tell by the way he looks at me . . . Maybe I'm just thinking the worst. I mean, I'm sure I am.'" He thought her about to cry.

Then, she said: "'Oh, I don't know.'"

But the most telling thing about the examinations, the officer said, was that the tests weren't telling at all. They couldn't tell him anything.

"Not one blessed thing." He pronounced it *bless-ed*.

He'd asked Driscoll and Colleen if they'd ever hurt the child.

No, they'd said. Inconclusive. He'd asked if they'd had anything to do with the disappearance. No, they'd said again. Inconclusive. He'd asked if they thought their son was kidnapped. Yes, both said. Inconclusive.

He'd asked if they thought Bobby was alive. Yes, they said.

"Let me guess," Caldwell said.

"Yup," the officer said, frustrated.

Inconclusive, Caldwell thought as he settled in to read the statement from Colleen. He hated the word. All cops did.

He hated it more now than he ever had.

"Fucking inconclusive."

For the record Colleen Goodson stated she was twenty-three, born September 25, 1932, in Cottonwood Falls, Kansas.

Stated she lived with her husband and two children at 8 MacArthur Terrace, adding: "I am a housewife. I am not employed."

Like her husband her statement began the day before the disappearance, on Sunday, October 30. Hers, around 4:30 p.m.

"I fed Bobby his supper because he hadn't been feeling well and had a fever. After I fed him I put him to bed. At about six o'clock myself and my husband ate supper. After we finished we sat and watched the television. I think that at about 9:30 or 9:45 p.m. I went to bed and a short time later my husband went to bed. Sometime during the night I heard the baby coughing and I went into the kids' bedroom and at this time found that Bobby had to go to the bathroom. He got out of bed and went into the bathroom because he knows how to go by himself and he did. At about 7 a.m. on October 31st myself and my husband got up because it was Monday and he had to get ready to go to work. I remember that I brought Johanna into bed with us before 7 a.m., maybe at about 6:45 a.m. At about 7 a.m., while my husband was in the bathroom, I took the temperatures of both children. They were normal. When I finished we both went into the dining room, myself and my husband, since I had made breakfast so he could get off to work. I think he got off to work at somewhere about 7:30 a.m. The children were still in bed."

Later in the day, maybe sometime close to noon, Colleen said she stopped across the street and Marjorie asked her to buy stamps and mail some letters. Colleen said she left the two children in the house while she did this. That was because Bobby was taking a nap, she said.

"Being that it was Halloween and he had just turned three I thought I would take him trick-or-treating in the afternoon, since he had never actually done this before. While he was asleep I thought maybe I would, then thought maybe I wouldn't. That I would wait until my husband came home so we could all go together. A short time later I fed both children and I remember Bobby ate vegetable soup, the kind you get in the can, and that he had an American cheese sandwich and a small glass of milk. I did the dishes and then at about one-fifteen or one-thirty we walked to the shopping center so I could buy food to make supper that night."

En route to the store Colleen said she noticed nothing unusual. A few cars, a few young women, some of them pushing carriages.

A few others were walking by themselves.

"I remember one woman," Colleen stated, "because she was wearing a red coat. It was well-fitted, not like those off-the-rack kinds you'd find in a department store. I'd guess she was older but no more than thirty.

"Her hair was nicely done, too."

Outside the store, Colleen said, she'd seen several carriages and decided to leave hers, too, since she was just running in.

"The weather was pleasant, I was only going to be a few minutes," she said. "Johanna was sleeping so I told Bobby to hold on to the handle, told him not to move. That he needed to stand and watch his sister.

"Mommy would be back soon."

It was hard to tell from the statement, Caldwell thought, how Colleen acted as she recounted this. The statement was a narrative; the words of the young mother, nothing more. He'd have to ask Johns and Spence about her state of being. Maybe listen to the tape. But he noted she'd stated: "A lot of mothers leave their children outside these stores and I never thought there was a problem doing this, though my husband, he would get upset when I told him I had done this, and he reminded me several times that I shouldn't, that just because other mothers did it didn't make it right. He said his own mother wouldn't approve and that's why he was saying this and that should be reason enough. I'd tell him Bobby doesn't wander. He's a good boy and does what he's told. I mean, there's times when he doesn't and he can be accident-prone. He's hurt himself playing on occasion, once breaking his arm when he fell off of his tricycle and landed wrong on the pavement outside our house. But he's a boy and I think this should be expected and, besides, the doctor told me he'd outgrow it eventually. The main point is he is a good boy and for the most part he listens and had never wandered before when I'd told him not to so I didn't see the problem." Until, she came out of the store. "You know how sometimes when something happens and you don't think there's anything wrong and other times you know it's something bad before you even know what it is? This was one of those times. I saw the police officer and I just knew. Call it mother's intuition. But I knew right then."

The rest of the statement, Caldwell thought, was to be expected.

Exchanges with police, the search. He noted Colleen thought it odd how Marjorie reacted when a group of trick-or-treaters came to the door, one a blonde-haired boy. Colleen said she knew immediately it wasn't Bobby, while Marjorie seemed almost unnerved by the sight.

"I should state," Colleen said near the end, "that my husband and I have never had any serious problems and that neither of us ever hurt our children and that both of us love Bobby and Johanna very much though sometimes I wish my husband would pay more attention to us. He works hard and I know he loves us. But he's always been quiet and he has a real hard time saying what he thinks and feels. I don't know who could have taken Bobby but I don't think he just wandered off since he doesn't wander and never had before. I don't know what to think except that maybe someone who lost a child took him or maybe someone else for some other reason only they know. I just hope the police find him soon."

Damn, Caldwell thought as he mashed out what was left of his unfiltered *Lucky*, not knowing what to make of any of it.

"Damn."

17

The woman in the red coat walked into police headquarters, walked in off the street, sometime Monday afternoon.

She walked straight to the front desk — to the desk sergeant, the duty officer — and said she needed to talk to the Inspector.

Caldwell hadn't expected to find her so soon, maybe not ever. Until now he wasn't sure she even existed. But, here she was.

Though, she said, she wasn't sure why.

Her name was Milagros Graciela Hernandez. A light-skinned Spaniard she was, from Spain, from a family once of some affluence.

As a girl she had come to the States with her mother and father snuck aboard a tramp steamer out of Barcelona harbor following the infamous Straperlo corruption scandal but before the chaotic elections of '36, the onset of the Spanish Civil War, the coming of the Second World War and the rise of Generalissimo Francisco Franco — fortunate enough to have gotten off the continent while the getting was still good.

Living with her boyfriend in a spartan artisan loft in the West Village, Manhattan, Milagros Graciela said she'd been on Long Island for some time with her family, now an aging couple of modest means.

Her father had read the story about the woman in the red coat earlier that afternoon. He thought it her and urged his daughter, begged her, not to get involved with police. She agreed to his wishes, then hopped the first bus she could, making her way to Mineola to see what the fuss was about.

The Inspector found her presence hard to describe; thought her poised and self-confident with fine, classic features, and deep olive-colored eyes. He offered her coffee. Graciously, she accepted.

He poured her a cup, asked if she'd have a seat.

"Please, Inspector," she said. "What is it you'd like from me?"

As he sat there, Caldwell thought back on all that had happened, knowing all he really wanted at that moment was some proof.

The interview with Lenore Terranova on Saturday lasted an hour, give or take. She'd barely stepped into the office when the Inspector shot her a look, said: "You didn't hear this from me, Lenore. Got that? You didn't hear this from anyone in this building." He thought her confused as she fumbled open her notebook. But, as she did, he said: "The police have reason to believe Colleen Goodson and her husband have been having . . . Well, let's call them 'marital problems.' There's also reason for police to believe Mrs. Goodson may have been involved with another man."

"Mrs. Goodson and another man, huh?"

"Looks like it," Caldwell told her, on the QT.

Lenore shook her head in disappointment.

"Who?" she said, finally.

"Jake Johnson."

"The dead guy?"

"The dead guy," Caldwell said, reaching for a smoke. "Witnesses saw them. She admitted to detectives she knew him, said they were 'friends.'"

"An affair?"

"Denied it. Said people shouldn't jump to conclusions."

Looking up from her notebook, Lenore said: "That's what she told me, too. Denied it, right to my face. Said I shouldn't make assumptions.

"I really wanted to believe her."

Caldwell tamped his cigarette on the desktop. "Understandable."

"Sure," she said.

"Don't beat yourself up, Lenore. You couldn't have known."

"Yeah." She glanced at her notebook, looked back at the Inspector. "Is there any reason to think this affair had anything to do with the crash?"

Caldwell sat there, mum.

"Inspector?"

"Investigators are trying to determine if the relationship had a role in it, a role in the disappearance. If it could have been a factor."

"You think it was?"

The Inspector shrugged. "Maybe."

"The husband know?"

"Hard to say. He did tell detectives he'd heard rumors."

"But?"

"But," Caldwell said, taking a drag of his cigarette. "Let me ask you this, Lenore. You ever talked to this guy, the father?"

"I saw him downstairs earlier. He gave me the brush-off."

"Sounds about right. From what I hear . . ."

Caldwell pushed back in his chair, suddenly uncomfortable.

"Inspector?"

"I'm sorry," he said.

"What?"

As cigarette smoke drifted up from the ashtray, Caldwell stood and, without a word, moved to the window. His back to Lenore, he reached into his pocket, then, in silence, stood there for the longest time. When he turned back he took two memorial cards, dropped them on the desk.

"What I was going to say is I haven't talked to him, either. But from what Farmer and Jones said, may they rest in peace . . ."

"I'm sorry," she said.

He didn't answer. After a lull, he said: "From what Farmer and Jones said, from what Johns and Spence told me, he's a strange character. At least, that's the impression. That he's very quiet, a man of few words. The detectives think he's detached, distant. Almost cold." Reaching for his cigarette, Caldwell added: "And his statement . . ."

"What about his statement?"

The Inspector leaned in, flicked embers into the ashtray.

"Let's just say it was very curious, Lenore."

"Why curious?"

He reached for a carbon, dropped it on the desk. "You didn't get this from me. Understand? But, go on . . . Take a look for yourself."

Lenore read. She jotted down a handful of phrases. "Wow."

"Yeah . . . That's a good word, too."

"You think he hurt his son?"

"The boy?"

She shook her head. "Sorry . . . The boy."

"You'd have to wonder."

"And what about the daughter?"

"What about her?"

"Come on, Inspector. Aroused? The baby 'aroused' him?"

Caldwell leaned back again in his chair. "Odd, huh?"

"Very."

"Yeah, well. I think you can say police found his statement, well . . . Unsettling. That investigators are going to bring both the husband and wife back in Monday for further interviews to . . . To sort it all out."

"I see . . . What about the letter he wrote to his parents?"

"No idea."

"Have you talked to the parents about it?"

"The detectives did, Johns and Spence."

"And?"

"There's reason to believe it hadn't arrived yet. You know, before they came East. We've contacted police out there. They're sending officers to the house to find it, to see what it said . . . They'll let us know, ASAP."

"What about Mrs. Goodson? About her statement?"

"Sorry. I can't tell you more than I've already said. But . . . "

"But?"

"But I do have one more thing for you, Lenore. Make it two . . . Mr. and Mrs. Goodson were given lie detector tests this morning."

"And?"

"The findings were inconclusive."

"Inconclusive? What does that mean?"

The Inspector recounted his conversation with the administering officer. Lenore was clearly stunned, didn't know what to say.

"I know. My reaction, too. It's something, isn't it?"

"I'd say," Lenore said, finally. "I mean . . . "

"I know," he said, reaching for what was left of his cigarette. "Not only are investigators trying to make heads or tails out of two confusing interviews, but you can say police are trying to locate a woman who may have seen Bobby Goodson minutes before he disappeared last week."

"Really?"

"Really," Caldwell said, mashing out his dying smoke. "Mrs. Goodson told detectives she saw a young woman while on her way to the shopping center who might be able to tell us if, in fact, the missing child was with her before he disappeared. We're looking for her . . . "

He dug into the dwindling pack of *Luckys*.

"Mrs. Goodson swore she remembered passing this woman as she walked with her son and daughter. All we know is she was wearing a red coat. A high-end coat, not one off the rack, Mrs. Goodson said. That's it."

"She didn't mention anything else? Hair color, eyes? Anything?"

"She said she was older, but probably no more than thirty."

"That's not much to go on."

"Don't I know it, Lenore. Bottom line is no one else remembers seeing this kid. If this woman did . . . Well, I'm sure you can see the importance."

"You want me to write a story."

The Inspector smiled. "That'd be nice."

"How can I source it? I'm going to need a source."

"Officials? That work?"

"How about a source close to the investigation?"

Caldwell leaned back.

"I can live with that. Look, I know you don't have a Sunday paper so none of this is much help if it's not kept under wraps until Monday. I'll make you a deal, Lenore. Anyone calls me between now and then I'm going to tell them we're having a news conference Monday."

"What's this going to cost me, exactly?"

"Did I say it was going to cost you?"

"You didn't have to."

He gave her a knowing smirk. "Look, this one's on the house. I mean, let's just say I need this out there . . . Besides, I owe you for last week."

"For?"

"For the night of the crash, how you handled the funeral."

"Fair enough," she said.

"Good, then. I think that should do."

He started to stand, to show her out. Lenore didn't move.

"One more thing," she said.

"Go ahead. Shoot."

"What about the neighbor? Taggart Woods."

"What about him?"

"What do you mean, what about him?"

"Just what I said, Lenore. What about him?"

A puzzled expression crossed her face.

"You know he worked on the plane, right?"

"The plane?"

"Yeah. He was the one who . . . "

"No," Caldwell said, before she could finish. "No, I didn't."

Lenore thought the Inspector looked about to be sick.

"Is there any reason to believe he could have done something to it? You know, to cause the crash?"

Caldwell leaned forward in disbelief.

"I . . . I don't know."

The headstones at Pinelawn National Cemetery, just over the border in Suffolk, stretched white and in ordered rows, far as the eye could see.

Aligned precisely in each and all directions — East to West, North to South; on the diagonal, even — they marked the final resting place for more than ten-thousand men killed in World War II, not to mention war heroes, Medal of Honor winners, anyone who'd once served; even dead Axis combatants once held prisoners of war by the U.S. government.

It was here on Sunday that the families of Holt Hamilton and Jake Johnson came to bid their goodbyes to the two dead men.

General Johnson was there, so was the Inspector.

The Hamiltons had flown in from the coast and stood stoic by, well-dressed, proper and polite.

The Johnson clan had come clear-to in their black bootlegger special, a late '40s flathead Ford, and stood graveside in their Sunday bests, Jake's Ma creating the biggest *through,* her wailing and a caterwauling, her ceaseless *clatterment* and carrying on, much to the consternation of those gathered for nearby funerals, who seemed to start with her every cry. Jake's Pa looked fit to be tied, thinkin' how all these big-city folk were sorry *good-fer-nothin's,* cain't even let a woman mourn her offspring.

When it was done he'd walked over to General Johnson and, after the Hamiltons said their piece, nodded to the commander and said: "Just like to say I'm much obliged for all y'all done for my boy, for all them kindly words y'all said 'bout him. Make me proud, it done." He reached out, shook hands. "When *we'uns* first heard Jake been killed like he were, well . . . I were so dang *dizzyfied* had to hold onto the grass *a'fore* I could lean again the ground. And his Ma? Lord, I ain't never see'd no kind of sorryful bones like that. Reckon she done thunk she outlive her time."

He pondered it all for a moment, thinking.

"Don't rightly know *if'n* she ever gone be the same, things still all *gormed* up'n all." He scuffed a foot in the fresh dirt.

Long after Caldwell stood talking with General Johnson. Both men had been moved by the funeral. That didn't mean there wasn't business to be done. The Inspector still had questions. About Jake Johnson, about

Taggart Woods; about the crash itself. The Inspector asked about Woods — and, about word he'd actually worked on the doomed bomber.

"Not a factor," the General said.

"And you're sure why?"

"He couldn't have known who'd be flying. Fact is, he'd already been granted his discharge before the crew was assigned the flight."

He noted the Inspector looked relieved.

"Besides, none of it had anything to do with the crash. Not Woods, not Johnson. Not any of the back-alley stuff we talked about.

"Not even the aircraft."

"What then?"

"A God-damned bird."

Caldwell stared at the General, confused. "I'm sorry?"

"God-damned *bird,*" Johnson said, again. *"Bird strike.* On climb-out, right after takeoff. Canada goose. Investigators said the damned thing must've smashed straight through the windscreen, hit Hamilton in the face. Damnedest thing I've ever heard. I'm told it probably killed him instantly. They think Johnson climbed from the jump seat to the flight deck, trying to save the plane. Poor bastard never had a chance."

Dumbstruck, Caldwell stood staring at the General.

It was a few moments before Johnson threw his arm around the Inspector's shoulder. "C'mon," he said. "First drink's on me."

Alongside his wife Driscoll Goodson sat, eyes locked on the Inspector. Caldwell thought him at a slow boil. "Why are we here?" he said.

Clearing his throat the Inspector said: "I've got some questions."

"Regarding?"

Caldwell shot Driscoll a hard look. "The statements you and your wife gave my detectives Saturday. I've got concerns."

"About?" Colleen Goodson said.

The Inspector noted she'd slid her hand over to grab her husband's thigh as she said this, thought it odd that he'd shifted, ever so slight, to avoid the contact. As he watched it all unfold, he said: "Your son, Mrs. Goodson. Your daughter. Circumstances. I'd like you both to clear up some things for me, things I'm not quite sure I understand."

Driscoll sat stiff-necked, anger rising.

"More questions. That's why you called us here?"

The Inspector pushed back in his chair. "Yes. That's exactly why."

Leaning forward, he reached for his *Luckys*.

"If you don't mind," Driscoll said.

The Inspector smiled. "Actually, I do."

He lit his cigarette, smiled again. Told Driscoll he'd sent officers out to retrieve the letter he'd written his parents.

"Why would you do that?"

"You worried?"

"Should I be?" he said.

"What then?"

"It's just I don't understand."

"You don't understand what, Mr. Goodson?" Caldwell said.

"Why you need to . . . I mean, it's private."

"Why I need to?" Caldwell flicked ashes into the ashtray. "I need to Mr. Goodson because it seems unbelievable to me."

"What?"

"The whole thing."

"Like?"

"The timing, what you said you wrote. All of it."

Driscoll scoffed. "You don't believe me."

The Inspector snickered. "Quite frankly, Mr. Goodson? No, I don't."

Driscoll shrugged. "I can't help that."

"That's what I thought." Caldwell turned to Colleen. "What about you, Mrs. Goodson. You've been awful quiet. What do you think about this?"

"I'm not sure what you want from us Inspector," she said.

"Do you know what's in this letter your husband wrote?"

Colleen turned to her husband. "What did you write Driscoll?"

As Driscoll Goodson sat silent, Caldwell rifled through a stack of papers, grabbed a few pages, dropped them in front of Colleen.

"Go on," he said. "You tell me."

For the next few minutes Colleen sat reading, the room filled with uneasy, almost unbearable silence. She fidgeted, gnawed on her lip. When she was done Colleen turned to say something to her husband, but he never even acknowledged her. Caldwell thought her crestfallen.

"What is it Mrs. Goodson?"

"I . . . I had no idea."

"Is it true?"

"What my husband wrote?" She took a tissue, dabbed her eyes. "Yes, I'm afraid it is. We've . . . we've been having problems."

The Inspector studied her. "And the kids?"

A tear ran down her cheek; Driscoll glowered at the Inspector.

"You both said the kids had been sick," Caldwell said.

"Yes," Colleen said.

"Has there been an issue with discipline?"

"What are you getting at?" Driscoll said, interrupting.

"What am I getting at? Did you hurt your children Mr. Goodson?"

Driscoll jumped up. "How dare you!"

The Inspector shot Driscoll a look. "Take a seat, pal."

"Pal?"

"I said take a seat Mr. Goodson. Sit down. Now! Explain the letter, explain your statement. Explain all of it . . . "

"Explain what?"

Caldwell reached for the statement.

"Explain what you meant when you told my detectives: 'I remember I mentioned in this letter something in regards to an argument my wife Colleen and I had, that we had been having some problems. That some of it had to do with issues over the care of the children, especially the boy. I wish to state we have had many arguments of late over the punishment of this child. If he was being dealt with as he should.'"

He stared at Driscoll. "Well, what about it?"

Driscoll didn't answer. He slumped back into his chair, closed his eyes. Colleen reached out and placed her hand atop his thigh.

This time Driscoll didn't move. She turned to the Inspector.

"I think you misunderstood."

"Misunderstood what, exactly?"

"Everything. I think you've misunderstood everything."

The Inspector reached for another cigarette.

"How's that Mrs. Goodson?"

"We didn't argue because my husband was too hard on our son," she said. "We argued because . . . Well, because, he thought I was too hard sometimes and because sometimes I was too careless. It's just sometimes I felt like I needed help. Because, I was at my wit's end trying to take care of our daughter and also make sure Bobby did what he was told. Because, sometimes I needed my husband to be more involved. To lend a hand."

"Because what? Bobby was bad? He made you angry?"

A tear rolled down her cheek. "It's not like that."

"Not like what?"

"It's not like you think. Bobby's a good boy. But, he's three. There's times he's going a mile-a-minute. Trying to keep track, well . . . before Jo was born it wasn't so hard. But there are days I've got my hands full."

"So you never hurt him Mrs. Goodson?"

Driscoll stared at Caldwell, Colleen took a deep breath.

"Once or twice, in recent months . . . I got frustrated."

"And?"

"I swatted him. Once in front of one of the cashiers down at the Five-and-Ten. Another, in front of my neighbor, Marjorie Woods."

Caldwell turned to Driscoll. "Did you know about this?"

Driscoll shook his head yes.

"And?"

But Driscoll didn't say a word.

"Driscoll's an only child, Inspector. He said his mother never had a problem. Never hit him. I just don't think he understood."

"Didn't understand what?"

"That it's different with two," Colleen said. "You know, than it is with one. You can't be everywhere. Months back Bobby was outside playing. Johanna was just a few days old and I had my hands full with her. Bobby fell off his bike. He broke his arm. It was terrible, just awful. I was beside myself. Driscoll was at work. I had Margie drive us to the hospital."

She clenched the tissue, tears streaming down her cheeks.

"The doctor said these things happen, that he's a little boy. But, well . . . I felt like Marjorie thought I was careless, that Driscoll thought I was."

Unexpectedly, Driscoll reached out took his wife's hand.

"I guess I just never realized," he said.

As Caldwell sat there not knowing what to think there was a knock at the door. An officer walked in, handed him a telegram.

It was from the Kansas State Police, the contents of the letter from Driscoll to his parents. It was everything he'd said it was; nothing more, nothing less. Nothing, it turned out, as extraordinary, inexplicable or alarming as Caldwell and his detectives thought it might have been when they'd first learned of its existence. When he finished the Inspector sat staring at Driscoll and Colleen. Amid the ashes of a half-dozen dead cigarettes the remnants of his latest *Lucky Strike* lay smoldering in the ashtray. It wasn't worth trying to salvage even one final draw.

All the questions, all the reactions, all the explanations. He was forced to admit it all made sense. Overwhelmed mother, aloof father. Two young parents faced with all the usual problems; problems compounded by their own very different natures. It explained a lot. And nothing at all.

All, just another detour in a case so far filled with them.

"Tell me about Jake Johnson," Caldwell said.

Driscoll appeared uneasy. Colleen stared at the floor.

"It was nothing," she said. "It was a mistake."

"Did you have an affair?"

"No," she said, barely audible.

"What then?"

"I just needed someone to talk to." Starting to cry, she turned to her husband. "I swear, Driscoll. It was all a big mistake. He . . . He wanted more. But nothing happened between us. Nothing, at all. I swear."

"Us?" Driscoll said. *"Us?"*

"I'm sorry," she said, a bare whisper.

Out of his chair, Driscoll wandered to the corner of the room — and fought not to cry. Colleen went to him, tried to hug him, still apologetic. But he ignored her attempts and, defeated, she took her seat, tears running down her face. Watching it all the Inspector went to Driscoll, whispered a few words then ushered him back to his seat.

The two of them sat there, husband and wife, mere inches apart. The rift between them, Caldwell thought, almost immeasurable.

"I never thought," Colleen said, finally. "I mean, I just never realized how badly I messed it all up. It was all just a really terrible mistake."

Driscoll sat, stone-cold.

"Do you believe her Mr. Goodson."

"Please," he said. "I don't want to talk about it."

"Fair enough. But I want you to understand none of this had anything to do with your son going missing. Or the crash. With any of it."

Caldwell reached for another smoke.

"Just one last thing before you leave Mr. Goodson," he said. "I'm sorry, but I have to ask. What did you mean by 'aroused'?"

"Excuse me?"

"Your statement. You said the baby *'aroused'* you."

"Yes."

"What did you mean, *'aroused'*?"

"What's the problem Inspector?" Colleen said.

"The problem?" He found it hard to believe. "So, let me get this straight. Your daughter 'aroused' you? From your sleep?"

"Exactly," Driscoll said. "I was asleep. She woke me."

The Inspector shook his head.

"You mean she *'roused'* you Mr. Goodson?"

Driscoll seemed confused. So did Colleen.

"Yeah, I guess. What's the difference?"

"The difference? You're kidding, right?"

"What do you mean?"

The Inspector banged his palm against his forehead.

"You really don't know, do you?"

"Know what?" Colleen said.

"When you wake someone, Mrs. Goodson, you *'rouse'* them from their sleep. When you *'arouse'* them, well . . . it means you excite them."

Young midwesterners, Caldwell thought. They didn't have a clue, not even the faintest. "You know, excite them in a, um . . . In a *sexual* way."

"Good God," Driscoll said, bolting upright. "Is this what you people think? What you've been doing, instead of searching for my son? Thinking . . . thinking we're some kind of . . . some kind of perverts?"

His face was beet with anger.

The Inspector had no idea what to say, what to do.

Cigarette burning in the ashtray he nevertheless reached for his *Luckys,* pulled the last one from the pack.

"I'm sorry," Caldwell said, finally. "I'm really, truly, sorry."

One by one the doors had all been opened. One by one, in most-unceremonious fashion, each of them had been slammed shut.

The Negroes and the gray Plymouth. The canine search. The hand-off in Bayport, a dead end when the woman at the farm stand, shown photographs, said she couldn't identify the car — or anyone else. Jake Johnson, Taggart Woods. The plane crash. The situation with Driscoll, with Colleen. Each of them, all of them. One after another after another.

Now, late Monday afternoon, more than a week into the investigation, the Inspector had one last lead left. And she was staring him in the face. The woman in the red coat: Milagros Graciela Hernandez. His last stab at something; maybe his last chance, he feared, at finding the fucking needle in the proverbial haystack. If not this, if there was nothing concrete here, what did he have left? He dreaded the thought.

He stared at Milagros Graciela. Sooner or later he had to ask the question. "Last Monday were you on Mitchell Avenue?" he said.

"Yes," she answered.

"At around one-thirty, one-forty-five in the afternoon?"

"Yes," she said, again.

Anticipation building, he said: "Did you see a woman pushing a baby carriage?"

"Why yes," Milagros Graciela said. "I did."

Caldwell took a photograph and dropped it on the desk.

"Is this the woman you saw?"

Milagros took the photograph, studied it.

"Yes. She looks familiar. I believe she is someone I saw that day."

The Inspector took a deep breath.

"Good. That's good. Now, I need you to think. I need you to think hard. Did she have a little boy with her, a little blonde-haired boy?"

The Inspector was all pins and needles as Milagros sat there, studying the photo, trying hard to remember. Before she even began to answer he knew it wasn't going to be the one he'd been hoping for.

"I don't know," she said, finally.

"You don't know?"

"I'm sorry. I'm not saying he wasn't there. I just don't recall."

And just like that the last door slammed shut.

18

The letter came in the mail on a Tuesday. It arrived in a plain white envelope, alone in the mailbox, and at first glance it seemed rather pedestrian, nondescript. The mailing information on the front of it, dead center, was clean, simple. Typed. There was no return address.

Had it been mixed in with the regular mail Colleen would have just tossed it on the dining room table. She'd just put Johanna down for a nap, was in the middle of doing laundry, trying to get her mind off everything: the accusatory looks from her in-laws, the growing rift with Driscoll; even the stares from the airmen sent to fix the house. All of it, the guilt, was beginning to overwhelm her. Still, no one knew the truth about Bobby.

Fact was, Colleen found the plainness of the envelope odd, so as she walked from the door she stuck a fingernail under the flap, pried it open. She got as far as the first sentence and, almost immediately, collapsed onto the living room floor. She sat there the longest time, sobbing, not knowing what to do. She had an impulse to run across the street to Marjorie's. Then she'd opened the door to find the burnt shell of the house staring her in the face — and it her like a sucker-punch.

Marjorie and Tag were, in fact, dead; being buried, actually, that very afternoon somewhere out near Bakersfield. And Driscoll and his parents were out searching, weren't due home until dinnertime.

Colleen ran to the kitchen, grabbed the phone, dialed police headquarters and demanded to speak with Inspector Caldwell.

She was rambling and the operator wasn't about to put her through. Not until she screamed something about her missing son.

Next thing, Colleen heard the Inspector ask: "Mrs. Goodson?"

She didn't answer straight off, her mind was going a mile-a-minute.

Finally, she yelled: "I've got a ransom note!"

He asked if he'd heard her correctly.

"Yes," she screamed. "A ransom note! They say they have Bobby! Do you hear me? They have him! Who? I don't know. Whoever sent it. What? Let me check . . . No, there's nothing. It just says . . . It says they want money." She was frantic, now; could barely contain herself. "Oh, my God. I can't believe this . . . This means Bobby's alive. Doesn't it?"

Hearing the hysteria the Inspector simply asked Colleen to take a deep breath, maybe even pour herself a drink. The Inspector said he'd be over with Johns and Spence as soon as they could get there. Wiping away tears she hung up the phone, sat at the table staring at the letter. Like the envelope, it was typewritten and neat. She began to read:

> Your son is now in my possession. Do the following. Obtain five hundred [ten-dollar bills] used, unmarked and unserialized. Place the bills in a large kraft envelope. Deliver yourself and the envelope to Key's Luncheonette [sixty-four Court Street near Borough Hall Brooklyn] Friday November 11th at exactly 2 P.M. Here await further instructions by telephone. Answer the pay phone on the second ring with "Kilroy is here" then listen for further instructions which will be given just once. To facilitate the immediate return of your son it is important that the preceding instructions be followed exactly. Unnecessary contact with law enforcement officers will hamper the transaction. Presence of said officers will invalidate it . . .

"Remember," Caldwell said, as he stood hovering over the dining room table, reading. "I am fair, follow my example."

"That's it?" Johns said.

"There is one thing," Caldwell said, turning the letter so they could see. "Anyone ever see anything like this?"

There, in black ink, underneath the typewritten demands and instructions, was a strange hand-drawn symbol: a circle with a dot in the center, a connected arrow leading from it that pointed straight off the page. All of them agreed they'd never seen anything like it.

All of them agreed it most-curious.

"Could be some sort of architectural symbol," Spence said.

The Inspector shrugged. "Maybe."

"An insignia?" Johns said. "He said whoever brought the ransom should answer 'Kilroy is here.' Could mean he's military."

"Possible."

Finally, Colleen said: "Maybe it's one of those . . . those zodiac signs."

The three cops eyed her, curiously.

"Like one of those horoscope things?" Spence said.

"Exactly," Colleen said.

"Check on that," the Inspector said. "Whatever it is, we've got to find out ASAP. At least, if we're gonna find this guy. Meanwhile, start making arrangements to get the money, to coordinate this with the NYPD. If we're going to go to Brooklyn we're going to need to run it by them . . .

"We're going to need all the help we can get."

He turned to Colleen. "When will your husband be home?"

"Dinnertime?"

"Okay. Here's what we do. Mike, Ike. Go to headquarters, set up a meeting with the city cops. I'm going to wait here for Mr. Goodson and his parents. Meanwhile, none of this leaves this room. That means no friends, neighbors. No *reporters*. Got me? No one . . . The press gets word of this and things can go bad real quick. Loose lips sink ships."

He turned to Colleen. "We're going to get this bastard."

Driscoll Goodson walked down Court Street like a condemned man headed for the gas chamber, aware of everything and nothing at all. He'd later tell detectives he'd felt every sensation — every fear, every breath, each and every agonizing step — as he walked toward that luncheonette. That he'd also felt a numbness, as if it were someone else walking in his shoes. So much so he later said he barely remembered the sidewalk.

The cops had given him a notepad and pencil, to write down the instructions he received in the phone call, and they had slipped a piece of carbon between the pages — so he could hand off a copy of those instructions to a plainclothes officer positioned as a customer in the luncheonette, should he be ordered to another location.

Detectives had been stationed along the block. One stood reading a newspaper. Another waited at the bus stop. One peered out from the window of a clothing store. Two more stood near the corner talking, like old friends who had bumped into each other on the street.

Driscoll barely stepped into Key's when the phone rang. He answered "Kilroy is here," and soon was scribbling down directions given by a man whose voice he later said he did not recognize. He tried to remain calm despite the apprehension he felt, knowing everyone around him, knowing all the cops, believed this was the man who'd taken his son.

Knowing that while everyone believed that no one knew for certain; knowing that none of them knew anything at all.

As he turned to leave Driscoll slipped the carbon to the officer in the booth. Headed out the door, down Court Street to Joralemon.

Turned right toward Adams.

He cut across the street leading to the Brooklyn Bridge, soon was on Willoughby. He walked past storefronts, parked cars, past people going about their workaday lives as detectives tailed him in an unmarked car. He didn't have time to consider what they might think if they knew what he was going through at that moment. If they knew the truth. He didn't have time to think about anything except trying to find the place he'd been told to go. Reaching Willoughby and Jay he stopped. Cold.

There he stood, kraft envelope crammed with five-thousand dollars in ten-dollar bills nervously in hand, down the block from the Polytechnic Institute and just a handful of blocks from where he'd begun his walk.

He stood there and waited. And waited. And, waited.

Stood there, but nothing happened. No one came.

It wasn't until the next afternoon anyone got the first inkling what'd gone wrong. It was then two boys — one nine, the other ten — walked into the NYPD Precinct with a man who told the sergeant he had a story to tell. His name was John DeAndrea. He was a bus driver, his son Tommy the older of the boys. The other was Tommy's friend, Billy Condon.

DeAndrea told the sergeant the boys had come home the previous day "out of sorts." When he got them to talk they said they'd been watching workmen near the bridge when a man approached, asked if they'd like to make two bucks. The boys said sure. The man gave them each a dollar, he said. Or, more precise, half of a one-dollar bill each. The bills had been torn in half, he said. He also said the man told the two they'd each get the other half once they completed the errand he would to send them on.

The man walked the boys to the new transit building near Jay and Willoughby. There, he stopped near the escalator leading down to the subway platform. He told the boys to stand under a Coca-Cola sign by a store on the other side, said a man would come and hand them a package. The man was his friend, he said, telling the kids it was all part of a joke. Once the man gave them the package the boys were to cross back to the subway entrance, take the escalator down to the platform. There they would hand him the package — and get the other half of the bills.

But as they waited Billy Condon told Tommy DeAndrea he was scared. Said maybe the package contained drugs, that maybe they were going to get in big trouble. It wasn't long before Tommy DeAndrea agreed and the two of them ran off, looking over their shoulders the whole way home, thinking maybe the man would chase after them.

The cops asked a lot of questions, were surprised how much the boys knew. The man was in his twenties, wore blue dungarees, shiny black shoes and a blue pea coat. Billy Condon said he recognized the coat because his uncle was in the Navy and had one just like it. He figured the man might've been a sailor, but didn't see any tattoos.

The boys went through hundreds of mug shots of known criminals. They didn't see anyone who looked familiar. And then all anyone could do was wait, to see if the kidnapper tried to make contact again.

They didn't have to wait long.

The second note came a few days later and it was much like the first — typewritten, with the same hand-drawn symbol at the bottom. It read:

> Mr. and Mrs. Goodson, I hope you have learned by now that our transaction can not possibly be completed when law enforcement officers are present. It is my wish your son be returned to you as soon as possible. Of course, this is now entirely up to you. I am doing my part. You have failed once. Return to the luncheonette at Sixty-Four Court Street on Friday November 18th. This time at exactly 4 P.M. With you at this time you will have a shoe box securely tied and containing seven-hundred-fifty [ten-dollar bills] used, unmarked and unserialized. Pick up the phone on the first ring. Answer "Kilroy is here." Listen for the instructions. They will be given only once. Do as I say. Remember, I am fair. Please consider fully any action you decide to take.

The first note yielded no fingerprints, save for those of the Inspector, Driscoll and Colleen, all of whom had handled the letter. The second was clean, too, and yielded none at all. The detectives still couldn't identify the strange hand-drawn figure. It didn't correspond to any zodiac signs, to any type of military insignia or architectural symbol. To anything anyone had ever seen. Which left them all at a frustrating loss.

Not knowing what else to do the cops got together the ransom, packed it into a shoe box, and sent Driscoll back to the luncheonette.

Again, he carried the notepad and pencil. Again, there were plainclothes officers on the block. Once again the pay phone rang as soon as Driscoll entered Key's and he answered, "Kilroy is here."

Again, he was given instructions on where to walk.

The cops, hoping the kidnapper didn't know they'd talked to Tommy DeAndrea and Billy Condon, arranged for detectives disguised as cleaning men to be positioned outside the transit station on Willoughby and Jay. But this time when Driscoll stepped out of Key's he turned away from Joralemon — and walked towards Schermerhorn. There was a drug store near the corner. It, too, had a pay phone. Driscoll walked into the store. The phone rang, he answered, "Kilroy is here." But instead of more instructions the kidnapper said: "I will call back in one half-hour. Wait."

Driscoll stood at the phone — and waited.

After a few minutes a man walked up, asked to use the phone. Driscoll told him no. The man, dressed in a suit, wearing a fedora, protested. Driscoll stood his ground. The man said he was a lawyer, that he practiced over at the court house; told Driscoll he'd make trouble for him if he didn't move away then and there. "I'm not in the mood," Driscoll said.

The man walked away. Moments later he returned with the druggist, who asked what the problem was.

Driscoll told the druggist: "I'm waiting for a call."

"You'll have to wait elsewhere. This man's a customer." The apothecary gave him the once-over. "Don't make me call police."

The lawyer stepped forward, reached for the receiver. Driscoll grabbed his wrist. He felt a hot wave of adrenalin surge through him.

"Touch that phone again," he said, glaring at the druggist and the lawyer in the suit, "and there's going to be more trouble than I think either of you want." And he waved them off.

Once they were gone Driscoll nervously checked his watch.

As he stood trying to calm himself he could scarcely believe what he'd just done. Before either man could return the phone rang.

Almost immediately Driscoll grabbed it and said: "This is Kilroy. I . . . I mean, 'Kilroy is here.'" The man on the other end laughed.

"Don't be so nervous," the kidnapper said.

The man told Driscoll to go to the D train on the Culver Line.

He told him to take the first car to Second Avenue, get off there; that there'd be a trash can on the platform against the wall, next to a gum machine. He said inside the can Driscoll would find his instructions.

As Driscoll walked to the station he still couldn't believe he'd grabbed the attorney to stop him from using the phone. He could remember once or twice, when he was a boy, how his father had been filled with such anger and rage. He didn't like it when he wasn't in control.

The D train arrived not long after Driscoll. He stepped into the first car and soon it was off. He tried to imagine the drumbeat noise the cars made as they bounded over the rails in the Manhattan-bound Rutgers Street Tunnel, that the screeching of wheels that accented every tilting turn, were the sounds of farm machinery back home in Kansas.

But, honestly, he couldn't imagine it at all.

It only made him more anxious, tense, and he was relieved to reach Second Avenue. The trash basket and gum machine were on the platform straight in front of him, just like the kidnapper said. He looked for the cops who were assigned to surveillance but saw no one and realized he'd forgotten to give anyone the carbon from his notepad. He thought to turn back but knew he had no choice despite his mistake. He peered into the trash can. There was a note. He reached in, pulled it out.

> Take this key. Proceed to Thirty-Fourth Street and Eighth Avenue [Pennsylvania Station] via the A train. Find the locker to which this key belongs, open it, and place the box with the money inside. Leave the key in the lock. Do not attempt to lock the locker again, but do make sure the door is closed. Return to the luncheonette. You will receive further information only when the money is safely in my hands. Remember, this can not occur if law officers remain with you. The locker is located below the stairway nearest the third-to-last car of the A train.

Driscoll made his way to the platform, got on the A train. He traveled toward Eighth taking note of the unfamiliar faces, wondering if anyone was the kidnapper who'd dispatched him; wondering if the cops were smart enough to figure out what was going on.

From what he'd seen he wasn't sure they were.

Stepping headlong into the madding crowd at Pennsylvania Station, shoe box cradled firmly in hand, Driscoll felt certain he was, indeed, alone. Men in business suits clogged the platform as far as the eye could see. More headed down the staircase to join them. Scattered in the mix a handful of women stood, high-heeled and in work attire, and Driscoll gathered from their looks most were secretarial. Some held compacts, which they used to adjust their hairstyles or their make-up and lipstick. Cigarette smoke tinged the air with a grayish hue and the smell of it was dense, stale, and not at all pleasant. Driscoll turned toward the lockers under the staircase. It was then he saw them.

The man wore a pea coat; the boy, of course, a head of blonde hair. The two were on the staircase, the man leading the little boy by the hand. As he moved to follow them, almost knocking a man onto the tracks in the process, Driscoll caught a glimpse of a uniformed patrolman. He thought to call for assistance but there was no time. He thought to call to his son but didn't want to send the man running off with no chance of making up the ground in the crowded terminal. He reached the foot of the stairs, heart pounding. The man turned back to look over his shoulder.

As he did, the two of them locked eyes.

Just then a swarm of men, briefcases in hand, came racing toward the stairs, blocking Driscoll's line of sight. He bounded forward, lost his footing, fell to a knee on the staircase. The shoe box slipped from his hand. He grabbed it, pulled himself to his feet, and raced toward the landing. In a few breathless moments he was in the main station. Panicked, he looked around. There, a hundred feet away, he saw the two standing — and started to run. As he did the boy turned toward him.

It stopped him cold. It wasn't Bobby.

And no matter how much he wished it was at that moment Driscoll knew there was nothing he could do.

He stood motionless as the masses, headed home from work, headed home to loved ones, breezed on past. He stood there until he could stand there no more then walked solemnly back down the crowded staircase to the lockers, found the one he was looking for and placed the box inside.

It wasn't five minutes, the cops would later say, before this man came walking up, peered inside, looked to see if anyone was watching, grabbed the box. As he strolled off, nonchalant as possible, detectives seized him.

Turned out the cops hadn't lost Driscoll in Brooklyn. He just was so preoccupied he hadn't noticed he was being tailed.

It also turned out, much to the disbelief of everyone, the man taken for interrogation wasn't the kidnapper. He was an ex-con just released from jail who told the cops he was a cook by trade and said he'd left utensils in the same locker before being pinched a day earlier on the high-charge of public intoxication. He'd just gotten out, had come back to get his stuff, seen it wasn't there. So, he said, he'd taken what was.

The cops didn't believe him. Until, that is, they checked his story. A mad scramble ensued to get the box back to where it was supposed to be: inside the locker, waiting for the kidnapper. They did. To their surprise not a half-hour later a second man came walking up. He, too, peered into the locker, looked around to see if he was being watched, grabbed the shoe box and strolled off as nonchalant as any criminal could. Unlike the cook, this time the cops let the man walk, following him as he headed out of Penn Station, walked to the corner of 34th Street and Eighth Avenue.

They watched as he stood at that corner and waited.

He walked up the block, he walked down the block. He scanned the sidewalk, looking for someone. He checked his watch. He walked some more. Finally, after more than an hour, he started back to the subway. As he did the cops grabbed him, dragged him off for interrogation, as well.

Galen Carroll was fifty-one years old, down on his luck, a drifter who told police how a man had come to him with an offer too good to refuse. All he had to do was go to Penn Station, remove a shoe box from a locker, bring it to him. For this Carroll would earn himself ten bucks and a bottle of Johnnie Walker. Cops wanted a name. Carroll didn't know. The cops took him to the station house, showed him mug shots from their files. Carroll drew blanks. They took fingerprints, just in case. But after hours of getting nowhere — and, with Carroll continuing to swear he had no idea about any kidnapping — it seemed like just another dead end.

So the cops took a statement and a description of the man Carroll said had asked him to get the box. A description that sounded an awful lot like the one given them earlier by the two boys, Tommy DeAndrea and Billy Condon. There wasn't much else to do but kick Carroll loose.

"Please, don't say that," Colleen said, looking at her husband with pleading eyes. "Don't you think I feel bad enough, already . . . "

She stopped mid-sentence as Driscoll turned from her, stared into the backyard, stared at the swing, thinking how he wanted to believe her, thinking he should. A thin coat of frost covered the old tire hanging from the branch. It glistened in the glow of the porch light as it stirred in the soft breeze, ever so slight. He thought about how he'd hung it there. How excited Bobby had been, filled with the exuberance only a child could know. How satisfied he'd felt. How he'd done something good.

Staring at it now all he could think was his boy was still missing. That no one had any answers, that no one seemed any closer to bringing him home than they'd been weeks before. That he had no idea if he'd ever see his son again. He thought about the entire mess, how everything had spun out of control so fast, sucked downward into nothingness with the vicious, unstoppable torrent of a whirlpool into a jack-rabbit hole. He thought about how his wife had set it all in motion. All of it. Had ruined everything. All with her recklessness, with her bad decisions.

His mom and dad had gone home to Bazaar.

Driscoll had taken them to the airport, seen them off. There was little more they could do on Long Island, was only so long they could leave the farm unattended. He understood. He'd shaken hands with his old man at the terminal and then his mother hugged him, telling him before she'd turned to head for the airplane that she just knew it would be all right.

He'd forced a smile, said: "I know."

He knew he didn't believe it then. He didn't believe it now.

"Driscoll?"

"What?" he said, still locked on the swing.

"Could you at least look at me?"

He shrugged but didn't turn back.

"We can't go on like this," she said. "I can't go on like this."

"I know," he said, finding it hard to believe he'd actually said it.

She put her hand on his shoulder. He thought how it reminded him of the first time she'd ever touched him and yet how it didn't remind him of that at all. It didn't seem like all that long ago he was actually in love.

All he could think now was the wrong person had gone missing. How he hated himself for thinking that; hated her for making him think it.

"Driscoll?" She wrapped her arms around his waist, pressed her head into the middle of his back. "Isn't there anything we can do?"

She started to cry, softly. He wanted to, but didn't.

"I'm not sure," he said. "I'm not sure things can ever be the same."

"I know," she said, low. "I'm sorry more than you know."

Driscoll didn't say a word, didn't know what to say.

He just stood staring out the window. Thinking about something his grandfather once told him back when he was just a boy. It was from *One of Ours,* the novel by the old plains writer Willa Cather.

He didn't understand it then. But for some strange reason it had come to him again — and, as Colleen clung tight, he just couldn't shake it.

Sometimes, even the wicked get worse than they deserve.

19

"A fucking travesty," the Inspector said, as he tossed the decision onto his desktop. "How could anyone in their right mind return no bill?"

"You knew it was going to happen," Mike Johns said.

Taking a long drag from his smoke, Caldwell pushed away the grand jury decision. "I can't even look at it, it's such horse shit," he said. "Gugliotta said it all came down to his mother. His own fucking mother. He said we had the evidence, that no reasonable person could honestly believe she didn't know it was her husband. I mean, he's in the doorway stark naked and she fires two fucking shots? Then his own God-damned mother cuts his balls out from under him? Her own dead son?"

No one outside of the grand jury knew for certain what had decided it, what ultimately swayed the members who'd been impaneled to hear the evidence against Ann Woodward. But the Inspector said he'd gone to see a man about a horse and from what he could tell none of it rested on fact; at least, not on the facts as anyone who knew anything about anything knew them to be. From what he'd heard it was the testimony of Elsie Woodward, Billy's mom, that ultimately set Ann free.

Everyone who heard her attestation was sworn to secrecy. That was law. But word around courthouse bars was she'd testified her daughter-in-law cherished her son. That they were the perfect couple, so very much in love. That she couldn't fathom any of it to be more than just a terrible, tragic accident. That it couldn't have been anything else.

Anyone who knew Elsie knew she didn't believe it, didn't believe her own words, not even for a second; that she simply wanted to muzzle what was growing society scandal. As if the whole dirty mess weren't already scandalous enough. But hearing it all the panel refused to indict and returned a decision of no bill — in under thirty minutes.

And just like that, Ann Woodward walked free.

That is, if you didn't count the whispers that now promised to haunt her the rest of her life; that promised to saddle her with the acclaim of a common horse thief. With emphasis, in the right circles, on common.

Caldwell couldn't get it out of his head how none of it was justice. Especially, since he wasn't convinced any of them — not Elsie, not Ann; not their high-society lawyers — had anything approaching a conscience.

"Unbelievable, that's what the whole God-damned thing is," the Inspector said, there with Spence and Johns. "Fucking unbelievable. I'm no bleeding heart. I certainly don't have to tell the two of you that. But, God as my witness . . . Even Billy Woodward deserved better."

What happened next was anyone's guess and all bets were on a third ransom note. But, as days became a week and nothing happened the cops began to wonder. Driscoll was growing more and more frustrated with the situation and with Colleen and no matter how hard she tried to make amends their conversations were limited to spare words.

Most interaction was out of simple necessity. And need. This included relations, which had come to nothing in the wake of it all.

Then one night Colleen sidled up to her husband in the dark, wrapping her arms around him from behind, kissing the back of his neck, insinuating herself tight against him, and for the first time since everything had gone south he relented.

It wasn't much. A few grunts and groans and, certainly, little softness. But maybe, she thought, it was a start. She thought this even as she lay alone in the darkness afterward, crying, Driscoll having excused himself without so much as a word once he was done. She could hear him in the kitchen, rummaging through the refrigerator for a beer.

He never returned and as she waited for sleep to come she stared at the ceiling. First to the sound of the television.

Then, to the sound of nothing but static.

All the while the cops were doing anything and everything that could be construed as even the least little bit useful. The Inspector had a wire tap installed on the Goodsons' phone complete with a tape recorder, which could be activated if the kidnapper called. No one did.

Johns and Spence checked stationery stores in search of the paper used for the ransom notes in hopes it might lead somewhere, to no avail. The NYPD kept surveillance on Key's luncheonette and the transit building at Willoughby and Jay, even on the lockers down at Pennsylvania Station, hoping against hope to catch a break. They didn't. The hotline operators continued to field calls, but most of the leads seemed useless.

Nevertheless investigators were ordered to chase even the wildest among them. On the off odd chance. All were odd, it turned out.

There was the report of a Chinese man seen with a white boy on the Staten Island Ferry, another of a woman whose daughter was approached by a man in a car who called out "Girlie!" as she sat on the front porch of her home in Malverne. There was the sighting of a small boy in a Buick with out-of-state plates. None proved worth a tinker's damn.

The Chinaman turned out to be a ferry worker who'd watched the boy when the kid's mother became seasick. The man in the car who'd called out was a mechanic out for a test drive who'd gotten lost — and, was looking for directions. The Buick belonged to a father-and-son from New Hampshire come to visit family out on Long Island.

Still, the calls came. One caller saw a black woman with a white boy in a car in exclusive Garden City, another saw a Negro woman with a blonde-haired boy in a local park. One caller reported to police he'd seen "an Aunt Jemima" — that's what he'd told cops, an *Aunt Jemima* — leading a blonde-haired white boy out of a store in Rockville Centre.

Detectives checked out all of them. Each proved to be a dead end, the result of what had long-been all-too-familiar innuendo.

And, the Inspector? He couldn't get it out of his head that so many black nannies had been left to raise so many rich white kids.

Especially, since he knew first-hand what a lot of those rich white folks said behind closed doors. Behind all their backs.

Then there was the case of Desdemona Lotharios.

It all started when a woman named Janice Buckwright called the police hotline to say her two-year-old daughter had been taken against her will. She informed the cops the perpetrator was Desdemona.

Investigators went to see Janice. They soon learned she was twenty-five; a twice-married, twice-divorced, chronic shoplifter who was mentally unbalanced and unstable. Problem was Desdemona was even worse.

A twenty-nine-year-old prostitute and bar-fly who frequented low-rent drinking establishments on the Queens border in Bellerose, it turned out she was a heroin junkie who sometimes crashed in flop houses in Manhattan. Often, with anyone who could afford the price of a room.

She said she didn't know anything about the girl.

The cops put the squeeze on her and soon she was talking a blue streak. She said she knew a guy, thought the two of them could score some money for drugs. They took the girl, called Janice to say they were holding her for ransom, told the young mother to bring them cash. But Janice just couldn't raise the hundred dollars they'd demanded.

Realizing they were in over their heads, and with no intention of ever caring a lick for the kid, the two left the little girl outside a housing complex somewhere in Brooklyn. Desdemona had no idea where. She told the cops she'd hustled a few johns, turned the tricks under the bridge, made some dough, scored some horse, then went to cook up.

The cops thought it all needle park.

Detectives checked every known associate in hopes of finding the guy, in hopes of finding the little girl. This included drug dealers, drug users, bartenders and bar patrons, confidential informants and neighborhood gossips. It was two days before they located the child.

Turned out she'd been taken in by a woman, who'd found her outside her apartment building wandering about — the girl, covered in bite marks from bedbugs, burn marks from cigarettes, and wearing a nightshirt that was shit-stained and urine-soaked. The woman bathed and fed the girl, then called authorities to report the shocking incident.

Desdemona was arrested, charged with kidnapping. Janice was forced to relinquish all parental custody. The girl was placed in a group home, becoming a ward of the state — marking yet another sad turn in a life filled with them. The guy just up and disappeared, gone with the wind.

None of which led anyone to Bobby Goodson.

As everyone waited and wondered what next the detectives in Mineola received a telegram. It was from police in Tucumcari, New Mexico.

The cops there had found a blonde-haired boy in the train station used by the *Rock Island Line*. He was the right age, but didn't know his name, didn't know how he'd gotten there, didn't know much of anything.

Still, he matched the description of little Bobby.

That the *Rock Island* and *Southern Pacific* serviced Tucumcari made it all the more interesting. You could catch the *New York Central* out of Grand Central Terminal or Pennsylvania Station in Manhattan, take the train to Chicago, transfer, run across Illinois into Iowa, Missouri, Kansas and Texas, and wind up in New Mexico. You could board the *Golden State* in Los Angeles, California, run across to Palm Springs, southeast through Yuma, Arizona, then through Phoenix, Bisbee and Douglas, on out to El Paso, Texas, and end up there. Or you could board the *Rock Island Line* any number of places in Kansas, where the railroad sometimes pulled trains for the circus run by the Royal American Shows — stations in Topeka, Herington, McPherson, Hutchinson, Pratt and Liberal — then get off at the Mission-style station where the boy had been found.

Certainly, it all suggested a range of possibilities.

But while a canvas of the terminal employees turned up clues, most seemed at odds. A janitor thought he'd seen the boy wandering through the station with a woman. A *Rock Island Line* ticketing agent thought she had seen him with a man. No one could recall his arrival in Tucumcari. Not the porters, not the station attendants. Not a taxi driver.

Frustrated, the cops contacted the local newspaper with the story of the lost boy in an attempt to locate passengers who might have arrived on the same train and soon an account was on the national wires. Back in New York reporters scrambled to get in on the action and before long headlines were suggesting maybe Bobby Goodson had been found alive in New Mexico. Certainly, the description provided by the Tucumcari cops made it seem possible, maybe even likely, and a photograph they sent along soon afterward left room for hope amid the doubt.

It wasn't long before those hopes were crushed.

Though Colleen and Driscoll said the boy certainly bore some resemblance both were dead certain it wasn't their son.

"I wish he were," Colleen told Lenore, sure to express her bitter disappointment. "But, trust me, a mother knows."

An onslaught of telegrams deluged police in the wake of Tucumcari. The story made national headlines and everybody and his brother had a theory they wanted to share with the cops via *Western Union*. There were hundreds of notes. Most were dismissed as soon as they'd been read.

Like the one from a man claiming to have a homemade "magnetic searcher" that identified map grids where Bobby could be found. "The U.S. police have no obligation towards me," he wrote, "financial or non-financial. Wishing you luck. My best esteem and faithful prayers."

He claimed to be a priest from somewhere in Minnesota.

Strangely, the telegram came from Beirut. Lebanon.

But if most of the leads were from crackpots — and, almost all were — there was one that piqued the interest of Caldwell and his detectives: from the sheriff's department in Waycross, Georgia. One of their deputies had seen a car in early November at a local diner called *Brother Billy Joe's*

Gone the Whole Hog. The car caught the attention of the deputy because he'd never seen one like it: a cream yellow-and-white Nash-Rambler with out-of-state plates. Caldwell called hoping for more information.

Waycross was in the southeastern end of the state, between Savannah and Valdosta. The deputy stopped, the sheriff told Caldwell, because the cops there had a little game they liked to play on outsiders. They'd pull over any car come through with out-of-state plates, escort it downtown. Drivers figured they were in for a ticket. Or maybe a night in the calaboose. Instead, they'd be met by the welcome committee, be treated to dinner and a room for the night — and they'd get a free tour of nearby Okefenokee Swamp. The deputy was just about to escort the vehicle into town, the sheriff explained, when a call came over the radio.

"A drunk Cletus Pike gone shootin' at the moon, a'gin," he said. "Least, what he thought were the moon." The deputy had to go.

No one ever saw the car again.

But there was one thing that stood out now having read the story about the missing boy, the sheriff told Caldwell.

The couple driving the car told his deputy they'd come down the East Coast, stopped somewhere near Savannah the night before, and were headed to somewhere in Florida. Panama City rang a bell. They had a blonde-haired boy with them; didn't seem like his parents.

Caldwell asked if the deputy got a license plate.

"Can't help y'all there, I'm 'fraid," the sheriff said.

It wasn't much, though Johns and Spence tried. There were a handful of Air Force bases in Florida, including Tyndall in Panama City.

It seemed like the best place to start.

One-by-one they went through the list, checking base records to see if anyone owned a yellow-and-white Nash-Rambler.

They found one at MacDill in Tampa, another at Eglin Field in Valparaiso; two more at Duke Field, an auxiliary base where the Doolittle Raiders trained in '42 for the historic *Thirty Seconds Over Tokyo* bombing raid on Japan. None proved a worthwhile connection and before long the car search got pushed to the back burner.

Turned out, there were more-pressing matters at hand.

The third note came in December. It was postmarked out of Brooklyn, affixed with a three-cent stamp. It was much like the others, typewritten and neat, with the same hand-drawn symbol in black ink; only this time the kidnapper demanded one-thousand ten-dollar bills and two-hundred-and-fifty twenty-dollar bills. Driscoll was ordered not to Brooklyn but to a tavern on Hillside Avenue, Queens. To do so the kidnapper told him to take the Long Island Rail Road to Floral Park, catch the Little Neck Parkway bus to Hillside Avenue. Driscoll was to walk to the tavern but was not to cross Little Neck Parkway or Hillside Avenue.

Instead, he was ordered to walk on the side of the street facing traffic. He was to answer the tavern pay phone on the first ring.

Again, with the words: "Kilroy is here."

"Remember, I am fair," the kidnapper wrote. "No cops."

Driscoll did as he was told, though the cops still followed him, watching his every move. Detectives used two cars to tail him; officers in plain clothes were stationed in the tavern, in a shoe store across the street, and in a nearby florist shop. Not long after Driscoll arrived the phone rang. The kidnapper ordered him to board another bus, take it to the end of the line, and wait at a phone booth outside a sweet shop in New Hyde Park. Driscoll walked to the stop, let two buses pass without boarding either, then finally stepped onto one and took it to the end.

He got off, walked to the phone booth and waited. The phone rang, he answered. He was directed to a nearby luncheonette.

There, at a pay phone, he found a note.

Driscoll was to walk down several side streets, through a park, onto a block bordered by a wooded area dense with undergrowth. There, the note said, he'd find a cardboard sign on the ground adorned with the letters B.G. — presumably for "Bobby Goodson." He was directed to leave the box containing the ransom on the sign, was directed to keep walking. The route from the luncheonette to the site was to be covered at a "normal pace," the kidnapper warned, adding: "You will be timed."

Driscoll again did as he was told.

Again, except for the cops. They continued to tail him at a distance in their unmarked cars until he reached the park. There, they lost him.

In a panic, they radioed for back-up. Soon the entire area was sealed off by units. Oblivious, Driscoll continued to the site, found the sign; nervously placed the box with the ransom money on top of it. Daylight was fading. It was getting cold. He looked around, saw no one. Just like that, he walked away. When he got back to the luncheonette Johns and Spence were waiting. They said the plain clothes officers had lost him and asked for the location of the drop site. Driscoll seemed confused but handed them the note. Quickly, Johns radioed all nearby units. Cops dispatched to the scene arrived expecting to find the money gone. Instead, it was still there; no one had come to claim it. Everyone was at a loss.

Hours later Driscoll arrived home. A half-empty glass of scotch sat on the table in front of Colleen.

"What happened?" she said, jumping off the couch as he walked through the door. "Where's Bobby?"

Before Driscoll could answer the phone rang. He and Colleen looked at each other, surprised.

"I have a call for Mr. Goodson," the operator said.

"This is Mr. Goodson," he said.

A man came on the line.

"Remember, I am fair," he said, in a stern voice. "I told you that. But you brought the cops again and, I have to say, you're beginning to try my patience. Next time is the last time, Mr. Goodson. No police!"

The line went dead.

Driscoll stood, visibly shaken. Colleen stepped toward him.

"What is it?"

He dropped the phone. "The kidnapper," he said.

She threw her arms around him, crying. He hugged her, too. They stood holding onto each other, crying.

After what seemed an eternity she finally asked what happened and he told her the story, all of it. She was still crying when he went to call the Inspector. As Driscoll dialed he realized he'd forgotten to turn on the tape recorder. Beside himself, he wondered if he'd ever see his son again.

The next day a story appeared in *Newsday*. Lenore Terranova wrote it and, much to the surprise of everyone involved, it cited a law enforcement source who detailed the history of the ransom notes, the failed meetings with the kidnapper, the call. The Inspector was outraged.

The cops had kept the whole ordeal under wraps and just like that, here it was, out in the open. Caldwell wondered what the kidnapper would think. If he'd be scared off, if he'd harm Bobby. If they'd have a prayer of catching him now. The Commissioner called him on the carpet, screamed at him until he was blue in the face. The first thing the Inspector did afterwards was to summon Lenore — and read her the riot act.

"You've jeopardized everything. Do you realize that?"

"So now you're blaming me?"

"You wrote it, didn't you?"

"Yes."

"Then why shouldn't I blame you?"

She stared at him in disbelief.

"So, what? I'm the reason the cops haven't caught the kidnapper? I'm the reason *you* haven't found Bobby Goodson?"

"God damn it, Lenore," Caldwell said, tossing the newspaper onto the desk in front of her. "Don't you understand? This . . . this story you wrote. It might have just cost us everything, everything we've been working for."

"Someone obviously didn't share that opinion."

"Who? Who told you this?"

"Why? It's not true?"

"I didn't say it was, didn't say it wasn't. That wasn't what I asked." He mashed a cigarette into the ashtray. "Who?"

"You know I can't tell you that."

"Why not?" She didn't answer. "I said, 'Why not?'"

"Because I can't. You, of all people, should know better."

Frustration building, Caldwell shook his head. "That's it."

"That's it?"

"That's it," he said, again. "We're done here."

"So that's how it's going to be, huh?"

"Yeah," he said, almost under his breath.

As she reached the door, Lenore turned to Caldwell.

"You ever consider this story might actually open some doors? That maybe it just might pry something loose?"

"Don't take this wrong," he said. "But go *fuck* yourself."

All of what happened next was pure misery for Caldwell. The phone calls from reporters, the questions. The denials. And he couldn't get it out of his head what he'd said to Lenore. He knew he'd hurt her; knew how unprofessional he'd been. He'd taken it all out on the wrong person.

But, he was just so angry. So pissed off.

Then came the call that changed his thinking. It was from a telephone company supervisor who said an operator had overheard the call to Driscoll Goodson. Johns and Spence immediately rushed in to tell him the news. The next few hours were nervous ones for the Inspector. He drank a lot of coffee, paced his office, chain-smoked a pack of *Luckys*.

Mostly, he waited. He hated waiting.

When the detectives returned he thought Johns almost giddy, while Spence wore a slight smirk.

"I think," Johns said, "we've got it. We've finally got it."

"Don't just stand there," Caldwell said. "Fucking tell me."

The operator said a man called requesting to be connected to the Goodson residence. She thought he sounded anxious and so, once she put him through, she stayed on the line. She wasn't supposed to do this; but, operators often did. She heard the man say: "Remember, I am fair." And once she heard that she'd decided to eavesdrop on the entire conversation. What she'd heard shocked her. She wrote down the number he'd called from, wrote down the time of the call, what he'd said.

She swore if the cops could find him she could identify him. By voice, alone. Her supervisor told the cops she had the uncanny ability to recognize a voice. "Her memory of voices is unusually accurate," he said.

"Unusually accurate?"

"Unusually accurate, Inspector," Johns said, again, recounting the conversation. "We've sent officers out to the address listed for the number she gave us. They're grabbing the guy as we speak."

Caldwell was near-delirious. Soon they'd have the kidnapper and, with any luck, maybe even Bobby Goodson. He couldn't believe their good fortune. The tables had turned so fast. He knew he'd owe Lenore a big apology. He could live with that if that was the worst of it now.

"Mike," the Inspector said to Johns, reaching out to shake his hand. "Michael," he said with a nod, as he shook hands with Spence.

"Good work, you two. Really good work."

He stepped back, lit up another *Lucky*. He looked like the weight of the world had been lifted from his shoulders.

"Let me know when they bring him in, okay?" Like a big shot he blew out a ream of smoke. "Where's the operator?"

"She's downstairs," Johns said.

"Good. We'll need to arrange for a line-up. One where we use only voices, have everyone read from the ransom notes or something."

"Sure thing."

"And we're sure this woman will be able to recognize his voice?"

"That's what her boss said."

"God, I hope to hell he's right," Caldwell said.

He grinned, ear-to-ear. The two Mikes had never seen him like this, turned to each other, smiled, knowing they'd done good work.

"One more thing," Caldwell said.

"Sure," Johns said.

"What's her name?"

"Who?"

"The operator. What's her name?"

Johns took a quick glance at his notepad.

"It's Helen . . . Helen Keller."

The cigarette fell from the Inspector's hand.

"Helen Keller? Helen *fucking* Keller?"

The two detectives stared at him, dumbfounded.

"Helen *fucking* Keller? That's what you said?"

Nervously, Johns glanced again at his notepad. "Yup. That's it."

Cursing under his breath, Caldwell turned and kicked the garbage can. It ricocheted off the wall, trash flying everywhere.

"What?" Johns said.

Caldwell leaned against his desk. "You don't know?"

"Know what?" Spence said.

"Am I talking to you, shit-for-brains? I'm talking to Mike, here. You really don't fucking know, do you? *Helen Keller?*"

He turned, reached for another cigarette from the pack on his desk, turned back. "God damn it. I've got *two* fucking idiots."

He took a drag from his smoke. "Unusually accurate, huh?"

The two men shrugged. Johns nodded yes.

"Helen Keller was deaf, dumb and blind, Mike. A God-damned *mute*. She couldn't see, couldn't hear . . . You *see* what I'm getting at? Do you fucking *hear* me?" The room was filled with silence.

Helen Keller silence.

Finally, Spence said: "But it's not her."

Caldwell flicked his cigarette at him. Spence ducked as it flashed past his head. "I know it's not her, you fucking moron."

"What's the problem, then?" Johns said.

"What's the fucking problem? The problem, Mike, is the God-damn lawyers, the fucking press." He stood, glaring.

"They're going to have my ass with this."

He was a student who, it turned out, lived with his mother and younger brother on Jefferson Street, a quiet block in Franklin Square. His father had been killed in a train crash on the Long Island Rail Road five years earlier; November, 22, 1950, the day before Thanksgiving. Seventy-eight died in the wreck, another three-hundred-sixty-three injured.

One witness said the victims were packed in the crushed rail cars like sardines in their own blood.

Neighbors said Joe Devlin was never the same after that, that he'd become a loner. After high school he went to Hofstra College, whose campus abutted Meadowbrook Field, a short drive from the IGA and the Goodson home. He was a senior now; was, by all accounts, managing.

Those who knew the family, though, said times were tough. The insurance settlement had only gone so far.

The cops brought Devlin in; ran him through the strange, unorthodox lineup, the one using only voice recognition as the identifying factor. They had him read from the ransom notes, along with four others.

Miracle of miracles, Helen Keller picked him, picked his voice, from the very first reading. So they took him down to interrogation.

From the start he denied any knowledge. He was twenty-two, had a future ahead of him. Why would he chance taking this boy?

Cops searched the house on Jefferson high and low. There was no sign Bobby Goodson had ever been there. Mrs. Devlin and Joe's younger brother both swore they had no idea what anyone was talking about when grilled by police. The Inspector needed answers, needed them quick.

"Where is he?"

"I don't know what you're talking about," Devlin said.

"Don't fuck with me," Caldwell said. "Where's the boy?"

It went on like that for hours. Until, finally, Joe Devlin began to crack. The cops had a typewriter, taken from his room. They had the paper. They'd found carbons of the notes tucked inside his dresser drawer. They'd even found the black pen used to draw the strange symbol.

It was only a matter of time, Caldwell told him, before investigators matched his handwriting. Before they found witnesses who could place him at the call locations. At the luncheonette in Brooklyn. At the transit station. At the tavern in Queens; at the pay phones in New Hyde Park.

At all the places Driscoll Goodson was ordered to go.

The Inspector said the cops had the two boys, Tommy DeAndrea and Billy Condon, both who'd identify him as the man in the Navy pea coat who handed them torn dollar bills. Which didn't take into account, he said, that they also had Galen Carroll, the drifter who'd Devlin promised a sawbuck and a good bottle of scotch — if he'd only retrieve the ransom money from the lockers down at Pennsylvania Station

Caldwell hovered over the table in the interrogation room staring hard at Devlin; seated across, Johns and Spence glared at him, too.

"I'm going to ask you one last time. Where's the boy?"

Devlin stared at the Inspector. "I don't know," he said.

Caldwell pounded a fist on the table. "What the hell do you mean you don't know? Where the hell is he?"

"I don't know," Devlin said, again. "I didn't take him."

Joe Devlin said he'd been taking a test at school when Bobby Goodson went missing. Further investigation proved he was telling the truth.

A professor swore Devlin was in class that afternoon and couldn't have taken Bobby. He brought in a test booklet and an attendance list of students as proof. The cops spent two days tracking down classmates. Each recalled Devlin; swore it wasn't possible he could've been anywhere else. It turned out Devlin had followed the stories; saw the chance to make some fast cash to help his mom. He didn't see the harm; he hadn't taken the boy. Besides, he'd read Driscoll's parents owned a big farm in Kansas. He told the cops he figured the Goodsons could afford it.

The police couldn't charge Devlin with kidnapping. He didn't do it. But they could charge him with extortion. And they most certainly did.

He faced a long prison sentence. It was all little consolation.

Bobby Goodson was still missing. And, still, no one had any idea what happened to him and now they seemed further removed from the truth than they'd been when they'd first started. Which was infuriating.

But what really angered Caldwell was not just the wasted time. It was that Joe Devlin considered it some sort of joke.

Proof was the symbol he'd used on the ransom notes.

Just before the cops had placed Devlin under arrest the Inspector took those notes, spread them out on the interrogation room table.

"I want to know," he said, pointing to the symbol. "What's it mean?"

Devlin smirked.

"I saw it on a children's show, *Space Funnies.*"

"And?"

"And it's the symbol for the planet Uranus."

He smirked again. *"Uranus."*

His mug shot later showed him sporting the nastiest black eye and when a shackled Joe Devlin was led into court to stand at arraignment there also were angry bruises on his back, chest, arms and legs.

The cops, to a man, all swore he fell.

20

Driscoll and Colleen were barely talking.

On Christmas Eve he came home, didn't say a word, and she went to bed alone while he sat on the sofa in front of the television. Hours later she awoke to the sound of him crying in the dark.

She found him leaned hard against the wall, all shadowy in the meager glow of the Christmas lights. He was staring at the tree, at the red wagon he'd promised Bobby, and it wasn't long before she bent down to cry alongside him. Shoulder-to-shoulder they sat — mother and father, husband and wife; two lost souls, two complete strangers — nary a word between them. They sat like that forever, it seemed; closer than they'd ever been and yet more distant. They ended up in bed, in the dark, and held each other through the night. When Colleen woke early Christmas morning Driscoll was gone. She walked out to the living room.

The wagon was gone. The tricycle, which had been in the corner since the afternoon of Bobby's disappearance, was gone, too.

Out in the yard she saw him at the tree, knife in hand. He'd cut the rope and she watched as he took the tire swing around the house, listened as he lifted the garage door. Getting back into bed she pretended to be asleep. It wasn't long before she heard the car engine and looked out just in time to see him drive off. She had no idea where he'd gone, when he'd return. She fed Johanna, brought her into bed and slept through to the late afternoon. She woke only when she heard the car door slam.

Still in bed, Colleen waited for Driscoll. He went to the refrigerator, made himself a sandwich, sat down to watch television. She found him asleep on the sofa when she went to get a bottle for Johanna. Then Colleen went back to bed thinking what a Christmas it'd been.

The second week of January Inspector Caldwell received a letter via certified mail. It was from Driscoll's father and it was as unusual as it was unexpected. Norman Goodson wrote to say he'd heard a carload of Negroes had passed through nearby Strong City in early November, stopping at a gas station in town. One of those Negroes, the driver, told the attendant he had no money for gasoline but offered to trade a suit for a fill-up and some food. The attendant hesitated, Norman wrote, but the driver was persuasive. He produced a receipt showing the garment had been purchased at a store in New York City sometime in October.

Sensing a deal, the attendant made the trade. But, pondering it all afterward the man at the service station found it odd. So did Norman.

In his letter he wrote:

> If this Negro was in such need of money he would sell the clothes off his back, I believe it possible he also might drive East to New York, possibly to Hempstead Plains, to snatch a young child for ransom. God knows this child could be my grandson. I think it the duty of the police to investigate this and trust you will do so immediately.

Caldwell thought it a crock. Still, he had his detectives contact the station attendant, get information about the clothing receipt, then track the purchase. It took Herculean effort. But Johns and Spence soon learned the garment had indeed been sold at a store on West 34th Street, Manhattan. The owner checked his records. He'd sold the suit in October. Paid for with cash. He didn't have a name just a telephone number.

The detectives tracked it all down.

It belonged to a man in Kansas City. A Negro man.

They made inquiries, first with the man's family, then with local police. The man was a doctor. He had no police record and, in fact, had served in World War II, decorated for his meritorious service.

Turned out, for saving a white officer in France.

When Johns reached the man he said he'd bought the suit in New York; that he'd been there for the funeral of his mother-in-law.

He'd offered to drive some relatives home to Hutchinson and, along the way, he'd lost his wallet. Out of cash he had no choice but to trade the suit. He said he was surprised the white attendant took the deal.

Old man Katsch died in February. Colleen went to the funeral. It was a few days after a snowstorm and she took a bus, then a cab, to the graveyard, a Jewish cemetery, and arrived as they were lowering the casket into the ground. It was frigid, a brisk wind blowing. Fresh dug dirt soiled the white snow and she stood at a distance, underneath an old oak, far from the crowd around the grave. She felt out of place.

She'd stopped going to the IGA after Bobby disappeared. It made her uncomfortable. Now as she stood there she saw all the old familiar faces: Edith, Myrtle, Jimmy Dodge. The women kept whispering, turning to stare. She thought to leave but decided not. Old man Katsch had been her friend, had believed in her. She owed him that much.

When it was over the women walked to a line of parked cars. None came over, though Colleen could see them staring like she was a common criminal. After most everyone had gone Jimmy Dodge came walking up.

"It's a good thing you weren't over there at the grave, Mrs. Goodson," he said. "I don't think you would have liked it."

"I know. It's so sad. I really liked Mr. Katsch."

"Not because of Katsch."

"The girls?"

Jimmy shook his head. "They were all talking about you."

"I can only imagine."

"I bet you can." He gave Colleen the once over, pulled keys from his jacket. "You look cold, Mrs. Goodson. Can I give you a ride?"

She smiled. "I could go for that."

She took him by the arm as they walked towards his car and once they'd gotten in he smiled, turning the heat on full blast. Soon it was nice and toasty and then they were headed back to Hempstead Plains.

"What'd they say, Jimmy?"

"The girls?"

"I saw them whispering. What'd they say?"

"I don't think you want to know."

"That bad?"

"They called you a murderer," he said. "Said you killed your son."

He heard her gasp and by the time Jimmy Dodge stopped the car on the side of the road Colleen was hysterical, tears streaming down her cheeks. He reached into his pocket for a handkerchief but she was too far gone. He sat there watching her, not knowing what to do.

Suddenly, she hugged him and Jimmy put his arms around her, held her tight. She grabbed even harder, pressed into him, sobbing.

It was some time before she'd calmed.

When Colleen let go she turned, stared out at the snow-covered ground, the snow-covered trees. The sun was low in the sky.

"What do you think?" she said.

"Me?"

She turned to him, eyes black where her make-up had run.

"What do you think?"

"I never believed it. I always thought you were swell."

"Really?"

He shrugged. "Sure."

Colleen leaned over, gave him a kiss on the cheek. Then, still sniffling, she hugged him again, this time tighter than before.

"Thank you, Jimmy," she whispered.

As she moved back to her side, she said: "We should go."

Neither said much most of the way back to Hempstead Plains, though it wasn't an uncomfortable silence. At one point Jimmy leaned his hand on the seat and Colleen slid hers over, squeezed. She felt a surge. It had been a lifetime since she'd felt like that, the situation at home considered. Things between her and Driscoll had been reduced to nothing, almost.

Sex had become random, rare; purely out of necessity. She glanced at Jimmy. He was so young, barely a high school senior, and she thought he looked sweet with his sandy blonde hair and smooth skin. But he was lean and muscular and she could tell he was fighting hard not to look at her.

Without a word Jimmy turned the car into a deserted school parking lot, stopped near the back of the building.

She didn't ask what he was doing, why he'd done so. She knew. And she knew at that very moment she wanted him to. Really wanted him.

As he grabbed her she whispered, "Thank you for believing me." He was too busy groping and didn't answer.

The two of them began to kiss and Colleen looked at him with bedroom eyes as she unbuckled his belt right there in the front seat. He fumbled open his pants, greenly, as she started to hike up her dress to remove her undergarments. The parking lot lights flickered on forming bright patches in the snow that fell off, ethereal, at the edges.

Then she saw them: a small group of boys carrying sleds, coming through the lot. Jimmy was sliding his pants down now.

But Colleen was frozen, staring.

There were four, maybe five of them, no more than twenty feet from the car. The windows had begun to steam and the boys were too young and too unaware to have the vaguest idea what was going on. But Colleen couldn't take her eyes off them, especially this one little boy with blonde hair. Jimmy reached for her, trying to pull her down onto him, anxious and forceful, but she resisted. She was fixated on the boy.

"Bobby," she whispered.

She felt Jimmy tug on her again but all Colleen could see was her son. She couldn't seem to get the image out of her head.

She began to cry.

Pants half-down, Jimmy looked out nervously, expecting to see a cop. Instead, he saw the boys turn the corner of the school, Colleen crying.

"What?" he said.

She looked at him like she'd seen a ghost. He tried to pull her back onto him. She pushed away, falling back against the door.

"What's going on?" he said, frustrated.

The parking lot lights caught Jimmy just right, blinding his face.

"Bobby?" Colleen whispered, again, crying harder now.

"I thought we were going to do this?" Jimmy Dodge said.

"I can't," she said, starting to fix herself. "I'm sorry, I just can't."

"What do you mean you *can't?*"

Colleen tried smoothing out her dress. "I just can't."

Jimmy slammed his hand against the steering wheel.

"So that's it? You *can't?*" She shook her head. "Maybe it's your guilty conscience," he said.

She started to say something but he just snickered. "That's what it is, isn't it?" he said. "You really *are* a murderer, *aren't* you?"

"Jimmy!"

He glared at her. "You are. You *killed* him."

She was near hysterical now but Jimmy had all he could take. He lunged toward her and it scared her. Instead, he pushed open the door.

"Get out!" he screamed, shoving her out into the cold.

She fell back out of the seat, onto the snow-covered ground.

As he started off, Jimmy Dodge yelled at her: "My mother thinks you're a murderer, too!"

Cold, confounded and confused, Colleen walked home in a daze. An hour later she stepped into the house, shivering, disheveled.

Driscoll ignored her.

It wasn't long before Driscoll neared the end of his hitch. And though it might have sounded callous there really wasn't any reason to stay on in Hempstead Plains. The cops weren't close to finding Bobby. Driscoll thought it time to go home. Then, just weeks before he was to be discharged, his thinking changed. It happened on the Fourth of July in nearby Westbury. Betty Weinberger had wrapped her one-month-old son Peter in a blanket, set him down in his carriage for a nap on the front porch. She'd gone inside to do errands. Ten minutes later she went to check on him — and, to her horror, he was gone. Simply gone. The ransom note was handwritten, in green ink. Scrawled, he wrote:

> Attention. I'm sorry this had to happen, but I am in bad need of money & couldn't get it any other way. Don't tell anyone or go to the Police about this, because I am watching you closely. I am scared stiff & will kill the baby at your first wrong move . . .

The Weinbergers were instructed to gather two-thousand dollars in small bills, place them in an envelope, leave it beside a signpost on the corner of Albemarle Road by ten the next morning.

The kidnapper promised once he'd gotten paid he'd return Peter "safe & happy." His sign-off was perverse: "Your baby sitter."

Despite the ominous warning Betty Weinberger called the Nassau County Police. Soon after Inspector Caldwell was on the phone with Driscoll and Colleen. Chances were the incidents were unrelated. Unlike Bobby's disappearance, the kidnapper had left a note at the scene. But, Caldwell said, the boy was taken from a carriage. The location wasn't far from where Bobby disappeared. There could be a connection.

The press got wind of the story soon after. Morris Weinberger pleaded with reporters not to run with it, fearing the consequences.

All the papers honored the request. All, except *The Daily News.*

It ran it on the front page.

Police made a drop-off. The kidnapper never came.

That morning Driscoll went to Meadowbrook Field, requested a three-month extension on his hitch. General Johnson made sure he got it.

Days went by with no word. The cops still had no link between the Weinberger kidnapping and the disappearance of their son.

Lenore wrote a story about how Bobby Goodson remained missing.

She quoted Colleen, who said: "I can't imagine what the Weinbergers are going through, though I know what it's like when your child is gone and no one knows what happened and everyone thinks you're responsible and maybe somehow you are. It's terrible. Really, just terrible."

Six days after Peter Weinberger was taken the kidnapper called with new instructions for a ransom drop.

Everyone did as they were told but he never showed. A blue cloth bag was found at the site. Inside was a note telling the Weinbergers where to find their son "if everything goes smooth." Police examined the note and decided it was written by the same person who'd written the first ransom note. That didn't mean they were any closer to catching him.

Because it was classified as a kidnapping from the start the Federal Bureau of Investigation stepped in on July 11 — a marked difference from the Goodson case. And unlike the search for Bobby investigators had hard evidence from the get — the handwritten notes. Investigators pored by hand through millions of writing samples in a myriad of official records: New York State Department of Motor Vehicle application forms, voter registration documents, probation files, even income tax returns.

They caught a break.

Six weeks in an agent at the U.S. Probation Office in Brooklyn thought the handwriting in the notes looked a lot like a handwritten statement in the file of a convicted bootlegger from Plainview, Long Island. Angelo LaMarca was a taxi cab dispatcher and a truck driver and he had two kids, a wife and a lifetime of unpaid bills. Agents went and arrested him.

It didn't take long before he confessed.

None of which meant a damned thing. The investigation found no link between the Peter Weinberger kidnapping and Bobby Goodson.

LaMarca did one, but he hadn't done the other.

Down on his luck, LaMarca said he'd been threatened by a loan shark, was desperate for cash. Out driving, he saw Betty Weinberger setting her son out in the carriage and decided that'd be a life-changing plan.

It'd all been on impulse.

He said he'd brought the boy to the ransom drop site the next morning but saw the cops there and panicked, leaving the child by the side of the road. Investigators rushed to the site and, in the undergrowth, they'd found the decomposing body of little Peter Weinberger.

He was just thirty-three days old.

For months Johns and Spence had been knocking on doors across Long Island. It was the Inspector's idea. And, it turned out to be the most-terrible of tasks. Not knowing what else to do the cops had compiled an unusual list. An inventory of victims. Victims lost to car accidents and to house fires, victims lost to drownings, incurable illness, deadly disease. In short, lost to any sudden, unexpected circumstance. The dead all had one thing in common. Just one, other than being dead. They were all kids.

It was a shot in the dark.

But Caldwell thought it might somehow lead his men to someone desperate or anguished enough to have taken Bobby Goodson.

First up was a family whose baby was stillborn. Scores of inquiries later the detectives decided they'd had as much as they could take.

"What's this one?" Spence asked, as Johns stopped outside a home one otherwise ordinary September morn.

"Smallpox, scarlet fever? Polio? Judging from the neighborhood, Mike, I'm sort of guessing the kid didn't drown in the family pool."

Johns glanced at the paperwork on the seat between them.

"Motor vehicle accident. That's all it says."

The woman who answered was no more than thirty. She was pretty, petite, and seemed surprised to find two strange men at her doorstep.

"Can I help you?" she said.

Johns forced a smile.

"Sorry to bother you, Ma'am. I'm Detective Johns, this is Detective Spence. We're from the Nassau County Police Depart . . . "

Behind him the rumble of an engine interrupted and he watched as the woman, staring past him into the street, went numb.

The detectives turned to see a big yellow school bus making its way up the block. Neither thought much of it — until they heard the gasp.

They turned back to find the woman, face ashen. She started to faint and, as she did, Johns leapt forward to grab her, catching her on the way down. Spence ran to the bathroom, grabbed a facecloth, soaked it in cold water — and brought it to Johns. As the detective placed the compress to the woman's forehead Spence ran back inside to grab a glass of water.

It was several minutes before the woman was again lucid.

"Why are you here?" she asked Johns.

"We're investigating the disappearance of the boy who went missing last October in Hempstead Plains. We needed to ask a few questions."

"Why me?" she asked.

"Because," Johns said, "and we're sorry to have to bring this up. But, well, our records indicate you lost your son in an accident . . ."

"Oh, my God! How . . . how could you?"

It was September, the first week of school, she told them finally. Her son had come home from kindergarten on the late-morning bus, excited as he stepped into the street. She'd been late getting dressed, watched as children crossed carrying drawings they'd made in class. And then her son dropped his artwork. The bus door had closed, all the kids seemingly free and clear. But he ran to grab the drawing blowing in the wind. Before she could mouth the words, he'd darted to grab it — her little boy in *exactly* the wrong place at *exactly* the wrong time as the bus lurched forward.

"He was such a sweet child. If only I'd gotten dressed sooner."

There wasn't much Johns or Spence could say.

They sat there, watching as she agonized over one solitary moment, an instant, that'd changed her life forever.

"Do you have children?"

Johns shook his head, no. "Neither of us do."

"Then I want to ask you something, both of you, and I want you to think about it before you do this to someone else who's lost a child. You two, knocking on their door, asking such thoughtless questions. Opening such a . . . re-opening up something that's such a terrible wound."

She clenched the handkerchief in her hand.

"How could you possibly know how bad I hurt, how bad my husband hurts? What this has done to us? How hard it's been? There isn't a day that goes by, not a day, when I don't die another death. Not one.

"I miss him so much. We miss him so much."

She was crying harder now. "You should be ashamed of yourselves, both of you," she said, finally. "You should really just be ashamed."

Persuaded, the Inspector called off the interviews. In a few short weeks it would be one year since the disappearance of Bobby Goodson. He was out of suspects, out of leads, out of ideas. He couldn't understand how Driscoll and Colleen could leave Hempstead Plains. Something about that seemed not right. He decided to call them in for one last meeting.

Johns made the call. The Goodsons arrived at headquarters the second week of October. The Inspector sat them down, asked if they'd submit to a truth serum test. Driscoll looked him straight in the eye and said: "I don't think so, Inspector. I don't think so at all."

And that was it.

On the afternoon of October 31, 1956, Caldwell, Johns and Spence met outside the IGA. None of them knew what else to do. By then Driscoll and Colleen were long gone back to Cottonwood Falls. Still, the Inspector thought someone should be at the market to remember Bobby Goodson. There was a chill in the air, Caldwell brought coffee. No one said much.

Mostly, they just all stood around.

Another Christmas came and went, uneventful except for a greeting card to Caldwell from Colleen. It was of a young boy and snow man.

Hope you're having a most pleasant holiday season, as we are. Little Johanna's gotten so big and is talking up a storm. It's been rather cold. We're hoping for snow. A white Christmas would be nice, we've agreed. Hope Santa Claus is good to you! The Goodsons.

"Sounds like they miss the boy terribly," Caldwell said, tossing it onto the desk in front of Johns and Spence. He reached for a smoke.

"You always said there's something not right about them," Johns said.

Caldwell reached into his drawer, grabbed a bottle of whiskey, poured shots into two mugs — one for Johns, one for Spence.

"There's an old Chinese proverb," he said, half-serious. "If you wait by the river long enough the bodies of your enemies will float by."

Spence and Johns eyed him.

He smirked. "Read it in a Fortune cookie."

As the detectives broke out laughing Caldwell held the bottle out, tipped it towards each. "To redemption. Whatever the hell that is."

He took a swig straight from the bottle, set it down, leaned back hard in his chair. Behind him, outside, a light snow had begun to fall.

"Mark my words," he said. "One of these days someone's going to find the body. They always do. Wonder how Mom and Dad will react then?"

They found the body in a box. It was a cold Monday morning in late February in a suburb outside Philadelphia known as Fox Chase.

Made of cardboard and marked "Furniture," it'd once contained a baby's bassinet. It was just in off the side of Susquehanna Road, a narrow rural lane, in dense, snarled underbrush, across from a crooked line of wooden telephone poles and not far from a stand of barren trees. The cops arrived not long after the call, placed by a student who said he'd been out in the field hunting rabbits. A gray winter sky hung in the air.

The ever-alert cops noted the site was a stone's throw from the Good Shepherd School for Wayward Girls.

Reluctantly, the detectives peered into the cardboard container. What they saw repulsed them. Inside was the body of a boy, naked, wrapped in a soiled blanket. His hair had been hastily and haphazardly cut, clumps of it littered in with the corpse. Angry bruises covered his face, stomach and legs. He hadn't been dead long but had been dying forever.

An examination revealed he was three feet tall, about thirty pounds, indicating he was malnourished, scarred. Likely starved. The medical examiner said he couldn't determine an exact age because of it but thought him four or five years old. Detectives pondered the time frame. It had been sixteen months since the news out of Hempstead Plains.

The Philadelphia cops thought he was Bobby Goodson.

Lenore Terranova was in with the Inspector working an unrelated story when Caldwell first got the call from the cops in Philadelphia.

"Give me a second," he said to her, answering.

"I see. You think it's our kid?" He got dead quiet as he listened. "Okay. Tell me where I'm going. We'll be there as soon as we can."

A cigarette smoldered as Caldwell wrote down the directions.

"They found him?" Lenore said, as he hung up the telephone.

He took a quick drag of his *Lucky,* mashed it out.

"Looks that way." Before she could ask another question Caldwell stood, grabbed his overcoat, headed for the door.

As she sat there, stunned, he turned back over his shoulder.

"Fox Chase. Outside Philly. Sorry. Gotta go."

Back in her office Lenore worked the phones. Finally, she got the captain who ran the Homicide Bureau down in Philadelphia.

She grilled him, he stonewalled her.

"Look Miss," he told her. "Not to be rude or nothing. But, I'm running a murder investigation here. I don't have time for this."

But before he could hang up she told him she'd overheard the phone call with Caldwell, knew his men thought they'd found Bobby Goodson.

"I'm not looking to name anyone. All I want to know is am I wrong?"

"No," the captain said, finally. "You didn't get this from me."

"I can't even remember who I called," she said.

Moments later she dialed the number for the Goodson residence in Bazaar. Harriet answered. Listening in, Bill McAllister sensed his reporter was onto something and pulled up a chair. Lenore shot him a look but he just grinned and sat there as she ran through her questions.

"They found the body?" he said, when she was done.

"Looks like it."

"Where?"

"Outside Philadelphia. In a box in some place called Fox Chase."

"And we've got it?" McAllister said. She smiled. "Good work," he said.

"That's not all. I talked to the mom. Goodson's mom, Harriet. He wouldn't come to the phone, but I heard him ask where they found him."

"And?"

"And when she told him he said, 'It's not him.' That's it. 'It's not him.'"

McAllister raised an eyebrow.

"Yeah," Lenore said, as she fed paper into her Remington. "Me, too."

She hesitated as McAllister eyed her, waiting.

"She told me the wife moved out, went to go live with her parents," Lenore said, after a moment. "They're getting divorced."

"The Goodsons?"

"That's what the mother said. Divorced."

McAllister took it all in. "I know that look," Lenore said.

"Write the story," the editor said. "Then go home, pack." He shot her a mischievous grin. "You got a passport?"

"A passport?"

"I can't recall, if Kansas is actually part of America," he said. "But come first thing tomorrow, Lenore, you're headed there on the train."

The train arrived on Friday, the first day of March.

It'd been three days since the Philadelphia cops found the boy in the box, two since Lenore set out from Penn Station bound for Kansas.

As the driver she'd hired pulled to a stop in front of the Grand Central Hotel, she began to wonder what she'd gotten herself into.

There were few streets in downtown Cottonwood Falls. The Grand Central, in a neat red brick building, was on Broadway, the biggest street in town. The stately courthouse sat at the south end of the block, wide and lined with stores. The north end ran smack into old Mill Dam.

Honestly, there wasn't a whole lot more to the place.

Lenore was dying for a shower as she set her bag down. First she needed to call McAllister to find out what'd happened in Philadelphia.

The operator connected the call. Bad news, Bill McAllister said. The Inspector had gone to Philadelphia, Johns and Spence in tow.

From the start no one liked what they saw. The boy was the right height and weight given the time elapsed since Bobby had gone missing and at first glance McAllister said Caldwell thought he bore a strong resemblance. But the hair color was off and the soles of the dead boy's feet were wrinkled, puckered almost, as if they'd been immersed a long time in water. Which made a comparison of footprints to Bobby's birth certificate all but impossible. The hair color could've been explained away, the Inspector said. After all, children born blonde didn't always stay blonde forever. But there was something about the shape of the dead boy's head. Somehow, Caldwell thought, it just seemed wrong.

There was one way to tell for certain if the dead child was Bobby. Colleen had told detectives her son had fallen off his tricycle, broken his arm. It was right there in the statement she'd given down at headquarters. The Philadelphia medical examiner took X-rays of the body: head, chest, legs, arms. Despite all the bruising it appeared the mysterious dead boy had never suffered any actual broken bones. Not a one.

"Which could mean only one thing," Caldwell told the reporter McAllister had call. "The dead kid isn't and never was Bobby Goodson."

Who he was, who he'd been, no one knew. At that moment the Nassau cops didn't much care and, truth was, neither did McAllister.

Sad to say, neither did Lenore.

"Look Bill," she said. "There's still a story, even if this kid down in Philadelphia isn't our kid. Dead or alive, Bobby Goodson's still out there. And his parents are still headed for divorce because of it. I need to talk to them, sooner the better. I'll call soon as I do. Promise."

Before McAllister could answer she hung up the phone.

Back in the car, headed to the Goodson farm down in Bazaar, Lenore began to think McAllister right.

She'd grabbed two books from the morgue before leaving. One a Willa Cather novel, the other an atlas. On the train she'd read a handful of chapters from the novel. It sounded so beautiful, the Plains of that time did, and yet so utterly foreign. Then she'd thumbed through the atlas, surprised to find Chase County was almost dead center in the middle of the country. Almost dead center east and west, north and south.

As the car rolled down Highway 177 she thought it unlike any America she knew. Kansas 177 ran just east of town. To the north it stretched a mile or two, past the depot that serviced the Falls, across the river, to the railroad station and rodeo grounds in neighboring Strong City. Past that was the Tallgrass Prairie. South, it sliced like a knife through barren, rolling hills and endless farm fields — some fallow, others gold with winter wheat — as it shadowed a lonely, solitary spur of the *Atchison, Topeka and Santa Fe* down to Bazaar. There were few houses.

She'd never seen such isolation.

Turning into the long dirt drive at the Goodson farm it took forever to reach the house. Driscoll and Norman were outside, working on a tractor.

"Hope I'm not intruding," Lenore said, as she walked toward them.

It was cold and a light snow dotted the air with a smattering of late-season flakes. Norman looked hot under the collar.

Polite-as-could-be, he said: "Actually Miss, me and my son are a bit busy at the moment, if you don't mind."

Before Norman could say another word Driscoll stopped him.

Reluctantly, Norman stepped away, announcing he was going inside to put on a fresh pot of coffee.

"I take it you're not surprised to see me," Lenore said.

Driscoll shrugged. "I suppose."

"Well, I suppose I'm surprised to be here." She looked around. "I'm not sure what I expected, but I'm pretty sure this wasn't it."

"How's that?"

"I've tried to talk to you a number of times, now. You haven't exactly been cooperative. I thought maybe you were just rude. Now I'm guessing you probably didn't do a whole lot of talking growing up out here."

"The police find my son?"

"You already know the answer, Mr. Goodson."

"Driscoll." He gave her the once-over. "My father's Mr. Goodson."

"Okay, Driscoll," she said. "I'm sure you're relieved about the news."

"I didn't think it was him."

"I heard you say that," she said. "How did you know?"

"I didn't," he said. "I guess I just didn't want to imagine it was."

Lenore stepped towards him.

Hands smeared with grease and oil from the tractor Driscoll thought about wiping them on his overalls, instead grabbed a nearby rag.

"I can't imagine."

"No, you can't," he said, wiping his hands.

"Look, I know it's been a roller coaster since day one." Driscoll didn't answer. Just took the rag, tossed it onto the nearby tractor seat.

"What's going on with you and your wife?" she said.

He shot her a look. "It's private."

"I'm sorry?"

"I said, 'It's private.' Let's leave it at that."

"So, that's it?"

The snow was falling harder now, cold enough to see your breath. Driscoll rolled down the ends of his plaid winter flannel.

"You might not understand," he said, finally. "But sometimes things are best kept to yourself. People around here respect that."

Lenore tried not to shiver, hands freezing. She closed her notebook, stuffed it into her purse. Down the drive, her driver sat waiting.

"Fair enough," she said, reaching to shake Driscoll's hand. It caught him by surprise. He seemed unsure what to do. "Thank you for your time, Mr. Goodson," she said. "I'm sorry if I've made things tougher."

"I love my wife," he said, after a moment. "I probably always will. No matter what you or anyone else thinks, we both loved our son. We've been through a lot. All of it's been far from easy. Fact is, it's been downright hard. What happens next, I have no idea."

His eyes were red. He looked down, not wanting her to see. He scuffed his foot on the driveway kicking up old dirt and new snow.

"They say everything happens for a reason," he said. "But I've done a lot of thinking and, pardon the expression, but I'll be damned if I know what it is. None of it makes any sense. I'm not sure it ever will. I blamed her, blamed myself. It hasn't solved a damned thing. I keep thinking he's got to be out there. It's the only thing I can think."

At that moment, watching him, agonizing, Lenore felt truly sorry for him. She thought to leave, to just turn and walk away, and for the briefest of instants she started. But in the end she just couldn't help herself.

"You just can't forgive her, can you?" she said.

He sounded defeated. And he never looked up, just stood there, staring at the scattered snow.

"I'd appreciate it if you let us be, now," he said.

"Please, just let us be."

The conversation was still playing out in her head a half-hour later, Lenore wondering what Colleen had to say about all of it, as her driver turned onto the block where the Tetherwoods lived in Cottonwood Falls.

Then she saw the police cars.

The old Homestead house had seen better days, need of paint being the least of them. Lenore stepped out, asked what was going on.

"And who might you be, Miss?" one of the cops asked.

She explained and the officer pointed to a man standing on the front porch. Late middle-aged, he wore a winter coat and black trousers.

"See the father," he said.

The father?

Walking across the lawn to the house, she said: "Mr. Tetherwood?"

The man and the officer he was speaking with turned, surprised.

The man wore a clerical collar.

"May I help you?" he said, stepping down off the porch.

"Mr. Tetherwood?"

"No, dear," he said. "I'm Reverend Elias."

"I came to see Colleen," Lenore said. "Is she okay?"

"Are you a friend?"

"Yes and no, Reverend. I'm a reporter. From New York. I came to talk to Colleen about, well . . . Please tell me nothing's happened to her."

"It's her father," the Reverend said. The minister took a glance over his shoulder, back to where the solitary officer was standing near the open front door, turned again to Lenore. "I'm afraid Mr. Tetherwood's dead."

It took a moment for the words to register. "Dead?"

The Reverend nodded. "Yes, dear. About an hour or so ago."

Excusing himself, the minister was up the front steps and into the house — leaving Lenore alone on the lawn in the falling snow.

The block was quiet. Dead quiet. *Mr. Tetherwood's dead.*

She took note most neighbors stood, hovering, on their comforting porches. Curious, but sure to remain a polite distance. Wood smoke billowed from chimneys, sweetening the air, and a thickening layer of snow drifted along the rooftops. A maze of footprints crisscrossed the lawn, blades of winter grass poked through where the new-fallen blanket of white had been crushed under the scurrying weight of men.

All of it seemed so at odds. *Mr. Tetherwood's dead.*

A crow cawed. Startled, Lenore turned but couldn't find it.

"Excuse me?" She turned back to find Reverend Elias. "I've spoken with Colleen, Miss. I'm sorry, but I didn't get your name. Are you Miss Terranova?" Lenore shook her head yes. "I've spoken with Colleen," the Reverend said. "She said she'd like to speak with you." Lenore noticed the Bible in his hand. "I think we should talk, first. She's devastated."

"I understand."

"I'm not sure you do," he said. "Her father killed himself."

Dumbstruck, Lenore stood speechless.

"We're all shocked," the Reverend said. "At least some of us are. It's just so horrific, after all that's happened, poor girl. The disappearance of her son. Her brother running off, like he did. Then, her mother. The situation with her husband headed where it is. Now this." Reverend Elias reached out, placed a hand on Lenore's shoulder. "You had no idea?"

"No, I didn't."

The minister told her about Franklin going AWOL, how Colleen's mother had run off the previous week — apparently, with another man.

"The father," Reverend Elias said. "To be honest, he's always been trouble. There's a lot of folks in town won't be sad to see him go, harsh as that sounds. Let's just say he was a complicated man. I think he'd just had enough of his . . . " He looked her in the eye. "Enough of his demons."

"Demons?"

"We all have our demons, Miss. I'm afraid Chardon more than his share. He was quite a drinker, a mean drunk at that. I think he didn't have much joy. And, I'm not sure he knew how to remedy that. At least that's what I got from my time with Colleen. We've talked a lot of late."

"That's sad," Lenore said.

"Truly sad," Reverend Elias said. "There's a lot of lost souls out there. Otherwise, folks like you and me, well . . .

"We'd be in some other line of work now, wouldn't we?"

Lenore forced a weak smile.

"One thing, before I go in. How did he die?" The minister hesitated. "There's not a lot I haven't heard, Reverend," she said.

Snow was coming harder, now. The Reverend breathed the chill air in deep, said best anyone could tell Chardon Tetherwood had taken a shotgun, sat down in a chair, placed the butt-end on the kitchen floor, leaned over the barrel — and used a big old switch to set the trigger.

Colleen said she'd been in the other room, heard the blast.

She'd found him on the floor.

"A bloody mess, it was," the Reverend said. "Just unspeakable, the poor thing. But when she finally calmed Colleen told me it was the same stick her father had used to beat her and her brother as kids."

"The same stick?" Lenore said.

"Same stick. Imagine that?"

Colleen was on a settee when Lenore walked in.

She looked relieved to see a familiar face and leapt from the seat like a child running to her daddy come home from work.

"I'm so sorry," Lenore said, as Colleen embraced her.

"Oh, Lenore. You have no idea," Colleen said, crying harder now. She held tight for what felt like an eternity. Then, releasing her hold, she smiled best she could. "It's so good to see you," she said.

"The Reverend told me what happened."

"It was just so . . . so awful, Lenore."

"I can't imagine."

"Don't." She wiped a tear running down her cheek. "I just can't tell you how good it is to see a familiar face. It's been a day."

Soon, Colleen was back seated, telling hide story.

"And then I heard the bang," she said. "I was in with Johanna, playing with some toys, and then there was this explosion." She shuddered. "After the plane crash, Lenore. Well, I thought the worst, of course. Like maybe the house had blown up or something. I was surprised when I ran out of the room and found it all still standing."

Her lip began to quiver. "Then I went into the kitchen."

She closed her eyes. "My God, it was awful."

Colleen began to weep and Lenore went to get some hand linens. She found herself at the kitchen door, a white sheet spread out in front of her, covering the body. Blood was everywhere: caked and drying on a kitchen chair pushed against the near wall; smeared across the wooden floor; puddled where it had run into gaps between the floorboards.

There were spattered droplets on the soiled white door.

Macabre as it was Lenore knew she just needed to see for herself, the corpse, and was about to step through when someone said: "Don't go in there." She turned to find a police officer walking down the hall.

"Don't go in there, Miss," he said, again.

Behind him two men wheeled a stretcher.

"These men have work to do, Miss. You need to go back inside and sit with Colleen, if you please. And please close the door."

She didn't want to, but Lenore went inside, closed the door. Nary a word between them they sat listening to the muddled voices, to the stilted movements, until all that was left was the sound of silence.

Then they heard footsteps coming.

"Sorry to bother, but I wanted to let you know we're on our way," the officer said. He motioned to the kitchen. "Is there someone who can take care of it? Maybe a neighbor? You shouldn't have to . . . "

Colleen dabbed at her eyes. "Someone will be over."

"Alright then, Ma'am. Look, if you need anything . . . "

She forced a weak smile but didn't answer. And then that was that.

Not long after there was a knock on the door. Lenore answered to find a neighbor woman, bucket and mop in hand. She smiled, slightly.

"Frightful day," she said. "Just frightful."

Outside, the light was fading.

Lenore knew there were still questions to be answered, work to be done. She had to call McAllister. She had to interview Colleen.

There was a story to write.

"I know this isn't easy," she said. "But, you know I have to ask."

"Seems like we've done this too many times, now, haven't we?" Colleen said, forcing a weak smile. "You know, it's just so . . . "

"What?" Lenore said.

"Such a mess," Colleen said. "My life is such a mess."

She let out a nervous laugh.

"Remember that first night," she said, "the night you first knocked on my door, and you were asking me about Bobby and I asked if you'd ever made a mistake? If you ever thought it was going to cost you?"

"Yes," Lenore said.

"Well, I've done a lot of thinking since then, a lot of growing up. I guess I never realized how much of it I had to do. How much of it I still have to. And I know, well . . . I know I'm paying the price for that. That no one believes me. That maybe the only person who's ever believed in me I hurt so bad . . . " She sniffled, dabbed her eyes with the linen. "That maybe I hurt him so bad he can't stand to be with me anymore."

She stared out the window. "I can only hope one day the truth will come out, that despite all the mistakes, the truth will come out. That I never wanted any of this to happen." She laughed.

"What?"

"It's all kind of funny, don't you think? How I've lost everything good in my life? All I ever wanted was a man. A *good* man. A man who I could have fun with, who would treat me nice, who would love me. Who would take me away from all of *this*. And now look. I lost my brother, my son. Driscoll left me. My father. The detectives who were trying to help me died. Jake, well . . . I don't want to get into it. I made big mistakes there.

"I never told you this, Lenore. But the boy down at the IGA. The stock clerk, Jimmy Dodge? He called me a murderer. Said I killed Bobby.

Kicked me out of his car on the way home from a funeral last winter . . . Every man in my life. Every one of them, Lenore. They turned on me, left me. Some of it, my own doing. Some not. But I lost every one of them. Gone. Just gone. Now, I'm right back where I started. Back here."

She turned again to the window. "Back here . . . Alone."

21

Monday, May 3, 2010

The story broke in *The Daily News* one otherwise ordinary morning, the photo of a late-middle-aged man with graying hair and a blue baseball cap beneath a bold banner headline that screamed: **EXCLUSIVE!**

Within hours it had gone national, gone international; gone viral.

Soon there wasn't a television channel, a radio station, a Tweet, blog or Internet search engine with ties to even the most-random Web site located in the far-most reaches of the globe where you couldn't hear about it, read about it. See it. All the news shows — ABC, NBC, MSNBC, CBS, CNN, FOX — interrupted regular programming to tease it.

It became, in that instant, the hottest story on the planet.

A man from Wisconsin had come forward to say he'd been kidnapped more than fifty years earlier from in front of a supermarket in Hempstead Plains, New York. He said he was dead certain he was Bobby Goodson.

That he was very much alive.

The story was that Robert Charles Landsness, a janitor from Kenosha, had been in search of the truth for years.

That he had hard evidence to validate his otherwise unimaginable claim. That he'd been in contact with his "sister," Johanna. That *she* believed there was "a good chance" the assertion was true.

The Federal Bureau of Investigation confirmed it had obtained a DNA sample, were attempting to match it at their lab in Quantico, Virginia.

A law enforcement source said a preliminary test indicated it was "entirely possible" Robert Landsness really was Bobby Goodson.

That this wasn't some hoax.

"I'm not saying this would be like finding Amelia Earhart," the source said. "But in the world of missing children, it'd be damned close."

Across the internet the world was beginning to ask WTF.

That morning Detective Dallas Storm was at a borrowed desk in the office of the Cold Case Squad down at Nassau County Police headquarters in Mineola, putting the finishing touches on breakfast when the squad's senior investigator walked in. Storm glanced at the clock. Almost eight.

"Nice a you to show," he said.

Dougal Skinner shot him a look as he set down his coffee, tossed a copy of *The Daily News* onto the desk.

"Ever wonder how a case can go so cold so long?" he said.

"Nah," Storm said, nodding to the stack of file boxes. "All this shit I put here 'cause I thought my desk looked kind a empty."

"Ass," Skinner said.

The African-American detective rose from his chair. He was a big man, not so much tall as imposing. Put together, cut. That's what he was. Cut. He stepped toward Skinner, got in, tight, nose-to-nose.

"Know you weren't talkin' to me, right?" he said, with a glare.

Try as he might he Skinner couldn't help but smirk. The two men grabbed each other in a big, brotherly bear hug.

"Dragged me out a Homicide for this, Doog?" Dallas said.

"Put in a special request, Cowboy," Dougal said, moving back to his desk, his coffee — and the morning paper. "Now I find first day down here and already you're making me look bad. Appreciate that."

"Anytime," his new partner said, with a laugh.

"This story's unbelievable, huh?" Dougal said.

"Mean they're not all like this?"

"Nah. Most of them are worse."

"Was 'fraid you were gonna say that, 'specially after I started readin' this." Storm tossed the first manila file across the desk.

"An' only a few hundred more like it."

He smiled.

"Told you you should have stayed in Homicide," Dougal said. "At least nobody's coming back from the dead down there."

"Be surprised," Dallas said.

Skinner smirked. "Bet I would."

The first file covered the basics. Incident reports, interviews, all sorts of documents involving all the officers who'd first worked the case back in 1955: O'Reilly, Ricks, Johns, Spence, Farmer, Jones. None of which answered the two begging questions: How'd it all happen? And, why?

No matter how many boxes he and Dallas combed through, no matter how many thousands of reports they'd read, Skinner knew those two answers weren't going to be there. There might be hints, clues. But they'd have to dig and dig hard if they were going to find the truth.

That meant talking to anyone still around, anyone still alive. It meant they'd have to go talk to Robert Charles Landsness.

Storm poured himself a coffee, turned back to find his partner and the file laid out on the desk wearing a most-quizzical expression.

"That look I know."

Skinner didn't say a word, reached for the newspaper.

"This guy said his father was Air Force. Let's dig up the old man's military records, see where he was. When. How long. Then let's run property records, a database on the family, see if anything pops. Maybe a sister, a brother, a cousin, an in-law — anyone who might be tied to this Goodson kid, Cowboy. If anyone in the family might have ever come in contact. Any links, anything at all. Then . . . "

Skinner looked up to find Storm staring at him.

"What?" he said.

Storm handed him a stack of papers.

"Civilian paperwork," Dallas said. "Put in a request with Records to try an' get all the military stuff. Said that's gonna take a little time."

"Anything good?"

"Shitload a nothin'," Storm said. "Twenty, thirty years back, most a the civilian records are, Doog. Worse, there's almost nothin' in the system, family moved so much. Had the guys check real estate, DMV, income tax. Anythin' I could think a. There's nothin'."

"No criminal convictions?"

"*'Fraid* not."

"No family connections from the property search?"

Storm took a sip of his coffee.

"Not a damn thing. Least, not local."

"We get any hits in Wisconsin? Kansas?"

"As we speak, searchin'."

Skinner reached for his coffee, took a sip. "Think we've got a shot?"

"Wouldn't get my hopes, Doog." He moved to the desk, set his coffee down. "Best bet's gonna be the military stuff, if anythin'. Long gone, the base at Meadowbrook is. Gonna have to go national, through channels. Request forms, the whole nine. Gonna be a big pain in the ass, ask me."

"Any idea how long?"

Storm shrugged. "Days, a week. More maybe."

Skinner pushed back in his chair, reached for his coffee.

He drank too much coffee, his one vice. He didn't curse a whole lot. Didn't drink much, at least not often. He didn't smoke. What he did was drink coffee. Lots of coffee. Times like this he knew why.

"I might know a guy," he said.

Storm stared at him, curious.

"Might be able to back-channel some stuff for us. Dealt with him on a deal last year, but if he's around he just might be able to tell us who was stationed where." He glanced at the clock. "Have to wait 'til at least nine. Meanwhile, hold off on an official request. Just in case."

"Knock yourself out," his new partner said.

Over the next two hours the two did what they could.

Skinner made his call. Storm tracked down contact info, addresses and numbers for Landsness and his father, as well as the Goodsons.

Dougal didn't like to fly but knew they had no choice and had Dallas check on flights to Kenosha. The nearest major airport was Milwaukee. Skinner told him to book it ASAP. To get a car, a hotel. He didn't like going in blind. That meant the two of them were going to have to cram, read as much of the initial case file as they could, catch a flight before the night was out, knock on doors come first thing in Kenosha. They'd also have to get to Cottonwood Falls, wherever the hell that was.

Pouring himself more coffee Dougal wandered back to the desk, took a quick run through the stack of paperwork they'd put together in little more than an hour's time: directions from Milwaukee to Kenosha, to the address listed for Robert Landsness; copies of old stories, copies of the 1955 police flier on Bobby Goodson; photographs of the Goodsons in their living room, search teams in the field, an old black-and-white photograph of a tricycle — an empty Halloween bag dangling from the handlebars.

"It's hard to imagine," he said, after a moment.

"How's that?" Dallas said.

Skinner nodded towards the boxes.

"That those guys who worked the case back then got so much stuff. How many more boxes you say were downstairs?"

Storm shrugged. "Half-dozen, at least."

"All, with no computers. Calling information, connecting to phone operators, knocking on doors. Typing out handwritten notes, forms."

"Must a been a bitch," Dallas said.

"Must have," Skinner said.

"Makes you wonder they ever solved a case," Dallas said.

"Even with all the resources we've got, Cowboy, can't help but wonder if it's not going to come down to the same for us . . .

"A whole lot of gumshoe detective work."

"Nike, Reeboks, An'-Ones [and1s] or Cons?" Storm said.

"*Waders,* Dal," Dougal said. "Before long, I've got the feeling you and me? We're going to be waist-deep in shit."

The return call from the military source came in just before 10 a.m. He'd been able to nail down some information, just not as much as he'd hoped. George Landsness trained at Lackland in late 1951, the contact told Skinner. From there he'd done a short stint at Fairchild Air Force Base outside Spokane, shipped overseas to Yokota Air Base outside Tokyo for the Korean War, had come back to the states and was assigned to Tyndall down in Panama City. He'd also served at Edwards, Davis-Monthan and Ellsworth. Which meant California, Arizona, South Dakota.

There wasn't a posting within a stone's throw of Long Island.

Meanwhile, after training in mid-1952 at Sampson Air Force Base in Geneva, Driscoll Goodson had been assigned to Meadowbrook Field.

He'd never served anywhere, it seemed, *but* Long Island.

There was one strange tidbit, the source said. Goodson declared two children during his years of service, a boy and a girl. So had Landsness. Thing was Landsness declared the girl at birth. The boy was declared at Tyndall in 1955. At age three. Maybe the kid was a relative who'd been orphaned, he said. Maybe he was just born out-of-wedlock.

Possible it was something more sinister, Skinner asked?

"It's not common under most circumstances," the source said. "Then again, all the records have him listed as the natural-born son."

Off the phone, Skinner sat pondering the information.

"Tell me what you make of this, Dal," he said. "Records claim Robert Goodson was born October Nineteenth, Nineteen-Fifty-Two. Geneva, New York. And my guy told me he's got a birth listed for one Robert Charles Landsness, also Nineteen-Fifty-Two."

Skinner leaned forward in his chair. "Except, it says he was born August Twenty-Eighth. In Kenosha, Wisconsin."

"Fake?" Dallas said.

"Could be, could be real. Either way, it's a problem."

Before either could say another word there was a knock at the door. The two turned to find an elderly man and woman looking over the room. The man wore khaki trousers, sneakers and a dark-colored golf shirt with a light windbreaker over the top. He was in his late seventies, if not older. The woman was of similar age, attractive, with silver-gray hair. Even at first glance, Skinner thought there something no-nonsense about her.

"Can I help you?" he said.

The man didn't respond. The woman gave him a nudge and he turned to her, as if to say. She motioned toward the detectives.

"Can I help you?" Dougal said, again.

"I'm looking for a Detective Skinner," he said, almost a shout.

Dougal gave Dallas a sideways glance as he walked over, extending a hand as he did. Trying not to yell, he said: "I'm Detective Skinner."

Loud, the man said: "Mike Johns, Detective. Retired. This is my wife."

"Same Mike Johns who worked the Goodson case back in Fifty-Five?" Skinner said, as the woman flashed a mischievous grin.

"Actually," she said, "we both did."

"Didn't have women on the force then," Dallas said, interjecting.

"I wasn't a cop," the woman said. "I was a reporter."

Turned out Lenore Terranova and Mike Johns had been married more than fifty years now, had four kids. She'd even quit *Newsday* to raise them. But writing was in her blood and so she'd taken to writing crime novels in her spare time; often, in the dark of night.

Nothing big, not one of them a best-seller.

Still, she'd had a few small successes — even if she'd never quite learned to write like Shakespeare. Or, Capote.

Between the kids there were ten grandkids, most of them grown.

Book sales had paid for a house out on the North Fork, Mattituck, bay side, on tranquil Deep Hole Creek, a short walk to the local airport.

Their eldest grandkid had just given birth to their first great-grandchild. They'd come visiting, seen the paper, read the stories about Robert Landsness. So Lenore suggested they stop by headquarters, see if anyone wanted to know what it was they knew about any of it.

Skinner and Storm listened, soaking it in.

The recollections of Johns were keen at times, meandering at others. Mike Johns was, to be certain, an old man. Dawdling, most-definitely hard of hearing. He told the detectives about the frustrating lack of evidence, the puzzling witness statements from Driscoll and Colleen. The bizarre plane crash that left six dead, hindering the investigation.

He talked about all the dead ends, said how he and Mike Spence always believed there was a good chance Bobby was dead.

If not from the day he'd disappeared then not long after.

Spence himself had been gone nine years, Johns said. Dead of a heart attack on 9/11. Over the years, between the afternoon Bobby Goodson first went missing and the day Spence died, the two of them had wracked their brains, the case eating at them, he said, sometimes consuming them, as they searched for the elusive truth. He couldn't get past his suspicion of the parents. Each had made troubling remarks, seemed so detached.

Nothing he could put his finger on, just a feeling.

The bottom line, Johns said, was no other suspects had ever emerged. And anyone who might have been considered was either dead — like Jake Johnson, Tag and Marjorie Woods — or had never been proven involved. For her part, Lenore was equally undecided. Except that, unlike her husband, she'd never been convinced Bobby was dead. Or'd been killed.

Though, she made it clear, she wasn't convinced he was alive.

The first of her novels was even inspired by the case, she said. In it the father had beaten the boy in a fit of rage, the hidden mother helping him cover up the crime. And though the secret had eaten at the two, leading to an inevitable divorce, both remained steadfast in their denials. Until, that is, a police investigation into the suicide of the mother's own father found it hadn't been a suicide, after all. That it had all been murder. Lenore said she'd gotten the idea after the sudden death of Chardon Tetherwood.

"He committed suicide?" Dougal asked, surprised.

"Strangely enough. Or so police there said."

Lenore was quick to add it was all theoretical exercise. She thought Colleen Goodson and her husband complex characters. Misunderstood — or, more likely, misinterpreted — by those who knew them.

Or thought they did.

"The truth is I've had trouble all these years believing either had a hand in it. That they really were anything but innocent victims."

"Why?" Dougal asked.

"That's the thing," Lenore said. "I don't know why."

Their actions after their son went missing certainly hinted Driscoll and Colleen had a role in it, Lenore said. And, she knew from interviews that most of the cops doubted their innocence, too. She said she'd always known her husband high on the list of doubting Thomases.

"But," she said, "then there were the conversations I'd had with each of them. At first I thought she was shallow, manipulative. And there were times she was. But over time I came to think maybe she was just young, confused. That she'd had a hard life without much direction and, from the one real conversation I had with him, that he was deeply private, almost awkward, and that only made matters worse between them.

"That it had only made it worse for them."

"Do you think they were involved?" Dougal asked.

"Before Robert Landsness came forward?"

"For argument's sake."

"For argument's sake? No, not then — despite what *he* thinks."

She nudged her husband, shot the detectives a look.

"Not now, either. I think the two of them were lost, maybe as lost as their son was . . . I think people made assumptions."

"*Sumptions?*" Dallas said.

"Where the truth lies, Detective," Lenore said. "That's where the lying began. The novel I wrote, in it the parents had both been lying. When investigators figured it out it led to the truth. Here's the thing. In the real case I don't think either of them lied. Not to the police, not to me. Not to anyone — except maybe themselves. Everyone thought they did. I think that's because everything everyone thought was true, everything they thought they knew to be true, turned out not to be. And yet someone, somewhere, had to be lying. *Had* to be. Me? I don't think it was Driscoll and Colleen Goodson. Do I know for sure? No. But, I always believed it. If it wasn't them, who was it then? Now that this Robert Landsness character has come forward I guess we're all going to find out.

"Won't we?"

Won't we?

The promise of those two words after more than five decades of not having one definitive answer in the Goodson case was seductive, to say the least. Yet, even if Robert Landsness was Bobby Goodson, it wouldn't answer all the questions that needed answering: like why he'd been taken in the first place; like how whoever took him had gotten away with it for all this time. Like how come the cops never had a clue?

To that end there was still much to be done.

And the detectives knew of no better place to start than to pick Johns' brain for specifics — things they'd need to focus on when time came to question Robert Landsness and those who knew him best. They were doing just that when the receptionist burst into the room.

"*The Morning Show!*" she screamed.

"The Morning Show?" Dougal said, confused.

"Turn it on!" she screamed, pointing to the TV. "That man. He's on!" Before anyone could move she grabbed the remote.

On screen Robert Charles Landsness was telling his story. He was hardly polished, far from it. That was the first impression Skinner had and all he could think was: *This* is the kid? He glanced at Storm, could tell

his partner was thinking it, too. Still, how Robert Landsness spoke —
roughshod, off-the-cuff; unbalanced, even — gave what he said an
immediate air of believability. Made what he said believable.

Then he described how he'd been taken down the East Coast to
Panama City in an old yellow-and-white Nash-Rambler. And, before
either of the detectives could even imagine what any of that might mean a
startled Lenore turned to her hard-of-hearing husband.

"The Nash-Rambler, Mike!" she said, only to have him give her a look
as he struggled to figure out just what she'd just said.

"The Nash-Rambler!" she yelled, again.

"What?" Skinner and Storm said, almost in unison. But Mike Johns
didn't say a word. Just stood there, shaking his head, stunned.

"What?" Dougal asked, again.

"Back in Fifty-Six," he said. "I think it was Fifty-Six. Me and Spence
had a lead on a yellow-and-white Rambler. From cops down in . . . "

"Waycross, Georgia," Lenore said.

Johns turned to his wife, again having not quite heard.

"Waycross, Georgia," she said again, louder.

"Right. Waycross," he said. "Cops down there — Sheriff's Department,
I think it was — they said they'd seen this car, this Rambler. There was a
couple. A bit older. And they had this little blonde-haired boy . . . "

He turned to Skinner and Storm.

"No plate, no way to trace it. We called around, every place we could
think of. Local air bases, all over the South. It's in the files."

"And?" Dougal said.

"And, not a damned thing. We found a couple cars. None was right . . .
Then we got another ransom note on the kid and so we dropped it."

"Ransom note?"

"Last of three, actually," Lenore said. "Long story. All fake."

Dallas shot his partner a look, raised an eyebrow.

"Too coincidental to be coincidence, you ask me," Dallas said.

Skinner nodded in agreement. It most-certainly was.

By now, Lenore had reached out to take hold of her husband's hand. Mike Johns just stood shaking his head in stunned disbelief.

"If that's the car," he said, his voice no more than a mumble now. "We were . . . Damn, we were that close." And he kicked at the floor.

22

Detective Dougal Skinner was raised on reclusive Shelter Island, son of a harelegger from a long line of hareleggers.

His mother was a fourth-generation Islander, his father a fifth, who'd earned his hard-fought living as a fisherman along the fertile backwaters and inlets of Southold Bay, Little Peconic Bay and Shelter Island Sound.

Declan Skinner owned a twenty-foot Jon boat and a lumberyard skiff and, sometimes, when the weakfish and porgies were running or when late-summer blues were slamming baitfish, churning hotspots across the bays, he'd go fishing in the old wooden skiff. Mostly he'd gas the flat-bottom Jon boat and crab for blue-claws or rake mussels, clams and bay scallops, maybe even run all the way over to Widow's Hole in search of those pure eastern oysters — those sweet *crassostrea virginicas*.

In winter he'd get to hauling flounder.

Sometimes, though, he'd just odd-job; taking work as a handyman — maybe work for a day's pay unloading trucks for cash.

Deck was a tough man, serious when it came to work, with little tolerance for those who didn't respect it like he did. He liked to drink when he could and the locals knew to tread lightly around him down at the tavern on both the coldest of cold winter nights and the hottest of hot summer ones. They knew he didn't like to talk out of school.

That he cared for it when others did even less.

Clemence Skinner dealt with the intricacies of her husband's personality. She made sure his clothes were clean and mended, always made certain dinner was on the table at a responsible hour.

She knew how to harp, never about family; had few close friends — though, those who were were as close as anyone could ever ask.

She sometimes worked at the salon in town, dyeing hair when times got lean. She was demanding and loved her son, made no bones about it. Dougal knew that as long as he did the right thing they'd always be there for him, his mother and father would. To defend him, to protect him.

That'd always meant a lot.

Life was good on Shelter Island. And though Doog didn't mind it much he knew his parents resented summertime when the Island was overflow with outsiders. There were little more than a thousand year-round residents on Shelter Island and it was isolated beyond that by the fact it was accessible only by boat. Smack dab between the forks on the East End, you had to take ferries from both North and South.

That geographic isolation made the Island even more small-town insular than those close at hand. Provincial, parochial, Islanders were religiously territorial when it came to who was an Islander and who wasn't, wouldn't ever be. Anyone didn't live on-Island was an outsider. Even if you weren't an outsider it didn't mean you were an Islander.

Hareleggers were born on-Island. That made *them* Islanders.

You could live a lifetime on Shelter Island. If you weren't native to it you might not be an outsider, but you weren't an Islander, either. Much of *that* owed to the fact Shelter Island was older than America itself.

West Indies sugar merchant Nathaniel Sylvester, along with brother Constant and two other men, bought the Island from the Manhanset Indians in 1651 and a year later he became the first white settler when he moved on-Island with his then-sixteen-year-old bride, Grissel.

Sylvester brought in slaves and built oak barrels to run tobacco, molasses, sugar and rum back home to England. Through the generations that followed Islanders became whaling men and, later, fishermen haul-netting menhaden and moss bunker for fertilizer and oil.

Through those generations Shelter Island remained much as it had been: wooded, deer-laden, with farmland and thriving marshes. As it had been, until the Long Island Rail Road came to Greenport in the 1830s.

An old whaling village, Greenport lay north across Shelter Island Sound. By century's end visitors had come, built a hotel on-Island, and soon tourists came flocking to Shelter Island on summer vacation.

California "Borax King" Francis Marion Smith made a fortune mining Death Valley, came east and bought a home on-Island.

Artemas Ward made millions selling advertisements on train cars and street cars in New York City. Before long he built one, too.

All Islanders could do was curse the influx. But ruinous as some saw it the boom brought with it modern amenities. Steam-engined ferries soon replaced the old rowboat ones and in no time Islanders were able to come across the bay to hit town, catch the train or just go to the theatre.

It was here Shelter Island was cemented forever into folklore.

Watching hordes scramble from the ferries the Porters, residents of Greenport, decided those Islanders looked like rabbits sprung loose from a cage. They took to calling them *hareleggers*. And, the name stuck.

Derisive as it was it wasn't long before Islanders had embraced it, the nickname; were referring to themselves as hareleggers, too.

It gave them distinction, gave them license. Gave them providence. Not just anyone could be a harelegger. Truth was, they liked that.

No one more so than the Skinners. Declan and Clemence knew their families had carved life from the land, and at no small cost, and being hareleggers was affirmation of that staunch resoluteness and resolve.

Their people weathered hurricanes and blizzards, shifting economics and political storms, the great wars and the great Depression, the latter which saw the housing market go bust — and still they'd borne it out.

Even as the summer folk started trickling back after the second war, then in earnest after Korea, Clemence and her husband took most-distinct pleasure in the fact that as a boy Dougal and his friends could roam the decaying shells of vacant vacation homes that littered the Island. That the tumbledown timber frames were an eyesore was certain. But nuisance as they were they also were reminder not all men were built so stout. That most were fly-by-night, fair-weather, and lacking in moral certitude. That and that alone kept them through the harshest of hard times.

Knowing friends had your back didn't hurt.

Dougal Skinner couldn't think of a better place to have grown up.

"Thought you'd want to read this."

Skinner looked up from the file he'd been lost in just as Dallas Storm dropped the latest copy of *Sports Illustrated* into his lap.

The four all wore pinstripes. Hated New York Yankees pinstripes. Derek Jeter, Jorge Posada, Mariano Rivera, Andy Pettitte.

"The Core Four," the headline proclaimed.

Dougal scanned the restless faces in the waiting area at LaGuardia Airport then looked up at his partner. "You really are an ass," he said.

"What?"

"The Sox in trouble, you bring me *The Four Horsemen?*"

"Four Horsemen?" Dallas said.

"Of the Apocalypse," Dougal said.

No, two World Series titles in the previous six seasons, God-send that they were, didn't soothe the wounds of a childhood spent dying with the Red Sox. Not with Big Papi in a slump, not with the Sox six-and-a-half down in a season barely a month old. Not with the Yankees the reigning World Champions for the twenty-seventh time.

Dougal glanced at the tote board. Still ten minutes until boarding. He started again for the file, caught another glimpse of the magazine.

Yaz. There was a ballplayer. Tony C., the Spaceman. Rice and Lynn. Pudge. Schilling, Ortiz, Youk. Pedroia. Ballplayers, each and every one.

He'd been a fan all his life. Almost all his life, it seemed.

He'd first seen Yastrzemski — Carl Yastrzemski — on a basketball court back on Shelter Island. Not even five, his father had taken him deep in the winter of '56-'57, Yastrzemski a senior at Bridgehampton High.

Bridgehampton had come over on the ferry from down on the South

Fork. Shelter Island was a season away from a league title. Dougal didn't remember much of it, but he'd seen pictures on the wall over at Joe's Clip Joint; heard stories from Joe Salerno, every time he'd been in town.

"Joey Scissors" had photographs of Yaz hanging on his wall. Later, next to the '57-'58 and '68-'69 Shelter Island teams that won league.

Dougal liked the latter since he'd been a guard, from off the bench.

Joey was a Bonacker, despite all the years he'd been on-Island. He'd gone to East Hampton, where he'd even once faced Yaz. He spoke of him like a God. Dougal thought it apt description. He'd been a fan since he was old enough to follow the Sox. He'd died when Conigliaro took one in the face, again with Gibson and the Cards. There was '75, despite Fisk and the foul pole in Game Six. And forever Bucky Fucking Dent, when Yaz went and popped out to Nettles. Of course, there was Buckner. And Boone.

He glanced back at the board. On Time.

"You took care of the car, right?" he said.

"For the *hundredth* time?"

Dougal shot him a look him.

"Nervous?" Dallas said.

"Me?"

"Know you don't like to . . . "

"It's not about flying, Cowboy."

"What?"

"Just thinking about the case. Cold so long, what we're even looking for. Still can't get it out of my head about what Mike Johns said. That he and his partner were that close. Could've saved fifty years of misery."

"Could a saved us a flight to Wisconsin," Dallas said.

Skinner was still pissed when they hit the gate.

It was just before 9 a.m., May 4th, when Skinner and Storm found themselves face-to-face with Robert Landsness — or, Bobby Goodson.

Or, whoever the hell it was he was.

The flight had been routine. Except Dougal really did hate to fly and so couldn't even nap. Landing in Milwaukee, he and Storm had driven the rental thirty-five miles to Kenosha, grabbed a late meal. They'd sat there, brainstormed, then gotten fitful sleep. After breakfast they'd gone out to the trailer park to talk to the man at the center of all the attention.

Robert Charles Landsness answered the door in a wrinkled, stained T-shirt and sweatpants, as reporters camped outside the knee-high planter's fence that bordered his small parcel unleashed a torrent of questions, hoping for answers. Landsness smiled and waved, soaking it all in, as he looked out over the media horde, at the television trucks with antennas and satellite dishes reaching high into the morning Wisconsin sky.

He motioned the two detectives inside.

The trailer was small and, to be kind, it was pretty much a shit hole. A slew of empty beer cans covered the counter; there were dirty dishes in the sink, junk mail and bills strewn on the kitchen table. The rug in the living room, the linoleum floor, the carpet leading to the bedrooms down back — all of them, worn and wearied. An old stereo, a bad hangover from the Seventies, sat precarious on a shelf far too small to hold it.

Like everything else it was covered in dust.

What Skinner noticed most was there were no pictures. Not one.

"You guys want a beer?" Landsness said.

Storm said pass, they were on the job. Skinner just watched as Landsness grabbed a *Pabst Blue Ribbon* from the fridge, stopping mid-turn to grab two cans of cola. He handed them to the detectives.

Skinner thought Landsness rather ordinary.

He had a face that was round but not too round, a light complexion and a head of unruly gray hair. He wasn't tall but wasn't short, was a bit on the stocky side and not lean. His eyes were blue.

As Landsness walked to the living room Storm leaned over: "Could be your brother, Doog — 'cept for the mess . . . an' the hair."

Skinner shot him a look. Not that he minded being bald.

The living room was at the front of the trailer. The detectives took a seat on the threadbare couch, Landsness in a worn armchair.

"I'm sure it's been a tough few days, Mister . . . " Dougal said. "I'm sorry, but I don't know how you'd like to be addressed.

"Mr. Landsness? Mr. Goodson?"

"Robert."

"Fair enough, Robert. Like I said, I'm sure it's been quite a time. You know, finding out the people you trusted most lied to you."

"I never trusted them," he said.

"How's that?" Dallas asked.

Landsness took an index finger and picked at the inside of his ear.

"Can't really say," Landsness said. "Just never did. Something about them never seemed right, you know what I mean?"

"Anything in particular?" Dougal asked.

"Everything," he said. "Always felt they had all these secrets, like they was hiding something. Any time I asked I got some bullshit, instead."

"Is that what made you go looking?" Dougal said.

Landsness shrugged. "More like the last conversation I had with . . . with that woman who raised me. She was in the hospital downtown and I went right at the end to talk with her, to get the truth out of her. Before she, you know . . . Before she cashed-in. Then she was rambling and stuff and I was trying to be understanding, since that's how I am."

"I understand," Dougal said, glancing at Dallas. "Anyone else there?"

"Nah. George and I . . . "

"George?"

"Her husband," Landsness said. "Me and him, me and their daughter, we haven't talked in years. We're what you would call 'estranged.' That's the word, right? Estranged?" He laughed, nervous. "Like I was saying, I was there, just me and her, and I asked her to tell me the God-damned truth. About what it was happened, how they went and got me."

Landsness lit a smoke, tossed the match, missed the ashtray.

"Then she was dead. After a while I realized she'd been saying how I was this Bobby Goodson kid."

Storm shot his partner a glance, but saw Skinner was dialed in on Landsness. "So what did you do?" Dougal asked, finally.

Landsness took a draw of his smoke.

"Wrote George a God-damned letter. Wrote the daughter a letter, too, telling them enough of this shit. I want the truth."

"And?"

"Neither of them answered. I tried calling. Didn't answer. Went to the house to talk. They kept telling me they had no idea what the hell I was talking about. The old man, he told me I should see a doctor. A shrink."

"Shrink?" Dallas said. "Why?"

Landsness laughed.

"I know, right? Why the hell do I need a damned shrink? Figured they were trying to make me think I was crazy — so it'd all go away."

"But you weren't about to let it go," Skinner said.

"Not on your life," he said. "I got sidetracked for a while, thinking what to do. Then like two years ago I went to down the library, since I knew they had computers there. I'm not real good with that but I knew I might be able to find information or something." His cigarette out, he reached for another, lit it. "Couldn't find nothing, least nothing useful. George'd been in the service, Air Force. Moved lots when I was a kid. Panama City, Edwards, Tucson, Box Elder. All over. Then I found all this missing kid stuff. Like old unsolved stuff, going way back. Started reading, going through all that. Stories, pictures. Anything might have a clue."

"Which is where you found Bobby Goodson," Dougal said.

"Fuck yeah," Landsness said. "Late last year."

Over the course of the next two hours Robert Landsness took them through his search. The documents he'd found, the cases he'd read.

Some of it fit, he said. Most didn't.

It wasn't until he'd read all about Bobby Goodson that he'd begun to believe. "Once I seen the photographs," he said, "I just knew."

It was then Landsness strolled to the back bedroom, returned with two pictures. One was of Bobby Goodson he'd found on-line. The other was him, same age. Both had the same shape faces. Same builds, hair, smiles. The noses seemed off, Skinner thought. Same with the eyes.

That could've been due to the angle at which the pictures were taken. Or lighting. A million things.

Landsness said that after finding the photographs he was going to call the cops, but didn't think they'd believe him. Instead, he'd gone to see his uncle. His aunt had passed away years earlier. But his uncle Thom had always been good to him, was someone Landsness knew he could trust.

"I told him I wanted to know about the God-damned car ride."

Skinner leaned forward on the couch. "The old Nash-Rambler?"

Landsness gulped his beer, let loose an Archie Bunker belch.

"I used to work down at the factory where they built them cars here in Kenosha," Landsness said. "Nash was long gone then. Rambler, too. Got bought out by American, the guys I worked for. Then they went and got bought by Renault." He said this *Ray-Nolt*. "Thing is those Frenchies wasn't the ones let me go." He looked around the trailer, suddenly pissed. "Chrysler. It was Chrysler, that shit Lee Iacocca. That's the guy screwed me. Had a nice house back then. Wife, too . . . Then it all got fucked."

"What about the car ride?" Dougal said.

Landsness reached for his cigarette, took a drag.

"The ride, Robert?" he said, again.

Landsness leaned forward in his chair.

"Had this cream-white-and-yellow Nash, an old Custom Country Club Hardtop. Fifty-One. Sweet car. Not like all them boats they was building in Detroit back in the Fifties, but like one of them Airstream trailers. All smooth, gorgeous. I remember being in the back of that car, the three of us driving for days. Driving, stopping to sleep, driving some more."

"And?"

"And I asked," Landsness said. "Thom said no big deal, they'd picked me up from family up in New York somewhere and took me to Florida — Panama City, he said — 'cause that's where George and his wife were since Thom said George had just gotten stationed at Tyndall back then."

"New York?" Dallas asked. "New York, where?"

"That's the thing. He couldn't remember."

"He couldn't remember?" Dougal said.

"He's fucking old," Landsness said.

They'd driven down through Jersey, Pennsylvania, Washington, D.C., Virginia, through the Carolinas into Georgia and then Florida. Most of it on old Route 1. Robert even had a map, highlighted, to show how.

He said the old man told him that crossing the Susquehanna River, over the top of Conowingo Dam, they'd gotten a flat.

He'd stopped to fix it, but they'd lost so much time Thom decided to stop for the night at a roadside motel in Bel Air, Maryland.

The Brownie Motel and Log Cabin Restaurant had green-and-white plaid bedspreads and an in-room television, Landsness said. He couldn't remember much else, except the restaurant was this big log cabin.

He'd had a peanut butter-and-jelly sandwich and a cold glass of milk, a dish of peppermint ice cream for dessert. Come morning they'd set off again and made Savannah, where they'd stayed the night in some place called The Dreamland. The Dreamland had an in-room radio and dark bedspreads that were solid pea-green, not plaid, Landsness said.

He noted how there was no TV. And no log cabin.

Skinner and Storm thought it odd a three-year-old could remember so much. Then Landsness said how they'd left the motel and stopped to eat maybe two hours later. He couldn't recall where, but remembered a police officer. They'd been sitting in a booth near the window when Thom noticed the cop eyeing his car. Thom whispered to Marie, then went out to talk. Landsness said he'd watched, then he and Marie went out, too.

The officer was saying what a nice car it was when his radio went off. Like that he was out of there, Robert said, tires screeching, siren blaring.

"And?" Dougal asked.

"Left, fast as we could. Didn't stop 'til we hit Panama City."

"You're sure," Dougal said, "about this officer?"

"Raced right out of there," Landsness said, tossing his empty beer can toward the sink. "What fucking kid wouldn't remember *that?*"

"Sure," Dougal said. "What kid."

He studied Landsness, pondering a question. As he did, Landsness walked to the kitchen, past the discarded can, grabbed another *Pabst*.

"Anything else you remember?" Dougal said. "From the ride, from before your aunt and uncle took you down to Florida?"

Landsness shrugged. "An old tire swing, hanging in the back yard."

"You're sure?"

"Don't believe me?"

"I didn't say that," Dougal said, shooting Dallas a look. He pulled out his cell. "You mind, Robert?" he said. "I forgot to check in."

"Whatever," Landsness said.

Skinner returned to find Landsness in a rant about corporate greed killing blue-collar guys, about September 11th conspiracies.

About women, about divorce.

"Why do you think these people took you?" Dougal said, finally.

"Honest? I think they had a kid and he died. Got no idea how. Maybe he was sick, maybe an accident. Maybe they fucking just killed him."

He looked over the detectives, sitting there.

"I think he died and they needed a kid to replace him or they were going to have a lot of answering to do," he said. "So I think they went out to look for a kid who looked like him — and they found me."

"Smokin' crack, he is," Dallas said, once the two men were back in the rental car. "Cracker-ass *son-a-a-bitch.*"

Skinner laughed. "You think?"

"If he ain't crazy, Doog, damn close."

Skinner turned to his partner.

"You might be right at that, Cowboy. But I think we've still got a whole lot of questions for George Landsness and uncle Thom."

Dropping the car in gear Skinner drove to the exit of the trailer park, turned onto the main road.

As he did he said to Storm: "I Googled the Brownie Motel."

Staring out the window, Dallas said: "An'?"

A few hundred yards down the block Skinner pulled to a stop, took out his phone and turned to show Dallas. An old postcard of the Brownie Motel, just as Landsness described it. Before Storm could say a word, Skinner typed in a new search, showed Dallas a shot of The Dreamland.

Storm shook his head. "How he knew."

"From vintage postcards. Bastard found it all on-line."

Storm turned again to the window. It was a beautiful spring day.

"Too good to be true, it sounded, Doog. Too much detail, all a it."

"But," Dougal said, "I also called Johns."

"An'?"

"Not only was there a tire swing, but the wife said Johns told her about the Georgia deputy and the radio call. Said details had never been released to the public . . . Which means this guy was there, Dal."

"Damn," Dallas said.

"One more thing," Dougal said. "She said one of the theories was the Goodson kid might've been taken by someone who'd lost a child.

"That he was taken to replace a dead kid."

Without another word Skinner flipped the car back into gear and pulled from the shoulder, again headed to the meeting with George Landsness. It was a mile down the road before Storm turned to him.

"What'd you think?" he asked.

"About?"

"Landsness, Goodson. *Whoever.* What'd you think a him?"

"Disappointing, Cowboy," Skinner said. "I guess after a more than a half-century of people searching for this kid I'd hoped for better."

Staring straight ahead, Dougal Skinner drummed his fingers on top of the steering wheel. "Better than who he is, Cowboy."

He let out a soft laugh. *"Fucking* better."

Deadpan, Storm glanced over at his partner, said: "Don't know, Doog. Had a certain charm 'bout him, I thought."

Skinner snickered. "Ass."

23

George Landsness leaned forward in his chair looking like he was itching for a fight. He and Thom Hardemann were old men now: George staring hard at eighty, Thom even older than that. Judging by the looks of him, Skinner envisioned George had once been a truly imposing character — not one to mince words, a real son-of-a-bitch.

"The kid's crazy," he said.

His brother-in-law jumped all over him.

"Enough of that shit already, George."

George just glared at him.

"Well, he is, Thom. You know it, I know it. Everyone in the family's always known it . . . "

"He's still your son."

"Damn it, Thom. Don't you think I know that?"

Uncle Thom shook his head.

"Sometimes, I wonder. The way you treat him."

"What do you want from me after all these years? You know how hard I tried . . . One fucking battle after another is all it ever was."

The elder man bit his tongue.

"Right, Thom. 'Cause you know I'm right." Landsness snickered as he turned to Skinner and Storm. "See . . . He knows I'm right."

"Yeah?" Dougal said. "And why's that?"

Thom started to say something. Landsness turned, gave him a look. Hardemann stared down at the tabletop, lost in the moment.

Without looking up at the men gathered around the dining room table he spoke. This time, softly. "The kid's been through enough, George."

"My son's got problems," Landsness said.

"George?"

"C'mon, Thom," Landsness said. "Stop it with the bleeding heart bullshit, already. I know he's your nephew, but he's my fucking kid. And it kills me to say it." He turned to the detectives. "It kills me to say it. But there's something not right about him. He's got problems. We tried to get him help for it, over the years. Me, my daughter. Even Thom here."

"Is that right, Mr. Hardemann?" Dougal asked.

"He's right," Hardemann said, defeated.

"My brother-in-law here," Landsness said. "He meant well. Trying to humor the kid, make him think he was helping him out and all. But my son? He's always been confused, thinking something that's not there. So Thom told him this story. About this car ride, going to Florida. That's all it was, a story. A story, figuring he'd drop all this craziness he's been talking all these years. All this stuff that's been tearing the family apart."

He stared across the table at his brother-in-law. "I'll be damned if then he doesn't go and find this thing about this kid — this Bobby Goodson fella — and all of a sudden he's sold it's him. That he's been kidnapped. You couldn't convince him it was all a lot of bullshit. No matter how anyone tried. You just couldn't convince him."

"We should believe that why?" Dallas said.

"Why? Because it's true."

"Not true."

"You callin' me a liar?"

"Yeah, George," Dougal said. "Because Thom here went and got Robert in New York, George. Got him in his old Nash-Rambler."

He smiled. "Isn't that right, Thom?"

The two old men sat, dumbfounded.

"New York?" Landsness said. "What the hell do you mean New York?"

"New York, George," Dallas said, leaning in. "Don't play dumb."

George looked confused.

"I don't know what the hell you two are talking about."

"Who's the kid, George?" Dougal said. "Who's he really?"

"He's my son."

"Prove it," Dallas said.

"You want fucking proof?" Landsness said.

"I got a lifetime's worth of headaches, all the bullshit came with it. But if you want proof I got a God-damned birth certificate."

"Could be fake."

"Whatever."

Skinner shot a glance at Thom Hardemann, then Landsness.

"Maybe it belongs to your real son, a kid who died."

Landsness exploded up from the table.

"You're fucking kidding me?" he shouted.

Then, turning to Storm, he said: "He's fucking kidding me with this, right? What are you guys, assholes?"

He turned to Thom. "These guys are *assholes.*"

The detectives both looked amused. Thom didn't say a word.

Skinner pushed back in his chair.

"How do I know you didn't have a kid and he died. Or maybe someone killed him and you guys grabbed this kid to take his place? Huh? You know, there's no statute of limitations on murder, George. And that DNA test, well . . . That DNA test is going to answer all the questions."

He smiled at Landsness. "It's going to be proof positive."

"Story's gonna be what then, George?" Storm said.

George Landsness just stood there, not knowing what to say.

Then, without a word, he slumped back into his chair. Skinner sat stone-faced. He didn't even look at Storm, didn't have to.

He knew both of them were thinking the same thing.

"It's gone on long enough, George," Hardemann said. "I told you it was going to come to this one day. That's what I said.

"It's going to come to this."

Landsness turned to his brother-in-law.

"Dumb son-of-a-bitch."

Before he could finish Skinner slammed his fist hard on the table, startling everyone. George sat trying to figure out just what to say.

"I knew my wife Gertie and Thom my whole life," he said.

"We were neighbors and I always liked her, really liked her. She was just fifteen and I was in high school senior and Thom had that car of his, this Nash, and he'd let us borrow it to go up to the lake."

He said it wasn't long before Gertrude turned up pregnant, how they didn't know what to do since she was just fifteen, her mother dead.

Her dad, a bad drunk.

"The war was on in Korea," he said. "I'd joined the Air Force and she was so young. There was no way we were gonna get married. How was I gonna explain that? But, we loved each other and there was no way she was gonna be able to have that child in the house, what with her father and all. Besides she wanted to finish school and I wanted her to, if she could." He looked at his brother-in-law. "Thom and Marie were working. I was heading off overseas. All of us were scared the old man was such a mean drunk he might do something dumb. I had an older brother down in Allentown, working for Mack Trucks. Him and his wife said they'd take the baby in, 'til I got back . . . 'Til Gertie and I could get properly hitched, get on our feet. Find someplace stable to live."

"Wasn't easy on anyone," Hardemann said. "Especially, my sister."

George took a deep breath.

"I shipped overseas. Base in Japan. Funny, huh? Japan. When I got back I stayed in the service, but before we could even find a place Gertie got pregnant again. I talked to my brother. We agreed it'd be best to wait 'til everything got settled for good. Then I got sent to Tyndall and me and her, we got married down there in Panama City, and she had the baby, a little girl. But Gertie, she was beside herself. It was all a lot to deal with, you know? After a few months we figured it was time and Thom and Marie, they went to Pennsylvania, brought Robert down to Florida. We did everything we could, but we'd all been apart so long. Gertie had to spend so much time with the baby. I was working all these hours over at the base. We were just trying to figure everything out.

"And Robert? It seemed there was always this distance. Didn't help Gertie wasn't real warm."

"Or that you could be a real bastard," Hardemann said.

"Or that I was a real bastard," Landsness said.

"Thing is," he said, "as the kid got older all of it was just a damned battle. He always acted like we didn't love him, there was all these fights. I'd tell him it was horse shit. His mouth, the fucking rebellion. All of it, not one fucking minute's peace. I told Gertie she needed to come clean to the kid, explain everything. But times were different and she, she was just embarrassed. Baby out of wedlock, not being around from the start. She couldn't bring herself to tell him, like if she didn't it'd all go away."

"So what happened?" Dougal said.

"I got sick of the bullshit," Landsness said. "Sick of hearing how he could've done better, could've had a better family. Sick of everything. Sixteen, seventeen, I sat him down one day, read him the riot act. Told him what the fuck happened. Me and him, we were so at odds by then he just didn't believe it. Thought I was making the whole thing up."

"After my sister died," Hardemann said, "it all really fell apart. Robert didn't get along with George, didn't get along with his sister. Felt like it was all one big lie. I told him about the car ride, going to Florida. That George had his birth certificate even. But by then he'd found that story — the one about that Goodson kid going missing."

"Dumbass was convinced we'd taken him," Landsness said, interrupting. "And once they found that girl out west, the one they found last year out there in California, remember that one?"

"Jaycee Lee Dugard?" Dougal said.

"She the one had been gone something like twenty years?"

"Almost."

"Well," he said. "My kid was convinced same thing happened to him."

Landsness got up, went down the hall.

They could hear him rummaging. When he came back all he said was, "There," dropping a birth certificate and some old photos on the table.

The birth certificate looked good.

Robert Charles Landsness. August 28, 1952. General Hospital, Kenosha. Father: George Albert Landsness. Age: 19. Mother: Gertrude Hardemann. Age: 16. Skinner thought none of it meant a damned thing. And the pictures? Some were out of focus, none were dated. The boy bore a resemblance. It might be proof, might be nothing at all.

Skinner turned to Thom. "When'd you get to Panama City?"

The old man thought for a moment.

"Early November. The second or third."

"You don't remember?"

"It was fifty-five years ago," Landsness said, interrupting.

"I know when it was, Mr. Landsness," Dougal said.

He turned back to Hardemann. "What day?"

"Honestly? I don't remember. I think the second."

"And when did you go to New York?"

"What's with New York?" he said. "You keep asking about New York."

"When," Dougal said, again, "did you go to New York?"

"But, we never went to New York," Hardemann said, confused.

"Right. You said that. Then how'd you get the kid?"

"We told you before," Landsness said. "He wasn't in New York."

"Where was he?"

"I told you. Allentown, Pennsylvania."

"So," Dallas said, "your son said Thom got him in New York, why?"

Thom stared at him. "He said that?"

"Yeah, Thom," Dougal said. "Robert said that."

"But that ain't what I said."

"Okay," Dougal said. "What did you tell him?"

"I told him we went east. That we got him back East."

"Then where did he get New York?"

Hardemann shrugged.

"Damned if I know. From what he read about that Goodson kid? He's from New York, right? Maybe he figured that shit just fit better."

Skinner leaned back in his chair.

"We've already contacted the FBI about the birth certificate and other records," he said. "If the DNA's a match, if Robert is Bobby Goodson, the FBI's prepared to come in and dig up yards in Kenosha and anywhere else they might need to dig for a body. You're deep in it, you two."

George shrugged. "Do what you gotta do."

"We will, George. Count on it." He smiled at the old man, then finally said: "I'm going to need to contact your brother."

"Good luck," Landsness said.

"Good luck? So what, you're not going to give us his info?"

George laughed. So did Thom.

"You want an address?" Landsness said, finally.

"Yes," Dougal said. "For your brother, the one in Allentown."

"And a phone number?"

"Yes."

"For the cemetery?"

"The cemetery?" Dougal said.

"You guys really *are* assholes,' he said. "My brother and his wife are dead a good ten years, now."

Skinner thought his smirk the biggest shit-eating grin he'd ever seen.

Back out in the car, Dougal Skinner sat staring at the steering wheel. It had been a day of such promise, too, he thought.

The Sox had won the night before. Twenty hits, four home runs. Better still, Dallas' team, the Mets, had lost on a walk-off homer in extra innings — and he'd been able to throw it all in his partner's face. Now?

"Guess I should have seen that coming, huh?" he said, blankly.

"Older brother, Doog? Yeah. Guess you should a."

"Then him saying the only one should be scared of the DNA results was his good-for-nothing kid, how he'd be up shit's creek then . . . "

"Nice touch, don't you think?"

Skinner sighed. What else could he do? He reached out, turned the key. Pulled from the curb still feeling like a horse's ass.

"Hard to believe any family could be that screwed up," he said. "Don't know about you. But it makes me thankful to have grown up normal."

Dallas stared out the window. "We do what now?"

"We check it out, Cowboy. All of it. We go to Kansas, we talk to the Goodsons." He glanced over at his partner. "I'm just hoping this Robert Landsness guy isn't our kid, terrible as that sounds.

"That our kid's still out there, somewhere."

As Skinner turned into the hotel lot, Storm said: "Those two guys better hope that DNA says Robert Landsness really is Robert Landsness, not this Bobby Goodson kid." He shot Skinner a quick glance.

"He's this Goodson kid, Doog? Those two motherfuckers gonna wish I was back in Homicide." He smiled. "Who knows? If he is, might be."

24

First thing Wednesday the detectives flew to Kansas City, Missouri, bound for Cottonwood Falls. They rented a car. Headed west on I-35 out through Olathe and Gardner, stopped for lunch a hundred miles or so down the road in Emporia. It was a beautiful morning, skies dotted with cottonball clouds, temperatures in the mid-sixties. Spring in the air.

The events of the previous day still gnawed at Skinner.

There were so many ways it could all still go. There'd been no word from the FBI on the DNA. He and Storm both knew who they thought had been lying and who'd been telling them the truth, but they also knew one thing you didn't do in these kinds of cases was jump to conclusions.

You let the clues guide you, banked on evidence. Understood things could change at a moment's notice.

Miserable over his rookie mistake with Landsness and Hardemann, Dougal had called home from the hotel in Kenosha.

His daughter was pregnant with twins and she'd had a tough go of it; confined to bed rest. But her husband had been a rock and that'd counted for a lot. This was the first grandchild — grandchildren, it was strange getting used to the idea — and that made Dougal understandably anxious. Donna had suffered through a tough first pregnancy, too, and it brought back all sorts of worrisome memories. Three decades and three girls later Dougal was finding none of it any easier. Logan was his oldest.

The call home calmed him. Somewhat. The obstetrician had issued a clean bill of health, had scheduled a cesarean.

At least now there was a due date.

Settling into a back booth at the lunch joint, he and Dallas sipped cold iced tea, waiting. They could tell it was a good spot from the moment they'd walked in. A hole in the wall, a dive, it was crowded with regulars.

Dallas ordered pork ribs, Dougal burnt ends. A sweetness wafted out from a smoker somewhere outside the door behind them. They'd covered all the strategies they could and all that was left now was to eat then drive the twenty or so miles on to Cottonwood Falls. See what happened.

"I talked to Donna last night. They finally got a date."

"Mireya said," Dallas said, taking a sip of tea.

"They talked?"

Dallas snickered. "They ever not?"

Skinner rolled his eyes. "I should know better."

"Nervous?" Dallas said.

"Over being a grandfather?"

"Yeah."

"You tell me. I'm not sure it's hit me yet, Cowboy. I keep trying to convince myself it doesn't mean I'm old, that I'm an old man."

"Are."

Dougal laughed. "That's the pot calling the kettle black."

"What's good for the goose, Doog. But you ain't black . . . *yet.*"

"Not a grandpa yet, either, Cowboy. Though I'll be in good company."

"Had good parents," Dallas said. "Gotta ask, though. *Lolita? Bong-Bong?* Mean, even Mireya sound scared a that."

"Didn't think could scare a Filipina with names."

Dougal reached for his tea, trying hard not to laugh.

"Logan and Dante, yanking chains." He smirked. "Of course, could've suggested *Dzigbode.*"

"Trust me," Dallas said. "Don't want to do that."

The smokey-sweet scent of garlic, tomato, molasses and vinegar wafted through the air as the waitress appeared shouldering plates overrun with burnt ends, ribs, baked beans, collard greens, fries. No sooner she'd set them down the two were digging in.

"I know Emporia?" Dallas asked, between bites.

"Essex," Dougal said.

Dallas looked suddenly annoyed.

"Right, Essex."

Mark James Robert Essex. Back in the winter of '72-'73, armed with a sniper rifle, he'd gone on a rampage in downtown New Orleans, New Year's Eve. Took root near police headquarters on Perdido. Ambushed two cops, killed a cadet. By the time it ended in a rooftop shootout a week later the Downtown Howard Johnson's was a raging inferno, its halls littered with dead and dying guests, and a military helicopter had been raked bow-to-stern with gunfire. Almost two dozen had been shot in a series of running gun battles, ten of them dead, five of them cops, among them the Deputy Superintendent of the New Orleans Police Department. Essex got blasted to kingdom come in an ear-splitting barrage that sounded an awful lot like war. Maybe, vengeance. The medical examiner said he'd stopped counting it all at two-hundred bullet holes.

The cops called it all "senseless." As if.

Then they'd announced Essex'd been a member of the Black Panthers, noted when they'd tossed his apartment they'd found white walls covered in racist graffiti: AFRICA. Hate White People Beast Of The Earth.

Almost all the victims were white.

Except, that was, for the dead black cadet.

It didn't take anyone in Louisiana long to do the math. Come up with two-dozen of one, two-hundred of the other. Give or take, take your pick. One side saw Essex as the victim of white supremacist racism dating to his time in the U.S. Navy, where fellow sailors said he'd been continuously taunted and harassed due solely to the color of his black skin; the other saw him as an unapologetic racist, despite all he'd been through.

"Essex was from Emporia," Skinner said. "Buried here, too, I think."

Dallas tossed a bone onto his plate, wiped sauce-stained fingers on a clean white napkin.

"Just 'nother crazy fucker givin' people a bad name, Doog."

"Every walk's got 'em, Cowboy. Least the barbecue's good."

Skinner's phone rang. A handful of uh-huhs, I sees and one not-so-grateful-sounding thanks later he was off.

"FBI?" Dallas said.

"Yeah."

"Bad, huh?"

Skinner didn't say a word. Storm leaned back in the booth.

"Can't say I'm disappointed, Doog. Want to, can't. No matter how much I want this thing solved, didn't want it to be that guy."

"Me neither," Dougal said, taking one last sip of tea. "Problem is, now we've got nothing. Not a damned thing. It's all back to square one."

Back to square one.

Aside from a momentary lapse, when it seemed emotion might get the better of her, Johanna Childress took the news in stride.

Composed herself, never shed a tear.

Robert Charles Landsness wasn't her brother, much as anyone might've wanted him to be — if only to answer the question. But DNA doesn't lie. And as the three of them stood there in the house where her mother was raised, Johanna, now a mother and grandmother, knew none of them knew where her brother might be. If he even still was.

"Is it wrong to say I'm relieved?" she said, finally. "Because, I think that's what I am, more than anything. As much as I want to find my brother, as much as I want him alive, in my heart I didn't want it to be *that* man." That's what she said, *that* man. "If I'm honest, I guess I didn't want it to be him almost as much as I did. Is that wrong?"

Neither Storm nor Skinner knew what to say.

"He just wasn't who I'd hoped to find," she said. "Who I'd pictured my brother might be. I wanted to believe it all, but he was just so damned unlikable. Now I don't know if my brother's still out there. Or, if he's . . ."

She didn't let herself finish.

"You can't blame yourself," Dougal said.

"Do you have any siblings, Detectives?" she asked.

Dougal shook his head no, pointed to Dallas.

"One a five, Ma'am," Dallas said.

"I always wondered what it would be like to have siblings," she said. "Someone you could count on like that. Dad remarried not long after everything. They have daughters; we know each other. I'm sure I could've done worse. Probably, a lot. But, it's not the same, if that makes sense. We're polite. But, we're not family. Do you know what I mean?"

Dougal thought how his own parents had always been with Donna. How they'd never really accepted her, never warmed.

"I do," he said.

Johanna Childress had turned fifty-five in April, had two daughters, the eldest in her thirties. That girl had two children, the other one. Three grandchildren in all. Johanna had showed Skinner and Storm pictures, ordered and in albums. Some included her mother, others her father and his second family. Johanna's own husband was a mechanic and for years he'd owned a service station over in Strong City. She'd spent most of her life as a housewife, though she'd also volunteered as a school aide in the Falls. Mostly, she said, because she liked kids. She wasn't beautiful, but from the photos shown it was clear she'd gotten any good looks from her mother. Looks that had overcome her father's ordinary ones.

She and her husband owned a big motor home, had for years. It'd taken them on countless vacations. She had galleries of photos she was eager to share. She had a keen eye for detail, no matter how minute, and had presented at a number of local shows throughout Kansas.

Someday, she said, she hoped for more.

Things had gotten sidetracked, first with her mother getting sick, then Robert Landsness showing up on her porch one night, out of the blue.

It was back in February. She and Dan had just sat down to eat when the doorbell rang. He answered to find this stranger asking for his wife.

Strangers didn't come calling on folks unannounced in Cottonwood Falls. Especially, come dinnertime. Dan asked who wanted to know.

He said he was Bobby Goodson.

Dan's first reaction was it was all some sort of scam. But it was soon obvious he knew details and after a few minutes Dan asked him in.

The initial shock gone, Johanna found herself confused with all of it. His mouth, how all over the place he was. Stories about his dying mother and her cryptic message and going on-line, finding photos.

"He did bear a resemblance to Dad," she said. "Then again so do you, Detective. To be honest so do a thousand others I've met."

That said, Johanna stood unconvinced. Dan, more so. But the two had to admit they'd found the tale about the car ride intriguing, the Air Force connection downright eerie. Johanna said she'd once been contacted by Nassau County Police seeking her DNA. Advances in technology had cops checking again for leads trying to resolve "The Boy in the Box."

Like with her brother that case remained unsolved. Except the boy in Philadelphia was confirmed dead and no one had claimed him — or been punished for his death. The cops said something about a problem with the old X-rays, that there was still a chance, and how it all came down to DNA. Johanna said she'd given hers then prayed the boy long-dead in Philadelphia wasn't her missing brother. Better to have him alive and not know than to need him dead to uncover some awful truth, she said.

When it all proved no match her first thought was relief, maybe even joy. Then came overwhelming sadness knowing a boy was still dead. That he'd been dead almost fifty years and was still anonymous.

That he might forever be.

She wondered if her brother shared the same fate.

She tried hard as she could to imagine him alive. That he might be on a beach somewhere, maybe married with a family of his own. That he hadn't become dust. That one day she'd get good news. That alone made her consider the story told that winter night by Robert Landsness.

The promise was too great, the risk of not pursuing too monumental. And so the two agreed to meet with her doctor for a simple blood test.

Then came word it was possible the two of them were, in fact, related. There were calls to police, the FBI. Investigators came, took DNA.

"I called my father," she said, thinking back on it all. "He told me not to get my hopes up. That was it. 'Don't get your hopes up, Jo.' I wondered if it was because he knew something. Then, I just figured it was because he'd been down that road so many times before."

She turned to the window. Such a gorgeous afternoon.

She loved all seasons, but adored spring when weather beckoned. Without turning back she said: "What makes someone do such a thing?"

"Take your brother?" Dougal asked.

"That, too," she said. "I was more thinking what would make someone pretend they'd been taken. What could make you feel so unloved?"

"Some people are just lost," Dougal said.

"This Landsness character," Dallas said, "no one more than."

"To go to such lengths?" Johanna said. "How much must you hate who you are, what you are? How bitter? It all just seems so sad."

She watched the mailman push his cart down the block.

"Mrs. Childress?"

No response.

"Johanna."

Still none.

"It's like I never knew my brother," she said, finally. "Even when I look through old pictures, I can't remember him. It's like I'm looking at a stranger. So why wouldn't I be hopeful this would be him? Who wouldn't have been hopeful over that?" She turned back to the detectives.

"I can't remember him. Nothing. My own brother, a few pictures, that's it. I can't even imagine what he'd be like now. If he's even still alive, if he ever lived past that afternoon. All these years and this is going to sound stupid, but all these years I've wondered: What if we were ever together in the same room? What if I'd wandered into a store somewhere and he was there? Would I have a feeling? Would I even know? Could you tell? Do you think you could tell?" She picked up the album, scanned the old photographs. "We've traveled so much over the years. Almost every state, at least in the lower forty-eight. And I wonder. Was I ever in any of those places and maybe my brother was right there, too? Maybe, I met him. Maybe, I just missed him. Maybe, he was stopped next to us at a traffic light. Or he crossed the street in front of us. Maybe he was the attendant at the gas station, the collector at the toll booth, the . . . "

"You can't do that to yourself," Dougal said.

"I know. That's what Dan said. Dad, too. That doesn't mean I didn't. It's only human and, well, I think I convinced myself I felt that when I met Robert Landsness. Despite something that seemed so wrong about him, despite how much I really *didn't* like him, I convinced myself. That he was my brother. That he'd felt what I'd felt all these years. That he'd cared enough to search for the truth. For his family. To search for me."

She turned back to the window, stared at the street. "Now, all I've got is what I've always had. Questions. It just doesn't seem fair, does it?"

"You can't look at it like that," Dougal said. "Fair, unfair. It is what it is. That doesn't mean something good can't come of it."

"How so, Detective?"

"We're here, me and Detective Storm. Because of Robert Landsness we've reopened the case, are taking a fresh look. To see if anything was missed, if there's answers. If we can find them. If we can find him."

"What if you can't?"

"We can't promise anything," he said. "I think you know that. But we promise we're going to try. That we'll do our damnedest . . .

"We'll leave no stone unturned."

No stone, Skinner thought as he and Dallas waited for Johanna to return. She'd excused herself, set a pot of coffee on the stove, and now she returned to the parlor with mugs, cream, a sugar bowl and a plate of homemade molasses cookies. She'd set it all down, fetched the coffee pot. Skinner spooned in the sugar and cream, took a sip. Just right.

"You said your mother's not doing well?" he said.

"Mom's in a care center, over in Emporia. It's been almost four years."

"Ma'am, what happened?" Dallas asked.

"A stroke. Mom had a stroke. She's pretty bad off."

The detectives thought Johanna about to cry, watched as she reached for a napkin, scrunched it in her hand.

"They said she's not going to get better," she said, finally.

After the disappearance, the accidents, the struggle, the suicide and the divorce, Johanna said her mother had fought to piece her life back together. It seemed like she'd done a damned good job of it, too.

Colleen first took work in town, made enough to get by, though Driscoll helped out time-to-time to make sure their daughter was cared for. There'd been a few relationships over the years. None ever stuck.

"Mom always seemed fine with that, though it was hard to see Dad having his own family and all, Mom still by herself like she was."

As the years went on Colleen stopped drinking.

She went on trips in the motor home with them, Johanna said, and even volunteered down at the First United Methodist Church over on Oak Street, near the Courthouse, teaching Sunday school.

There was a sadness to her, one that came and went, often when you least expected, Johanna said. Could be something in the morning paper, news on TV. Young boys playing in a schoolyard, a mother wheeling a carriage. Maybe a visit to a supermarket in whatever city they were in.

"She was a good grandmother, warm in ways Dad never could be," she said. "I think she'd always wished Dan and I had a son. You know, just because. Still, she had herself a life. She made herself a life."

The trouble began one Sunday morning, Johanna said. Her mother was outside church after service let out and kids were running about when one darted toward the street. There wasn't much traffic in the Falls, but Sunday mornings after church passed for what of it there was.

The little boy was named Douglas, had blonde hair.

He ran toward the street right in front of Colleen. As he did she grabbed his arm, latched on. She was in her early seventies then and as she swung the child back towards the sidewalk she lost her balance. The car didn't strike her mother hard, Johanna said. This was Sunday morning, Cottonwood Falls. Folks didn't drive like maniacs. Still, it knocked her down. Broke bones. And Colleen hit her head.

"They rushed Mom to the hospital over in Emporia," she said. "For the longest time it seemed she'd make a full recovery. And, despite everything, Mom remained in good spirits. Looking forward to getting out, to getting back to the day-to-day."

Then, Johanna said, Colleen had a stroke.

"They said she was lucky to survive. But I don't know I'd call it luck. It turned her into an old woman overnight. Unable to talk, unable to fend for herself. She'd been so strong. It's been downhill ever since."

Funny thing, Johanna said, was Douglas was one of the Hinkson boys. What would have been a great grand-nephew of Bobby Boy Hinkson.

"Mom said Bobby Boy was Dad's best friend growing up, before he got killed in Korea. She always said she'd named my brother after him."

She pressed her lips. "That just made it all even worse."

Once things sorted out Johanna began going through her mother's belongings. Doing so she'd uncovered a host of old black-and-white photographs, handwritten notes, even diaries she'd kept. She gave them to the detectives on the promise they'd eventually be returned.

"I think you'll find the diaries interesting," she said.

"Because?" Dougal asked.

"Just read them," Johanna said, her smile ever-so-slight.

That was all she said. Just read them.

25

The next afternoon found Storm and Skinner wandering through the parking lot where the old shopping center once stood out on Eisenhower Boulevard. The IGA was gone. The mom-and-pop stores that once called the lot home gone, too. A massive modern supermarket now anchored the site, its parking lot stretching from the corner to cover an area bigger than two asphalt football fields. It all seemed so very suburban.

The detectives had come to do what all good investigators do when they reopen any long-cold investigation: return to the scene of the crime. That a lifetime had elapsed between then and now, that it had changed, was no doubt a hinderance. That didn't mean you couldn't at least gauge the situation, couldn't retrace the route Colleen Goodson said she'd taken that fateful afternoon. Couldn't imagine it all as it once had been, couldn't imagine the disappearance as it allegedly had taken place when. You never knew. Maybe somewhere down the line it'd all prove useful.

The two were on little sleep, the flight back to LaGuardia getting in late the night before. Skinner spent much of that flight thinking about Driscoll Goodson. He and Dallas had gone to see Driscoll after leaving Johanna's. The old man had been standoffish, matter-of-fact, didn't seem the least-bit surprised Robert Landsness wasn't his long-lost son.

All he'd said was: "I didn't think it was him."

There'd been a look of resignation, sure. But no angst, no tears. Not much of anything of consequence at all. Without emotion he'd walked them through the events as he recalled them, from the moment he'd been notified back on base to the time he and Colleen returned to Cottonwood Falls. If he was frustrated by any of it — the lack of answers; the failure of the cops over the decades to find his son — it didn't show. It was all cold, antiseptic, Skinner thought. Certainly, it'd gotten him to wondering.

Driscoll had no strong reactions to his ex-wife, either. Didn't seem angry over what'd happened, didn't sound bitter.

Maybe it was because he didn't hate her. Maybe it was because it was all so long ago. It crossed Skinner's mind maybe it was something else, altogether. Like the odd chance the old man knew what'd happened to his boy. That maybe he'd even had a hand in it, whatever it was had.

Criminals did that, Skinner thought. At least, almost all who weren't sociopaths. They compartmentalized. Exercised what psychologists, sociologists and even cops called "criminal dissociation." Talked about their crimes from afar, with distance. As if they'd heard stories about the crime from some acquaintance but hadn't actually seen it — or, for that matter, committed it. That was how Driscoll told it, what'd happened.

In the car driving back from the house, Skinner and Storm had to admit it all sent chills down their spines.

Skinner had decided going in everything was back on the table. If the situation with Landsness hadn't been proof enough he and Storm needed to keep an open mind, the conversation with Driscoll Goodson made him certain it was the right call. Dallas agreed. Everyone was again a suspect until they weren't. Nothing, no matter how incredible or unbelievable, would be considered improbable or impossible. Until it was.

On the way out of town they'd stopped in to see the local cops.

They explained who they were, asked for the case file on the suicide of Chardon Tetherwood. There wasn't much crime in Cottonwood Falls, not serious anyway. Even with fifty years gone it wasn't long before the file was located, photocopied, and signed for, and they'd again hit the road for Kansas City. But not before Skinner made two inquiries with the chief. Did he know Driscoll and Colleen? What did he think of them?

Dougal knew the answer to the first question. The population of Cottonwood Falls was barely a thousand. He waited on the second.

"She was a good woman," the chief said. "Good woman. Always a hello and a smile, no matter which way the wind."

And Driscoll? Skinner asked.

"Hard man to get to know," the chief said, shaking his head. "Don't know how else to explain it. Just not someone you'd ever feel real close to. Never says much, never shares much. Kind of like talking to a wall. If the man didn't leave a shadow, I'd swear on my mother, sometimes you'd have to wonder if he'd even been there. You really would."

None of that made Driscoll guilty of anything Skinner thought as he sat in the darkened cabin on the flight back home. Except, being a loner. Or maybe being painfully shy — or, socially inept. And still . . .

Skinner knew he needed to get his hands on the novel about the case, no matter how Lenore Johns told them it'd all been theoretical exercise. He also knew they'd need to comb through every line on every page of every file back at headquarters to determine what was missing. His mind raced. What about anyone killed in the plane crash? What other suspects and scenarios had been considered then ruled out — and why?

Johns and Spence had dismissed the lead on the Nash-Rambler down in Waycross. History now proved them right. But no one could have known that until just now. What else had been missed, overlooked?

Not even considered?

What about the fact Driscoll Goodson was a farm boy, which meant he knew how to operate heavy machinery. The Meadowbrook Parkway was being built around the time of the disappearance.

Was the unthinkable even possible? Skinner didn't know.

What he did know from his years as a cop was random kidnappings are rare, maybe the rarest of all crimes.

Sure, there was the Weinberger Case, Lindbergh, Jaycee Lee Duggard. Most of the rest no one could figure you could count on one hand. Most children are taken — or, in the worst of the worst-case scenarios, are murdered — by someone known to them. Mother, father, family, friend, neighbor. Someone close. Someone with access but above suspicion.

Someone you'd least suspect.

Before meeting Dallas, Dougal had gone and talked to the Inspector in charge of the Missing Persons and Cold Case Squad, then paid a visit to the Commissioner. The case had become a national sensation, what with the emergence of Robert Landsness and now with proof he wasn't Bobby Goodson. The media was now having a field day, wanting to know just what the cops were doing to see if the case might ever be resolved.

Shouldn't the department do some prospecting, Skinner asked?

Archaeologists had long-used ground-penetrating radar to map a host of underground features — dig sites and grave sites; searches for dinosaur bones, fossils, even human remains. Forensic archaeologists used it to search potential crime scenes without having to excavate first.

So, Skinner said, why not use the non-intrusive system to search the section of the Meadowbrook being built at the time Bobby Goodson went missing? Why not use it to check the old Goodson house, maybe scan the basement, the yard? Maybe the site of the old Woods home?

Radar would allow investigators to see through the rock, soil, asphalt, concrete. A team wouldn't have to dig unless they'd found something of interest. The Commissioner wasn't warm to the idea. Not with the county in time of fiscal crisis, taxpayers screaming about bureaucratic waste. But after some persistence he said it just might show what a fine, professional department he ran; a department willing to pull out all stops, even now, to solve even the coldest, most long-forgotten case. Without making a promise he knew he'd later have his feet held to the political fire to keep the Commissioner said he'd take it all under consideration.

To see what he could do. If he could do it. Which, he'd try to do. If he could. For now *almost* a promise was good enough for Dougal.

As Skinner and Storm walked up the block toward Mitchell Avenue, toward MacArthur Terrace, Dougal sipped on a coffee he'd bought across the street at the 7-Eleven, already his fifth of the day, wondering just how different things all must've been back then; the scene. How surely there'd been fewer homes, fewer strip malls, fewer cars. Fewer people.

How that alone suggested why no one had seen anything.

Turning onto MacArthur Skinner thought it all so familiar. The street, the houses, even the sidewalks. He thought of all those old photos he'd seen chronicling the birth of suburban Long Island, all the neighborhoods with their aging cookie-cutter tract homes where he'd investigated cases during his career across Nassau County. He thought of his block, where he'd raised his own family — all, so different than Shelter Island.

All, so different than this neighborhood must've been then.

The detectives didn't stop in at the house the Goodsons once called home. No reason to. They just stood outside for a bit, looked around, then walked on over to Hughes, where the neighbor told police she'd found the carriage. It was good to have a sense of it all, Dougal told Dallas: the time it took to cover ground, the surroundings. Yet he thought it also seemed so useless, so futile. Everything was just so . . . so *ordinary*.

As the two of them walked back up Glenn Curtiss toward the shopping center, Dougal took one last sip of his coffee.

"Where the lying began," he mumbled.

"How's that?"

"Where the lying began," he said, again, this time so Dallas could hear. "Just thinking about what Mike Johns' wife said, about that line from her novel. Can't help but think the lying began right here, Dal."

He tossed his coffee cup into a nearby trash bin.

"Somewhere out here that Halloween, Cowboy," he said. "Right here. That's where someone took the first step toward that first lie."

The next morning found Skinner and Storm in the office sorting through boxes, taking inventory of what they'd have to work with.

Most of what they'd read about the case so far was from the narrative, a file of more than three-hundred pages detailing the main components and focus of the investigation. The boxes contained all of the additional interviews, statements, leads. The vastness of the paperwork was in itself staggering. But, much to their chagrin, there was almost no physical evidence. No clothing, no items of interest. No nothing, really.

It made sense when you thought about it.

Johanna was left in the carriage and the cops hadn't found any evidence there. The boy had simply vanished without a trace.

But something bothered Skinner. While the files contained a bunch of old notebooks — from Johns and Spence, from Farmer and Jones — the last entries in the notes belonging to Farmer and Jones were dated November 1, 1955. He had Dallas check them all again.

"First, November First. Fifty-five," Dallas said. "Nothin' other."

"Be right back," Dougal said, rushing out before Dallas could say another word. He returned minutes later. "November Second."

"Second?"

"November Second," Dougal said, again. "I just checked the memorial plaques. The two of them were both killed November Second."

"Figures each would a had 'nother notebook, don't it."

A smile creased Skinner's face.

"It most-certainly does, Dal, since they were out in the field doing interviews when it all went bad. Which . . . "

"Which makes you wonder what happened," Dallas said.

There was only one way to find out. Since they weren't in the boxes that meant there likely was just one other place they could be: with the families of the two dead cops, somehow overlooked by investigators in the wake of their horrific deaths. If not that evidence was gone.

Forever.

Skinner was soon searching on-line records trying to locate family. The widows were long-dead. Farmer's daughter was dead now, too. Real estate records showed Jones' son had sold the house years before, moving to Carolina. Skinner called the listed number. Busy.

He called back three times before getting the son's wife. Sorry, she said. They'd sold the contents of the house before the move.

The records listed all potential descendants of the dead men. Sons, daughters, grandchildren. Nieces, nephews, cousins. Even distant relatives. Some of the addresses and numbers were good. Most weren't, properties long-since vacated; numbers, long out-of-service.

The detectives kept digging. Finally, they found a listing for a woman who was one of Farmer's granddaughters. They called, she answered. Skinner explained the situation. She said that when her mother died she'd taken the belongings, stored them in her attic. Did she still have them? Yes, she did. Buoyed by the prospects Skinner asked if there were any old detective's notebooks in the boxes. She said she didn't know.

She'd never had the heart to check.

She didn't live far from headquarters, twenty miles or so.

Skinner asked if he and Storm could stop by, take a look. He told her how critical to the investigation the stored items just might be.

"Okay," she said, finally. "Let me know when."

How about within the hour, he said.

It was a shot in the dark. Most detective work is.

How big a shot Skinner and Storm had no idea until Doreen Parrish led them to the ladder staircase fitted through the ceiling of her upstairs hall — and Dougal turned his flashlight on the darkened attic.

Light bounced off a handful of cartons, dying at the edges, the rest of the room filled with shadows and silhouettes.

A light breeze kissed the back of Skinner's neck and he flinched. Not knowing what it was, he took a hand, swatted at it. Nothing there.

He tried hard to dismiss it, though circumstances considered, for the briefest instant it crossed his mind he'd been touched by a ghost.

"There's a light switch," Parrish said. "On your left."

Skinner angled the beam, found it, flicked it on. The light revealed dozens of boxes stacked floor-to-ceiling and a fine dust that blanketed the plywood floor, cobwebs drifting from the rafters. Skinner followed the breeze back to the louvres of a window-sized vent cut into the gable end of the attic and half-laughed, realizing his "ghost" foolish invention.

"What?" Dallas said, hearing the reaction.

"Nothing," Dougal said.

The first cartons held little interest. Nicknacks, books, ornaments, old clothes. An hour in, Skinner and Storm were beginning to think the whole task futile. Then Dallas opened the box that changed everything.

The navy sport coat was sealed in a clear plastic bag.

As Dallas pulled it from the box the first thing that hit him was the faint smell of smoke. He unfolded it to find the jacket soiled, charred, and felt to see if there was anything in the pockets. There was.

He reached in. Out it came, a detective's notebook. Careful as he could he tried to open it, but the pages were fused.

"Don't force them," Dougal said.

It was frustrating being so close to a clue of such magnitude, not knowing if it was important. But the two of them knew it was best to leave what came next to the professionals — and decided to take the jacket, notebook and contents of the box to the lab for examination. To let the technicians uncover what it was they could. If they could.

Back in the office the two settled in, began to go through the remaining files, one by one. A few hours in Skinner looked up from a file he'd been reading — wearing, Dallas thought in that very instant, an expression that seemed almost pained. Before Dallas could ask Dougal reached out and, visibly shaken, handed the file to his partner.

"I'm sorry, Dal," he said. "But, I think you'd better read this."

26

"Diz!"

The old woman broke into a joyous smile no sooner had she laid eyes on him. But Dallas Storm just stood there, wearing a bothered look.

"Diz?" she said, again.

He held up the manila file folder. "Southern State Parkway," he said. She studied him, not knowing what to think. He waved the folder again. "Nineteen-Hundred-Fifty-Five, Ma?" he said. "Southern State? Cops?"

"Sweet Lord Jesus, child," she said, as she cut him short.

She motioned him in and, of course, he did as asked.

Slowly, achingly, she coursed the living room. His blood was at a boil now, but she was his mother and he helped her take a seat in her favorite armchair, the old brown cloth one with the worn armrests, before he sat down on the sofa across from her continuing his stare. She knew how it was when he got that look to him and she took a deep breath.

He laid the file down on the table. She nodded to it.

"Where you *fine* that at, Diz?"

"I'm a cop, Mama."

She started to say something, thought better, thinking back on the years. She'd had nightmares the longest time after, the longest. But truth was she hadn't much thought about it since her boy Josiah been lost to Vietnam. Since her husband had gotten sick with that diabetes and the doctors killed him off, one piece at a time — first that leg taken, then the other, until her dear sweet Ozzie, he'd simply lost the will. She'd given life to five children; two boys, three girls. Still had four of them and she knew, in her heart, she'd done right by each. They were all good people. She was proud of that. But she'd never told *none* of them about that night. The girls had been too young. Diz, her youngest, hadn't even been born.

"What you think a me, Dzigbode?"

Dzigbode. Dallas leaned forward on the couch. "Mama?"

"Ever know me be anythin' but a God-fearin' Christian woman?"

"No Ma'am."

"Ever know me be anythin' but a woman a *respec'fulness* an' *considerations?*"

"No Ma'am."

"Then Diz, got to understand had my reasons didn't tell you none 'bout that night," Alile Storm said. "That your daddy an' me, we had our reasons. Was all good intentions. Didn't want you *get* the wrong impression a people, that they was *all* like that. Didn't want you *think* the *worse.* That *kine* a thinkin' Diz, it ain't no good for no one."

"But . . . " he started to say.

He'd always hated it when she'd done this, made him question his thinking, when he was so sure he'd figured it out. He was just a boy when Josiah'd gone off to Vietnam, not even ten.

His brother was an athlete and a fine one at that. A defensive back on the football team at Roosevelt High School in the late Sixties, a guard in basketball, ran track in spring. Never the best student but one who gave his best, an honest effort. He'd always been the protector, kept trouble at bay, made sure his brother and sisters never had a worry, a care, a concern. Now Dallas wondered how it was his brother had gone off to war, wearing the uniform of his country, had fought for it, defended it — had died for it — all at the hands of an enemy he'd had no quarrel with, that he didn't even know much or care much about, when back here, back home, back in the country he'd loved enough to die for, men in uniform once held him at gunpoint, held his own at gunpoint. All, for a wrong they'd been perceived to have done when they hadn't done it at all.

To think those men wore the same uniform Dallas himself had worn. Had worn the same badge. Had pledged to uphold the same law.

"Diz?"

He didn't answer. She knew he wouldn't. He'd always been a stubborn child, the one most like her, and she knew he was keen on trying to figure it all out, as he always had, knew she needed to let him. That he'd answer in due time, when the time came. Only once the time came.

Diz. She was the only one who still called him that.

Dzigbode, when she was trying to make a point, get his attention. *Diz,* when she was just being his mother.

Funny thing was she was the reason he'd come to be called Dallas in the first place. A teen in the Seventies, he'd grown up a fan of the NFL Pittsburgh Steelers with their black-and-gold uniforms and that defense known to America as "The Steel Curtain."

The Steelers not only wore black. Though most in the neighborhood didn't care much for the team's quarterback, Terry Bradshaw, who was blonde-haired and straight out of Shreveport, Louisiana, the Steelers had stars. *Black* stars: Franco Harris and, later, Lynn Swann on offense; Dwight White, Ernie Holmes, L.C. Greenwood and "Mean" Joe Greene as the face of that feared defensive line. Their other face, their *black* face.

That Christmas he was sixteen she'd bought him a jersey. He'd opened the box thinking it was that of his beloved Steelers only to find the white jersey of their arch-rival, the Dallas Cowboys. He hated the Cowboys. Tom Landry and that hat; Roger Staubach. That lawman star. But this was his mother. Torn, he'd worn that shirt to school one day.

Then Murphy, always the comedian, saw him in the hall. Shouted: "Hey, you. *Dallas!*" And everyone fell out laughing.

All these years later he'd grown comfortable with it, maybe even grown to like it. He leaned forward again on the couch, staring, anger still there. She was his mother. He opened the manila folder.

"Held guns on you, on you and Daddy. On Josiah. These men did."

She didn't say a word. "Held loaded guns on you. Held guns on the *Negroes.* Says so right here."

She looked at him, serious. Like she did when she did.

"Held guns on us *niggers*, child," she said. "Didn't call us no *Negroes*. Them men, *theys* called us *niggers*. To them folk was all we was. Wasn't Black, wasn't Negroes . . . All we was was *niggers*."

He felt a rage he hadn't felt in the longest time welling up inside him. "Those policemen, they called you . . . They called you the N-word?"

"Didn't call us no *N-word*," she said, stern now. "Called us . . . "

She told him the story in every hurtful detail, explaining to him, to the only son she had left in this world, why, despite it all, she'd never once tried to stop him from becoming a policeman like them — though there were times, she soon said, when she'd thought she should.

"Got to understand," she said, "much as I had my *conflic's*, knew deep in my heart was a good thing not to say nothin'. Let you do what *you* need be done." She sat there, still, a lone tear running down her cheek.

"Understand what is I'm sayin', Diz?"

"No, Mama," Dallas said, finally. "Not sure I do."

Driving out along an endless stretch of Sunrise Highway through the pine barrens of mid-eastern Suffolk County, Dougal Skinner was lost in thought. The road stretched before him two lanes wide to the horizon and in a few weeks it'd be bumper-to-bumper with the pretentious summer crowd bound for their holidays in the Hamptons. Right now it was almost desolate, but a handful of cars in either direction.

Before leaving the office he'd called Dallas. It was no surprise when the call bounced to voice mail. He left a message, anyway. Nothing much. Just a reminder that if Dallas needed anything he knew where to find him. He wondered how his friend was dealing with it all.

He wondered how he would have dealt with it, had it been him.

It had been a twisted day. The Commissioner, realizing the value of good public relations, had authorized the survey search by the forensic archaeology team. To the surprise of just about everyone they'd actually located a site of interest. It was just in off the shoulder of Meadowbrook

Parkway, a quarter-mile as the crow flies from the shopping center where Bobby was said to have disappeared and the house where the Goodsons once lived. Dougal went to the scene to watch the excavation.

Bones and bone fragments were unearthed just a few feet under the surface. The lead forensic archaeologist said they appeared human.

There wasn't a full skeleton and the team could find nothing else of import in the area, between the shoulder and old Barnum Creek. But the bones had been taken to the lab for analysis, to be dated and examined for DNA. Everyone was already thinking the worst and the media, having sniffed it out, was reporting the cops were trying to determine if the find marked the final, tragic end to the long-unsolved Goodson case.

For his part, Dougal was hopeful. Not that he wanted the boy dead, he just wanted some firm clues, firm answers.

He knew, despite it all, nothing had been solved.

Knowing resolution was days off, knowing Dallas would be out-of-pocket until he'd gotten his feet back, Dougal went to the office after the dig. He'd packed all the evidence boxes he could fit into the trunk of his car, packed the photos and diaries given them by Johanna, grabbed the novel by Lenore Johns, called Donna and told her he was spending a long weekend out on Shelter Island. A long weekend alone.

She wasn't happy about that, not with everything else going on in their lives at the moment, impending grandparenthood high on the list.

But she understood. She'd been a cop's wife a long time.

The sun was low in the sky and off in the distance headlights began to flicker in the dusk as Dougal reached out, absentminded, turned his on, too. He didn't drive this way often, not to Shelter Island.

Once in the last ten years, to be exact. Just once.

The usual route took him out along the North Fork, the Long Island Expressway to the end — an end that hadn't even been built back when he was a kid. From there it was the old main road, through a myriad of East End towns: Riverhead, Aquebogue, Jamesport, Laurel, Mattituck,

Cutchogue, Southold, out past Port of Egypt to the North Ferry hard by the railroad station in downtown Greenport.

Once, the road had been lined with potato farms, vegetable farms, duck farms and farm girls who sold cabbage, turnips, brussels, fresh eggs, homemade pies and jams, all from hand-built roadside farm stands.

It was so different now.

The Elbow Room was still there alongside the road in Jamesport and the old red school house still stood on that small hill near the railroad bridge in Laurel. But now there was that massive outlet mall at the end of the LIE threatening to swallow up the old race track where locals ran weekend stockers and from there, clear out to the traffic circle, the blacktop was lined with stripmall stores and fast food restaurants and car dealerships; most that once was old farm land, now leveled and paved over. Some old farms had become vineyards, farmers in their overalls and work-stained white undershirts given way to gentrified vintners in designer jeans and scotch-plaid flannels from L.L. Bean. Traffic no longer got snarled by rusting old tractors moving barely faster than a farm horse or by overburdened potato trucks hauling in from the fields. It was now standstilled by day-trippers in their Land Rovers, BMWs and Porsches come to antique or just spend a lazy afternoon tasting wine.

Sad, Dougal thought, those old days long-gone. That that Long Island pretty much now survived only on Shelter Island. And, barely at that.

Truth was, that wasn't why he'd avoided going north.

He'd driven out on the South Fork because he was in one of *those* moods. The dig site, the find. His daughter, soon to become a mom.

The situation with Dallas. The case.

All of it had gotten him to thinking about his life.

His mom once told him, when he was a kid, how good things happened to good people; how bad people got theirs in the end. On a night like this he wasn't so sure. So he'd decided to take the South Ferry across instead of the North. Decided to take that drive, once again.

The drive he hadn't taken since that night so long ago.

A cop will always tell you that of all the tough parts of the job the worst is having to knock on someone's door in the middle of the night, break the news. They'll tell you no matter who answers the reaction is always the same, how they'll pray those officers are there to tell them their loved one has been arrested. That maybe they're even at the hospital, seriously hurt. That they're anything but dead.

Truth is, cops don't go knocking on doors that time of night unless there's notifications to be made. Unless someone is, in fact, dead.

Truth is, no one knows that better than cops.

So when Dougal heard them that night, when he looked out the window half-asleep and saw the cruiser, he knew. His two youngest were in bed. He went to check on them, anyway.

But Logan? She was in the dorms over at Hofstra University. As he raced down the stairs he was sure she was gone.

He opened the door, trembling. Found the officers, nerve-wracked as he was. Near collapse, he said: "Please, tell me it's not my daughter." No, one of the officers said. And just when he began to breathe again, filled with indescribable relief, the cop said: "I'm sorry. It's your parents."

What happened next was a blur. Donna rushing to comfort him, his two youngest, stirred from their sleep, taken up on the couch in disbelief. Everyone, in tears. Him, walking the floor like a condemned man, calling Logan, breaking the news. No one having the vaguest idea what to do, what to say, as they'd waited for her to arrive home from campus.

Declan and Clemence hardly ever went off-Island and, even then, only out of necessity. That night they'd taken the South Ferry over to have dinner, take in a movie in Southampton. It was raining and heading home they'd had a blowout. Deck changed the tire, but it'd set them back.

The ferries didn't run all night to Shelter Island. Last one on an off-season Thursday was quarter-to-midnight. The road was slick from the rain. Declan pushed it, anyway. The car skidded off the wet pavement, across a shallow ditch, crashed into a small stand of trees.

Neither was wearing a seat belt. They'd never had a chance.

The cops offered to drive him out. Dougal refused saying he was fine, that he had to go it alone. He reached the scene on Ferry Road sometime after 4 a.m. It was black, the night sky dense with low clouds, the ground soaked, the crash site the only thing lighted. Two white sheets stretched over the earth. He went numb as he stepped from the car. He knew what they were, those sheets, what was under them. *Who.* He'd been here before at a scene like this. Those had all been strangers.

These weren't strangers this time.

Investigators are hard to such things. But Dougal was a cop, like them, and when he hit the ground everything stopped. Every one of them, dead in their tracks. Knowing. Knowing but for the grace of God what might've been. How it might've been them. After a moment some officers ran to him, got him upright. Wrapped him tight in a warm blanket.

Steadied him as he sat there sobbing, weeping like a child.

Weeping, until he could cry no more.

He stood there now, leaned hard against the car, unexpected tears welling in his eyes. The flashers were on, it was pitch black.

This time nothing was illuminated except the glow of those hazard lights, dancing on and off like lightning bugs; except for that of the smallest area illuminated by his flashlight. It didn't matter. He could see it all in his mind as he had seen it a million times since that God-awful night. He walked across the ditch, to the stand of trees, shined his light on the scarred trunks; trunks scarred where the bark had been gouged a decade before. Otherwise, it felt all so barren.

The light caught the outline of one small cross, then another, and in that instant he was dumbstruck. He hadn't left them. He'd never had the heart to come back at all. He knew it hadn't been Donna. Or the girls.

They would have mentioned.

He bent down, shined the light on one cross, then the other. A small envelope in a sealed plastic bag was fastened to the back. He set the light on it. Inside was a card from the funeral home and a hand-written note:

> *"Someday, when the hurt and anger over how they died is gone, remember the good they've done. Raised a good cop, a good friend, a good . . . "*

"Son of a bitch," Dougal said, barely a whisper, as he finished reading. It wasn't signed, but that didn't matter. He knew the handwriting.

As he stood watching the ferry an hour later the words still echoed. He'd stuck the note in his pocket, gotten back in the car. Sat there, speechless, not knowing what to think, what to do. He wasn't sad. How could he be sad? All he could feel at that moment was thankful. Thankful he'd had good parents. Thankful he had such a good family, a good friend. Thankful he'd had a good life. A blessed life. A truly blessed life.

The last few miles to the ferry were mindless. He'd reached the slip, parked the car off to the side of the road, walked to the landing and leaned hard against the rail watching the ferry make that crossing, the shortest crossing in the history of ferries, the distance between where he stood and Shelter Island barely the length of a football field — far shorter than the distance crossing from the north. It was still early. He had time. So he'd stood there, watched trip after trip. After trip. Taking it all in, thinking.

Thinking about how close his parents had come, about how fast his life had changed. Thinking about how the briefest of instants can change the course of a lifetime. A daughter, poised to give birth. Parents, killed in a car crash. A Negro family, held by the cops at gunpoint.

A boy, vanished from in front of a suburban supermarket.

Each, in no more than the time it took that boat to make it across.

Hours passed by the time Dallas walked back into the living room. He'd gone inside to the bedroom he and his brother once shared as boys, shut the door, sat there staring at the old pictures. Josiah in his football uniform, Josiah playing basketball. Josiah at his graduation, family gathered around: his mother, father, sisters, aunts, cousins; all the kin.

Josiah when he'd joined the Army.

He tried to imagine what had happened that night long ago, how it had all gone down. The account had been sanitized in the official file, the story his mother told anything but. Those officers, training their guns. His father trembling, his mother trying to will herself to be strong. His brother cowering in the back seat. Ducked down, hiding.

That was the hardest part, he thought. The harshest part. He'd never known Josiah to be anything but a rock, to be anything but strong.

To think those men had made his brother wet himself, that they'd laughed at him, mocked him, just a boy, as he did.

How he wished just one of them was still alive, that he could hunt him down. God forgive him what he would do to the man if he could find him, then. If he could find any of them, God forgive him what he would do.

Then Dallas found himself staring at the verse, the one fastened neatly to the wall amongst all the photographs of Josiah hanging there.

And he sat there reading it, over and over and over again.

The words of the Reverend Dr. Martin Luther King, Jr.:

> *"Darkness cannot drive out darkness. Only light can do*
> *that. Hate cannot drive out hate. Only love can do that."*

His mother had hung it there fresh home from church one Sunday. One Sunday amid the sadness not long after word had come Josiah was dead in Vietnam. One-by-one Dallas looked over all those photos again. His mother and father, his sisters, his cousins, his aunts, his brother. His family, himself. All of them joyful as Josiah became the first of them to graduate high school. The shot of him there alongside his brother, his brother dressed in his Army uniform, the two of them so proud.

He could still remember how he'd felt back then.

How proud he still was now, a man of fifty, that his brother had managed so much in so short a life. At the impression he'd made on so many in so short a time. Then he'd walked back out to the living room to find his mother sitting in that armchair, having not moved an inch. As he walked past he'd placed a hand on her shoulder, given a gentle squeeze.

"Ma?"

She stared straight at him. "Diz?"

"Still think you should a told us 'bout what happened that night."

"Would a just angry up the blood child," she said.

"Still angry now, Ma."

"Y'all get over it."

He took a deep breath. "An' you know that how?"

He couldn't quite be certain and, even later, he wasn't sure if he'd imagined it. But, he thought she'd almost smiled.

"Cause I figure if you done heard it as a boy was gonna stay angry a *lone* time, Diz. A lone time. Heard it as a man, well . . . Then I figure you was gonna have 'nough sense to understand. Put it in its right place."

She pointed to the manila folder still laid out on the table.

"Two *kines* a hate in this world, Diz," she said. "*Kine* a hate jus' because. *Kine* a hate jus' because don't know no better. One can't never change. The other? The other maybe got hope you show him the light.

"Can't do that you fill with hate, too."

She gave him that look. "Y'all my son, Diz. An' this hate, it got to end somewheres. A man, he can't live a right life with a hatred in his heart. Man a anger, man a hate. That's a man a small-minded thinkin'. Jus' small-minded, understand? Didn't want you become a man like that.

"Didn't want none a my *childrens* grow up be like *that*."

Dallas reached for the folder. "Held guns on you, held *loaded* guns on you. Held guns on . . . Held guns on the *niggers*."

She stared at him. "Rather had become one a *those* men, Diz?"

Those men. One of those men.

As Dallas sat there not knowing what to say, that phrase a drumbeat in his head, all he could think of was those damned white cops.

And also God-damned Essex.

"Know your Mama's right, don't you child."

This time she smiled, definitely smiled.

And in that moment Dallas wondered if she'd really bought him that Cowboys jersey on accident, after all.

27

The face in the old black-and-white photograph stared out across the worn butcher block table, across the years, stared out at him, straight through him almost, and at that moment Dougal Skinner felt a million things and nothing at all. Mostly, he thought, he felt inadequate.

He sipped what was left of morning coffee, mind a blur.

What happened to you, Bobby?

It was the only lucid thought he could muster and in that instant he knew he had no answer, had no idea where to find one.

He'd been staring at that face for hours, off and on, since late into the night before, and he couldn't bare to look at it any longer.

He turned, walked to the kitchen, poured himself still another cup from the coffee maker, wandered out back. He'd set the photo on the table, hard against a vase, no sooner had he come in from the ferry.

Not that he needed to be reminded what the case was all about. Rather, experience told him that sometimes all it took was a glance to jar loose a thought and that sometimes something as innocent as a picture did just that — connecting some unconnected wire in your brain when you least expected. For hours he'd sat and read *Sweet Child of Innocence*, the novel by Lenore Johns. Imagined it a correct assessment of Driscoll and Colleen Goodson. Him, somehow sinister, with an abusive bent buried 'neath an even-keeled, reserved exterior. Her, shallow and manipulative, with a fierce loyalty to her controlling husband. The two of them strangely unaffected by any and all of it, the disappearance of their son, knowing full well the truth only the two of them knew. That one of them had beaten the boy to death in a fit of rage, that together they'd dug the hole. Buried him beneath the slab in the basement. Covered their tracks.

Yet even as Dougal got to thinking throughout the night and his eyes soaked in that picture, the one of Bobby Goodson as he had been — not fictionalized, not sensationalized; but in the flesh, of the living — that one instance when the wires might connect simply failed to materialize.

No lightning, no magic.

Despite a million wanton thoughts there was still no way to navigate the maze; the sad truth, even after all this time, every reasonable scenario, every reasonable answer, leading to the same inevitable dead end. To the same deadest of dead ends. The jury was still out on the bones found along the Meadowbrook. But the forensics team had checked the house and, at Dougal's insistence, abutments to the parkway bridge. The old-timers reminded him the foundation was under construction back then; rumor had it the boy's body was buried deep in the wet cement.

Dougal thought it urban legend. Jimmy Hoffa stuff, all this Christ in concrete. Still, he'd felt obligation and, truth be told, not much relief when the teams struck out. What to make that, as in the book, Colleen's father died of a shotgun blast under most-curious circumstances, circumstances even more curious as a result of the work of those small-town cops. Cops who'd failed to answer all but the most-basic questions.

Dougal had no idea.

He'd read the report, wondering if the cops missed something, but found the lone smoking gun to literally be the smoking gun.

He stood at the mooring sipping coffee, looking out on the backwater. It was dark and tranquil and an early-morning haze clung to the surface. Within the hour, as the sun rose, it would burn off in the building heat and the water would glisten and gleam, full of promise only a fisherman could truly understand. For now the mist lingered. He thought how it reminded him of that morning. The one so long ago, now.

He was just a kid, not even fifteen, and that morning he'd taken a wood bucket and a long-handled crab net, had poled along the quiet edges of the solemn creek in the Jon boat. Through the shallows, through the eel grass, hunting blue-claws by the glow of a kerosene lantern; on the shoals, clinging to the dock timbers. Wherever he could find them in the flickering pre-dawn light. He was almost home, half a bushel full, before the sun ever cracked the horizon. And then he saw him.

Face down in the water, not far from his boat. Old Lester.

He didn't know it was Old Lester, straight off. Didn't know it until he'd reached him, grabbed him, turned him over. Seen his face, ashen and lifeless. But he'd known long before he'd even moved an inch the man was gone. Just gone. Stone cold dead.

His old man hated Lester. It had been that way for years, though it hadn't been that way forever. Declan and Lester had once been friends. Then Lester's wife ran off without so much as a word and never came back and Old Lester got irritated with everything, with everyone, picking fights, wearing out whatever welcomes he had left in the bank. Deck held out hope Lester'd come around; gave him every chance. Said Lester had repaid the kindness by crossing the one line he shouldn't have ever crossed. He'd poached his grounds, threatened his lifeblood.

The two men had come to words, rumor had it maybe more. No one seemed to know for certain. But Lester said something and Deck, he took it worse even than the poaching, warned Old Lester it'd better end then and there. Weeks went by, then months, then maybe a year or more, and nothing happened. Then Old Lester had come up a floater — and a bad one, at that. The volunteers from the local fire department ran out an ambulance to help, just in case. One look was all it took.

The cops came around, asked a lot of questions.

Folks kept secrets on Shelter Island. That didn't mean there weren't many, just that folks kept them. There had never been a murder on-Island, not one in more than three-hundred years, least not one that'd ever been charged. Folks weren't saying this was the first — though behind closed doors they weren't saying it wasn't, either.

Investigators from the Suffolk County Sheriff's Department, the Greenport Police, the Town of Southold Police, the New York State Police and even the fledgling Suffolk County Police Department were brought in to keep an eye on the local cops from Shelter Island.

Those investigators said it looked like Old Lester had been smacked in the head with a bat or an oar, something hard — that he'd been knocked overboard, had then drowned — though the cops also conceded Lester could have slipped, conked his head on his scow.

Could have fallen into the creek unconscious, drowned like that.

The cops sat Dougal down at the kitchen table. Asked him a lot of questions: Where'd he find the body? How'd he find the body? What did Old Lester look like when he'd found him? Was he sure he'd been dead? When did he last see Old Lester alive? Did he suspect foul play? Did he think his father could have done it? Was he certain? Why?

Dougal was nervous. He'd never been questioned by cops before. He listened to the questions, answered each best he could, honest as he could. Then he sat there as the cops asked them all over again, each in some different way, until he realized what they were getting at; that they were trying to make him stumble, trip him up. And finally he asked why they were doing that since he'd told them the truth, the whole truth and nothing but, and then they sat there finding it seriously hard to believe they'd just been upbraided by what they thought some punk-ass kid.

So they told Dougal they were going to arrest his old man. Now or maybe later, they didn't know, but they were going to arrest him, were going to throw his ass in jail. And all Dougal could think at that moment was how they were wrong. How it was all just coincidence and bad luck and how surely there had to be some way to prove it. Just had to be.

The thing was there seriously was no way to tell.

The Medical Examiner declared Old Lester could have been murdered or that he really could have slipped in the darkness, slammed his head, gone in. That his findings were all somehow inconclusive. And so his old man was never charged, though he also was never cleared, and for the first time Dougal thought he might become a cop just so he could find answers those guys couldn't; so he could really do cop work.

The funny thing was, he thought as he stood here now, all these years later he couldn't find any answers, either. Just nagging questions. He wondered how that was possible. He found it all disturbingly ironic.

The first pages of the diaries were achingly pedestrian. A young girl's life, as it were, from the age of fourteen. Colleen, on which boys were really swell; on what girls were regular *dumb Doras.*

Colleen, on life in school; on life in the Falls.

"Girls bellyaching," an entry from January 15, 1947, read. "They hate it boys think I'm the cat's meow. They disremember when it wasn't so. No sense why. Not going to get all-overish because they're all wet and mean."

Some of it was rife with references, meanings, lost to the years. A boy who was a real "oil can." A man known around town as a "Sunday man." One woman who, Colleen noted with disdain, was "all seven-by-nine."

Dougal hadn't the vaguest. And still . . .

Colleen wrote how this boy in school had confided to her he'd gone "almost all the way" with a girl she knew. How the boy warned her to "keep that dry" and how she'd written, afterwards, how she loved secrets but wasn't always so good at keeping them. How Dougal figured that's what'd been meant by "keep that dry." Though, who knew?

Some of the descriptions were obvious, even after all these years.

The local hotel was "swanky;" one local banker was known to dress "rag proper." A teacher Colleen disliked was "an old fuddy-duddy."

Mostly, Dougal thought, Colleen came across as frank in her assessments. That she wasn't one to mince words. Like this entry:

> "Daddy came home again mean. The
> situation's all beer and skittles. Said
> mother was no better than a catalogue

> woman and said he should clout her one.
> She yelled go boil your shirt and said you
> can't come it over me, so. He said what's
> going on and she said it's nothing to
> nobody and he said so now I'm nobody,
> I'm your husband, damn it, and she said I
> want to be shut of you you're so damned
> infernal. Don't know what started it, but
> daddy threatened to clobber me one and
> Franklin stepped into it. Father beat him
> with a switch, making for a terrible scene.
> It's all May hay, it is. I truly hate them.
> Thank goodness for Franklin . . . "

No less candid were accounts of boys asking for dates, of Colleen leading them on without concern. She wrote about using them to take in movies in far-off places like Emporia and Topeka and for dates to the county fair and to the state fair and to the stock-car races all the way over in Hutchinson; to sporting events and the like.

One entry about a boy Colleen liked came with a confession: "I want to kiss him a lot and good." When another boy took her to a movie, she wrote: "He tried to do stuff, touch me. I kind of let him think he could before we went. Kind of, so he'd take me. But I wasn't doing THAT."

She mentioned still another, then wrote: "Now he's angry with me saying I did him wrong. Boys. They're D-U-M-B."

Boys might be dumb at that Dougal thought, Colleen making no bones about being unabashed, unashamed and unapologetic. Still, boys marched onward like lemmings toward a cliff edge; single-minded in their focus, blind to the inevitable. She preened, they swooned. She played the hand, they protested. And then come the inevitable realization they'd reluctantly folded. Each and every one of them. Sent home in defeat.

Calculating to a fault Colleen seemed early on. Determined, those entries as testament, to change her lot.

No matter how cruel she need be, to what end.

As far as Dougal could tell that's where Driscoll Goodson came in. Targeted, all indications were, because he was nice enough, steady enough, naive enough. Because he was available and, it seemed as certain, because he came from money. Yet as time passed it became clear from the telling something unexpected had happened, that Colleen had genuinely become enamored with her new beau. It was obvious she'd even begun to fall in love. Recounting their first date, she'd written:

> "He's so shy, but very sweet. Bought me
> cotton candy, soda pop. Held my hand.
> Didn't force it like those other boys."

Before long, that had evolved to:

> "Glad Driscoll wants to see me as much as
> he does. Still not much of a talker, but I
> can tell he likes me and I like him. Wish
> his parents were keener on me, especially
> his mother. Also, his friend Bobby Boy.
> We've had quite a few months so far. Find
> myself daydreaming of us. Us? Think we're
> going to have the time of it still."

Within a matter of pages she'd gone from day-dreaming and little else to making out, touching, getting hot and heavy. Getting lost in the moment. She wrote how excited it made her feel, how alive. How good the two of them felt afterwards. How things had gotten to going almost all the way — and how nervous both of them were, how scared, neither having ever done anything close to that before and how Driscoll promised he'd be careful and how he was and how thankful Colleen was that she could trust him to keep his word and show restraint, when all those other boys only tried to make her. Then, Driscoll was off to college and Colleen seemed certain Harriet Goodson was trying to put distance between them.

Two years and a hundred pages down the line Colleen had come to the conclusion she was still no closer to getting out of her situation, out of Cottonwood Falls, than she'd been at the start. That she was losing her grip on Driscoll; the nagging feeling the two were at a crossroads. That there was a chance she'd be out of the car, left by the side of the road.

> "All this time, now maybe nothing? Can't bear the thought, back on my own. Things bad at home. All mother does is drink. Daddy threatens to beat me. Think how lucky Franklin is, having run off as he did. The Goodsons have become a constant annoyance, especially H-E-R. Harriet the Lariat! She wants me G-O-N-E! Doing all she can to persuade Driscoll she's dead-on. I love him and think he loves me. But, he's a momma's boy and I'll never be his mother. What to do?"

What Colleen did next was turn up pregnant. Which made Dougal wonder since what happened soon after was Driscoll and Colleen hastily married — and, lo and behold, she'd written that she'd lost the baby. From the reading there seemed to be a lot more to the story than met the eye, with hints much of it was pure invention, borne out of what Colleen saw as necessity. Interestingly though there was no admission. Yet there was an argument, recounted in entries, when she recalled a confrontation with Harriet, her mother-in-law most-accusatory in all her assertions:

> "I said, What, you think I made it up? She said it crossed her mind. I told her not by a long chalk. How dare you? She LAUGHED. Said maybe I should go crawl back under the rock my family crawled out from under. I want to strangle her. And I mean STRANGLE! The nerve! What a terrible, terrible, horrible woman she truly is, Harriet the Lariat!!! Told Driscoll we need to leave. SOON!"

Then Driscoll was in the Air Force, Bobby Hinkson was dead and little Bobby was born — the three of them moved far from Kansas.

To Hempstead Plains.

From all Dougal read things seemed fine. Not epic, not earth-shaking, not story-book romance. But fine. Driscoll was working, Colleen was making friends. Little Bobby was growing. Other than the fact he had a slight lisp, Colleen wrote, all was right and good with the world.

Then Johanna was born. And it all seemed to change.

There were entries about Johanna crying for days on end. About fruitless days; fitful, sleepless nights. Entries about Bobby acting out, Driscoll agitated and aggravated; about Colleen at the end of her rope. About a world crumbling more with each passing minute, no relief in sight. Along the way Colleen told of Bobby falling off his tricycle, breaking his arm, lamenting she'd failed to prevent it.

She'd written about how thankful she was for neighbor Margie being there when she needed her most — calling the doctor, driving them to the hospital — and how Marjorie stepped in to smooth things over with Driscoll, who'd thought Colleen irresponsible for letting it all happen in the first place. She'd confessed how she'd gotten so out of sorts, struck Bobby one day; lost her temper, swatted him a good one on the backside. How he'd cried. How awful it had made her feel afterwards, thinking to herself what a terrible mother she was. No better, she wrote, than her own feeble parents, who on their best were all fits and starts.

She'd written how she'd had a drink to calm her nerves, which had been frayed to threadbare. How she'd admonished herself to do better, be better. And still she hadn't realized all along Jo had been crying with the sufferings of colic, common gas, and how it'd taken the doctor to tell her all she needed to do was change her formula. She'd resolved the issue.

But, she noted the growing chasm was swallowing her marriage.

> "Driscoll's grumpy again. Maybe I should say
> all the time. It's been a long time between us.
> You know, a long time without THAT. I think
> he's tired of trying. Certainly, he hasn't tried
> anything of late and some days I think he
> could care less and some days I think I could,

> too, I'm so tired of trying to explain that I'm so
> tired. Is this what happens to married people,
> that they just stop trying? He's SO difficult to
> talk to. Sometimes, I just don't think he wants
> to be bothered. Maybe it will pass. One can
> only hope. I never imagined it would be like
> this, married life. He made a point to say he
> didn't think his mother would be so
> overwhelmed. His MOTHER? I told him that
> was mean. NO ANSWER. What else is new."

It was obvious what was coming next, Dougal thought. Within a handful of pages, there it was. "Met someone," was all it said and it wasn't a time before entries evolved into complaints about Driscoll and about how he complained she drank too much and about how he had accused her of being like her mother and how angry that had made her.

Enough that she wrote:

> "I asked what he meant by that and he didn't
> say a word, just sat there. I'm not my mother,
> that's what I told him, and he saw I was hurt
> and he said that he understood but still said
> my drinking concerned him and said they say
> the apple doesn't fall too far from the tree for a
> reason. He told me I needed to STOP!"

The drinking hadn't stopped. Neither had this notion of Colleen running around because before long there was a notation about a doctor's visit. And there was one simple question: "Pregnant?"

The doctor's appointment was for the Friday before Bobby went missing. An entry from the very morning he disappeared noted the doctor had arranged a follow-up. "What a TERRIBLE mess I've made. Really screwed up this time." Underneath, Colleen wrote: "Driscoll or Jake?"

Driscoll? Or Jake?

It wasn't clear, straight off, what Colleen meant by that, though Dougal thought there was an obvious assumption to be made.

Just as obvious was that the answer was soon irrelevant. Within hours of having written those words Bobby was gone. Within days Jake Johnson was gone, too; dead, along with Marjorie, Tag, Holt Hamilton, Farmer and Jones. It was some time before Colleen wrote about any of it again. By then it turned out she hadn't been pregnant after all and nevertheless Driscoll had learned of her running around, informed by the police, and then Driscoll and Colleen were back in Cottonwood Falls and things had gotten so far twisted that soon it was all over but the shouting.

And then even that.

He'd read on, Dougal had, read as much of those diaries as he could stand to read. Johanna was right, it explained a lot.

More than he could have guessed.

If Colleen was to be believed she'd never actually slept with Jake Johnson. She'd confessed how she'd thought about it, been tempted. How she'd come close. How in the end she just couldn't bring herself to do so because when she thought about it, really thought about it, she'd decided she really did love her husband. That she'd considered life might be better with Jake, then realized it wouldn't. That the man she wanted was Driscoll. Which was the crux of the matter, Driscoll or Jake?

That it had all gotten so out of hand, so misconstrued, was because Colleen had let it. She knew that, had agonized over the fact she could never convince Driscoll she really hadn't cheated. That she had no way to prove it; how the entire mess was of her own doing. That she truly had only herself to blame. Which, it turned out, was what she did.

She blamed herself for all of it.

She'd written about how she'd come close to having an affair with the stock boy, Jimmy Dodge, how she'd wanted him, right or wrong, if only just because the situation with her husband had become so strained — no relief, no resolution, in sight. Written how Jimmy had turned on her in the car once she'd become paralyzed by visions of her son.

How he'd called her a murderer. *A murderer!*

Intriguing, Dougal thought, was Colleen wondered if in some strange way she really was. If her son was dead; if that did make her his killer.

It struck Dougal how it all jibed with the accounts in the original case file. Witnesses at the time noted Colleen seemed distracted, distant even, and most-certainly hinky the afternoon her son disappeared.

Which led to speculation, led to assumptions.

Now, it all made sense.

Her actions weren't sinister, they were confused. Colleen had been overwhelmed. Two children to take care of, not enough time, not enough assistance. Not enough understanding. Not enough of a husband. She'd mishandled the situation, sure. Had gotten in over head, gone rolling in the deep. She was involved with another man, at a crossroads on what to do — who to choose, what life to choose — and the kids had gotten sick. Then the call from the doctor suggested she might be pregnant. Or, at least, that he'd suspected she might be. It had sent her over the edge.

It was easy to see how, distracted by it all, she might've made a bad decision; left Jo and Bobby outside the IGA. How she'd failed to consider the consequences of her actions; had failed to take heed of her husband's concerns. How life had gone seriously wrong from that moment on. How the police, the witnesses, how even Driscoll, might've assumed something else entirely. Assumed Colleen no better than the boy who cried wolf.

That might be the wrong take. Somehow, Dougal didn't think so.

The entries were too honest.

Seeing Colleen, seeing it all through her eyes, only reaffirmed what Dougal knew from his years as a detective: there's two sides to every story. Sometimes common sense was the key to understanding where all stories touched truth, where they didn't. Through countless entries, saddled with guilt, Colleen's voice rang true. She'd wondered what might've happened if the situation had been different, if she'd done just one thing different. She'd been anguished, knowing she might never get the chance to make any of it right again. How she didn't know how to make it right, how shameful that made her feel. She wrote how Driscoll was a good father. Distant, yes. But a father who truly cared, more than he'd ever let on.

How she'd taken all of it for granted — having a good husband, a good man, good children; a good life — and how all of it had vanished.

Had vanished in one careless instant. Like that, gone.

> "If I could know one thing, if I could ask God one thing, it would be why? Why did someone take Bobby? Why did they do this to us? What I wouldn't give to know what happened to my sweet little boy. To have him back, to have it all back, how things were. I can't imagine who could be so terrible, what kind of person could be so terrible. If only I had known, if only I knew what I know now. But I was blind to it. How can I begin to ask for forgiveness, ever be forgiven? How can I ever forgive myself? I can't. I am reminded of that all the time."

And still there were two most-curious entries that continued to haunt Dougal long after he'd set the diaries aside, thinking how Colleen was not close to who he'd imagined her to be. Thinking how she was far better, far more complicated, than anyone had ever given her credit for being.

Than he had given her credit for being.

One came a decade after Bobby had first gone missing, after a decade without word of any kind, and long after Colleen had resolved to get her life in order. The case was long cold by then and Colleen had written how she'd stopped drinking, become a regular church attendee. Had begun to teach Sunday school. On the tenth anniversary of the disappearance, Colleen wrote how the old butcher down at the IGA once told her there was something about Marjorie Woods that troubled him:

> "I cannot say this for certain, he told me, and I will not tell you how to choose your friends. I will only say choose them wisely and I am not convinced this woman is a wise choice. I had

no reason to believe him. Margie was always good to me. Still, I wonder. When it came to people, Mr. Katsch was seldom wrong."

Curious, Dougal thought, this warning about the neighbor, how Katsch was "seldom wrong." What to make of that? What to make of the account Colleen wrote in the days after Chardon Tetherwood was found dead. Of the note, recounted in detail, from her own mother. How Colleen had found it, spattered with blood, beside her father's lifeless body.

How she'd taken it, kept it from the police. How she couldn't bear the thought of anyone ever reading it. Not ever.

> "Time to acknowledge the corn, Char. All you ever been is a lick and a promise, a barrel-boarder, but I ain't addle-headed and by good rights you should a done better by me. Don't care a continental no more what you think. I'm done gettin' my back up and found me a man thinks I'm cream gravy and that ain't no flannel-mouth talk. We's hand in glove, we are, me and him. Go tearin' up jake if you want, but I'm givin' you the mitten. p.s. Coll ain't your daughter, Char. Ha!"

Colleen wasn't his daughter?

Thinking back on the account for hours afterward Dougal found it a truly terrible thing — that a mother could be so cold. That a child should have to learn such harsh news in such bad fashion.

What do you ever know about your life? What does anyone ever really know? You think you know the answer. But, Dougal thought as he sat there, most people never even know the question. They take what happens at face value, rarely thinking it might be just part of the story, not the whole. Rarely thinking the life they've lived might not be the truth at all. That some of it might be something else altogether. Dallas had no idea the secret his family held for so long and only now was he finding out, trying to piece together the puzzle, hoping it came out right.

And Colleen? The diaries made it clear she'd always wondered why she didn't look like her brother, like her father, but had never pressed her own curiosities. Then her mother left that note and her father killed himself and there she was. Left alone to sort it all out. Just as she'd been left to sort out all of it, the mysteries and miseries of her life.

And how did someone do that, exactly — sort it out?

Robert Landsness misread the circumstances of his family secret and it had come out all twisted in his head, so much so he believed he'd been abducted. Look at the saga of Ann Woodward, handed it all on a silver platter, a real-life rags-to-riches story, and how she'd created a secret so deep, so dark, so *secretive,* it'd cost her family everything. Because then Truman Capote went and wrote an article for this famous New York magazine pretty much saying how Ann had killed her husband in cold blood and she got wind of it before it hit the newsstands and dropped cyanide. Simply, it turned out, to save herself further embarrassment.

Far from distraught her loving mother-in-law told the press: "Ann shot Billy and now Truman's killed her. And, well, that's that."

And, well, it might've been. Except that then one of Ann's sons leapt from the upper-floor window of a high-rise apartment and Dominick Dunne went and penned *The Two Mrs. Grenvilles,* a most-eloquent novel so-obviously based on the whole sordid affair, and it became a big best-seller and a television mini-series and then it wasn't long before the other son had jumped, too. Then all of the Woodwards were rightfully dead.

William Sr., Billy, the two boys, Ann. Even Elsie. All, stone cold.

What about those who, like the Woodward boys, took the pieces and got so lost amid the puzzlement of them they couldn't ponder the question at all? Who became alcoholics, drug addicts, suicide victims, making themselves miserable, hoping to deaden the pain, kill it, not knowing how else to resolve the issues that saddled them, not knowing where to even begin, how to begin — destroying lives that, under different circumstances, in a different light, might have otherwise been lives of promise, lives of fulfillment? Lives, in the end, instead laid waste.

What about the true outsiders, the ones for whom, Dougal knew, that confusion turned to anger, hatred even. Who became rebellious, became criminals. Became monstrous, became monsters. Became the most-heinous of their kind imaginable. Who became unimaginable.

As a cop he'd studied histories played out all the time in a manner so abhorrent, so offensive, so contemptible, so alien; often, beyond all belief. Charles Manson, Arthur Shawcross, Ted Bundy, John Wayne Gacy, Jeffrey Dahmer. Joel Rifkin, Son of Sam killer David Berkowitz.

The Columbine Killers, the Virginia Tech gunman. Mark James Robert Essex. Richard Cottingham. Colin Ferguson.

Little Hitlers, each and every one. Misguided, not miscast.

Not misunderstood, misunderstanding.

Dougal had come face-to-face with Ferguson back on December 7, 1993, a date which, for families on Long Island, would live in infamy.

Delusional, Ferguson decided to take out his fallacious vengeance on a crowded Long Island Rail Road train as it slowed into Merillon Avenue Station in Garden City during the evening rush, killing six, wounding nineteen. All he'd said, over and over, was, "I'm going to get you," as he fired bullets into strangers in three minutes of hate-filled gunfire.

The biggest shame of it, Dougal thought, was all Colin Ferguson got was three-hundred-and-fifteen years. And eight months.

He would have killed him if he could have. And, he knew, so would've any cop, given the chance.

Yet somehow the root of such evil often remains lost on those closest. How else to explain Jeffrey Dahmer's pitiable mother telling the media after her son was killed by a fellow inmate two years into the first of his fifteen life terms: "Now that he's bludgeoned to death, is that good enough for everyone? Now is everybody happy?"

Not quite, Dougal thought. But, he'd slept better that night.

The evening sun was dying in the sky. The old creek tranquil. And gray. Dougal set his coffee down on the dock, down on the steps next to him where he sat. Thinking. *Good things happen to good people? Bad people, they get theirs in the end?* Maybe so, maybe not.

Then again, what does anyone ever really know about their life?

What, he thought, do you really know about your own?

Straight out of high school Dougal went to work for the Greenport Police. The department had approached him senior year, after the local paper wrote how he'd wanted to become a police officer following the unfathomable incident with Old Lester. His parents objected, asking why'd he'd ever want to work off-Island. Asking how he could become a police officer after all that'd happened. But Dougal said it was his life, that they needed to respect that. For years it was a point of contention.

The job wasn't much. But he was a kid, barely eighteen, and he liked it even if mostly what he did was write tickets, process reports, once in a blue moon assist with the arrest of a shoplifter, a vagrant or some other not-so-notorious local criminal. Three years in, he'd realized he wanted more. He'd socked away some money, had heard about a school that trained students for a career in law enforcement.

John Jay College of Criminal Justice had opened in the early 1960s as the College of Police Science and classes were in a building downtown, East 20th Street, Manhattan. It was a small school and most old-school cops, the real old-timers, thought it a joke that someone needed to go to college to learn how to be a policeman. But Dougal sensed the world was changing and he wanted to know how to do things right because they were right, not just do them because that's how they'd always been done.

He enrolled in the fall of '73; had no idea how it'd change his life.

The education alone was worth it. He learned basic law enforcement skills and also found himself learning the latest techniques on crime-fighting and investigative detective work from some of the best of the old breed and new. But that wasn't the best thing that happened to him.

It was a Saturday night and he and a handful of classmates had gone to Chinatown to eat. They'd walked around, found a restaurant.

He met Donna no sooner had he walked through the door.

She was the hostess and she was Chinese. It was a hole-in-the-wall; her family owned it. Dougal had never seen a girl like her, certainly not back on Shelter Island. He tried not to stare but then she caught him.

He wasn't certain but he thought as he'd left she'd smiled.

He'd gone back the next week and then the week after that until he'd worked up enough courage to talk to her. Her given name was Dao-Ming: *Shining Path*. Friends called her Donna. He was surprised by her English, found out she'd been born in New York. That her family fled China before the Communist Revolution in '49, abandoning their home in the Longting District of Kaifeng, an ancient city on the Huang He, the Yellow River; had abandoned a dumpling house they'd run on Earth Market Street, a short walk from the synagogue of the historic Kaifeng Jews.

Dougal was taken by her strength, her steadfast loyalty to family. He asked her to a movie. She apologized to him, explaining how her parents wouldn't approve. He said he understood, sure his own parents wouldn't, either. He also said sorry, but he wouldn't take no for an answer.

It took a handful of months. And, dozens of heartfelt conversations with her parents, Donna acting as his interpreter. In the end Dougal not only got permission for a date. He got himself a wife.

More than thirty years down the line here he was, father of three beautiful daughters — soon to be a grandpa.

Feeling nostalgic he decided to go inside, look through old family photo albums. It'd be a nice break from all the questions weighing on him. He pored through those albums, as well as boxes of unbound pictures, and late into the evening he finally downloaded the disks given him by Johanna — beginning to look through them, as well.

It was closing in on midnight when he found himself staring at an old black-and-white photo of Colleen Goodson and Marjorie Woods.

"I'll be damned," he said. That's what he said: I'll be damned.

Mid-morning found Dougal digging up the front lawn, near the old well. Not long after breakfast he'd gone next door, a begging question on his mind. When she answered, he stared hard at her — and, asked.

"What was it Old Lester said to my father?"

Caerwyn Stone was well into her eighties, but swift as ever. Still it was obvious the question caught her off guard. Sixth-generation on Shelter Island, she'd been a lifelong friend of Clemence. No one, Islanders said, had been more devastated when Clemence and Declan passed.

"Dougal?" she said, not knowing what else to say.

He just stood there, staring at her hard.

She took a deep breath, thinking back. "You know I can't do that, son. I made your parents a promise."

"But," he said, "you're the only one left to ask."

"Your mother would kill me," she said.

"She'd understand."

The old woman stonewalled him. He persisted.

Finally, she told him how Old Lester got drunk one night not long after his wife disappeared, said how maybe his wife wouldn't have run off if it weren't for Clemence and Deck. How it was their fault she'd done him like that. Deck told Lester to watch his mouth, she said.

But, Old Lester . . . he just couldn't help himself.

Dougal pushed for more but the old woman was a tough nut to crack. A dozen ways from Sunday, he asked; his best detective. She avoided answering all she could. Staring hard at dead ends he tried one last time.

Obviously torn, she wavered.

"Said he'd *never* raise a boy *wasn't* a harelegger."

Dougal eyed her, curiously. "What does that mean?"

"I've said too much already," the old woman said, shut the door.

Left standing there Dougal didn't know what to think.

He thought how he and his father had once dug up the lawn near the well so they could bury the family dog. He began to wonder if, in fact, that's what they'd buried after all — or if it'd all been something else, maybe someone else. Like, maybe, Old Lester's wife. Or . . .

The strangest thought came over him. Panicked, he'd raced back home, grabbed a shovel. Started to dig. It was near noon when he uncovered the first of more than a dozen bones. Before long he fell back onto the ground, speechless. He was still staring into the abyss when Dallas called to tell him he'd gotten the findings from the crime lab.

Before his partner could even say a word, Dougal interrupted.

"It isn't him, Dal" he said. "Those bones . . . It isn't him."

28

Dougal was right. The bones found alongside Meadowbrook Parkway weren't the remains of Bobby Goodson.

And neither were those he'd found in the front yard.

The lab determined the first set of bones were that of a Native American girl, an Indian, and likely had been placed for burial some two hundred years earlier. The jury was still out on the second set and, with ties to the investigation, Dougal recused himself from all that followed so as not to taint the findings. But, he was a cop. And he was convinced from what he'd seen of those bones, those skeletal remains, they were those of Old Lester's wife. He was also dead-certain she'd been murdered.

The investigators thought so, too, and had gotten a court order to exhume a grave located in a small private cemetery on the far side of Shelter Island. That grave belonged to Old Lester's mother-in-law.

The news created quite a stir, all this talk about officials testing DNA. And anger was building amongst the locals, anger at the mere suggestion of murder. All across Shelter Island hareleggers hunkered down, saying whatever happened when was ancient history. That what was done was done and so be it. The media, of course, was having a day of it.

One New York tabloid headline screamed: **SKELETON ISLAND!** Another: **SHELTERED CRIME-LAND!**

The story was all over TV, the radio. The internet.

As hours passed into days, then into a week, Dougal, dead-center of the firestorm, grew tortured as the hard questions tore at him: Was Old Lester to blame? Was Declan? He knew chances were investigators would never be able to tell. Either way he thought it terrible stuff — despite the knowledge he'd been an unwitting accomplice, just a boy who'd believed he was burying the family dog. The thought kept him up nights.

At least it had until he'd come to the conclusion that while the answer might change how he'd gotten to where he was in life, it didn't change him. Others might not have seen it like that, might have let it destroy them even. As it had the Woodward boys, as it had Robert Landsness.

But Dougal was too strong for that. No matter the outcome, Declan and Clemence had raised him to be strong enough not to let it eat at him. Ruin him. Not if *he* wasn't guilty of anything. Even if *they* might be.

His biggest saving grace, of course, was the many believers. Donna, the girls. Dallas and Mireya. His son-in-law, his boss, all his friends on the job. All of them made it clear they knew what he was — and were steadfast in that belief. Still, he continued to ponder the curious statement Caerwyn Stone told him about what Old Lester had said back when.

What the hell did *that* mean?

Dougal was still working through the plausible scenarios when the lab came through with pages from the notebook found in the suit worn by Farmer. As he and Dallas sat poring over those pages two things jumped out at him. One was an entry by Farmer about a car — a gray 1949 Dodge belonging to Taggart and Marjorie Woods.

Next to that entry Farmer had scrawled one word: Plymouth?

The detectives knew what it said in the original case file. Especially, Dallas. Tag and Marjorie told of a gray Plymouth near the IGA before Bobby disappeared. It was the very reason why those cops had stopped Osias and Alile Storm later that night. A gray Plymouth, a gray Dodge? Apart from small details, they were near-identical.

The old cop truism came to mind. Suspects *always* have a *dodge*.

"We need to take a ride," Dougal said.

Dallas stared at him, not quite understanding. Minutes later the two were stepping from their unmarked car on MacArthur Terrace.

The woman who answered the door at No. 8 was surprised to see them. Dougal explained they needed to take a look around and she let them in. He stood for a moment in the living room thinking it unfamiliar, not at all as he'd envisioned it. The walls were painted eggshell, the windows modern and new. There was luxurious wood planking covering the floor. The back of the house had been expanded, an expensive kitchen with rich wood cabinets, stainless steel appliances and a formal dining set filling the addition. Windowed French doors led to a large rear deck.

Through the glass Dougal could see a huge in-ground pool.

He'd thought to ask if they could see the attic, but it was obvious there'd been construction, the original doghouse dormers gone in favor of a full second floor. He asked to see the basement, instead.

The woman said sure.

Dougal walked downstairs, Dallas and the homeowner in tow, and when he reached the bottom of the landing he saw the space had also been refinished. There was a giant flat-screen television, an entertainment system and six oversized leather theatre chairs. A wet bar owned the entire far corner of the room. Dougal pointed to a door.

"The water heater and burner are back here?"

The woman said yes.

He opened the door, flicked the light switch.

The walls were unfinished, the foundation still bare concrete. Original concrete as it had been built. He asked the woman for a flashlight.

She went and got him one. He took it, pointed it along the back wall, into a narrow space between it and the oil burner.

There, in faded crayon, scribble covered the foundation.

"Doog?"

He didn't answer, just stood there staring. He squeezed in as far as his frame would allow, leaned over — and touched the scrawl with his hand. He stood there shaking his head in disbelief, not even the faintest notion of what to say. The woman had no clue what was happening. Dallas, either. Without a word Dougal turned and walked past them, out of the small utility room, and then in silence made his way up the stairs.

Both thought he looked like he'd seen a ghost.

Dougal was out on the front lawn staring vacantly at the house across the street when Dallas reached him.

"Want to tell me what it is that's goin' on?" he said.

Dougal didn't answer.

"Doog?"

"The neighbor woman," he said, finally. "She said the boy had a burn on his backside, from an iron falling on him. That's what Farmer wrote."

Dallas stared at him, confused. "An'?"

"I read the diaries. Read them, all Colleen Goodson wrote. She never mentioned an iron, never mentioned the boy getting burned."

Dallas shrugged as if to say. Dougal turned to his partner.

"Let me ask you a question, Dal. The mother, she writes all these diary entries, accounts as honest as I've ever seen in all my years on the job. She writes about the kid falling off his bike, breaking his arm. About swatting him a good one on the backside . . . About how bad it makes her feel."

"So?"

"So as far as I can tell she doesn't pull any punches. Not one. Not when it comes to her life back in Cottonwood Falls, not to when it comes to getting what she wants. Not to what she thinks about her husband, her mother-in-law; her family. None of it. She writes about her problem drinking, about seeing another man. About how her mother left her father a note just before he killed himself, saying she wasn't his daughter."

He felt a tremble come over him. "So why doesn't she write about the kid getting burned with an iron?"

Dallas raised an eyebrow. "'Cause it didn't happen?"

"Right, Cowboy. Because it didn't happen."

The woman was at the front door now watching the detectives standing out there on her front lawn.

She called out: "Can I get you guys something?"

Dallas motioned no thanks, he'd be in to talk to her, then watched as she stepped back inside. Dougal moved toward the stoop, sat down.

"Made it up, the neighbor woman did?" Dallas said.

Dougal pulled an old black-and-white photograph from his pocket. Dallas gave it the once-over, not quite understanding.

"I'm lookin' at who?"

"Colleen Goodson," Dougal said. "Colleen Goodson and the neighbor woman, Marjorie Woods." Dallas started to ask but Dougal cut him off. "Found it the other night, when I was going through those old photos Johanna Childress gave us. Her mother, when I saw that picture I thought, 'She looks vaguely familiar.' Vaguely, like maybe I'd seen her somewhere before. Probably from pictures in the old case files."

"Makes sense."

"The other woman," he said, without so much as a glance. "The Woods woman? She looked *really* familiar to me, Dal. I just knew I'd seen her somewhere before . . . And her picture *wasn't* in the case files.

"It wasn't anywhere."

He reached into his pocket, pulled out a second photo, handed it to Storm. It was a picture of two girls, also black-and-white. The two of them were really young — one in her late teens, the other younger even than that. They were at a rock-strewn beach, out at the end of Long Island.

Underneath it said: "Me and Cousin Margie. Orient Point."

Without a word Dougal motioned for his partner to turn it over. On the back, it said: "Marjorie Stallworth, August 1941."

The Stallworths came from New Suffolk, out on the North Fork, Dougal said. On Peconic Bay, a hop, skip and a jump from Orient Point — just a stone's throw and a short ferry ride from Shelter Island.

Not long before Pearl Harbor they'd pulled roots, headed for the land of opportunity. For California. Landed somewhere not far north of Bakersfield, a small town in the San Joaquin Valley. Porterville.

He'd confirmed it through Census records, real estate records.

Had confirmed Marjorie Stallworth was, in fact, Marjorie Woods.

Dallas had no idea where Dougal was going with any of this. It crossed his mind Marjorie Stallworth — that is, Margie Woods — might somehow be related to Lester's wife, maybe even Old Lester himself.

He was sure that wasn't good.

He shot Dougal a look and his partner reached out, handed him still another photo. This time, a black-and-white of an old sedan.

Dallas had no idea whose car it was. Had no idea what, if anything, it had to do with anything. He just knew it wasn't a Dodge.

Or, for that matter, a Plymouth.

"Whose car?" he said.

Dougal took a hand, scratched the back of his neck; absentmindedly ran it across his bare scalp. "You know, I had hair once," he said.

"Doog?" Dallas said, beyond lost.

Sitting there on the front lawn in Shelter Island, right after he'd found those bones, Dougal said he'd thought back on his childhood as he'd waited for Crime Scene Bureau detectives and the Medical Examiner.

Said how he'd thought back on instances that hadn't really struck him before, that he'd taken for what they were. Then how at that very moment they'd seemed like something else altogether. Something important.

"You know, sometimes the obvious isn't so obvious," he said. "That's what I was thinking, Dal. How sometimes the obvious is obvious. How sometimes it isn't." He nodded to the photo of the car.

"My old man . . . When I was growing up, my old man had a Nineteen-Forty-Four Chevrolet. That car, there."

He squeezed his hands, balled them, trying to quell the tremble.

"Remember the case file? The woman at that farm stand, the one in Bayport? She said she saw this green car and gray car the day Bobby Goodson went missing, saw a man and a woman and a blonde-haired boy. That the woman and the boy drove off in one car, that the man drove off in the other." He pointed across the street. "The neighbors had a gray

Dodge, Dal. Marjorie and Taggart Woods, gray Dodge. We had that Nineteen-Forty-Four Chevrolet . . . A *green* Chevrolet."

Dallas struggled to get his head around it, all of it.

The question that came to mind seemed so inconceivable — so much so he couldn't believe he'd even thought it.

"You sayin' *your* mother and *your* old man had somethin' to do with this? That *they* were the ones took Bobby Goodson?"

Dougal moved from the stoop, stepped past Dallas.

"My neighbor out on Shelter Island," Dougal said, his back still turned to Dallas. "She told me Old Lester said how he'd *never* raise a boy *wasn't* a harelegger." He shook his head. "I knew he didn't mean me, Dal. I was born on the Island, right there in our house. Upstairs, on the bedroom floor. My mother said so. I've even got a birth certificate signed by an old doctor friend of the family says it's true."

Dallas stared at him not knowing what to say.

"You know how when you're just a kid and your mother, she throws you in the tub and washes your hair?" His voice quavered. "Clemence used to say all the time how my hair was so brown I looked like the milkman's son and how she was going to lighten it if it killed her. Then she'd throw me in the bathtub, scrub my hair good, and the color would run down and turn the water dirty." He thought back. "She worked at the salon, in town. Dyeing hair when times got tough, you know? I never thought much about that . . . I never thought about it much at all."

"Doog?"

"Thing is, no matter how much she'd wash it, no matter how brown that water got, it never got lighter. Not a shade. It stayed the same."

He was fixated on the house across the street, now. "It wasn't until I'd gotten older, ten maybe, that it started to turn. I was showering on my own by then, of course, and it was only then that that brown color started to fade. That it got this dirty blonde. It stayed like that 'til I lost it and . . . And, believe me Cowboy, I started losing it young."

The woman was at the door again. She started to say something but Dougal waved her off. He pulled out a note, handed it to Dallas.

"Doog?"

"Read it," Dougal said. "Read it out loud."

Dallas knew what it was the second he saw it and fought to compose himself, hands trembling. "Someday . . . " His voice cracked, stopping him dead in his tracks. Dougal nodded, pressing him on.

Dallas drew a long, hard, exaggerated breath.

"Someday, when the hurt and anger are gone, remember the good they've done. Raised a good cop, a good friend . . . a good *son*."

As Dallas sat there in stunned silence Dougal stepped back to the stoop, sat down beside him. The two of them sat there the longest time not a word between them, just sat there, looking out over the street.

Looking out over the scene on MacArthur Terrace.

"The basement, those drawings?" Dallas said, breaking the silence.

"Marjorie Stallworth," Dougal said, matter-of-fact.

"Marjorie Stallworth?"

"Those two girls at Orient Point?" Dougal said, turning to Dallas. "Marjorie Stallworth and her cousin from Shelter Island, *Clemence*."

"Fuck," Dallas said. That's really what he said: *Fuck*.

A jetliner broke through the scattered clouds. Dougal sat and watched until it was long-faded from sight. "That scribble in the basement?" he said, finally. "I knew it was there, Dal, because . . . Because, I drew it."

Epilogue

The old woman was on her deathbed.

She was comatose, as she had been for some time now, and at this moment he thought her feeble, frail. Vulnerable.

More so than he could've ever imagined.

An intravenous tube hung down from a drip bag tethered to a bedside stand and the line disappeared beneath the blanket, directing fluids into her arm. The hose from the tracheal intubation stretched from the hole in her throat to the life-critical ventilator — a ventilator that filled the hospital room, a room of such otherwise unimaginable quiet, with the most-disturbing, heart-rending sound. Dead-time rhythm, he thought.

He stared, thinking her so close to the end, the very corpse of a woman he'd come to know from old photographs and diary entries and case files and interviews, and he perished the thought.

He wished he could remember her when she was who she'd been in those old black-and-white photos; wished he could remember her then.

Try as he might, he couldn't — and it filled him with sadness.

For more than a week he'd envisioned this moment, had wondered what he'd find once he got here. He leaned in close, caressed her hand.

"Mom," he said.

No sooner had he said it than he was overcome with the strangest sensation he'd ever known; this woman, the mother he didn't know.

Tears welled in his eyes.

"There's so much to tell you . . . " he said, his voice reduced to a near-whisper. "I wish . . . I just wish I knew if you could hear me."

Outside the hospital room, outside of the windowless door, Johanna Childress waited with her husband, daughters, grandchildren.

With her father.

As he sat there beside Colleen Goodson he realized he had no idea how even to introduce himself. All his life he'd been Dougal Skinner; Shelter Island native, son of a harelegger, from a long line of hareleggers. Dougal Skinner. Husband, father. Cop. *Doog.* Now here he was, Robert Goodson — Bobby Goodson — and truthfully he felt as lost as the little boy he'd turned out to be. All of it so infinitely far from easy.

He'd come west straight from the hospital on Long Island. Left them all there, gathered in the maternity ward, driven to the airport, caught the flight. Dallas offered to go with him, to the terminal at least, but he'd told them he needed to go it alone. He knew that. Then again, so did they.

It had all been so joyous, becoming a grandfather. The doctor had performed the caesarean, delivering a healthy boy and girl, and Logan had come through it all like the trouper he'd always known her to be. Dante played proud Papa, handing out cigars, and once the anesthesia had worn off, he'd helped Logan into a wheelchair and pushed her down to the window outside the nursery to get a look at their new family.

Dallas and Mireya and Alile Storm were there, of course. And there were hugs and kisses and celebration and jokes about how they'd all gotten old overnight. Donna and the girls were overjoyed, seeing Logan as a new mom, and Donna remarked how it seemed like yesterday they'd themselves first become parents. Just like yesterday, she'd said.

As he drove to the airport, boarded the plane for Kansas City, it'd hit Dougal how he really *wasn't* Dougal anymore; that he really never was, never had been, and never would be again. That he was Robert.

That he'd somehow shared a birth, as well.

He'd made sure not to call anyone, no one in his new family, his long-lost family, to tell them of his pending arrival. The Commissioner agreed to withhold it all from the press until he could tell them face-to-face.

There'd be plenty of time for a news conference, now that the DNA tests had confirmed what he already knew to be true.

The first thing he'd done after reaching Cottonwood Falls was take Kansas 177 south to Bazaar to see the man that, strangely enough, would be his father. As he'd stood outside the farmhouse door he'd hesitated — and it took him a lifetime to summon enough courage even to knock.

He waited, thinking that though he'd rehearsed it a million times by now he strangely had no idea just what to say.

Then he'd found himself face-to-face with Driscoll Goodson and all he could muster was, "I don't know if you remember me . . ."

The old man was confused at first, then his eyes grew wide, waiting for something more. "Please," Driscoll said, motioning him in. As the two of them walked to the dining table, the old man turned to him.

"You came to tell me he's . . . *dead.*"

"No," he said. "No, not at all."

The old man stared in disbelief. "You mean, he's . . . Is he *alive?*"

"Yes," he said, the rest of it caught in his throat. "Yes."

No sooner had he said it than the old man collapsed into this big wooden armchair, sobbing, tears streaming down his cheeks.

"My God. Really? My boy's *really* alive?"

He shook his head, yes, best he could. "He's . . . he's here."

Trance-like the old man pulled himself from the chair, moved fast as he could to the window. He peered out, saw nothing; turned back.

"Where?" he said. "Where is he?"

His eyes begged — no, they *pleaded* with him — for explanation.

"I'm . . ." he said, in a cold sweat. "I'm your son."

When the shock of it wore off, and, more than an hour later, neither man was all that certain it had, the clock found them still at the table, talking. That his father hadn't fainted surprised him, though maybe he was also surprised he, himself, hadn't, either. There'd been this strangely surreal moment as the words sank in, and so both had just stood, frozen, staring at each other, ears not believing what one of them just said.

Not believing what the other had just heard.

What followed was a long, emotional hug, one the detective had imagined since he'd first put it all together; the clues.

One his father, across those long decades since that darkest of days back in Hempstead Plains, never imagined he'd ever share again.

As the two of them began to settle in Driscoll reached into his back pocket, drew out his wallet. From the fold he pulled out an old black-and-white photograph. It was creased and crinkled and finger-worn at the edges and he sat there for the longest time staring at it, just staring, before he finally took it, handed it to his son. *His* son.

Dougal, now that very boy, shook his head.

It was a wallet-sized portrait of the same photo Colleen Goodson had given the police the day he'd gone missing back in 1955.

"I can't begin to tell you," Driscoll Goodson said, "how many days out in the fields I'd stand looking at that picture, wondering what'd happened. Wondering if he was still alive, if you were. Where he was. You . . .

"If I'd ever see *you* again."

Then it came crashing down, the weight of an emotional tidal wave, the two — two grown men; an aged father and his aging son — crying like babies. Each knowing *exactly* how the other felt in that moment.

Neither knowing the least how the other felt at all.

Finally, Robert took to his feet. Moved to his old man — *his* old man — and placed a hand on his shoulder. Gave a reassuring squeeze. Then Driscoll had gone to the phone and called his wife, off visiting their daughter and grandkids up in Topeka. He'd told her the news, incredible as it was, and Robert could tell it was still all so overwhelming.

Then he watched as his father, a jumble of nerves, called Johanna. Johanna didn't answer. Driscoll left a message.

Tongue-tied, he didn't know what to say. So he said, simply: "It's your father. Please call me. It's . . . it's important."

It wasn't a minute before she called back and Robert listened as his father told her there was news, that she needed to come soon as possible. Fifteen minutes later Johanna was in the foyer, shaking like a leaf. He looked at her and said: "You said how you'd always wondered if you were ever in the same room as your brother if you'd even know it was him?"

"Detective?" she said.

He stepped toward her, wrapped his arms around her in a deep, smothering hug. "You know now," he whispered.

When the commotion finally died down he told them all he knew.

About the photograph he'd found amongst the pictures Johanna had given him, the one of Marjorie and her mother. Their mother. The one he'd found of Marjorie in his own family album, the one with Clemence at Orient Point. About how the neighbor had hinted there was more to the story of his life than he'd ever imagined. About how he'd found the bones — and how DNA tests had confirmed it was Old Lester's wife.

How the diaries and Farmer's old notebook had suggested the truth about what'd really happened that long-ago Halloween.

The first thing he'd done after finding the crayon scribble was have an X-ray of his arm, which showed it'd once been broken.

He gave a DNA sample, matched it to the one Johanna had given detectives investigating "The Boy in the Box."

"I think the original detectives would have solved it," he said. "If . . . "

His father interrupted. "If it wasn't for the plane crash."

Then Driscoll explained how all his life he'd had this fear of airplanes; back to stories his dad told of the Knute Rockne crash, back to the crash at the old Glanville place. It struck them how tragically ironic it was.

Especially since, Robert noted, he himself had also always had this inexplicable fear of flying.

"Thing is," Robert said, finally, "even growing up I always knew there were a lot of secrets on Shelter Island. People were private about private matters and I always wondered, especially after I became a cop, if they were *too* private. I knew some of it felt too secretive. Then I saw places where it wasn't like that, where people had no respect for boundaries, and I thought that seemed worse. That there was no distance.

'I guess I never saw it as sinister," he said. "Even though I was a cop, it was my life. We had a house. There were never any fights, at least not bad ones. The neighbors, the ones we talked to, were always friendly. Were there when the chips were down. I never gave it a thought."

Once he understood what'd happened, who he was, Robert said he'd gone back to talk to Caerwyn Stone. He'd convinced the brass she'd never talk. Not if they'd sent ten investigators, not if they'd threatened to charge her and drag her to court. The only hope he'd said was for him to talk to her, one-on-one. To convince her to tell him what she knew.

It'd taken all he had, he said. He'd shown her the photographs, the case files, the statements from the woman at the farm stand.

Told her about the man, the woman and the little boy the witness had seen. About the cars, about all of it.

And then Stone said, simply: "It wasn't your mother's idea."

He'd asked what she meant by that and the old woman told him how Clemence said her cousin was afraid the boy — "How you," she'd said — was being neglected. How she needed to do something to protect the child, the *children,* so she'd planned to take them. Take them both.

"Both?" Johanna said.

"Yes," Robert said. "The plan was for Marjorie to take both of us."

Marjorie and Taggart Woods, two people who couldn't have children of their own, were going to grab Robert and Johanna and run off to Mexico, Caerwyn Stone said. That's how Clemence explained it.

That Clemence and Deck would watch the kids was temporary, she said. Except then Marjorie couldn't loosen the straps to the baby carriage and, when she saw this old man gardening in his yard, panicked. Left little Jo there. Even after they'd handed off Bobby, they were still trying to figure how to grab Johanna without raising suspicion.

Then the bomber crashed into the house. Clemence and Deck had no choice then. Or so they believed.

They'd had no idea Majorie Woods had made it all up.

"Your parents loved you," Caerwyn Stone said. "They thought they were doing the right thing, keeping you safe. We all did."

"That 'we' not only included Caerwyn Stone, Declan and Clemence," he said, as he sat there staring at his dying mother. "Caerwyn Stone said it included the family doctor, Old Lester — even Old Lester's wife."

He gave his mother's hand a gentle squeeze. Told her how Caerwyn Stone said how she, Clemence and Declan had explained to their closest neighbors how he'd been adopted. How those neighbors vowed never to tell him he really *wasn't* one of them — that he *wasn't* a harelegger.

Clemence and Declan even persuaded the doctor, their old friend, to forge a birth certificate. As for the rest of those in town?

Well, to them they'd simply lied.

But then Old Lester killed his wife when things went south between them, when she'd threatened to go to the authorities — and tell them the truth. Lester told Declan he'd done it to protect him, protect their secret, then begged him to bury the body. Caerwyn Stone said Deck berated Old Lester for being so terrible. Told him none of it, not even going to jail, was worth the cost of a murder. He'd helped bury the woman, since the deed was done. But then Deck told Lester that was it between them.

Had told him that was all, had written him off. She swore Declan didn't kill Old Lester, that he'd really slipped, hit his head, drowned.

"I don't know," he said, "there's any way to ever tell."

He sat there knowing there was no way to tell if she could hear him, knowing any chance he had to share a moment with her, to make up for lost time, was forever gone. His father, sister, all of them, were still out there in the hall. He listened to the sound of the ventilator, its incessant rhythm pounding in his brain and tried to imagine that she'd found peace

— had found it, amidst the suffocating turmoil that'd plagued her life.

He pulled a picture from his wallet, turned the photo so his mother could see it — knowing full well, in his heart of hearts, she never would. It was the photograph of her two newest great-grandchildren, a little boy and his adorable sister, surrounded by family. Their family.

He leaned in, ever close to his mother. To his mom.

"This is Robert," he said, "and his sister, Colleen Storm."

About the Author

A national award-winning reporter for *Newsday* and author of the critically acclaimed *Swee'pea and Other Playground Legends,* about former All-American Lloyd (Swee'pea) Daniels and New York City playground basketball [Published by Michael Kesend Publishing, Ltd., 1990 / Reissued by Simon & Schuster imprint Atria Books, July 2016], John A. Valenti 3rd has appeared on hundreds of television and radio shows, including NPR and *Good Morning America* with Charles Gibson. He's had featured roles in *The Legend of Swee'pea,* an award-winning documentary by Benjamin May, and the Emmy-winning ESPN 30-for-30 *Big Shot* by Kevin Connolly — the latter the story of how John Spano fleeced Fleet Bank out of $80 million to buy the NHL New York Islanders while claiming to be a Dallas multimillionaire and how Valenti headed a team of *Newsday* reporters and uncovered the truth, leading to the federal conviction of Spano. A veteran of four decades with *Newsday,* Valenti has been honored with national first-places finishes in the prestigious Society of the Silurians, Associated Press Sports Editors and National Headliner Award competitions, including APSE Best Enterprise Reporting in 1996 as part of team that reported a ground-breaking series on concussions and for Best Investigative Reporting in 1997 for his investigation of Spano. He was the lead columnist on *Newsday's* "Death on the Roads" series that earned the esteemed Silurians Community Service Award in 2004, was part of a team that took first place in the 2007 Silurians competition for "Death of a Yankee," the reporting of the plane crash that killed New York Yankees pitcher Cory Lidle, and the 2012 First Place award by Silurians for Online Breaking News coverage of 2011 Tropical Storm Irene. He also was part of the *Newsday* team that won the 2024 National Headliner Award for breaking news coverage of the arrest of alleged Gilgo Beach serial killer Rex Heuermann. Valenti has covered Major League Baseball, the NBA, NHL, the 1994 World Cup Soccer Tournament, major-college sports and breaking news events and *Newsday* submitted his work for Pulitzer Prize consideration at least 10 times between 1987 and 2024. Among notable figures Valenti has interviewed include: Michael Jordan, Magic Johnson, Billie Jean King, Mike Tyson, Mario Andretti, Wayne Gretzky, Pele, Maradona and the first two men to walk on the Moon — Neil Armstrong and Buzz Aldrin. He was a candidate for the 1986 NASA-sponsored "Journalist in Space Project" and made his critically acclaimed debut as a poet in *13 Poets from Long Island* in 2023. *For Nothing Is Hidden* is his debut novel. Valenti lives in Elmhurst, Queens, with wife and longtime companion Elizabeth Eser Jose. He has one son, Jarek.

Author's Note

It would be unmindful not to acknowledge language used by characters in this book can be vulgar and offensive at times, especially their use of racial epithets. I can only offer that, as the writer, this was a carefully-weighed and thought-out decision; that my consideration was that to sanitize such dialogue would have minimized the offense and therefore would not have been an accurate representation of the times — or, of those portrayed. This is a historical novel. It is inspired by real events. Hopefully, from history — and, from honest portrayals of history — we learn. And so I trust that, as a reader, you'll understand these decisions made, no matter the offense.

While bigotry, racism, hate speech and racial animus sadly remain ever-present, I would offer there's always hope — or, so I've been told.

FOR NOTHING IS HIDDEN

BUSHWICKBORN PRODUCTIONS, INC. / POPE BROTHERS INK